In Too Deep

SHANNYN SCHROEDER

Print ISBN: 978-1-950640-25-6

Cover created by The Killion Group

Editor: Jen Prokop

CHAPTER

One

Ronan Doyle never imagined a kids' game of Truth or Dare could fuck with his head as an adult. But that was before a very grown-up Chloe McCarthy sat across from him as a temptation. So much more than she had as a teenager.

He didn't belong sitting around a bonfire in the middle of the street, pretending to be happy, making jokes as he listened to childhood friends play Truth or Dare. He'd been gone for years, back only because his family had summoned him to make decisions about their father. Today, though, he'd hoped for the comfort of home. He hadn't realized he'd be walking into the annual block party. As a teen, this party had defined his summers.

Until his fourteenth summer. That year changed everything.

The summer his dad had disappeared. Twenty years ago today, in fact. Hence the reason for the visit home. Most of his siblings, headed by his older brother Brendan, had been pushing to declare their father dead for years. On his last visit home, the twins mentioned that since it had been twenty years, it no longer made sense to wait. He couldn't let that happen. It was too final, and they still had no idea what really happened.

So he decided to move home. Not here, home. This neighborhood held too many memories. Instead, he bought a house nearby, but far enough to not have constant reminders.

The day his dad went missing hadn't been during the block party. The party had been the weekend before. It was the last good memory he had of his father.

So here he was, sitting on a crappy lawn chair as Maggie, the youngest of the O'Learys who was about his sister's age, circled the fire looking for her first victim. He'd already witnessed some steamy revelations about which neighbors had hooked up with each other over the years, as well as a few sexual dares. It was a little weird, even to his alcohol-filled brain to see people he knew as kids, now grown, still playing the same games they had twenty years ago. Some of the faces had changed, as younger siblings aged into the group. When he was fourteen, it was Spin the Bottle, not Truth or Dare, and he'd been lucky enough to plant a kiss on Maureen Lynch. He studied the faces around the fire. No Maureen.

"Ronan," Maggie said, pulling him from his memories. "Truth or dare?"

Someone on the other side of the fire called, "No fair. Everyone knows the Doyles will do anything. A dare won't scare him."

"Especially a dare created by Maggie. But I'll take truth." There was nothing Maggie could ask that would make him appear worse than how most of these people already viewed him.

And it might be a good reminder for Chloe to stay away.

Maggie rubbed her chin in thought. "What's the worst thing you've ever done to someone in this neighborhood?"

Funny how she had to qualify it. As if they all assumed he'd done much worse away from here.

They weren't wrong.

He laughed and looked across the fire at Jimmy O'Malley, who grew up to be a cop just like his dad. "Hey, Jimmy, what's the statute of limitations on grand theft auto?"

A few people laughed and someone let out a low whistle.

"That's my cue to bow out. I'll be back. Anyone need a refill?" Jimmy asked, holding his plastic cup.

Ronan rested his elbows on his knees. Chloe leaned forward, attention riveted on him. He focused on the O'Leary sisters running the game. "When I was fourteen, I stole your father's car. Crashed it into the liquor store so I could get some more beer. Needless to say, I was already drunk."

And angry. So fucking angry.

Everyone stared at him slack-jawed. Mr. O'Leary had been a pillar of their close-knit Chicago neighborhood.

He took a swig of beer. "Your dad was cool about it. Pissed, but cool. Didn't call the cops or tell my mom." He paused. There was no dad to tell at that point. That was the summer he disappeared. "He just made me work off the cost of the repairs."

He raised his cup. "To Patrick O'Leary."

The crowd howled in laughter and smiled as they toasted the man who had died a few years ago. The whole time he told the story, Chloe sat on the ground, staring at his every movement.

Her denim shorts rode to the crease of her ass cheek as she shifted her legs and her t-shirt with the sleeves cut off clung to her curves, serving her up as a distraction. Nothing about her reminded him of the sweet, quiet girl afraid of her own shadow.

She'd always been off-limits, first as his older brother's girlfriend, then because her parents had unjustifiably threatened him with arrest. None of it, however, had stopped the temptation.

So when it was his turn to ask, he wanted to scare her off. Test this new, bolder version. Teach her it wasn't nice to tease. A quiet voice in the back of his mind did its own taunting, telling him that he just wanted a chance to touch her. She shouldn't let him. Turning, he asked, "Chloe. Truth or dare?"

"Dare." One reddish-brown eyebrow arched in a dare of its own.

Definitely bolder.

"I dare you to let me do a body shot off you." Holding her gaze, he searched for the flicker of fear, a flinch to begin the flight, but saw nothing.

"Who's got the tequila?" she asked.

Had her voice always had that sexy rasp?

Fuck. Of all the responses he might've imagined, that wasn't one. He'd expected her to blush and decline at worst or run off and hide at best. He'd wanted to remove the temptation and it backfired.

Someone passed a bottle and another person ran off and returned with a salt shaker and limes. Keeping eye contact with him, Chloe twirled her hair and tied it on the top of her head. Then she poured the shot, lay down in the street, and pulled her shirt up.

His mouth went dry. She sprinkled salt on her skin just below her breasts and balanced the shot glass on her stomach before putting the slice of lime between her teeth.

With everyone's eyes on them, he rose from the creaky chair and lowered himself to her prone body. His mass cast her in darkness despite the flickering fire beside them. His shadow completely swallowed her.

Her eyes continued to speak to him. *Go ahead. This was your dare. Are you chicken?*

The problem was that Chloe wasn't the kind of girl who taunted and teased. She'd always been the girl to help a neighbor, went to church every Sunday, never spoke a mean word to anyone. But laying splayed out before him, she didn't look so innocent. Sweet? Yes. The kind he wanted to devour.

He licked his lips and lowered his mouth to her abdomen. When the tip of his tongue made contact with her skin, she quivered slightly. He stroked slowly, allowing her time to change her mind. She smelled like summer: sunscreen and bug spray and youth. Completely fitting for this moment.

The rough grains of salt on his tongue rubbed against her as he lapped them up. Goosebumps rose across her skin as his tongue moved, but she held still. He picked up the shot glass and downed the tequila. The burn of alcohol slid down his throat, tasteless. He concentrated on savoring her and the silky feel of her skin on his tongue. Then he moved to her mouth to take the lime from her lips.

He hovered above her face for a second, staring into her eyes, still full of dare. Leaning in, he couldn't help but allow his tongue to sweep into her mouth to sample her forbidden taste. He pulled back with the lime at the same time she gasped.

Silence surrounded them as if they'd been swallowed by a bubble. Only the crackle of fire behind him spoke of time continuing. He waited for the slap that didn't come.

She simply sat up, tugging her shirt in place. She shot

another arched brow in his direction. Chloe had definitely outgrown her shyness.

The crowd began to murmur, but no one spoke of what they'd witnessed. Chloe rose to take her turn. He tossed the lime into the fire.

Chloe turned her attention to the crowd. "Kevin."

"Truth."

"Why didn't you ever ask me out when we were younger?"

Seemed like Chloe was trying to push everyone's buttons tonight. If the Doyles were the worst in the neighborhood, the O'Malleys came in not too far behind, and Kevin was an O'Malley.

"You were a good girl, like your sister."

"So?" she asked. "I dated Brendan Doyle," she added with a wave over in his direction.

Ronan burst out laughing. Of course, she wouldn't get it. While Brendan had had a rough year or so right after Dad disappeared, he straightened up, became the model son. He bought into the whole, I'm-the-man-of-the-house-now thing. Everyone loved him.

Some people around the fire focused on Chloe and Kevin. Others stared at him, wide-eyed and open-mouthed.

He hated the added attention, so he went to refill his beer at the keg. He didn't know what he'd been looking for from that stunt. The ability to finally put his tongue in Chloe's mouth without repercussion? Give her reason once again to fear being near him? He got neither. She simply handled it as part of the stupid game.

Footsteps slapped the pavement behind him. He turned to see Chloe striding up, the sway of her hips causing her shirt to ride up a little, baring a strip of skin he'd had his tongue on.

"It's good to see you back in the neighborhood."

He gave a non-committal hum. He wasn't sure how good this was. She ran a finger over the rim of her plastic cup.

"So, that was pretty hot," she said, lifting her chin toward the fire.

"If you say so."

"Oh, I definitely say so." She stepped closer. "How long are you in town for?"

"Not sure." *Until I can find answers about my dad.*

"Maybe we can get a drink together. Or something."

"What are you doing, Chloe? How drunk are you?" In his recollection, being drunk was the only way she was ever attracted to him.

"I'm not drunk. A little buzzed. And that body shot got me humming. I just thought we could continue."

"Really?" He pushed their history from his mind. If he was going to hell, he planned on making it worth it. He dropped his cup and slipped a finger through the loop of her shorts at her waist. He tugged her closer until her body brushed his. He lowered his mouth to hers. Her breath fluttered against his lips, and he could almost taste the size of this mistake.

Before making contact, someone yelled, "Chloe? Where are you?"

She jumped away from him like he'd expected her to when he suggested a body shot. She licked her lips. "That sounds like my mom. I'll be back."

The hell she would. She was playing games and he wanted no part of it. Running as her mom beckoned, no different than a kid being called in for the night.

Instead of returning to the fire, he walked toward his mom's house. Sitting on the concrete steps, some of which were missing chunks—why hadn't she asked him to fix this? —he watched the happenings of the end of the party from a safe distance.

He'd grown up with most of the people at the bonfire. Unlike him, they'd kept in touch with each other, returned for the annual party, remained close. He'd turned eighteen and ran. He couldn't wait to get away from here. The weight of people's stares was too much for him.

The sympathetic glances, the pitying head shakes, the questioning looks—as if he had answers about what had happened to his father. Between the scrutiny of the neighborhood and the brokenness of his family, he couldn't stand it, so he'd left. Chloe's parents and their threats hadn't helped.

He'd been back periodically over the years, never able to totally stay away. He loved his siblings. And his mom needed him. But he couldn't be involved with the neighborhood the way some did: going to church as a family (church? The place might burn if he crossed the threshold), family barbecues that included the neighbors (he wasn't much of a cook), and of course, planning this block party (far too full of memories for him).

The front door behind him opened and he looked over his shoulder. His younger brother, Killian, stepped out.

"Hey, man. Mom said you were here. It's been a while."

"Yeah."

"What's going on down the street?"

"Truth or Dare." He wished he'd grabbed another beer so he could remove the taste of Chloe from his mouth.

Killian descended the stairs and leaned against the rail. "Why are you here?"

Every time one of his siblings questioned him, it always

felt like an accusation. "You know why." *To make sure Brendan didn't try to pull anything.*

Killian nodded. So they wouldn't discuss it tonight, wouldn't fight about it. They'd save that for tomorrow.

"How are you?" Killian asked.

"Fine."

"Don't fucking lie to me. I know the date."

"Yeah? So?"

His brother sighed and crossed his arms. "You're not the only one who misses him. We all lost him that day."

"I'm well aware."

"Are you? Because you show up here acting like you're the only one he left."

"He didn't just leave." He sucked in a deep breath, readying for the argument he'd often had with his family.

His siblings, led by Brendan, had wanted their mom to have Dad declared dead years ago. Ronan was the only one to side with Mom against doing that. They didn't know where Michael Doyle was or what had happened to him. The one thing Ronan believed to the core was that his father wouldn't have left them. The others were younger. They hadn't had the relationship with their dad that he and Brendan had had.

Instead of arguing, Killian said, "It doesn't matter now, does it? But it might help if he had a place at the cemetery where we could let go of him."

They were all grown. Time to let go of hope.

Fuck. This again? "Did Brendan send you to talk to me?"

"It's been twenty years."

Ronan had known his siblings would make this play. On the anniversary, pull the strings to press for the declaration that he'd fought for years. But there was something different about this year. Twenty years. Time to move on. But he needed answers. He was only surprised Brendan wasn't here doing the dirty work himself.

"Mom needs to let him go," Killian added.

He also heard the unspoken words. *He* had to let his father go.

"She'll never let him go. He was the love of her life." He couldn't imagine ever having that. A person who fit so perfectly that without them, a piece of him would be gone. But that was who his parents had been for each other.

"She might be better if she said goodbye and accepted that he's gone for good. He's not coming back."

Ronan knew that. He was also aware that Killian could just as easily have said the same about him. If their father had been able to come back to them, he would have. So, yeah, he was probably dead. But without proof, knowledge of what happened to him, Ronan couldn't bury him. He couldn't let him go without answers. Why couldn't his brothers understand that?

Chloe looked down the block to where Ronan had disappeared. She didn't know what she'd hoped for after the body shot. That he would grab her and kiss her properly? In her dreams. As it was, that non-kiss was the hottest thing she'd experienced in a long time. She'd give almost anything for more.

She hadn't seen Ronan in years. And after he'd rescued her from her own stupidity, Ronan became the subject of many, many teenage dreams. There was something about his quiet broodiness that drew her to him. Always the bad boys.

He'd been a hulking brute as a teenager and he'd only filled out with solid, defined muscles as a man.

As she neared her parent's house, she saw her mom standing on the porch.

"What do you need, Mom?"

"It's late. What are you doing down there?"

Chloe clenched her jaw before answering. "We're catching up, playing games. You can go to bed." She didn't bother mentioning how much alcohol was being consumed.

"You need to make sure our chairs are brought in and put in the garage."

"I'll do it soon. I promise." The downside to being back in the neighborhood with the people she grew up with was that her mother still made her feel like a kid.

She looked across the street to the Doyle house. Someone joined Ronan on the front steps. Probably one of his brothers. She went to the keg and poured three beers. Offering a drink was the neighborly thing to do, and she was nothing if not polite. The fact that delivering beer down the block would put her back in Ronan's orbit was a pleasant side effect.

As she neared the men, the glow from the streetlight hit them. Chloe recognized the second man as Ronan's brother Killian—or his twin Kieran—which to guess?

"Is that you, Kieran?" she called from the sidewalk in front of the neighbor's house.

When he turned, she immediately knew she'd guessed wrong. Although the twins were identical, Killian was the serious brother, while Kieran was quick with a wink and a smile. With seven kids, the Doyles were one of those families where you could run through a list of names before landing on the one you needed. But she and the twins had been in the same grade, so she knew them better than the younger siblings. She'd watched as they always tried to prank teachers. It made her home in on their differences.

"Sorry, wrong brother."

"I know." She sighed. "I knew it as soon as you turned. In my defense, it's really dark out here." She neared and held up the red plastic cups. "Beer?"

"I'd love one. Thanks." He took a cup from her.

Tension surrounded the brothers, cloaking them in the darkness that had been cast over this house for years. It made her sad because they were good people, a loyal family. She'd always been a little jealous of the Doyles and how they readily accepted each other.

She turned to Ronan. "I figured you could use a refill." *You know, since you dropped yours before almost kissing me.*

"You figured, huh?"

She leaned closer, extending a cup to him. "I thought you might be thirsty."

"Thanks."

When he reached for the cup, their fingers touched, sending a charge up her arm. Their gazes were locked and something zipped between them, but then he blinked and it was gone.

Stepping back, she took a drink of her own beer.

"Whoa. You drink?" Killian asked.

She nearly sputtered. "Yeah. I'm a thirty-two-year-old woman. I work in a bar. Of course, I drink."

Ronan shot her a look. "As I remember, you don't handle your liquor well."

"That was one time and I was sixteen!" Had he not gotten over the events of that night? How many times had she apologized?

Both Doyles stared at her. Pointing a thumb over her

shoulder, she added, "That wasn't even the first body shot I've ever done. Given or received. I *did* go to college."

"Wait. I missed a McCarthy doing a body shot? Why didn't anyone let me know?" Killian said with a rare smile.

"What's the big deal?" she asked.

"It's just that—" Killian started.

"The McCarthys are the good kids. We all know it. Always have. You guys never did anything wrong," Ronan finished. His eyes still held the accusation: *Except for that one time.*

"Here's a newsflash, Doyles, I'm not a kid anymore. I'm a grown-ass woman. And as such, I drink, I fuck, and yes, I occasionally swear."

Somehow that sounded better in her head than it did when it came out. She hated the need to defend herself.

Killian raised his glass. "To all the women who drink, fuck, and swear."

She took another drink. But they were right. The McCarthys were the perfect family. Her siblings naturally held up their end to make everyone look good. It required effort from her. Back in high school, it had been easy. She just did whatever she was told and whatever was expected of her. But once she went to college, she realized that wasn't who she was or who she wanted to be. But for her family, she continued to pretend.

Which was exactly why she shouldn't be here.

Hadn't she just listened to her mother talk about all the wonderful, *nice* men she could be dating? Unfortunately, no matter how many times Chloe had tried to tell her that just because guys seemed nice didn't make it so, her mother didn't listen.

Seeing her with Ronan would probably give Mom a stroke. So much for her vow to try to do better. Be the child her mom wanted and life would be so much easier. It wasn't like her mom was asking for anything ridiculous. A steady job and a nice man. That was all that was missing from her life for her mom to be happy. She went to church, did Sunday dinners, doted on her nieces and nephew.

"What do you want, Chloe?"

Hearing Ronan use her name in the dark sent a shiver down her back. She returned her attention to his face. He had the beginnings of a beard and his black hair, overdue for a cut, curled in waves at his collar. "Nothing. I'm being neighborly. That's what the block party is all about. If you don't like it, you shouldn't have come."

"Ouch," Killian said with a smile. "I think you can add being mouthy to your list."

She sucked in a sharp breath.

"I like it," Killian continued.

Nothing from Ronan. She didn't know why she bothered. He would never make a move to sleep with her—of course, that's all it could be. Just enough to scratch that itch.

Maybe it was time to actually let her mother set her up. Bad boys got her blood racing but it could never be more than a few wild nights. At least with them, she knew what she was getting. Her mother might have the ability to find a truly nice guy. Lord knew Chloe failed in that mission spectacularly. The nice guy she'd found had been worse than all of the bad boys.

"Enjoy the beer, Doyles." She turned and walked back to the bonfire to play more games with childhood friends.

CHAPTER

Two

Ronan watched Chloe walk away, knowing it was for the best. It didn't stop him from studying the sway of her sweet ass in those tiny shorts though. He drained his beer and stood.

Killian glanced down the block. "I think I'll go say hi."

"See you later."

"Will I?"

Ronan tried not to hear it as a dig about his lack of visiting. "You could call me if you want to get together."

"We've tried that."

"I've never been one for big groups. You'd have better luck if we're one on one."

Killian burst out in laughter. "Our family is a big group. There's no avoiding that."

"That's the reason I don't like groups. Give me a call when you're free."

"Will do."

Ronan turned and went back into the house, glad there were no hard feelings between him and his brother. Killian had tested the waters to see if Ronan was willing to give in. He'd report back to Brendan that he was as steadfast as ever.

His mother had gone down the block earlier to visit but came home early. Inside, he'd expected that she might've gone to bed, but she was sitting on the couch in the living room, the blue glow of the TV illuminating her face. "Hey, Mom."

She reached over to the end table and flicked on a lamp. "You're overdue for a haircut."

Was he? He ran his fingers through the mop on his head.

She stood. "Come on. I'll give it a trim now."

"It'll keep. It's late."

"I'm not asleep, am I? Downstairs."

He didn't bother to put up any further argument. When Ann Doyle gave a command, it was wise to do as you were told. She moved ahead and turned on the basement lights. He followed her down the creaky stairs, ducking as he neared the bottom as he'd done since his teens. Whoever built the house hadn't considered anyone over five foot six.

He turned the corner where his mom stood holding a cape beside her wash sink. He remembered how she'd used the utility sink beside the washer when she first started doing hair from home. It had been like that for a couple of years after Dad disappeared. She'd scraped together enough money to get a proper wash sink and a real salon chair—used—to set up shop.

That first year she'd had a lot of clients from the neighborhood. He'd figured they'd come mostly out of pity. She was a rare single mother in this area and she had seven mouths to feed. It wasn't until he was in his twenties that he realized she had so much business because she was damn good.

He sat in the chair and let her drape the plastic cape over him, but when he slid back to rest his neck against the basin, he felt like Godzilla trying to squeeze into a closet. Didn't faze Mom though.

"I'm glad you came to visit. You should do that more often. Your brothers miss you."

"They know where to find me."

She turned the water on and waited for it to warm. "Street goes both ways."

He closed his eyes and sighed. He'd never win this argument or any other for that matter. She was right. He didn't come home because he didn't like how he felt here. Too many memories.

Her hands massaging his scalp were hypnotic and his shoulders released tension he hadn't realized he'd been holding. His mom had been cutting his hair his whole life. The handful of times he'd paid someone to do it had felt like a betrayal, so he didn't do much to his head until he saw her.

When the water cut off, he opened his eyes. She roughly wrapped a towel on his head and pointed to the other chair. He moved in silence, wondering why it was imperative for her to cut his hair tonight. She squeezed out the excess water and tossed the towel into a basket near the washer.

As she ran a comb through his hair, she said, "Sometimes you look so much like him I have to do a double-take."

He remembered his father's face clearly and while he didn't notice the resemblance when he looked in a mirror, pictures didn't lie. His father had always been clean-shaven, though, which was part of his reason for sporting a beard.

As much as he'd loved his dad, he didn't want the constant reminder.

"How are you?" she asked.

He knew those three words were asking more than the state of his life. The anniversary of his dad's disappearance hit them all hard.

"This one is harder than most," he admitted. He thought he'd have answers by now.

"Maybe it's time for all of us to let go."

"Damn, Brendan," he muttered. Meeting his mother's eyes in the mirror in front of him, he said, "Don't let him pressure you into doing anything."

She arched a brow at him. "My children have never been able to pressure me into giving in on anything. I'm not about to start now."

She clipped hair around his ears. Lowering her voice as she concentrated on the task at hand, she continued. "A long time ago, I accepted that he's gone. He's never coming back. In truth, if he were to show up on my doorstep today, I don't know that I'd have him."

What? He'd always thought she couldn't move on. "Then why haven't you declared him dead? Why haven't you gone on with your life?"

She stopped snipping and rested a fist on her hip. "Who says I haven't?"

Her steely gaze met his and he realized he had no idea what his mom did with her life.

"You don't date. You haven't remarried."

She took a slow deep breath. "I never made the official declaration because of you kids."

She meant him. He'd been the one arguing about it for years.

"At first, there was the hope he would come back. Later, it was...you needed it to be a possibility." Picking up another lock of hair, she went back to cutting. "And as for dating, I've done my share. I've never remarried because I didn't want to. More than the fact that I'm still married to your father, I decided I never wanted to be in that position again. I like my life just fine, thank you."

The truth spilling in this basement was a little too much to handle. He felt like nearly half his life was a lie.

He watched his mother's quick movements as she cut wayward curls but remembered that he didn't like it too short. No need to look too much like Brendan either.

When she seemed satisfied with her work, she nodded and knocked loose hair to the floor. But as he moved to stand, she pressed a hand to his shoulder. "Let me clean up that thing growin' on your face."

He settled back and she tilted the chair. With a straight razor, she cleaned up the lines of his beard and trimmed it close. While she didn't mind the facial hair, she didn't like it wild. This time when she finished, she stroked his cheek. Then she stepped back and pulled the cape from around his neck.

He stood and ran a hand over his head. Then he bent and pressed a kiss to her cheek. "Thanks for the haircut. As for the rest, I need answers. I need to know what happened."

"It won't change anything."

"It might not. But at least I'll know. We'll all know. Just give me a little more time."

She nodded. At least she had his back. She wouldn't let Brendan or Killian make a move. She'd hold them at bay and take the heat for it.

Which meant he needed to press harder to finally get the answers he'd been searching for.

THE FOLLOWING MORNING, WHILE MOST OF THE NEIGHBORHOOD was off to church, Ronan was climbing the steps to his childhood home once again. The twentieth anniversary meant something to all of them. Brendan called a family meeting. Between racking his brain for ways to find answers about his dad and thinking about Chloe, he hadn't gotten much sleep last night. He hoped Mom had a pot of coffee on.

He rapped twice on the front door before pushing it open. "Hey, Mom. Just me."

She stood in the kitchen doorway, wiping her hands on a towel. The scent of warm cinnamon rolls wafted toward him.

"Good morning," she said. "Coffee's ready, but since you'll probably take the last of it, start a new pot."

He followed her into the kitchen and drained the pot into a mug. "I'm the first one here?" he asked as he prepared the maker for another pot.

"The twins and Brendan are on their way. Gavin went to the basement to look for something, but I haven't heard from Declan or Nessa."

"I don't suppose you have any insight into how I can convince them that we need answers." He turned and leaned against the counter and sipped the hot coffee.

She sat at the table and stared at him. "I told you last night that they won't do anything I don't agree to."

"I'm not trying to start a war here. I want them to understand why I can't go along. I don't understand why they don't need answers."

"Let's see what they all say when they get here."

Thumping on the basement steps caught his attention

and he turned to see Gavin twist through the door, carrying an old wooden crate.

"Hey," Ronan called.

"Good to see you." Turning to their mom, he said, "I assume it's cool for me to take this junk?"

"I don't save junk. What's in there?"

"Rusted old coffee can. A bent framing square. Some other tins and hunks of wood."

She sighed and didn't even bother to inspect the contents. "Go ahead."

"Building your next great sculpture?" Ronan asked.

"Thinking about it. There's a gallery that wants me to do an installation and I'm toying with the idea of doing something with the contrast of old and new."

Ronan respected his brother but he didn't understand most of what he did. The front door opened announcing the arrival of three of his other brothers.

Mom stood. "We should move to the dining room so we can all fit at the table."

Ronan smiled. The kitchen wasn't big, but it had always been a gathering place. They would all come in with friends, grab food or drinks, and instead of going to the living room, more often than not, they'd stand around jaw-jacking in the middle of the kitchen.

And it drove Mom nuts. She considered them underfoot, even when they towered over her.

He picked up his cup and went to the dining room table. Mom followed with a heaping plate of cinnamon rolls. He sat with his back to the windows as his brothers filed through. Gavin came in with the coffee pot and mugs.

"I only have two hands, so if you want milk or sugar, get

off your ass and get it." He set everything on the table and took a spot beside Ronan.

Ronan took that as a good sign. Maybe he wasn't totally alone in this.

Killian poured coffee in the cups and passed them around.

Brendan said, "Should we just get started?"

"What about Declan and Nessa?" Ronan asked.

"Who knows if Declan will show? And I haven't heard from Nessa either."

Just then, the front door opened again and Nessa and Declan came through.

"Sorry we're late. Someone had a hard time getting his ass in gear this morning. Anything before eleven is iffy for him."

Declan rolled his eyes at their baby sister. Then he plopped into a chair and grabbed a cinnamon roll. "You're a saint, Mom," he said with a mouthful of food.

"Now that we're all here," Brendan began, "I'm sure you all know why I called a family meeting."

"Because you want to make decisions for everyone like you're the king of the world," Ronan muttered.

"It's been twenty years since dad disappeared. Mom could have declared him dead more than a decade ago. It doesn't make sense to not finish this."

"We still don't know what happened to him."

"Uh, he took off." Declan shot him a look that said he thought Ronan was stupid.

"He didn't."

"Then where the hell has he been for twenty years?"

"I don't know."

"Does it matter?" Declan asked. "He wasn't here. That says enough."

Gavin, who was typically pretty quiet, said, "Declaring him years ago would've made sense for Mom to get money. We're all grown. What difference does it make?"

Ronan didn't know what side of the argument that was supposed to help. Brenden grunted.

"I think what Gavin means is that what can it hurt to wait a while longer?" Kieran added.

Him, Gavin, and Kieran on one side, Brendan, Declan, and Killian on the other.

He looked at Nessa. "You haven't said anything."

She stood. "I know I'm supposed to care about this. But I don't. I don't even have too many memories of him. So this argument doesn't matter to me. What does matter is that even after twenty years, his disappearance is ripping this family in half, and that sucks."

She left the table and went into the kitchen.

"How long are we supposed to wait, Ronan?" Brendan said.

"Until we get answers. I've always thought the Cahills knew something. Maybe they'll finally tell the truth."

Mom suddenly spoke up. "No, they wouldn't have kept anything from me. They were so helpful after Michael went missing. Alan Cahill came to visit. He gave us money. I was so worried in those first weeks. About all of you. About money and how to afford the bills without losing the house. I asked him if your father was doing extra work for him that night as he often did. Alan said no."

"See?" Declan said. "He took off."

"But Dad told you he was doing something for Alan, right?" It had been Alan's denial that sparked the rumors of a mistress.

She nodded.

Staring at Declan, he said, "Dad wasn't a liar."

Tension and anger rolled across the room from Brendan. "That solves nothing. It's time to finally move on."

Ronan thought fast. "Give me until the end of the summer. Let me try to find some answers."

"Summer's already half over," Brendan pointed out.

Gavin countered, "Then waiting shouldn't be a problem."

"Whatever," Declan said, as he rose and grabbed another cinnamon roll before heading to the kitchen to find Nessa.

Ronan rose, thoughts racing through his mind. He kissed his mom on the head as he passed. "Thanks for the coffee."

When he reached the front door, Brendan stopped him. "What are you planning?"

Ronan shrugged. "I'm going to find answers."

He knew better than to let Brendan in on any ideas he had. As the oldest, Brendan felt the need to tell everyone what to do and how to do it. He sure as fuck wouldn't like Ronan getting a job for the very men they had questions for.

Three

Chloe slapped at the phone to turn off the alarm and closed her eyes again, longing to return to the dream that had gotten her ramped up. She arched up and into a kiss with Ronan Doyle. So much more than the quick swipe of his tongue when he'd taken the lime from her mouth. She moved slowly, stroking against his tongue, pulling away with a bite of his lower lip. She moaned and writhed against him. His big, strong hands held her hips, his fingers pressing into the soft flesh. Her own hand slipped into her underwear to give herself a much-needed release.

She'd enjoyed many an orgasm over the last couple of weeks thanks to Ronan. She told herself she'd get some new material, but he was serving her so well.

Ringing pulled her out of the moment. She glanced at the phone. *Mom. Ugh.*

She was hot and ready and needed to get some relief, but if she didn't answer, her mom would just call back until she did. The woman didn't believe in leaving a message or sending a simple text.

"Hi, Mom. What's up?"

"Apparently, not you."

Does she have a camera on me? "I worked last night. I have to go into work soon, so I was taking a nap." *One that was supposed to have a happy ending that you're cheating me out of.*

"How are you supposed to find a better job if you're sleeping all day?"

"I'm not looking for a different job right now. I like working at the Black Rose. It suits me. I enjoy it far better than I ever did working in an office."

"But what kind of career is that? And what about starting a family? You can't very well work at a bar while raising children."

Chloe laughed. "I'm nowhere near a position to think about children. Sorry to fail you again. Chalk it up as yet another disappointment." She sat up, giving up on the orgasm she thought she'd be giving herself.

Her mother heaved a sigh. "You are not a disappointment. I worry about you."

Chloe clenched her jaw. They'd had this exact conversation so many times, she knew how it played out. "I'm happy with my life, Mom."

She could almost hear her mother's head shake in disbelief.

"I was calling because I saw Mrs. Nelson today. You remember her son, Lance, don't you?"

Oh, God. She was *not* up for fighting her mother's matchmaking. Did she know this guy? She scanned her memory. She wasn't even sure she knew who Mrs. Nelson was.

"They live over on Orchard. He was a little gangly as a teen. Red hair."

Recognition suddenly hit. "You mean Pizza Face?"

"Chloe Marie. I taught you better than to talk about people like that."

"I'm sorry. I didn't mean it that way. It's just what everyone called him growing up. I'm sure he grew into a fine young man." She had to hold in the snicker at the use of her mom's words.

"He is a lovely man. A podiatrist. A *doctor*."

"I know what a podiatrist is. I don't need an explanation."

"That makes him stable. Regular hours. He goes to church every week."

"If he's so fabulous, why is he still single?" Lord knew in her mother's mind you were only single in your thirties if there was something wrong with you. Chloe being her prime example.

"He's recently divorced." Her mother's voice dropped to a near-whisper.

Chloe didn't know what to attack first, but she went the safe route. "I don't want to be some guy's rebound relationship. Those never work out."

"It would be good for you, even if he's not your soulmate. He's the kind of man who can take care of you, who's kind and gentle."

"I can take care of myself."

"You haven't had a serious relationship since Tim."

How many times had she tried to explain? She couldn't just come out and say Tim had been abusive, because although he was, he'd never hit her and that's what her mother would want to know. It would just be another instance of her overreacting. Not knowing a good thing when she had it. "We just weren't meant to be."

"But it gets lonely. Even for you."

Her words stung because they were true. She thought

back to Ronan. He wasn't a bad guy, wasn't really good, either. He would never be kind or gentle. It wasn't in his nature. And that was exactly what had always drawn her to him, even though for the last fifteen years he'd barely acknowledged her existence.

Until the block party.

She shoved out of bed. "I have to get ready for work."

"What's there to do to get ready for a bar?"

Chloe ignored the jab. She'd gotten good at that. She'd thought things would be different this time because her dad had gotten her the job with Mr. Byrne. She liked working there. "I know you think working at a bar is beneath me and I should shoot for something higher, but I enjoy my job. And I'm good at it." *Why can't you just be happy for me? For once.*

"If you have coffee with Lance, I promise not to mention your job again."

"For how long?"

"As long as I can."

Ooo...she must be desperate to offer that up. Even though Chloe knew it was too good to be true, she agreed. It was only coffee after all. Nothing could happen on one simple coffee date. She told her mom to tell Lance to stop by the Black Rose. Mom reluctantly agreed even though that was not a place for a proper date.

Maybe the guy wouldn't even show. Then again, maybe he would and they might have a nice time. It would make her mother happy with her for a change.

The problem with that was she never really enjoyed a *nice* time.

AFTER THE FAMILY MEETING, RONAN WENT TO CAHILL Construction and got a job. Although his last name would've opened doors for him at Cahill if he needed, he simply relied on his years of running crews away from Chicago. He'd worked for an Indiana company that sent him on the road as a superintendent all over. Taking a job on a crew was a huge step down. But he didn't mind. Thomas Walsh had questioned that when he interviewed Ronan. Ronan told him he wanted to be back home and was willing to put in the work.

Although Alan Cahill's name was still on the company, even Ronan knew he didn't have a hand in the day-to-day business. Not long after Michael Doyle's disappearance, Alan was elected alderman and eventually moved on to mayor. His son Danny had taken over operations. As far as he knew, Danny and his father didn't cross paths, other than with Alan.

Ronan had focused on getting in with the old-timers, guys who had been working for Cahill in some way or other for more than twenty years. Any time there was overtime to be had, they let Ronan take it. He never turned it down. He also never turned down the chance to go out for a drink after work. That was where the most important business took place—over a Guinness at the pub.

For as much as things had changed in Chicago, some stayed the same.

But he was no closer to figuring out what happened to his dad than he was when he'd been before he came home. He'd burned through the last two weeks and had nothing to show for it. He was beginning to think Brendan was right. He was never going to get answers.

This afternoon when Thomas Walsh, his immediate

supervisor, called him to the trailer, he knew something was up.

Thomas sat back in a creaky chair that rocked under his weight. "Take a seat," he said, pointing to the only other chair in the tight space.

Ronan sat. "Is there a problem?"

Damn. If he got laid off already, he'd be pissed.

"Not at all. Just the opposite. We're offering you a promotion to superintendent." The look on Walsh's face didn't exactly express happiness.

Ronan blinked, unsure if he'd heard correctly.

"Ronan?"

"I'm sorry. Did you say promotion?"

"Yes. Congratulations. I'm assuming you'll be taking it since you jump on any job we've offered."

"Of course. Thank you. It seems kind of sudden. Is that going to be a problem with the guys?"

"Not my call. The day's about done. Go out and buy a drink for your crew. Then head on over to the Black Rose. You know where that is?"

"Yes." The Black Rose was the bar where Alan Cahill had conducted all of his off-book business since the beginning. While it wasn't a private bar, you only went to the Rose as an employee of Cahill's if invited. It was not a drink-after-work establishment for most of them.

"Meet Danny Cahill and he'll go over the specifics of the new position." Thomas stood and extended a hand.

Ronan shook hands and thanked him again. This was it. His chance to finally find some answers. And to think last week he'd been almost ready to call it quits on his quest for the truth. He'd never had a face-to-face with Danny Cahill. They'd met in passing, but Ronan doubted the man would recognize him. Meeting Danny Cahill was the first step to getting closer.

He headed back to where the crew was rolling up the tools for the day.

"What'd the boss man want?" Drew asked.

"To tell me I'm being promoted. First round is on me tonight, boys." He spoke cheerfully, as though these men were his friends, when in fact, they weren't. He didn't have anything against them, but the young guys wouldn't be able to get him any closer to finding the information he needed, and he didn't know if he could trust any of the older guys.

A deep cheer traveled across the group as word spread that they'd get a free drink. Ronan smiled as he gathered his stuff and loaded his truck.

At the bar, he rushed through a beer, anxious to get to the Black Rose. Thomas hadn't given him a specific time, which wasn't unusual. The Cahills could hold court there most of the night. He accepted congratulations from guys on his crew, but his mind was on the next step. He slapped backs on his way out of the bar and headed to the Black Rose.

Danny Cahill was the connection to his dad. He considered how to approach Danny, what to do to get closer, admission to the inner circle. In his gut, he knew that inner circle, Alan Cahill and friends, knew something about what happened with his father. Chicago politics and construction were dirty business.

Brendan had tried going at them head-to-head when he was younger and came up empty. They protected themselves and Brendan had been labeled as someone not to trust. It was one of the rare occasions Ronan could remember his brother acting rashly. That was usually his move.

He circled the block near the Black Rose, looking for

parking. Nothing available, which was normal for a Friday evening, but it didn't help calm his nerves. His stomach churned for a multitude of reasons. A first meeting with Danny Cahill, not wanting to leave his boss waiting, worrying that Cahill wouldn't be able to tell him anything about his dad. Worse, getting all of the answers he believed he wanted. He looped around twice before finding a small spot that took three tries to parallel park into.

He pulled open the heavy mahogany doors with the engraved black roses centered in the wood. The interior was dark but inviting. Couples sat at small tables enjoying dinner, singles gathered at the bar. Ronan looked around for Cahill. The hostess walked up to him.

"One?"

"I'm meeting someone. Danny Cahill?"

"Oh, Mr. Cahill is expecting you. This way." She led him to the back of the restaurant to a round corner booth.

It was the kind of booth he'd imagined a mafia boss used to conduct business. He swallowed a chuckle. The Cahills weren't Italian mafia, but they were definitely connected. In Chicago, you no longer heard stories of the Irish mob, but that was only because they all owned legitimate businesses.

Didn't make them any less "mob."

No one was at the table, so Ronan was unsure of his next move. It felt disrespectful to sit when his host wasn't there, but where was he? The hostess said Cahill was expecting him. Fuck. He was not made for this kind of interaction, where every move would be scrutinized. He preferred to plow ahead and do what he wanted.

Instead of sitting, he stood, leaning against the edge of the booth, and took out his phone to appear less anxious. A moment later, Danny Cahill was standing beside him.

"Ronan Doyle?"

"Yes, sir." Ronan extended a hand.

As they shook, Ronan took a long look at Danny. The man was about the age his dad had been when he disappeared. In his mind, Michael was frozen in time at the age of forty-three.

"Please take a seat." Cahill gestured toward the booth.

Ronan thought he caught a glimpse of appreciation in the older man's eyes that Ronan had waited to sit. They sat across from each other and Ronan fisted his hands in his lap to keep from moving.

"I have to say that I was surprised to find out that Thomas had hired you. I didn't know you were back in town."

Cahill had known he left? "I just came back. I've been rehabbing a house, thinking about flipping it, but missed a regular check."

"You're way overqualified for the job."

"I know. Like I told Mr. Walsh, I'm fine with working my way up."

"I've heard a lot of good things about you." So he'd been checking up on Ronan.

"Thank you."

"Superintendent is a big step up, both in pay and responsibility. But given your experience, you know that."

"Yes, sir."

"I have little doubt you can run a crew. Thomas can show you the ropes for the rest. If there's anyone from your old crew you'd like to bring under you, let Thomas know. Otherwise, he'll decide and then fill in with new hires. You'll start on Monday at the site on LaSalle."

"Okay." He waited, sure there was more to this meeting than letting him know what site he'd be working. After all, that was information Thomas could've given him. His mind raced. He had the chance to spend hours every day with men who knew his dad. Guys who might know what was going on back then.

"The reason for meeting with me tonight is the responsibility part of the job. As I'm sure you know how business is done. We sometimes do jobs off the books, favors to people who can help us."

Ronan nodded. It wasn't something that was explicitly said, but you'd have to be an idiot not to know that working for cash on the weekends was an off-the-books job.

"As superintendent, it'll be your job to get those done for the money I give you. One-time cash payment that you pick up from me here. Give as much or as little to the crew as you want. What you work out with them is between you. You keep the rest."

And that explained how Thomas Walsh could afford to live in a swanky house in Park Ridge, even though he was just a blue-collar guy. These were the kind of jobs he and Brendan had worked on with their dad as teenagers. All the weekend jobs taught them about construction and hard work. Dad paid them cash and taught them valuable skills.

Cahill waved a server over.

"Hi, what can I get for you, Mr. Cahill?"

Ronan knew that raspy voice. He looked up and swallowed hard. Chloe. What the hell?

"Guinness?" Cahill asked him.

Ronan nodded.

"I'll be right back with those." She paused and stared at Ronan until he looked up at her. "How are you doing, Ronan?"

Her bright smile was like a stab to his chest.

"Good," he answered, wishing like hell she would let him pretend they didn't know each other.

She nodded and turned away.

"You know Chloe?"

"We grew up in the same neighborhood." *She'd always been a pretty little thing that was a hundred percent off-limits. Until his stupid dare.* He licked his lips, feeling the phantom brush of her mouth against his.

Cahill slid an envelope across the table. "Here's a little bonus for you. A welcome aboard."

"That's not necessary."

"We take care of our own. You're one of us."

"Thank you," Ronan said, swallowing bile at the thought of being one of them. They were shady as all hell and he'd always known it. Now that he was getting what he wanted, to be part of the inner circle, he began to wonder what it would cost him.

CHLOE WALKED TO THE BAR TO POUR TWO PINTS OF GUINNESS. She didn't usually wait tables anymore unless they were swamped, but she always took care of Mr. Cahill. When Alastair Byrne, owner of the Black Rose and her dad's friend, had promoted her to manager, he gave her a list of customers who expected special treatment. Danny Cahill and his father Alan were at the top of that list. That meant when she was on duty, she took care of them.

Seeing Ronan with Cahill had been a bit of a shock, but hearing him refer to her as some girl from his neighborhood irked her. She supposed it wasn't a lie, but since he'd done a body shot off her, it felt like she should be more than some neighborhood girl. Although they had history, she was being irrational because her flirtation with Ronan had always been one-sided and thoughts of him had taken up permanent residence in her rub club for getting off.

She should've just let him pretend they didn't know each other. It was what he wanted. But there was little in the world that bothered her as much as being dismissed. A huge part of her wanted to go back to that table and make sure he couldn't ignore her.

However, she also acknowledged that it was that kind of impulsive thinking that got her into trouble. And Mr. Cahill was here for business. She couldn't risk upsetting him even if it meant driving Ronan crazy.

When she delivered the beer, Mr. Cahill was no longer at the table. She set the glasses down without a word.

"Thank you," Ronan said.

"Will there be anything else?" she asked stiffly, staring him in the eye, challenging him to dismiss her again.

He leaned back in his seat. "Is there a problem?"

She glanced over her shoulder for any sign of Mr. Cahill. When she saw the coast was clear, she spoke in a harsh whisper. "Your tongue was in my mouth two weeks ago. You licked salt from my stomach. But I'm just some girl who grew up in the same neighborhood?"

"We'd both been drinking. It was a party. What was I supposed to say?"

She opened her mouth but realized she had no comeback. They weren't anything to each other. This was why she should've kept her mouth shut.

She turned to leave and he grabbed her wrist. The rough calluses on his hand rasped against her sensitive skin. When she twisted, he tucked some cash in her apron, his fingers causing a tingle to spread across her abdomen even though there were layers of material between his hand and her stomach.

"Thank you for the beer."

She gave a quick nod because if she said anything, it wouldn't be nice. Not that anything she said would offend Ronan. But she didn't want Mr. Cahill overhearing. Without much effort, Ronan had managed to treat her like no one, pushing cash at her in that stiffly polite way. He was different at the block party. At least he'd made her think so. He was every bit into that body shot as she was. But now, he was pretending otherwise. She wondered why.

She went back to the bar and wiped down the counter. Normally at this time of the evening, she would go to the office and get some work done, but until Cahill walked out the door, she would have to remain out front.

Watching Ronan, she tried to figure out why he was meeting with Cahill. Had Ronan started working for him, like his dad had? She hadn't known he planned to stay in town. This was the first time she'd seen him in here. The Black Rose was known in the neighborhood as the place for business meetings for the Irish community. More deals were made across these tables than happened in boardrooms or offices. These men liked cordial conversation over a pint. It was a litmus test she'd witnessed hundreds of times. Talk of family preceded business. Points of the contract discussed after two pints when everyone was more relaxed.

She could probably write a book on the dealings of Irish businessmen. Older men drank only here, rarely at home. Alcohol didn't have a place with the family. She briefly wondered if it changed through the generations. Did Danny

Cahill do things differently than his father? Or did Alan expect Danny to keep everything the same?

Ronan ran a hand through his dark hair and she realized that he'd gotten it cut. His waves were tamer, no longer curling at his collar. His hands were broad, his fingers thick and blunt. What he could do with those hands...

"Someone you know?" Alyssa said as she leaned against the bar beside her.

"Yeah."

"He's hot. You know, if you go for the broody, grunting type."

Chloe looked at the waitress.

"Which based on the attention you're giving him, you're totally into." She threw up her hands. "Hey, no judgment here."

"I'm not into anything he has. I'm just waiting for them to finish up so I can go in back to get paperwork done."

"Sure. Whatever you need to tell yourself. I'll just ignore the eye fucking I saw when you delivered his beer." She paused to wink. "While I have you here, can I get next Thursday off? My sister is coming in and my mom is planning a family dinner."

"It should be okay. Let me see who I can get to fill in."

"You're the best. Thanks." Then she spun to go pick up her drinks from the bartender.

Chloe took out her phone and pulled up the schedule to see who might be able to switch with Alyssa. As she texted Brian to see if he could cover the shift, she considered Alyssa's words. Sure, Chloe spent too much time staring at Ronan and thinking about him naked. But eye fucking was a two-person sport. He was painfully uninterested. After making rounds to check in with tables, she stopped back at Mr. Cahill's booth. Ronan was gone.

"Is there anything else I can get for you, Mr. Cahill?"

"Can you get another Guinness for me? My father'll be joining me for dinner. He should be here soon."

She smiled and nodded, even though inside she cringed. If the Cahills were staying for dinner, she wasn't going to be getting any paperwork done tonight. As she poured another beer, her phone dinged.

A text from Lance Nelson asking if he could stop by for a drink. Her night was shot anyway—might as well get all of the punishment out of the way at once. Glancing back at Cahill's table, she considered the time. Alan Cahill had arrived and was already sitting in the booth. She texted Lance back letting him know she could take a break soon.

As she set the beer in front of Danny Cahill, she looked at Alan. "Good evening, Mr. Cahill. What can I get for you today?"

"Just a coffee. How are things?"

"Good. Thanks for asking. Would you like menus?" Not that they needed them.

Alan shook his head. "I won't be staying for dinner."

She did a mental fist pump. Maybe she could get rid of them and Lance so she could finally get work done.

Danny Cahill said nothing, so she turned to face him. "Would you like anything to eat?" *Please say no.*

"If my father's not staying, I guess I'll head home for dinner. I might even be able to see my kids before they disappear with friends."

She smiled, nodded, and went to get Alan's coffee.

When she returned, the tension at the table was tangible.

Alan was not happy. She set the cup in front of him and backed away. Curiosity had her lingering nearby.

"What the hell were you thinking?" Alan asked.

The muscle in Danny's jaw twitched. "It was the right thing to do. Thomas had already hired him and he has the experience to lead."

Were they talking about Ronan? The timing led her to believe they were, but she supposed it could be anyone. They employed so many people she'd met over the years.

"I've been telling you he's up to no good."

"He's not like his brother Brendan. He's no trouble."

Chloe stifled a laugh. Now she had confirmation they were talking about Ronan, but to say that Brendan was the troublemaker and Ronan was the good brother was laughable. She'd never heard a peep about Brendan doing anything terribly wrong. Fights and stuff as a kid. In fact, he was so upstanding that her parents didn't mind that he was a few years older than her when he'd asked her out at sixteen.

He'd grown up, joined the military, and then the FBI. In the meantime, Ronan, if the rumors held any truth, had done pretty much every bad thing he could think of.

Their voices quieted for a moment and then Danny stood. His face was tight as he leaned down over his father. "It's been twenty years."

"At least if he's that close you can keep an eye on him."

Danny shook his head, and then he walked past Chloe with a stiff nod. She returned to the table to see if Alan needed anything else. She was usually a little awestruck seeing him up close and personal. He'd been mayor of the city when she was younger. He'd only been in office for a single term, but he was connected to so many people and families she knew it was kind of like seeing one of your own in charge.

Now he just looked old. She supposed he was in his seventies because Danny was in his forties. Danny had kids who were in high school and college. Alan was older than her parents, but they had friends in common.

Alan turned to her, his face as stormy as Danny's had been. She briefly wondered if he felt like he was staring in a mirror when he looked at Danny.

"I'm done, Chloe. Thank you for the coffee. Tell Alastair I stopped by." He paused. "I assume he's not in?"

"No. He's at least halfway retired. Mrs. Byrne wants him to retire all the way, but you know how it is when you own your own business. He can't just walk away. I'll be sure to tell him you said hi."

He patted her arm with his wrinkled, pale, spotted hand. "You're a good girl."

She forced a smile. "Thanks."

Always the good girl. She was so tired of that label. It was like a jacket that didn't fit. No matter how hard she tried, she just couldn't get it zipped.

As the old man left, she wiped down the table. Someone tapped her shoulder. She turned and a tall, lanky redhead stood in front of her.

"Chloe?"

"Lance." She forced another smile. His face had cleared up since adolescence, and his hairline was receding. Other than that, he looked much the same.

"Is now a good time?"

"Sure. Let's grab a table. What would you like to drink?"

"I'm good with coffee if that's okay with you."

"Take a seat," she said, pointing to a small table. "I'll be right back."

She ran to the bar, poured two cups of coffee, adding a shot of whiskey to hers. She sat across from Lance.

"I remember seeing you when we were growing up, but we never really knew each other. Tell me about yourself."

"Not much to tell. I'm manager here."

"Your mom was telling me that this is temporary while you figure out what's next."

"Well, that's what she'd like to believe. You know moms. I like it here." She took a gulp of coffee.

"What do you do outside of work?"

She thought for a minute. She hated first date small talk. "I'm a master binger?"

"Binger?" His whole forehead—and there was a lot of it —crinkled.

"I find a new TV show to stream and plow through every episode of every season in record time," she said with a smile. It was a joke. Mostly.

"Oh. I don't have much time to watch TV. What else?"

"I like to cross-stitch."

He screwed up his face. "You mean the needlepoint stuff old ladies do?"

"Uh, yeah. It's relaxing." She had nothing to add. All this guy did was make faces at what she liked. "Tell me about you."

"I'm newly single. I've been divorced for three months."

"Kids?"

"No. That was part of the reason for divorce. I wanted kids and my ex didn't."

"Wasn't that something you talked about before getting

married?" She tried not to sound judgey, but how did he marry someone without knowing that?

"I thought we were on the same page." He shook his head and Chloe felt bad for him.

"What do you do for fun?" she asked.

"I don't have much time for fun. I'm still building my practice. I thought I'd be in a different place in my life. Divorce messed with my plan. I'm trying to get my life back on track."

She leaned forward on the table. "What does that plan look like?"

"I want to meet someone who wants the same things I do —kids, a house, regular family vacations."

"Sounds nice." She tried not to sound sarcastic, but it wasn't anything she was looking for. Not after Tim. She wished like hell she did. Life would be so much easier. He needed to find someone like her sister Erin. Too bad she'd been off the market for years.

"What's your plan?"

"I don't have one."

"Surely you have some idea. Where do you see yourself in five years?"

She sat back and thought for a minute. She had no plans. "I'm playing it by ear for now."

He stared at her.

This conversation suddenly made her feel like a total loser. She'd promised herself that she would never let a man make her feel that way again. He wasn't worth her time. Taking a slow breath, she said, "Thanks for the coffee, Lance, but I should be getting back to work now."

"Oh. Sure." He stood. "How about dinner some time?"

She drained her cup. She wanted to say, "Hell no. I'm not

what you're looking for," but there wasn't enough whiskey in her coffee to loosen her tongue that much. Instead, she said, "Maybe. If our schedules line up. We both seem pretty busy, and we work opposite schedules."

"Sounds like a plan. It was good seeing you."

She nodded, picked up their cups, and dropped them off in the kitchen. Then she went to the office to finally start the paperwork she'd been trying to get to all night. Unfortunately, she couldn't focus. Lance's question dogged her. Where did she want to be in five years?

In the back of her head, she figured she'd be married with kids at some point. Like her sister Erin. Maybe. After three years with Tim, who was a master planner, who told her what her life should look like and where they were headed, she found too much planning made her skittish. Part of her missed having those kinds of long-term dreams and aspirations.

Right now? She had nothing. But she wasn't even having all that much fun.

Maybe it was time to make some changes.

CHAPTER
Four

A week later, Chloe sat in her living room and debated how to spend her time this afternoon. She had to work tonight, and she had an appointment to get her hair cut, but beyond that, she had nothing. Everything about her coffee date with Lance last week still bugged her. She'd been more restless than usual. She put on her latest binge-worthy show—space bounty hunters—and toyed with the frame for her current cross-stitch. It was a silly hobby, but she loved it.

Her grandmother had taught her when she was young and Chloe had taken to it immediately. Something was soothing about the counting and making precise little x's that turned into a phrase or a picture. In general, Chloe had never been terribly creative. That had been Erin's specialty. Her little sister could make up stories about anything.

Chloe, however, liked logic and patterns, which was why her parents pushed her toward business. To a certain degree, they'd been right. Math came easy to her. And she was good with people. But it was completely unfulfilling. She was bored out of her mind at every job she'd held. It made going back to get her MBA a nonstarter, much to her mother's disappointment.

The Black Rose might not be sophisticated work, but at least she wasn't bored. She picked up her cross stitch and watched TV as she worked. Her mother had been proud when Chloe learned this skill. She used to brag about how beautiful her cross-stitch was. Good enough to sell at the church bazaar.

Then Chloe's grandma had taught her how to make her own patterns instead of buying them. It opened the door to more interesting things because Chloe could create her own sayings and designs. Cross stitch had always been her getaway. When her mom was nagging and her siblings were bragging, she could retreat to a world of counting and thread and pouring her aggravation onto a piece of material. Then she tucked it away where no one would see. By the time she was living on her own, she had piles of cross stitches to fill her online store.

Now she had a moderately successful online business selling NSFW cross stitch. Her parents didn't know anything about it. They'd be mortified by the sayings she made and sold.

She'd told Erin about it, and Erin made her promise never to tell anyone. Chloe promised and then turned to Garrett. If anyone would tell her if she was making poor choices, it would be her brother, the priest. Garrett had laughed. He said there was no harm in writing inappropriate things. It was not the kind of offense that would send her to hell. Not that she fully believed the place existed. However, he agreed that their mother wouldn't handle it well.

She looked at the red lettering she had yet to finish.

Everyone needs the kind of friend who will help hide the body. It wasn't like she was encouraging someone to commit murder.

When she was frustrated, she made a new cross stitch. After her date with Lance, she came home and made one that said *Fuck the Status Quo.*

The sheer number of "fuck"s on her cross-stitch these days would send her mother to confession on her behalf.

Looking at her unfinished project, she couldn't get motivated. She wasn't feeling friendship. Today she was feeling naughty. She picked up her extra hoop, ignoring the on-screen couple who were flirting but who she doubted would end up in bed together. She thought about Ronan and her run-in with him at the bar when he'd grabbed her wrist. She remembered the feel of him over her in front of the bonfire. She knew then what she wanted to cross-stitch. *Do all the dirty things.*

She worked for over an hour on her idea and then decided to head to her mom's house before her haircut. Her appointment was with Mrs. Doyle, so Chloe usually liked to knock out a quick visit with Mom beforehand. She could be a good daughter without being tied up too long.

On her way out, she picked up the small cross stitch that she'd finished for her mom. It was a simple bible verse—*Let all that you do be done in Love ~Cor 16:14*—her chance at convincing Mom she wasn't going to hell.

She drove home and as she got out of her car, she saw a couple of trucks over at the Doyle house and guys taking sledgehammers to the front porch. Inside her childhood home, she yelled, "Hey, Mom."

"You don't have to holler, Chloe. The house isn't that big. What are you up to today?" her mom asked as she came from the kitchen.

"I just stopped by to say hi before I get my hair cut." She held out the cross-stitch. "I made you this."

"It's beautiful. I always wished I had my mother's skill in embroidery. I guess I'll just have to be content to know all of it was passed on to you."

"Mmm-mm. What's going on across the street?"

"I think Ann is finally replacing that porch. It's been a trip hazard for her in the winter for years." Her mom swept aside the sheer drapes and they both looked out the front window at the men working. "I'm thankful I've always had your father to take care of such things. To be on her own for so many years..."

"What does being alone have to do with a bad porch? I'm just as capable of making a phone call to find a repairman as a man is. That's all Dad would do. It's not like he would fix it himself."

Her mom turned to face her. "One day, you'll understand."

Her dad came through the front door, handed a bakery bag to her mom, and kissed her cheek. "Looks like they're getting that porch done. And on a weekend. I bet that costs extra."

"Not if Ronan's doing it," Chloe responded.

Her mother shot her a glare that clearly said, "*That* boy," full of contempt. Then she looked in the bag as if she didn't know it held a bear claw.

For as long as Chloe could remember, her dad took a walk every Saturday, stopped by the bakery, and bought Mom a bear claw.

"Hi, sweetie," he said to Chloe. "How are things?"

"Good."

He nodded and went to his home office.

Her mom reached into the paper bag and broke off a piece of pastry.

"Don't you ever get tired of bear claws?"

"What?"

"Every week, Dad brings you the same thing. Haven't you ever thought 'I'd really like a chocolate doughnut'?"

"I don't particularly like chocolate."

She didn't get it. Chloe looked at her parents and knew they loved each other, but she never saw any sparks between them. Not good or bad. They just were. Maybe that was because they'd been married for thirty-five years. Maybe at some point, there was no more excitement to be had.

"What are you asking?" her mom said.

Chloe shook her head. She wasn't even sure she knew. "Don't you get bored?"

"Of what?"

"Everything. Life. Being a mom. A wife. Bear claws every freaking Saturday."

"No. I like my life. I'm very fulfilled. When you find what you want, you don't need to change it." The look of total confusion on her mom's face said more than her words. She couldn't imagine any other life.

Chloe let that sink in. She didn't know if she believed it. Her mother was content to just accept things in her life. She'd never known her mom to want anything. Chloe used to want things. It was time to figure out what she wanted now.

RONAN WAS QUICKLY REMINDED WHY HE BOTH LOVED AND hated being the boss. Running a crew wasn't so bad, but the bullshit business part, he hated. The paperwork was killing him.

One perk, however, was that he got first pick on all left-over materials. He'd gotten his first off-the-books job this week, which entailed pouring a patio for some guy who Cahill owed a favor or who would owe him. The leftover concrete would be enough to repour his mother's front porch, so he planned to give up what free time he had to work on her house.

And with it being the weekend, he could get the whole thing demoed and repoured without pulling a permit. He could've asked Cahill to get him a permit (or grease the right palms to ignore the project), but he was the last man Ronan wanted to owe. Of course, that also meant he had to oversee both jobs. He left a couple guys at his mom's house to demo the porch and haul away the mess while he got the other customer's patio started.

Concrete wasn't his expertise. He preferred demolition, but he'd worked on every crew possible over the years, so he was a jack of all trades, master of none. Doing so had given him an advantage here. He caught Cahill's attention, but he didn't know how to poke around to get information without drawing the wrong kind of attention or getting fired.

He needed a plan and that might require him to ask the one person he didn't want to talk to: Brendan. Maybe he'd ask Mom about Brendan. He rarely saw his older brother. They parted ways when Brendan became the perfect son. He'd decided on law enforcement for his career and used the military to get him there while Ronan was still busy stealing cars and getting in fights. Even after Ronan had straightened out, Brendan had kept his distance.

The patio pour went off without a hitch and Ronan paid the guys out while they were still finishing. That way, he could follow the truck to his mom's house to make sure they didn't have any problems. Unfortunately, things were not going his way this time. Leroy and Tanner were still busting out the old porch when he got there. Which meant the truck was going to have to wait on them. Which was going to cost more money.

Fuck. He slammed his truck into park and jumped out. "What the hell is going on? This should've been done."

Leroy wiped the sweat from his forehead. "You're thirty minutes early."

Ronan checked his phone. Damn. Leroy was right.

"Fuck. Sorry. Let's see how fast we can get the rest of this out of the way." He moved next to Tanner and began tossing chunks of concrete in the wheelbarrow. Then, when Leroy moved to the dump truck, Ronan helped empty the wheelbarrow while Tanner began filling the next one.

He should've had a couple more guys to make sure things moved fast enough. He considered having the guys from the patio come here, but by the time they arrived, the job would be mostly done. He'd just have to suck it up and move the rocks. He offered the truck driver some extra cash to sit and wait, which he did easily so he wouldn't have to worry about being sent to another job after this one.

It only took twenty minutes of busting his hump alongside his guys to clear the debris and another ten minutes to ready the frame. The sun beat down on them and his shirt stuck to his back. Sweat rolled down from his forehead and he questioned allowing so much hair to grow on his face.

As the concrete poured into the form, he yanked off his sweaty t-shirt and wiped his face. Leroy sent out a long, high-pitched whistle. Ronan opened his mouth with a retort, but another voice responded.

"Thank you," a low, husky voice answered.

Damn. Why couldn't he escape this woman?

"Hey, baby," Leroy continued.

Ronan smacked his arm. "Shut the fuck up."

"Hey, Ronan. What are you doing here?"

He turned and looked at Chloe. She wore tight blue jeans and a tank top with a deep scoop in the front. It was the color of dark wine and reminded him of her hair. He pointed to the porch. "I'm working."

"Uh, yeah. I'm not that dumb. I'm just wondering why you're doing this on a Saturday instead of enjoying your weekend."

"It needed to be done. I had time today."

Leroy tapped Ronan's chest with the back of his hand. "Gonna introduce me?"

"No." Turning back to Chloe, he asked, "What are you doing here?"

"Your mom's going to cut my hair."

He looked at the long reddish-brown ponytail swinging behind her head. He almost told her not to cut it too short because she looked good with long hair, but it wasn't his place.

Wiggling her fingers, she said to Leroy, "Hi, I'm Chloe."

"Hey, Chloe. I'm Leroy."

"Leroy needs to get back to work." He wasn't quite sure why he needed her to leave, but he did. He glanced over his shoulder where Tanner continued to work, ignoring what was happening with them. Why couldn't Leroy be more like Tanner? To Chloe, he said, "You can go around back to get to the basement."

"I know the way," she said sweetly. "Always so pushy, Ronan. Don't you ever relax?"

Not often enough. And not in any way I'll admit to you. "We need to get this done before the concrete sets up. And you probably don't want to be late for your appointment. My mom is usually pretty booked on Saturdays."

"I'm early. I saw the truck and heard the noise, so I wanted to check out what was going on." Her left eyebrow shot up in challenge. "Is that a problem?"

"When you're distracting my employees, yeah."

She looked him up and down, letting her gaze roam his bare chest and torso. "*I'm* a distraction?"

In ways you'll never know. He pointed to Leroy, who was still grinning at her. "Obviously, to Leroy here, you're a distraction."

She winked. "See you later."

Not if I see you first. He poked Leroy and pointed to the porch to get him moving. He couldn't let Chloe be a distraction to him either. He hadn't seen her more than a handful of times in years, and that was usually in passing from opposite sides of the street. Now, it seemed like he couldn't shake her. He'd taken her parents' warning to heart. While they'd been fine with their daughter dating Brendan as a teen, Ronan would never be welcome. Even though they were grown, she was still hands-off. She wouldn't fit into his life. Not like she would expect to.

Maybe if he'd found the answers he'd been searching for about his dad...but that hadn't happened. So Chloe was off the table.

He watched Leroy and Tanner smooth the concrete. He was no longer needed here, but he wanted to talk to his mom when they were finished. He had to give her instructions on how to care for the fresh concrete.

And then there was asking about Brendan. His stomach churned at the thought of that conversation. He didn't want to owe Brendan any more than he wanted to owe Cahill. He'd hoped with this job he might be able to get information on his own.

Just the other day, Old Man Mulroney had talked about his dad. They called him Old Man Mulroney because he was one of four guys named John that Ronan knew of and he'd been around longer than most. The guy was only about ten years older than Ronan, but compared to most guys who worked construction, Mulroney was old.

It started as an offhand comment about how much Ronan looked like his father. Mulroney said he'd been on the same crew as Michael and that he talked about his boys all the time. It was a he'd-be-proud-of-you kind of comment that Ronan wasn't interested in, but Ronan figured he could pump the man for insight.

Mulroney said he'd share a couple stories with Ronan over a beer next week. While part of him wanted to hear stories to better understand his father, he really wanted to get to the relationship between Cahill and his father. One of them had lied twenty years ago and he bet it was Cahill.

He needed to find out why.

Chloe bounced down to the basement of the Doyle house. Mrs. Doyle had cut her hair most of her life—except for a brief time during her teenage years when she wanted to go to a *real* salon like her friends. She quickly learned that the extra money didn't give her anything special over what she got from Mrs. Doyle.

And today, the added perk was seeing Ronan without a shirt.

Good things all around.

"Hey, Mrs. Doyle," she called out as she plopped on a battered loveseat.

"I'll be done a bit," Mrs. Doyle responded over the head of an older woman with white fluffy hair.

"No hurry." She picked up a magazine and flipped through the pictures. Every time she got restless, she came to get her hair done. She needed a change, and hair was an easy thing to attack. While she studied photographs of hairstyles, she said, "The new porch looks good."

Not to mention your hot second son.

"It's nice of Ronan to do that," she added.

The woman in the chair said, "That's what a good boy does. Not like my good-for-nothing grandson. Never lifts a finger other than to text or play video games." She pointed in the mirror. "I tell you, Ann, I don't know what it is with this generation. No sense of family."

Chloe's back went up, but she didn't respond. She knew her family was strong. They might not always understand her, but her family loved her.

"You get out what you put in," Ann answered. "Kind of like being a beautician. Anyone can hack at hair. But if you care about your clients, learn who they are, what they like, what matters to them, they always come back."

And that was why Chloe trekked back home to get her hair cut. Mrs. Doyle's chair was about comfort.

Mrs. Doyle handed the woman a mirror and spun the chair. "What do you think?"

"Perfect."

Mrs. Doyle took off the cape and helped the woman up. "Do you need to call your daughter?"

"No. I told her when to be here. I'll wait outside." She handed Mrs. Doyle some cash and went out the way Chloe had come in.

Mrs. Doyle brushed off the chair and swept the loose hair on the floor into a pile. "Have a seat, Chloe. What are we doing today?"

Chloe sat and yanked her ponytail out. "I don't know. I want something different."

Mrs. Doyle ran her fingers through Chloe's hair. "Did you lose your job?"

Chloe laughed. "No."

"Do you plan to quit?"

"No. I like working at the Black Rose. Why do you ask?"

"Girl, do you think I haven't put two and two together? I usually see you right before you quit your job or right after you lose it. Whenever your life is in flux."

"I thought bartenders were supposed to be the intuitive ones."

Mrs. Doyle winked. "I'm pretty sure you are. That's why you keep coming here."

She picked up Chloe's hair to check the ends and let it cascade down her back. "It's healthy. How about some highlights?"

"Sure. Maybe a little shorter too?"

"How short?"

"Not too much. I still want enough for a ponytail." *Or enough to hold onto.* That thought conjured images of a shirtless Ronan again.

"Okay. Let's choose a color."

Chloe enjoyed the process of getting her hair done. The smooth movements of Mrs. Doyle, who had Chloe's hair wrapped and set in record time while she chatted with her next client. The woman had endless energy. She was the kind of mom Chloe wanted to be one day. Not that her own mom was bad. But Laura McCarthy projected perfection. Ann Doyle did not.

There was comfort in accepting people as they were.

Chloe flipped through another magazine while she half-listened to Mrs. Doyle gossiping with the other client. They swapped stories about everyone's kids. She wondered what was said about her when she wasn't around.

Heavy footsteps echoed through the basement. From her spot in a chair by an old dryer, all Chloe could see were a pair of work boots, but she knew it was Ronan. "Hey, Mom. We'll be done soon. When will you be free so I can go over instructions?"

Mrs. Doyle looked at the head of the woman in the chair and then over at Chloe. "Give me about thirty minutes."

"Once you rinse me," Chloe said, "you can go. I'll wait. I'm in no hurry."

"No date for tonight?" Mrs. Doyle asked.

Her cheeks became warm. "No date. I have to go to work later."

"It's not good to work so much."

"You're one to talk," Ronan said from the stairs. "I'll be here whenever you're done."

Mrs. Doyle finished cutting the woman's hair and had Chloe rinsed and cut in under thirty minutes. Her hair now swung above her shoulders and she had some long layers. The red highlights blended well but brightened her hair. It looked sassy. She liked it.

"Thank you. This is exactly what I was hoping for." She handed Mrs. Doyle cash.

"Before you leave, can you head upstairs and send Ronan down?"

"Sure." With her sassy new hair swaying, she ran up the stairs. She wasn't sure if Ronan would still be outside, but she figured she'd either see him in the house or call him from the front door.

She didn't have to go far, however, since he was sitting at the kitchen table drinking a beer, still shirtless.

"Hi. Uh, your mom said to go down."

His gaze shot up and she replayed the words. *Go down.* Oh, how she'd like him to go down. His broad hands on her thighs. The rasp of his beard...

"Like what you see?" She paused with a smirk on her face. Teasing Ronan was something a younger Chloe would never dream of. "My hair, I mean. What do you think?"

"I liked it long."

Her heart thumped at the acknowledgment that he had a preference about her hair. He wasn't as immune to her as he'd like to pretend. She lifted a shoulder. "It's still long enough." To prove her point, she wrapped a hunk of hair around her fist.

He rose from the table and moved toward her. Head tilted while he assessed her, he spoke quietly. "I can't seem to escape you lately. Why is that?"

"I don't know. Three times in less than two weeks. Maybe fate is telling us something."

"What's that?" He crossed his arms expectantly, his pecs flexing with the movement.

"Maybe we're supposed to be in each other's orbits." She circled her arms to mimic the idea of planets colliding.

"Sounds dangerous for me."

Her blood raced and her heart thumped in her ears. How could she ever be a danger to him? "How so?"

"In my experience, hanging around you lands me in handcuffs."

The accusation in his voice was like dumping ice in her pants. "Seriously? That was more than fifteen years ago. I said I was sorry."

"Doesn't change the fact that your one night of acting out got me arrested."

She sighed. That night had gone so wrong. She'd snuck out of her house, borrowed her brother's car to go to a party, and got drunk. "And in my experience, being around a Doyle causes heartbreak. We all get past it, right?"

"Sure," he said, but his eyes didn't reflect forgiveness.

Something she couldn't read stared back at her, making her itchy. "It's gotta be fate. I mean, what's the likelihood of you being at the Black Rose? I've never seen you there."

"I just got a promotion. Mr. Cahill wanted to go over some things."

Mentioning Cahill reminded her of what she'd over-heard. "About that...I probably shouldn't say anything, but they talked about you after you left."

His brow furrowed and his eyes narrowed. "They?"

"Danny and Alan Cahill. Alan was not pleased with Danny promoting you."

Ronan stepped closer still, and she smelled the sweat and dirt from the work he'd done. Heat radiated off him as if he hadn't been sitting here in the air-conditioned house.

In a low voice, he said, "Can you tell me exactly what they said?"

She blinked a few times. "I never figured you for one to gossip, especially if it was about you."

Ronan Doyle never cared much about what anyone thought of him.

"Can you tell me or not?"

"I'll try to remember. Stop by the Black Rose tonight and buy me a drink. I get off at two."

"You think I should buy you a drink after the hassles you cost me years ago?"

"No, you should buy me a drink because I have something you want." She turned to leave out the back door without waiting for an answer. Her heart thudded and her ears were probably red, but luckily, they were hidden beneath her fabulous new hair. She couldn't believe she just told Ronan Doyle to buy her a drink.

CHAPTER
Five

Ronan watched Chloe leave, mesmerized by the sway of her ass. The things he'd like to do to her...But what he'd said was true. Chloe McCarthy spelled trouble. He'd tried to do the right thing that night almost 16 years ago. She'd been falling over drunk and every guy at the party was eyeing her. She wasn't safe there alone, but she hadn't wanted to hear it. He'd wrestled the car keys from her and forced her into the car. On the drive to her house, she caused such a scene that the cops pulled them over.

It hadn't taken long for Ronan to be in cuffs for driving a car that wasn't his with a drunk minor in the passenger seat. Chloe said nothing as they put him in the squad car because she was too busy puking her guts up all over the cop. Sure, he'd been released immediately, her parents weren't that dickish, but he'd never forget the total look of disdain in their eyes when they'd warned him away from Chloe. They said they'd have him charged with statutory rape if they found him with her again.

Damn. He'd never even kissed the girl.

When the door closed behind her, he pulled his T-shirt back on and went to the basement, determined to put Chloe out of his mind. After explaining to his mother about watering the porch, he planned to ask about Old Man Mulroney and if she remembered him working with Dad. But then his sister showed up. He only knew it was Nessa because the back door slammed and her footsteps stomped through the kitchen and living room.

"Mom?"

"Down here," Ann called. "As I am every Saturday," she added.

Ronan smiled. All of the Doyle children had inherited Ann's sarcasm. But unlike their mother, they often lost control of the snarkiness and got themselves in trouble.

The stomping from upstairs came down the wooden steps toward them. "You're not going to believe that asshole, Tony. I don't know what I ever saw in him."

Ronan turned in the salon chair he was sitting in and eyed his sister. Nessa was passionate about a lot of things, but rarely a drama queen. If some guy was fucking with her...

She pulled up short when she saw him sitting there. "Hey, Ronan. What are you doing here?"

"We poured the new porch today. What did Tony do?" Ronan scanned his memory to try to figure out if he'd met this guy. He came up empty. "Who is Tony?"

"Current boyfriend," his mom answered. "Emphasis on *boy.*"

"Yes, Mom, you were right. I should've listened to you." She flopped on the couch. "Can one of you drive me home?"

"Where's your car?" Ronan asked.

"Tony picked me up and we were at a barbecue at his friend's house. I left."

Ronan's muscles tightened. "What happened?"

"Nothing important. Can you drive me or not?"

"Of course." He'd get her to spill in the truck.

"Thank you."

Ronan got up and kissed his mom on the cheek. "Don't forget the porch. I'll be back tomorrow to check on it."

"If you need to stay, I can wait," Nessa offered.

"I'm done. I need to go shower anyway."

He led the way out the back of the house and toward his truck. "How bad is whatever this Tony did?"

"What do you mean?"

"Like do I have to pay him a visit?"

One side of her mouth angled up. "No. Not that bad. We've only been going out a few months. He turned out to be an ass."

Screeching tires at the curb caught their attention.

"Oh, fuck," Nessa muttered. She reached out and grabbed Ronan's arm. "I'll handle this."

He stopped but shot her a look.

At the curb, the driver climbed out of the car. The guy was tall, at least as tall as Ronan, but not as wide. He had sculpted muscles, the kind you got from working out at the gym instead of from lifting heavy shit.

"What the hell, Nessa? Do you have to embarrass me everywhere we go?"

The fuck? Ronan took a step forward, but Nessa held up a hand.

"What?" she yelled. "You were the one dancing and hanging on every woman at the party. You're half-drunk and it's not even dinnertime."

"It's a party. We were having fun."

"No, Tony. You were having fun. I was trying to fend off your drunk friends."

This was getting worse and worse. He didn't care what Nessa thought she was going to handle, Ronan was done with this. "It's time for you to go."

Tony's chest puffed. "Who the fuck are you?"

As if she knew exactly what was going to happen next, Nessa spun and held up her hand again. "Ronan, no." Turning back to Tony, she said, "This is my brother. I suggest you leave."

"Come on, babe. Let's go back to the party."

"I'm not going back there. I'm not going anywhere with you. It's over."

"Let's talk about this. Alone." His voice lowered and he closed the distance to where Nessa stood.

"There's nothing to talk about. I'm tired of you being an asshole and then telling me I'm being unreasonable."

Tony's gaze shot over her shoulder to meet Ronan's. The man lowered his voice even more. "Babe. Come on. This is no one else's business."

Then he had the balls to grab Nessa's arm and try to pull her away. Nessa yanked her arm back and shoved both palms into Tony's chest, sending him back a foot. "Keep your hands off me!"

Still off-balance, Tony struck out to backhand Nessa. He had no chance of making contact because Ronan rushed forward, leading with his fists. He punched Tony twice before the man hit the ground. Ronan lowered himself and hit him again before Nessa grabbed his arm.

"Damn it, Ronan. Stop. The neighbors are gonna call the cops."

That was enough to stop him. He hadn't been arrested in years, but an assault charge might be worth it to keep this dirtbag away from his sister.

"He's not worth it."

Ronan straightened and poked at Tony with the steel toe of his boot. "Stay the fuck away from my sister. Or I'll make sure she's not around to save your sorry ass next time."

Nessa was still tugging him toward his truck. They climbed in but didn't pull away until Tony stumbled back to his car and drove off.

As he started the engine, Ronan looked at Nessa, who stared out the passenger window. "Are you okay?"

"I'm fine. He's just an asshole."

He reached over and touched her arm where Tony had grabbed. "He do that before?"

She turned her head. "What? Grab me?" She nodded.

Ronan threw the car into drive and gripped the steering wheel. He kept his mouth shut because right now, he wanted to lash out and Nessa didn't need that.

"He never hit me, Ronan."

He grunted. He wasn't even sure if he believed her.

"Can we just drop it?"

"No. We can't. What the fuck, Nessa? How could you be with a guy who treats you like that?" He was glad they hadn't gone out long, but the fact that it lasted even a couple months was too long.

"Here's a newsflash, Ronan. Guys like him don't walk around with a sign that identifies them as abusive. They're sneaky. They start off sweet and kind and thoughtful. Then they start making demands. They want you all to themselves." She took a shuddering breath. "You don't see it at first. Hell, most women don't see it for far too long."

"You keep saying 'they' and talking about how this goes. You've been with guys like him before?"

She gave him a one-shouldered shrug. "Nothing serious. I don't need you to go all *Punisher* out there."

"I knew we should've locked you up when you were little and we had the chance."

She laughed loudly. "As if you ever had the chance. I was too sly for all of you."

He wished he could call it a lie, but she had been. Still was.

"You can't protect me from the world, Ronan. We all have to navigate life. Every relationship is a learning experience. Some are more meaningful than others. Some are a lesson. Tony was one of my lessons."

"When did you get to be so smart? The Nessa I know would've been plotting how to attack the guy's car with a baseball bat."

She chuckled again. "That's not off the table. But we're getting a little grown to react like that, don't you think, old man?"

"I am not old."

"Too old to be fighting in the street," she said, pointing at his swollen knuckles.

"He had that coming."

"He did. But I can fight my own battles. You taught me well."

Obviously not well enough if she'd thought Tony was good enough for her.

"So, how's work? Mom said you got a job working for the Cahills," she asked, shifting the conversation.

"Got a promotion. Superintendent."

"Congratulations. I still can't believe you went to work for the same company Dad worked at. But I guess it put you on a fast track for promotion. Like those rich people whose kids automatically get into Ivy League schools."

"Not quite like that. I've been doing this kind of work for over a decade. I've put in my time. When are you going to learn that people like us have to work for everything?"

"I know. I'm just saying. How many guys go to work for the same company their dad worked for?"

"Danny Cahill followed in his daddy's footsteps."

"But it's his father's company. That's not the same. Fifty, sixty years ago, sure. But today? People go all over. Even if it's the same industry. Like a doctor's kid might become a doctor, but she's not going to work at the same hospital. She's going to look for her own job."

"Are you going somewhere with this?"

"Do you think that giving Cahill your time is going to lead you to answers?"

He glanced at his sister out of the corner of his eye. Yeah, she'd always been the smartest. "I'm not sure. But at this point, I have to try. I know they know something."

"Why does it matter?"

"Because it does." He was tired of having to defend himself. He expected it from Brendan. That was just the way their relationship had always been. But Nessa was his little sister. Most of her life, she'd looked up at him with stars in her baby blues like he could do no wrong. "Don't you want answers?"

"I did. When I was a kid. Sometimes you just need to accept things. Answers won't change the fact that I grew up without a father."

He often forgot that it had been different for her. He'd

been a teenager while she'd only been a little girl when their dad went missing.

Pulling up in front of her apartment building, he said, "Call me if that asshole shows up."

"I doubt he will. You're a scary guy."

"I'm serious."

"I know. Thank you for being a good big brother. Congrats on the promotion. But maybe it's time to look for a new job." She swung the door open. "Thanks for the ride."

She hopped out and he watched as she went into her building. He considered her words for a minute. He couldn't think about looking for a new job. It had always been about Cahill and getting answers, but now he wondered what would happen once he had answers or reached another dead end.

Could he move on?

CHLOE WAS BUSY AT WORK ALL NIGHT. IN ADDITION TO managing, she had to fill in for Joyce, who had called in sick. More like called in because of a party, but whatever. It was the nature of the business when you hired young people. She'd been the same way at twenty-two, much to her parents' dismay. But she grew out of it, as most did.

As manager, she tried to be understanding, but this was Joyce's third time calling in this month. If she didn't have a really good reason, Chloe would have to let her go. Firing people was one thing she didn't like about this job. She'd only had to do it one other time and her stomach had been in knots for days. She liked Joyce, so she hoped there was a good excuse for the absence.

Saturday night at the Black Rose was busy. It wasn't a club, so the atmosphere wasn't loud music and sweaty bodies dancing, but there was a constant flow of customers. After dinner, which often consisted of families or friends eating before a night out, the bar filled with many regulars. They talked and drank. Sometimes there was a game on TV—international soccer or rugby—or local teams depending on the season. Chloe tried to stay on top of enough of it to chat with patrons, but sports weren't her thing.

She was beginning to wonder if she had a thing.

Her apron was filled with cash. It was one thing she missed from being a full-time waitress. She was a damn good waitress and tips came easily to her. She was so busy talking with her customers and reminding them that it was last call, that she hadn't thought about the time. She'd told Ronan she got off at two, but he hadn't committed to coming here.

Now that the time neared closing, she couldn't get him out of her mind. Images of Ronan shirtless, sweaty, muscles bulging ran through her head.

Focus on work. Closing the bar. Chances were he wouldn't show up. He didn't want to have anything to do with her. He said as much in his mother's kitchen. She doubted her bit of gossip from the Cahills would draw him to the Black Rose at two in the morning to buy her a drink.

As the clock struck two and there was no sign of him, she called herself stupid for thinking there had been a possibility he would show. At two-thirty when customers were gone and the cleaning crew was setting up, she was resigned to having a drink alone to forget she ran into Ronan Doyle.

She locked up the front door of the Black Rose and when she turned, she saw Ronan leaning against the passenger door of his truck.

Damn. He came.

"I didn't think you'd show."

"You said you finished at two. I figured that was your way of saying you didn't want to drink here." He opened the door he'd been leaning on and waved her in. "Did you have somewhere specific in mind?"

"There's a four o'clock bar around the corner. We can walk."

His only answer was to engage the alarm on his truck.

She turned toward Last Shot. It was a total dive bar, but since they were open later than the Rose, the staff often went there for a quick drink before heading home. As she walked, she glanced down at her clothes. She looked like she just finished working. If she had known he was actually going to show up, she would've changed into something nicer. She would've put on makeup.

Ronan quickly caught up to her and then slowed to match her stride. If she wore heels, she wouldn't feel so short next to him, but in her sneakers, she had to crane her neck to look into his eyes.

"How was work?" he asked.

"Good. Busy." What the hell was she doing? She'd wanted to go on a date with Ronan Doyle since she was a teenager—even before she dated his brother. They were finally alone and she had nothing to say. *Way to seduce him, Chloe.*

"How long have you been working at the Rose?"

"Over a year. After I lost my last job, my dad asked Mr. Byrne if he could use me. Now he has me doing management stuff. What made you decide to get a job at Cahill?"

"I'm rehabbing a house and missed the regular paycheck."

They walked the rest of the way in silence. At the next

corner, green neon lit the doorway. Ronan reached across and opened the door for her.

"Hey, Nate," she called to the bartender.

"Hi, Chloe. What'll you have?"

"Beer?" she asked Ronan.

"Why don't you grab us a table and I'll get the drinks."

"Okay." She turned and found a table in the corner.

Ronan followed a minute later carrying two drafts. Sliding one in front of her, he said, "I held up my end. Now tell me what Cahill said about me."

Her heart sank. He did only come because he wanted to know what she'd overheard, not because he had any interest in her. She didn't want it to bother her, but it did. She sipped her beer before speaking.

"Alan laid into Danny about you. Not yelling, but you know the way dads do when they're pissed and want to make sure you know." As soon as the words left her mouth, she realized her mistake. Her gaze shot up to meet his. No, he wouldn't know that tone. "Sorry," she mumbled.

"Nothing to be sorry about. My father had plenty of time to use that voice with me before he disappeared."

She took a deep breath. "Anyway, it wasn't clear why Alan was mad. He said he thought you were up to no good, like Brendan. That made me laugh. I mean, come on. If he thinks Brendan is trouble?" She paused but got no reaction from him. The ominous way Danny had spoken still kind of spooked her. She lowered her voice for the next part. "Then Danny stood up, said it's been twenty years. Again, no explanation."

Ronan said nothing. He studied her with intensity as she spoke. Like he didn't want to miss a single syllable.

"Alan made a comment about keeping an eye on you. A

few minutes later they were both gone." *And I had to suffer through a miserable date.*

Ronan sat back in the booth, slowly turning his beer while staring at her.

"Why does it matter what Alan thinks of you? He doesn't run the company anymore, right? I thought he stopped back when he was mayor."

Ronan huffed. "He might not have an office but make no mistake that Alan very much still has a hand in everything."

She cringed. She knew what it was like to have people think poorly of you. "But if he really thought you were a problem, he would've had Danny fire you."

No other response from Ronan. The man was so damn frustrating. "Sorry. Probably not the juicy tidbit you were hoping for."

She thought she did a pretty good job of keeping her disappointment from her voice.

"What are you doing?" he asked.

"What do you mean?"

"What game is this? You listen in on a conversation and when I ask about it, you want to meet for a drink at two in the morning."

"Going out for drinks isn't unusual for most people. I just happen to work late."

"Why not just tell me at my mom's house?"

She leaned back in the booth to give herself breathing room. His dark blue eyes stared at her with such intensity she felt itchy all over.

"Why, Chloe?"

His insistence annoyed her. "Because I wanted to see you again. Alone. I thought maybe there was something between us. Attraction."

"What did you think would happen?"

She opened her mouth to respond but paused. He didn't say he wasn't attracted to her. He'd skimmed right past that. "Are you attracted to me?"

"You know damn well I am."

No, I didn't. You aren't easy to read. She held her tongue and pushed back the burgeoning grin. Leaning forward again, she reached across the table to run her fingers over the back of his hand. His knuckles were battered and bruised. Again, something that shouldn't be a turn-on, but was. She said, "If that's the case, what are you going to do about it?"

He was close, but not quite close enough.

Then he surprised her by leaning in, his lips within touching distance. Closer. Closer still, but his eyes were open, staring into hers. His breath wisped across her lips. The corner of his mouth tilted up. "Not a fucking thing."

When he shifted back, it was like cold water splashing her. She swallowed the humiliation that felt no different than it had years ago when she'd made a play for him. "Who's playing games now? You say you're attracted to me. I saw it when you licked my body and put your lips on mine."

"Just giving you a taste of your own." He stood and tossed a few bills on the table. "Let's go. I'll walk you back to your car."

"Wait," she said. Standing, she had no idea what possessed her to pursue him and this attraction. Maybe it was the abysmal date with Lance, maybe she still wasn't over what had happened with Tim. But as she reached for his arm, she found herself offering, "What if I keep eavesdropping for you?"

He froze and she knew she had him. He stared at her. Yeah, he was interested in her offer.

"What's the rush?" she asked. "We can stay and have another drink."

"It's late," he answered as he ushered her out the door.

"Really? Party boy Doyle can't stay up late?"

"I'm an old man now. I usually go to bed pretty early."

"Aw. I feel special that you stayed out just for me."

"Not my choice. You blackmailed me into coming."

"I'm sorry the information wasn't what you were looking for." They walked back down the block toward the Rose. "He's there all the time. Danny. Like every day. His dad shows up a few times a week. He has meetings with all kinds of top city officials. Even more guys that I don't know, but I could find out."

He spun on her so quickly, she lost her footing and he grabbed her arm to steady her. "Stay out of it, Chloe. I don't need you risking your job to feed me useless information."

"If you tell me what you're looking for, I can pay attention, and then maybe next time, it won't be useless."

He practically growled. "Stay out of it."

She heaved a sigh and crossed her arms. They stared at each other for a moment.

His voice softened. "Look. I just got the promotion, and it happened fast, so when you said the Cahills had been talking about me, I was curious. I'm not looking for anything specific."

She shot him a look that called him a liar.

"I do know that the Cahills are vindictive and ruthless. If you like your job, just do what you're supposed to do and leave it at that."

She dropped her arms. Turning away, she waved a hand at him. "Whatever."

He followed her back to her car behind the Rose. She

pulled keys from her pocket and unlocked the door. "Are you okay to drive home?"

"I'm fine, Ronan. I had one beer. I drive home every night." She didn't even turn to look at him. She swung the door open, but he braced a hand on it to stop her. She finally looked up. "What?"

"Thank you."

She softened a little. "For the record, the Cahills don't pay my check. Alastair Byrne does. I know the power the Cahills wield. I'm not stupid."

"I wasn't suggesting you are. Just naïve."

"I'm not naïve either. I wish you would stop looking at me like I'm a child."

"What do you want from me, Chloe?"

How could he not see? Determined to show him, she surged up and her lips met his. She gripped his T-shirt tightly in her fists. Her tongue stroked his lips tentatively, afraid he'd push her away, but he opened and kissed her back.

Her heart thudded. He was everything she'd thought he'd be—strong yet gentle, determined and questing. His tongue stroked hers. His beard bristled against her lips in delicious friction. His mouth lingered on hers for long moments.

Gently, he pulled her hands to release his shirt.

When she opened her eyes and met his, he said, "This isn't going to happen, Chloe."

"Why the hell not? We're attracted to each other. That kiss says you want it as much as I do."

"I'm not what you're looking for. We both know that."

"I disagree. You have no idea what I want." *Hell, I don't even know.* "I'm not asking you to marry me. Just fuck me."

The words didn't seem to have an effect. No look of shock.

He chuffed and stepped back so she could get in her car. Shaking her head, she got behind the wheel.

"Good night, Chloe. Drive safe." He closed the door.

As she pulled away, she was filled with frustration. He continued to think she was playing a game, and she didn't know how to change that. Maybe she never would. She was not so pathetic that she'd chase a man who didn't want to want her.

Six

Walking back to his truck, Chloe's words echoed in his head. *Just fuck me.* As if Chloe McCarthy had ever been a girl who just wanted to fuck. It didn't stop his imagination though. His entire ride back home was filled with thoughts of Chloe naked and screaming his name. If a simple kiss had that effect on him, there was no way he could sleep with her. She could be mad or disappointed, but she wouldn't have regrets. He, however, might.

He crawled into bed with her taste in his mouth and his hand on his dick.

The following morning, he made the call he'd been avoiding, but Brendan was his best bet.

"Hello." The dude sounded wide awake and freshly pressed even early on a Sunday morning.

"Hey, Brendan. It's Ronan."

"I know. We have this fancy thing called caller ID."

"Wasn't sure you had my number." Ronan had figured Brendan didn't have it since he avoided Ronan at all costs. "Are you free today to meet up and talk?"

"About what?"

"Cahill and Dad."

"Stay out of it."

His choice of words sent suspicion creeping into Ronan's thoughts. He wasn't talking about declaring Dad dead.

"I can't. You know that. Besides, I'm working for Cahill and they just promoted me, which puts me even closer to them."

"Fuck. Why can't you ever listen?"

He'd known Brendan wouldn't like his plan, but he was on a timeline. "I didn't like what you were saying. Will you meet me or not?"

Brendan's irritated sigh cut through the phone. "I promised Mom I'd stop by, so give me an hour and I'll see you at Super Cup."

Super Cup was the neighborhood diner that was a couple of blocks from their childhood home. The food wasn't great, but the coffee was pretty good. Ronan took a shower and did his best to scrub Chloe McCarthy from his mind.

If he planned to do whatever necessary to get close to Danny Cahill, he'd be spending more time at the Rose, which meant their paths would cross again. He couldn't deal with having a hard-on every time he saw her. He would just have to convince her that she didn't want to have anything to do with him.

An hour later, Ronan was sitting in a corner booth at Super Cup waiting for his older brother. He'd shown up a few minutes early and Brendan strode through the door exactly on time. The diner wasn't packed because the after-church crowd hadn't yet hit, but the early morning regulars were sprinkled throughout the place. Ronan didn't bother to wave because he knew Brendan would've chosen this same booth

—one in the corner with a full vantage point of the exits to watch who came and went.

Brendan saw him and joined him at the table. The waitress immediately hustled over, filled Brendan's cup, and topped off Ronan's.

"Would you like to see a menu?" she asked.

"I'm good," Ronan answered.

"Coffee's fine," Brendan followed. When she stepped away, Brendan looked at him. "What did you want to talk about?"

"Why does Alan Cahill think that you're trouble? And why does he want Danny to watch me?"

Brendan sat back in his seat and turned his coffee cup slowly with his left hand. "Where did you get that information?"

"Does it matter?"

"Maybe."

Ronan studied his brother. "Chloe McCarthy."

Brendan hadn't been expecting that. There wasn't much of a response, but Ronan knew his brother. He sat a little straighter and tightened his grip on the cup. A reaction, but Ronan didn't know why.

"How?"

"She's manager of the Rose. She waits on them and after I met with Danny about my promotion the other night, she said Alan was there and their conversation was heated."

Brendan sat with that a moment, and Ronan's irritation notched up. He'd come for answers, but as usual, his brother wasn't very forthcoming.

Finally, he leaned forward, his arms on the table. "What do you hope to get?"

"From you? A reason why Cahill thinks you're trouble. More than me. Chloe got a good chuckle over that."

Brendan smiled. "Could be because the summer after dad went missing, I went to see Alan Cahill. I'd talked to the guys on Dad's crew and I knew Cahill knew something."

It was Ronan's turn to be surprised. He'd almost forgotten that Brendan had worked for the Cahills. "You never told me that."

"Well, I was pretty hot-headed back then. Caused a scene. Lost my job. It didn't help." He drank his coffee.

"You've always acted like I was crazy for thinking they knew something."

"I just wanted you to drop it. If I had told you my suspicions, especially back then, you would've done something really stupid and landed your ass in jail."

Ronan didn't have words. All this time, all these years. "I haven't been a kid for a long time. Why not tell me?"

"Because it doesn't matter. No one talked. No one gave me any information to continue that line of thinking." He looked over his shoulder out the window. "They made me think it was all in my head."

"So you did the same to me."

"It was safe."

"Do you still suspect them of knowing something?"

Brendan remained silent for a few moments. When his gaze met Ronan's again, he said, "I think it's more than knowing something. I think they did something."

"What the fuck?" Ronan growled. Everything he'd thought about his brother was off. "Why admit this now? All these years, I've been looking for answers and your sole response has been to declare Dad dead."

"You never asked what I thought."

"Would you have told me?"

His brother shrugged. "Look. Declaring Dad dead made sense. Still does. It gives Mom closure. It's obvious he ain't coming back. At least this way, she can get his social security and his pension."

"Money isn't going to fix anything. If she wants to retire, it's not like we would ever let her live on the street." He sipped his coffee. "It feels like giving up."

"I never said give up on finding answers. Declaring him dead shows that we've all moved on. We don't need to hold on to the false hope Mom gave us twenty years ago."

"It was never about hope. Something bad happened to Dad. We all have a right to know."

Brendan finished his second cup of coffee. "I agree. That's part of the reason I became FBI. Local cops can't be trusted when it comes to the Cahills."

"Have you been investigating them this whole time?"

"Not since the beginning of my career, but damn close."

Ronan leaned back. "I guess I'm not trustworthy enough for you to have told me?"

"I never told anyone. There's not much to tell. I'm going on my gut instinct, just like you." He slid his empty cup to the edge of the table. "But between you and Chloe, we have an inside track I haven't had since I was seventeen."

"Chloe isn't part of this." He didn't know why he needed to make that clear to Brendan, but he did.

"You said she came to you with that information. If she's working at the Rose, she can eavesdrop. Hell, if I ask her nicely, she might plant a bug."

"Leave her out of this."

Brendan's eyes narrowed. "You two got a thing?"

"No." *Just fuck me*, her words echoed again. "She can't risk her job to break the law for you."

"Fine. We'll try it your way. I'll get you a list of names of guys who were around back then. You can talk to them, but don't get pushy. The minute you do, and they think you're suspicious, they'll all clam up. No one wants to cross the Cahills." He rose and tossed a few bills on the table.

"I don't give a fuck about crossing them. If they've been keeping secrets for twenty fucking years, they can go on and be pissed."

"I gotta head to Mom's. You know how she gets if we don't visit regularly. Wanna come?"

"Shit. We walk in together actually getting along, she might have a heart attack."

"True."

"I'll stop by in a bit to make sure the porch is good."

"I'll call you." Then he headed out the door.

Ronan finished his coffee and thought about everything Brendan told him. What did it say about his relationship with his older brother that he hadn't known what Brendan had been thinking? When they were young, they had been inseparable. Right after Dad disappeared, they'd grown closer as they did everything they could to help their mother hold the family together. But as time wore on, they both reacted differently. Brendan was determined to do everything right. Ronan had broken every rule he came across because he was just so angry.

Maybe it was time for brothers to start acting like brothers again.

CHLOE RELUCTANTLY DRAGGED HER ASS OUT OF BED SUNDAY morning to join her family at church. Although her family had always been churchgoers, her mother's expectation of Chloe's attendance had increased tenfold ever since Garrett had moved back to Chicago and their parish. Now, she was expected to show her face at least once or twice a month. It wasn't that she hated Mass or didn't believe in God. It was mostly that she worked late and hated getting out of bed early.

The rest was routine for her. In times of stress, she often prayed, because that was what she'd been raised to do. As an adult, she'd questioned her beliefs, but it always came back to just doing what was easiest. And making Mom happy was easiest.

Plus, they would have lunch together as a family, and that counted as a visit, so two birds. As they walked back to the house—it was a beautiful summer day—Chloe listened to Neil talk about a big new job his firm was taking on. Some downtown renovation and he hoped to be on the team. Erin and Mom were chatting about the kids, who were running ahead down the block.

The rumble of a truck coming down the street caught her attention and Chloe looked over her shoulder. Ronan. She was torn between wanting to jump onto the back of his truck to escape and wanting to hide from him because she was embarrassed. She couldn't believe she had the nerve to tell him to fuck her. She didn't know where that had come from. Well, she'd known, of course—she'd always had a thing for him—but to just say it? Last night, it seemed like honesty was a good thing. In the light of day, not so much. Maybe it was because he saw her as the good girl, or maybe it was the fact that she was just coming from church.

She wasn't one to verbalize her desires. But it had felt good to be honest with Ronan, even if he did ultimately reject her. What would have happened if she had been that honest with Tim? Or her mother?

The thought was so bizarre that her brain froze.

She slowed her pace as Ronan parked. Her mother was already opening the front door. Ronan stepped from the truck and Chloe felt her whole face get hot.

Her dad yelled, "Porch looks good, Ronan."

Chloe rolled her eyes at her dad's neighborhood manners. She didn't believe he liked Ronan any more than Mom did.

"Thanks," Ronan responded. His gaze met Chloe's.

She forced a smile she didn't feel, and then put her head down and went into her family's house. Erin's kids already had the TV on, and Chloe debated sitting with them or going to help in the kitchen. Erin decided for her when she looped her arm through Chloe's and said, "Let's get lunch." Then she lowered her voice and said, "Ronan Doyle is looking good."

Chloe rolled her eyes. "I didn't notice."

Erin nudged her. "Liar. I heard all about what happened after I left the block party."

"What did you hear?" she asked as she paused before stepping into the kitchen. They had five minutes at most before their mother joined them. Mom always changed out of her church clothes and into something more casual once she got home.

"All about a smoking hot body shot between you and Ronan. The way I heard it, people were expecting clothes to melt away."

Chloe shook her head. "It was Truth or Dare. Ronan

thought he could get under my skin, but I'm not a skittish teenager anymore."

Erin laughed. "Oh, I wish I could've seen the look on his face when you agreed to let him do that."

"Well, if you weren't an old married fart, you would've been out there getting drunk with us."

"I'm not old."

Just then, their mom came downstairs. "What are you standing around here for? Lunch isn't going to make itself."

After Mom walked by, Chloe stuck her tongue out at her sister. While they might be living completely different lives, they were sisters and Erin would never talk about Ronan being a hottie in front of their mother. Chloe didn't understand why her mom didn't like Ronan. She couldn't imagine it was because of the night Chloe had gotten drunk and Ronan rescued her. She'd explained what had happened right away.

In the kitchen, Mom had deli meat set out, along with a pile of fruit and salad fixings. "Erin, set the meat and cheese out on a tray. Chloe, cut up the fruit to make a fruit salad."

The sisters worked side by side at the small island while their mother worked on the other side of the kitchen.

"Seeing anyone these days?" Erin asked.

Chloe shook her head. "I had coffee with Pizza Face."

"Chloe," her mother admonished.

Chloe smiled. "If I used his name, Erin wouldn't know who I was talking about." Turning back to her sister, she added, "His skin is totally cleared up now, but the date was horrible. He made it painfully obvious that I'm not interesting enough for him."

"What?" Erin said. "You're fun."

"Hmm," her mother said. "Lance's mother indicated there was going to be another date."

"Well..." Chloe started with a chuckle. "I was at work and didn't want to be rude. So when he asked, I said maybe. But I will be busy indefinitely."

"But—" her mother started.

Erin cut her off. "You know who I saw this morning on my way here?"

Chloe shook her head, but mouthed, "Thank you" to her sister for stopping Mom from talking more about Lance.

"Brendan Doyle. He was on his way into Super Cup."

"Should've been on his way to church," Mom said. "Those boys need all the help they can get."

"They aren't boys anymore, Mom. They're grown men and Brendan works for the FBI. I'm pretty sure he stays out of trouble. And Ronan works construction. They're not running the streets."

"Hmph."

Chloe set her knife down with a clink. "Why do you hate them? They had a rough time when their dad went missing. But—"

"Ran off, you mean."

Chloe paused. "That's rumor. The Doyles don't think he ran off. Do you know something the rest of us don't?"

"I know the type."

"What type, Mom? What did any of the Doyles ever do to you?" Her voice was louder than what would be considered appropriate, and she waited for the scolding.

"Brendan broke your heart by running off. You were drunk and vulnerable. And his brother took advantage."

Chloe scoffed. "I wish."

Erin's jaw dropped and her eyes went wide. She shifted and angled herself to be able to see both Chloe and Mom.

"As if you could remember. You were blackout drunk."

Chloe laughed. "I think I would've remembered if the guy of my teenaged fantasies showed any interest in me. The sad thing was, I threw myself at him. He could have had me. Instead, he shoved me in the car and was bringing me home. I told you this, yet you still think he's evil. It was fifteen years ago. How long can you hold a grudge?" She stepped away from the counter. "You know what? I'm not hungry. I have to go to work this afternoon anyway, so I'm going to head out."

Her mother said nothing. On her way through the house, she said her goodbyes. She got to her car when the front door to the Doyle house opened and Brendan stepped out. Ronan's truck was still at the curb. Neighborhood wisdom said the oldest Doyle boys were never in the same room together. Not in years. The cop and the criminal. They butted heads all the time.

"Hey, Brendan. Long time."

He paused, squinted at her, and crossed the street. "Hi, Chloe." He offered a genuine smile and leaned in to kiss her cheek.

Nothing. No urge to turn her head and catch his lips. "Visiting your mom?"

"Yep. She gets cranky when we don't come by enough."

"She's been seeing a lot of her boys. I mean, that's two days in a row for Ronan."

He shrugged. "Ronan tells me you're working at the Rose."

"I am. You should stop by some time." She pulled out her phone and handed it to him. "Put in your number. Give me a call so we can have a drink and catch up."

"I will." He thumbed in his number and returned her phone. The front door opened again and Ronan leaned on the frame. Brendan glanced back at his brother, who glared at him. Then he flicked a thumb over his shoulder. "I should get going."

"See you." She opened her car door slowly to see if Ronan would say anything. He didn't. She climbed in and drove off.

The best thing she could do for herself would be to put all Doyle men out of her mind.

UNFORTUNATELY, THE UNIVERSE HATED HER. CHLOE WENT TO work, still pissed off that her mom disliked Ronan. She didn't even know why it irritated her. It wasn't like Chloe was dating him. Hell, she wasn't sure he even liked her. And having him ignore her on the street just made it worse. Why did she care?

It was probably her lustful imaginings of him and allowing her hormones to get the better of her, but she was drawn to him. Which made it difficult to put him out of her mind. She'd spent a good chunk of her afternoon scrubbing shelves and reorganizing inventory in a desperate attempt to clear her head. Anything to avoid thoughts of why he didn't want her.

When Danny Cahill came in and took his usual seat at the corner booth, Chloe knew she had no chance of removing the case of Doyle on the brain. As much as she wanted to pawn the Cahills off on another server, she didn't shirk her duties when it came to work. With a deep breath, she dried her hands and crossed the room. The Cahills were the only people who took a booth without being shown. It suddenly bothered her that they strode in as if they owned that booth. They never waited for the hostess and never requested a server. Danny and Alan alike sat like kings waiting for someone to take care of them.

Swallowing her sudden anger, she plastered on a smile and went to the table. "Good afternoon, Mr. Cahill. What can I get for you?"

"Working on Sunday, too, Chloe? Doesn't Alastair give you a day off?"

"Sure, but it varies depending on how I have other people scheduled. Plus, Sundays aren't too busy, so I can catch up on things."

"Can you get us two Jamesons? Neat. My father will be here soon."

She nodded and went to pour the drinks. By the time she returned to the table, Alan was there. Setting the glasses down, she said, "It's good to see you again, Mr. Cahill. Can I get you anything else?"

The older Cahill grunted and shook his head. She was barely two steps away when Alan laid into Danny.

"I tell you to watch out for Doyle and the first thing you do is hire him for an off-book job? What the hell were you thinking?"

Chloe slowed her gait. Ronan had told her not to eavesdrop, but she couldn't help herself. They were talking about him again and Alan was pissed. Way more than last time. But why? It wasn't like under-the-table work was unusual around here. Everyone knew it happened.

"And on *that* job, too."

"I split the work around to all my men. What better way to test his loyalty? He didn't question a damn thing. Took that cash and then used the concrete remainder to build his ma a porch. He's just here to work."

What else would he be there for? What was special about that job?

"I'm telling you, boy. He's there to dig."

"If I see any sign of trouble, I'll fire him immediately. But he's a good worker. Keeps his head down and does the job."

A glass clanked loudly against the table. "Given the circumstances—"

"That doesn't make sense. Why now? He's just a regular neighborhood guy. It's fine. You retired, remember? Let me run the company as I see fit."

"I won't let you ruin everything I worked my life to build. I wouldn't let it happen then. I sure as hell won't let it happen now." He finished his drink and set the glass down with a clink. "Ronan Doyle is looking for answers."

"He's looking for steady work is all."

The older Cahill shook his head. "One wrong step and I'll have him blackballed."

"This isn't the eighties anymore, Dad."

"Things still work much the same. Where are we on the Armitage development?"

"Snail's pace. More red tape."

"You're not speaking to the right people then. We're supposed to break ground within the month."

"Not we. Me. I've got it handled."

The conversation shifted then to more construction talk, so Chloe moved farther away. Walking to the back office, she paused and asked a waitress to check on the Cahills in a few minutes. Then she considered her next move. Since starting her job at the Rose, she'd heard some questionable conversations between the Cahills but nothing that felt threatening like this. What had Ronan done to draw Cahill's ire?

She didn't have a way to reach Ronan, but she did have

Brendan's number. But the whole neighborhood knew the brothers didn't get along. No one knew why though. Just some kind of falling out. Today was the first time she could remember seeing them at their mom's house at the same time. Maybe they'd patched things up. Without giving it too much more thought, she texted Brendan.

Hey, Brendan, it's Chloe. Can you please pass my number on to Ronan?

Are you asking me to be your wingman? I'm wounded.

She shook her head. Trust me, Ronan has no interest in me. I just heard something that I think he needs to know about.

I can pass a message if you want.

She could do that. Would Brendan tell him? It shouldn't matter. Ronan had told her not to eavesdrop. If he didn't get this message, at least she'd done what she could to make sure he didn't screw up his job. Just tell him that the Cahills are looking for a reason to fire him.

Got it.

That wasn't much of a response. She didn't know why, but it felt important that Ronan understand. Make sure you tell him. They aren't playing.

I'll make sure I tell him. How about that drink? Can I stop by tonight?

Amazing. A Doyle who wanted to spend time with her without being tricked into it. Sure. I get off at eight.

Meet you at the Rose?

No. I'll be at Last Shot down the street.

See you then.

Brendan might not quite scratch the bad boy itch she had, but it would be good to catch up with him. Until the block party, she'd forgotten how much fun she'd had just hanging out with the neighborhood families. Because she'd gone to

Catholic school, she hadn't spent her days with her neighborhood friends. The weekends and summers gave her freedom. Playing Truth or Dare at the block party reminded her of all the summer fun she'd had with those families.

She had wanted that. The sense of belonging among big sprawling families where there was always someone around for company. But it wasn't in the cards for her. She mostly liked her life, and she knew she wasn't meant to live like her mother and sister. She didn't know exactly when she'd had that revelation—probably when she left Tim. Until then, her mother's life was pretty much what she had expected for herself.

So she'd take a few drinks in a dive bar with an old boyfriend where there was no chance for her imagination to run wild.

CHAPTER
Seven

When Ronan's phone rang and he saw Brendan's number, he debated answering. He could count on one hand how many times his big brother had called him in the last decade. Given that they'd seen each other this morning, this wasn't a good sign.

"What, Brendan? Miss me already?"

"Oh yeah. Maybe we can get together to braid each other's hair."

"Funny."

"Guess who I just got a text from."

Fuck. He didn't want to hear. He'd seen Chloe give her phone to Brendan.

"Chloe McCarthy. When I saw her earlier today, she said we should get together for drinks and catch up."

"Stay away from her."

Brendan hummed in that irritating way their mother did when she thought she knew something. "I would, but I promised to give you a message. She said that the Cahills are looking for a reason to fire you."

Motherfucker. That girl didn't listen for shit. Not when she was sixteen and not now.

"How you managed to piss them off a week into your promotion is a feat. I underestimated your ability to anger all the wrong people."

Ronan took a deep breath and ignored his brother's condescending comment. "What else did she say? I haven't screwed anything up."

"She sent a text, so there was no context. But I'll ask when I meet her for a drink at eight."

"I told you to stay away from her. She doesn't need to be caught up in this mess. Definitely not with you."

Brendan laughed. "Like she'd be better with you?"

"Fuck no. But I didn't break her heart."

Brendan dropped into silence. It might've been a cheap shot, but he didn't care. Except for running a little wild as a pre-teen, Brendan had always been on the straight and narrow. He'd done what was right for him. He didn't intentionally hurt Chloe.

"I'm just having a drink with an old friend. Nothing else. And she reached out to me. I didn't track her down."

"Then pick me up. I'm going with you."

"In case you've forgotten, I'm FBI. I know how to ask questions."

"But I'll be there to make sure you don't pressure her into doing more. Drawing her deeper into this mess we're trying to unravel."

"I'll pick you up at seven-thirty. I'm supposed to meet her at Last Shot. You know where it is?"

He remembered the crappy bar where they'd had a beer. Where she'd told him to fuck her. "Yeah."

They disconnected and he kicked the bucket of tools he

had sitting in the middle of the room. After visiting his mother this morning, he had planned to start working on his kitchen. He'd bought this foreclosed house before moving back. He'd told himself it was an investment, a way to move on. But since then, the only rooms that he'd completed were the master bedroom and bath.

He worked long days and drank too much at night. He'd been thinking more and more about selling it. He wasn't the kind of guy who owned a house. But fixing his mother's porch made him feel accomplished in a way his job didn't. It was time to make progress here.

Brendan's call fucked with his head, though. He couldn't decide if his brother was trying to fuck with him by making plans to drink with Chloe. Even though they didn't have anything going on between them—no matter how much they thought about it—Brendan had no business with her.

He grabbed his sledgehammer and went to work knocking down everything in his path.

By the time seven-thirty rolled around, Ronan was running late. He'd made a mess of his kitchen, which he was now regretting, but he felt better physically. His head was clear enough to face Brendan and Chloe. He'd just gotten out of the shower and was half-dressed when there was a knock on his front door. Figured Brendan was exactly on time.

He answered the door in his jeans. "I'll be ready in a minute."

Brendan stepped into the living room. "Interesting look you have going here," he said, pointing to the single chair in the room. "I guess you don't do much entertaining."

"If I do, it's not happening in here. The place needs a lot of work. Gimme five." Ronan turned the corner and went into his room to finish dressing. He heard his brother moving around. Part of him was embarrassed. Construction was the one thing he was good at, but his house was a mess.

A moment later, Brendan was leaning against the doorframe to the bedroom. "Did a hell of a job on the kitchen."

"I just did that today. Time got away from me."

"You should call Declan. I think he's looking for work. He'll be cheap labor."

"I thought he had a gig at a bar or something." Last he'd heard, their little brother was bartending. Declan had bounced through so many different jobs, Ronan couldn't keep track.

"Well, you know how it goes with him."

"Yeah." He wondered if that meant Declan didn't have a place to live again. He moved apartments almost as often as he switched jobs. The man never signed a lease. He crashed with friends or did monthly rentals. Always said he didn't want to be tied down. He'd laughed when he helped Ronan move in here.

Ronan shoved his keys, wallet, and phone in his pockets. "Let's go."

Brendan blocked his path. "We need a game plan."

"For Chloe?"

"Yeah, for Chloe. You keep telling me to stay away from her, but based on what's been happening, she seems intent on sticking her nose where it doesn't belong. She sure as hell isn't doing it for me."

"We need to convince her to keep her nose out of it."

Brendan pursed his lips. "You think she'll listen?"

"We'll make her."

"You're awful protective toward some girl who doesn't mean anything to you. Unless, of course, you're doing a body shot off her." Brendan pushed off the frame and stepped back.

"How the hell do you know about that?"

"Some things never change. People in that neighborhood talk. It's why I won't live there. You can't escape who you once were."

"Ain't that the truth." They headed out to Brendan's car. "As far as Chloe goes, she's toying with me. Like I can be her walk on the wild side."

Brendan turned and pointed up at Ronan's house. "Yeah, real wild here. Homeowner, project manager at work."

Ronan laughed. "Like you said, can't escape the past."

It felt weird joking with Brendan like they had when they were young.

"Believe me, I tried. That's what the Army was about. And when that didn't work, I went to the FBI."

Ronan settled into the passenger seat. "And yet, we're both back here. For as far as we ran, we ended up where we started."

"This is home. I decided to stop running and face the shit that made me who I am." He started the engine but didn't put the car in drive. "I'm glad you reached out. I've wanted to but figured you didn't want to hear from me. Listen up, because I'm only going to say this once."

Ronan looked at his big brother.

"You were right. I should've stayed to find answers a long time ago."

Ronan hadn't seen that coming. A knot formed in the middle of his chest. This was all he'd wanted. He nodded. "We'll find them now."

Brendan pulled into the street.

"And Chloe?" Ronan said.

"What about her?"

"Stay away from her."

"Dude. She has no interest in me." Brendan shot him a look as he made a left onto Addison. "You can't be that dense."

"What?"

"Even when we dated, I was the runner-up. She'd come over to the house and stare at you even though she was my girlfriend."

"What the fuck are you talking about? She was head over heels in love with you. The Doyle who was going places. Had a plan. Wasn't a shit ton of trouble."

Brendan chuckled. "You don't know Chloe at all. She went out with me because I'm safe. She could bring me home to the family. But it was you she wanted. The girl had a wild streak of her own. You were what she wanted but was afraid to go after."

Ronan flashed back to the night of the party where she'd gotten drunk and crawled all over him. He'd felt dirty for being turned on by his brother's ex-girlfriend, thinking she was using him as a substitute. Now, though, Brendan's words painted a different picture.

"Why tell me this now?"

"Because you seem concerned that I'm going to make a move on her or some shit. I'm only interested in Chloe McCarthy for the information she can provide. I'm not about to step in your way."

"That's not a path I'm on."

"Maybe it should be."

Ronan laughed. "I've never been parent-approved. So

that's a non-starter. Chloe is still very much a mama's girl." The night of the block party when they had been a breath away from making out, her mother's voice had her running away. "Turn right up here. Last Shot is down the street from the Rose."

"Just sayin' if you both want each other, you're adults."

If only it were that easy.

CHLOE WAS SITTING AT THE BAR BY EIGHT O'CLOCK. SINCE IT was a Sunday night, the Rose was slow, so she took off a little early and was already working on her second beer. When the door to Last Shot opened, she turned to see if it was Brendan. It was so much better. And so much worse. Brendan and Ronan strode in and it was like watching a movie in slow motion. Other heads turned because the Doyle boys—no, men—drew attention. Tall and broad, scruffy and sexy. And they walked with a cocky confidence like they belonged anywhere they stepped.

Both men's gazes landed on her and she immediately felt warm. She tried to convince herself it was the alcohol, but even she wouldn't buy that lie.

When they stepped close, Ronan's deep, rumbly voice sent a shiver down her spine. "Chloe."

"Didn't expect to see you here."

"When I passed on your message, he insisted on joining us," Brendan said.

"Don't see why. We already did our catching up." She waved the bartender over. "Three more." She reached for her purse, but Brendan put his hand on hers.

"I got this round. Why don't you guys get a table?"

Grabbing her half-empty bottle, she slid off the barstool and brushed against Ronan as she walked to the tables in the back. Was that a grunt she received in response? She slid into a booth and waited to see if Ronan would sit beside her or across from her. She glanced up at him as she took a pull on her beer.

He sighed and then sat next to her.

"Put on your big boy pants tonight, did you?"

"Why do you keep pushing me?"

"Because it's fun. I've had a rough day and you interrupted my evening with your brother."

"What made today rough?"

She'd expected him to balk at her talking about Brendan, so she was thrown for a minute that he'd asked about her day. Remembering her argument with her mother, she just shook her head. "Nothing important."

"I told you to stay away from the Cahills and eavesdropping on their conversations."

"I can't stay away from them. They're part of my job. When I'm there, I'm like their personal waitress because Alan is good friends with the owner." She drained her bottle as Brendan set the three fresh beers on the table.

"Did I miss anything interesting?" he asked.

"Nope. Just your brother trying to boss me around."

"I'm not trying to boss you around. It's for your own good."

She snorted. "I get to decide what's good for me."

"Nice to see you haven't lost your spunkiness," Brendan said. "What is he getting bossy about?"

"I told her to stop listening in on the Cahills' conversations."

"And I pointed out that taking care of them is my job. If I

happen to overhear something, so be it. And I'm telling you, Alan Cahill is out to get you. Did you piss in his Cheerios or something?"

Ronan opened his mouth, but Brendan raised a hand. Instead of saying anything, Ronan took a drink of beer.

"What makes you say that?" Brendan asked.

Chloe watched as Ronan's lips wrapped on the bottle. She wanted to feel those lips again. "Alan was mad that Danny had given you an off-book job. Especially that job."

"Did he say anything else?" Brendan said.

"Yep." She stared at Ronan. "He said a few interesting things about Ronan."

She shifted in the booth to sit at an angle. She drank from her bottle and waited for Ronan to give her his attention. The muscle in his jaw ticked, causing a ripple in his beard.

"Are you going to share?" he asked without looking at her.

"Didn't your mother teach you it's rude to avoid eye contact when you're talking to someone?" she pushed.

He swung his head to face her, and she suddenly regretted forcing his attention. His eyes bore into her, hot and intense.

She licked her lips. He tracked the movement. Then did the same. Her breath fluttered. She swallowed hard.

"Alan said he thought you were there to dig. That you wanted answers. He was mad and told Danny that he wouldn't let him ruin everything he built. Something about then and now."

Brendan's muttered, "Fuck" pulled her attention from Ronan's face.

"What is all this about?"

"Nothing," Ronan said.

"What's Alan's problem with you?"

"Don't know."

"Bullshit. I think I deserve honesty. I brought you the information."

He leaned closer, looking menacing, but she wasn't afraid of him. "I told you to back off."

"Ronan," Brendan said quietly. "Ronan."

Ronan turned his attention to his brother.

"I think we should tell her," Brendan said.

"No."

"Tell me what?" There was something brewing between the brothers. As much as she told herself it didn't matter and she shouldn't care, the reality was she was nosy. She wanted to know what would get Ronan so worked up.

"We think the Cahills know something about what happened to our dad."

"Fuck," Ronan growled. "She has to see them all the time."

Her head was reeling. Their father? He'd been missing for twenty years. She replayed the conversations she'd heard them have about Ronan. "Wait. You don't think they *know* something, you think they *did* something to your dad?"

"We don't know," Brendan said, calm as ever. Ronan, however, slammed his fist on the table and walked away.

"Why is he so mad?"

Brendan leaned back in his seat and put his arm across the back of the booth. Lifting his beer, he said, "If I had to guess, he's worried about you getting caught up in a mess that isn't yours."

"Should you maybe go after him?"

"Nah. He'll be fine. He just doesn't see it yet."

"See what?" She was only three beers in and she was having a hard time following.

"That you can be useful."

"Me?"

"You've already been privy to two different conversations without even trying. Imagine what would happen if you put in some effort."

Ronan took that moment to reappear. "Fuck no." Reclaiming his seat beside her, he pointed at his brother. "I told you she needs to stay out of this." Then he turned to her. "Go home, Chloe."

She leaned closer, fury bubbling in her chest. "I am so freaking tired of people telling me what to do. You don't make choices for me, Ronan."

"I won't take your calls. I won't see you here or at the Rose. Your information will be useless."

She smiled sweetly. "I think Brendan will be interested." She glanced at Brendan, who said nothing but answered with a smile.

"I'll kick his ass if he talks to you again."

Brendan laughed.

"That's real mature of you. Especially since I'm a grown woman who can speak to whomever I want."

Ronan's hand flexed into a fist on the table. "Didn't he hurt you enough the first time?"

"I didn't intentionally hurt her. You know that," Brendan said.

She reached out tentatively and placed her hand on Ronan's chest. His heart raced and his muscles were rock hard. "*I* know that. I was a kid and thought I was in love. We weren't going to be a forever thing. I'm fine."

His hand gripped hers for a brief moment against his chest before pulling it away. "You might not be this time."

This made no sense. She was no one to him. A neighborhood girl. He'd said so himself. Why did he care?

"I want to help. Think of it as letting me pay you back for rescuing me when I was sixteen."

"She's the best thing we've got. Pressure from you on one side, her listening from the other to know how it impacts them," Brendan said.

"See? All I'm going to do is listen. It's kind of my job as a bartender. Nothing's going to hurt me."

CHAPTER

Eight

Ronan couldn't believe he was considering this. Everything was getting blown way the fuck out of proportion. He shouldn't be trying to tell Chloe what to do. If he'd learned anything about women, it was that making demands like that simply ensured she was going to do the opposite. He might just kick Brendan's ass for going along with this.

Chloe raised her hand and called a waitress over to get another round. Ronan looked at her. "Are you sure that's a good idea?"

"Didn't we just cover that I can do whatever the fuck I want? You don't have to stay."

Brendan chuckled.

"Shut up."

"What should I be looking for with the Cahills? Danny comes in every day, but Alan doesn't. He's only with Danny a couple times a week."

"Danny's never suspicious on his own?" Brendan asked.

"Mom said Danny and Dad hadn't been friends," Ronan said. "Did Danny even know Dad?"

Although Brendan was only a year older, he'd worked more weekend jobs with Dad, and he'd spent the summer working for the Cahills after Dad had gone missing.

Brendan shrugged. "I remember Danny hanging around sometimes, but he never worked the jobs. And when he showed up, the crew was more irritated than anything. They didn't like him, but I don't know why. I was too young to know what to ask or where to look."

"Alan doesn't trust you, Ronan. He not only wants Danny to fire you, but he said if he sees any problem, he'll blacklist you. You'll never work construction again."

The waitress dropped off their beers, and Chloe drank quickly.

"That might've been a threat back in the days when the union was strong. All he can do is keep me from working with the big union outfits. There are a ton of non-union guys doing just fine. Someone always needs work done. I'm the last person you need to worry about."

She reached over and wrapped her cool fingers around his forearm. "He wasn't playing. It wasn't just being irritated by Danny like he was when you got the promotion. He's worried about you. About you digging. Which now I under-stand he thinks you're looking for information about your dad." She took another swig of beer. "Which means they're hiding something."

She'd arrived at the same place he and Brendan had before this little drinking session. Which was why he was worried about her involvement.

"What do you think they did?" she said quietly, the serious nature of the topic finally hitting her.

"We don't know. Things were different back then. A lot more political wheeling and dealing. A lot more people looking the other way when shady shit was happening," Brendan said.

"Oh my God!" she said, sitting up straight. "You think they're Irish mob."

"I didn't say any such thing," Brendan said, finishing his first beer. The man drank slow. "What I will say is that you need to do nothing more than listen. And then, only when it's not obvious. If Cahill gets suspicious, he'll stop talking at the Rose. With that, I'm going to say good night." He rose and tossed some money on the table.

"You're my ride, asshole."

"I'm sure Chloe can take you home. That'll give you two the chance to work out whatever this is," Brendan waved his hand between them, "so that you're not snarling at each other every time we talk. Fuck or fight. Do something."

Then the asshole turned and left. Again, he heard the echo of Chloe's words, *Fuck me*. His throat went dry so he gulped some beer. Now that he focused, he could smell the scent of her perfume. It made him want to bury his nose in her neck.

"Brendan agrees with me."

"What?" He spun his head to look at her.

"Even he thinks we should sleep together."

Ronan closed his eyes on a groan.

"What's the big deal, Ronan? We're attracted to each other." She slid her hand on his thigh. "It could be a lot of fun." Her fingers inched up the inseam on his jeans.

He slapped his hand on hers. "You don't want a relationship with me."

"You're right. I don't do relationships anymore. I mean, I

suppose if the perfect man dropped in my lap, I might give it a go. But I've learned that there is no such thing as the perfect guy." She flexed her fingers on his leg. "In the meantime, I like to have fun with whoever strikes my interest. And you always have."

It was the second time tonight that he was led to believe she always had a thing for him. He set his beer down. "What do you mean by always?"

Her eyes narrowed. "As long as I've known you, I've thought you were hot." She smirked.

"Earlier tonight, Brendan said that even when you were dating him, you were looking at me."

"That's not true. Sure, I had a crush on you then. If you had asked me out, I would've wanted to go out with you. But Brendan was safe."

"Why not hit on him now, then?"

"I'm not into him." She pulled her hand off his leg and he missed her heat. "What's wrong?"

"Seems weird that you're suddenly hitting on me. When we were teenagers, you walked around like you were afraid of me. And you dated my brother. I don't think I could have the same woman he has."

Chloe burst into laughter. "Oh my God. You're such a man. Brendan and I never had sex. We kissed. Never even made it to second base."

Kissed and she'd thought she was in love? Teenage girls. Go figure.

"Don't look at me like that. I was sixteen. He made me feel special. And when I looked at you, it was more awe than fear. Well, maybe a little fear. You were big and mean and power-ful. But I never felt unsafe around you. More than anything, I wanted to soothe you."

He took a pull on his beer. "Soothe the savage beast?"

"More like comfort the hurting boy."

"I'm no boy anymore and I don't need comfort."

"We all need comfort sometimes." She nudged his arm. "Come on. I'll take you home."

He slid from the booth and waited for her to join him. "I can call a car."

"I don't mind driving you. Maybe you can invite me in for a nightcap and show me around your place."

"That sounds like an invitation for trouble."

"Are you saying you can't control yourself around me?" she snickered.

That was exactly what he was worried about.

CHLOE LED RONAN DOWN THE BLOCK BACK TO WHERE SHE WAS parked by the Rose. Although he wasn't talking, the air around them was charged. She knew it wasn't just her wild imagination. He felt it too—he just didn't like it. She unlocked the doors to her car and walked around to the driver's side. Ronan stood and stared.

"You're kidding, right?"

"About?"

"I forgot you drove a little shitbox."

"Come on, big boy. It won't be that bad. I'm sure you can fit."

He heaved a sigh. "At least it's a short trip."

Chloe got behind the wheel and swallowed a laugh as Ronan had to fold almost in half to fit. He banged his knee on the dash while trying to shift the seat back. Even in its furthest position, his legs had no room.

"This is a death trap."

"Not for normal-sized people. I have plenty of room." She waved her arms around to prove her point.

"If I do that, you're gonna lose a window."

"I guess no car sex for us."

He groaned and she snickered as she started the engine. "Where to?"

He gave her directions and she pulled into the street.

"As long as you're trapped in the car with me, will you explain why you avoid me? You admit to being attracted to me, and while there was an issue in our past, we're both adults now. Nothing illegal. We're both consenting."

He sighed again, as if out of patience. "Because you're Chloe McCarthy. You're sweet. Although with as bossy as you've been lately, I might reconsider that description. Besides, you've never been a no-strings kind of girl."

"I'm just looking for a good time. Aren't you? We can spend a night together." She glanced at him out of the corner of her eyes. "Maybe a few nights if it's good."

"It would be better than good."

"Is that a promise?"

"I've never had any complaints. But it still ain't happening."

She huffed. "Whatever. Your loss."

They drove the rest of the way in silence. Although she was far from drunk, she was mellow because of the alcohol she'd had, and she was trying not to let his constant rejection sting. She wanted to play it off like it didn't matter because it shouldn't. It wasn't like she couldn't find a guy to screw. But Ronan was like Holy Grail level. Something she'd wanted for so long that he became a fantasy.

Maybe it was time to let the dream fade into obscurity.

Even without a chance of fulfilling her fantasy, would she still be willing to help him? She wished she could be petty and say no, but she would because it was the right thing to do. If she could help him find the answers he'd been waiting twenty years for, she'd do it.

"I have to say that this ride has been pretty unsatisfactory. Brendan said we should fight or fuck and you just took one off the table." She turned to look at him. "I bet I could take you now, seeing as you're all scrunched up in my car."

"You could take me even if I wasn't. I would never hurt you."

While she'd been joking, his comment was serious. Then again, so much about Ronan was always serious. But she believed him. Regardless of his stance of keeping his distance, he wanted her. She just couldn't understand why he kept pushing her away. It made her want to keep poking at him.

When they got to his street, she slowly inched down the block. "You have a house?"

"Yeah. Why do you sound so surprised?"

"I don't know too many people our age who own a house. A few, like Erin, who are married, but no one single."

"That's me up on the right. It's a fixer-upper, so it's not much to look at."

"Really?" She couldn't keep the excitement from her voice. She loved home renovation shows. "Can I see?"

He gave her side-eye, but said, "Sure."

As she inched past his house, she saw someone sitting on his steps. "Looks like you got company."

"What the hell is Declan doing here?"

She found a spot to park near the end of the block—her small car was able to squeeze into a tiny spot, but she didn't point that out to him. They got out and he waited for her on the sidewalk.

"I haven't done much work yet. Mostly demo, so it still looks like an abandoned house."

"Is that your way of warning me off? Not gonna work. I watch all of the home makeover shows. I'm fascinated by the before and after."

"This is mostly before." He stopped in front of the small, yellow brick bungalow. It was cute and nothing like she would've imagined for him.

Declan stood. "About time."

"What are you doing here?" Ronan asked.

"Brendan said you needed some help on your house." He pointed to the bag at his feet. "I figured I could crash here while I work." Then he leaned around Ronan. "Hey, Chloe."

"Hi." She didn't know Declan well. He was a couple of years younger than she was. She had been in the same grade as the twins and Declan had often wanted to hang out with them, but she'd preferred spending time with Brendan and Ronan. Still did.

Ronan led them up the concrete front stairs and unlocked the door. "Brendan had no business calling you. I planned to do that tomorrow. And I don't have a spare bed."

Declan hefted his bag and lifted a shoulder. "I'm not picky. The floor's good."

Didn't he have a place to sleep?

"But, uh, you know, if Chloe's spending the night..."

"No worries, Declan. Ronan and I are just friends. I want to check out his renovation. I won't be spending the night."

No matter how much I might want to.

RONAN WAS GOING TO KILL BRENDAN. OR MAYBE HUG HIM. He couldn't decide which. He didn't know if he had the restraint he would need to keep his hands off Chloe—especially since she kept talking about them fucking. How was he supposed to see her only as a friend when her words made him picture her naked and writhing beneath him?

Lucky for him, Declan's presence doused all thoughts of sex. So while he might consider thanking Brendan for sending Declan over, mostly he wanted to punch his brother. Declan was a pain in his ass at best, a free-loader at worst. The man hadn't held a steady job or place to live in years.

He flicked on the light in the living room to reveal the bare space. His recliner and TV were the only fixtures in the room.

"Uh, this is kind of sad, Ronan," Chloe said.

"In my defense, I've been focusing on other rooms. The bathroom and my bedroom are done. I've started the kitchen." He continued walking, turning on lights as he went.

Declan went straight to the kitchen. "Holy shit. This is your idea of started?"

He clapped his brother on the shoulder. "I got the demo done. Now it needs to be cleaned up. That's what you're here for."

"The demo's the fun part."

"Yeah, well, talk nice to me and I'll let you help with the demo when I do the upstairs."

Chloe squeezed by, the curves of her body brushing against him. "Wow. I bet this will look amazing when you're done."

"That's nice of you to say, but I don't even have a plan yet. I just knew I needed to get rid of the counters and cabinets from the seventies."

She spun and held up a hand. "Have your mom or Nessa help you figure out how to do this. You need a woman's touch."

Declan laughed. "That's sexist of you. Men can be very good in the kitchen."

She scoffed. "I'm sure there are men who love to cook. However, I've been around Doyle *boys* my whole life and I've never seen any of you help your mom in the kitchen."

"Ouch." Declan slapped a hand on his chest. "Words hurt, Chloe."

She burst into laughter. It was deep and throaty and made Ronan's imagination get dirty all over.

Ronan turned away. "The upstairs is old bedrooms and I haven't done anything up there yet."

"Dude. You've been here, what, a couple months?" Declan asked.

"Some of us have regular jobs. By the time I get home from work most days, the last thing I want to do is put my toolbelt back on. Besides, it's my own place to live." He led them down the short hall and pointed. "Bathroom. Bedroom."

Chloe peeked into the bathroom and then strode fully into his bedroom. He had taken his time in here. He wanted a place to relax.

"I'm impressed. I half expected to walk into a TV-comedy-level bachelor pad. You know, beer bottles and pizza boxes covering all the surfaces, dirty clothes piled on the floor."

"I haven't lived like that for a lot of years. Regardless of your Doyle boys comment, I am an adult."

Her cheeks flushed pink. "I take that back. You are obviously a grown man."

Her eyes met his and there was no mistaking the heat exchanged between them.

"Dude. You have a king-size bed. That's huge," Declan said.

Ronan closed his eyes. "Don't even think about it. I'm not sharing my bed with you."

Declan sighed. "Fine. You got anything to drink?"

"In the fridge." Once he walked away, Ronan looked down at Chloe. "So that's the whole tour. Like I said, not much to look at."

"There's plenty to see here. Thanks for letting me in."

Ronan couldn't help but think she was talking about more than the tour. They stood for a minute, their breaths synchronizing.

She licked her lips. "I guess I should be going."

"I'll walk you out."

But neither of them moved. Locked in a trance.

From two rooms away, Declan yelled, "Jackpot! Pizza and beer."

It was enough to jolt Ronan back.

"What was that?" Chloe asked.

"Fuck if I know."

"But you felt it too," she said with a smirk. "You're not as impervious as you'd like to make me think."

"I never said I was impervious. Just that I wouldn't act on whatever this is."

"Even if I promised it wouldn't go anywhere? That I wasn't looking for anything serious."

"I wouldn't believe you." He swung out an arm for her to lead the way from the hall. "I'll walk you to your car."

"I can get to my car alone. I'm not scared to be out after dark."

"I know." Over his shoulder, he said, "I'll be back in a minute."

Declan nodded with a piece of pizza in one hand and a beer in the other. "Now you two behave yourselves."

Outside, Chloe picked up the conversation again. "I meant what I said. I'm not looking for a serious relationship. We have some hot chemistry here. I'm just suggesting we act on it."

They arrived at her car and she leaned against it.

"How do you see that working out, Chloe?"

"We have some great sex. Work it out of our systems, and then go on to be good neighborhood friends."

He inched closer to her, not touching, but the heat from her skin called to him. He braced a hand on the roof of her car. "And what? When we see each other in the neighborhood, I smile and nod and pretend I'm not imagining you naked? Wave and forget the feel of your hot pussy on my dick, the taste of you on my tongue?"

She swallowed hard and nodded. "I can do it if you can. Pretend I don't think about the ripple of your muscles beneath my fingers. Forget the press of your body between my thighs."

All thought flew out of his head and he pressed against her. Their mouths crashed together with mashed lips and thrusting tongues. She gripped his shirt in her fists and wrapped her leg around the back of his thigh, pulling him into her. His cock throbbed. She tasted like summer—sweet and hot.

He reached under her shirt and palmed her tit, squeezing her nipple a bit, just enough to cause a gasp. When her mouth left his, he trailed open-mouthed, wet kisses across her jaw and down her neck. Her hips bucked as he sucked on her pulse point.

"Oh, God. Ronan."

He straightened and focused on her beautiful, lust-filled face.

"Let's go back inside," she said.

"Declan's inside."

"Fuck." She leaned her forehead on his chest. "At a time like this, I wish I owned a minivan. Something big and sprawling so you could stretch out for a proper fuck."

He groaned. He'd never thought he'd hear Chloe McCarthy with such filthy words dripping from her tongue. It turned him on more. Maybe Brendan was right. They could fuck their way through the tension. "What time do you get off work tomorrow?"

She closed her eyes. Squinting, she said, "Midnight, unless it gets busy."

"On a Monday?"

"Anything's possible."

"Not if I drive them all away. Any chance you can get off a little earlier?"

"What are you suggesting?"

"I can meet you at your place when you get home. Then we can finish this."

She smiled. "I'm supposed to wait twenty-four whole hours?"

He skated his fingers down her front, circling each breast before moving to the juncture between her thighs. He rubbed his whole hand against the rough denim, applying enough pressure for her to sink against him. Her leg muscles clenched and moist heat radiated through the material. "Play with yourself tonight when you get home. Think about me and all the things you want me to do. Then tomorrow night, I'll do them."

He stepped back and took her hand. "Drive safely."

She walked around to the driver's side and got in. He waited on the curb until she pulled away. What the hell had he just gotten himself into? While he hoped Chloe would be able to sleep with him and forget it ever happened, he wasn't sure he could.

CHAPTER
Nine

Chloe didn't sleep well. No matter what she did, even following Ronan's very explicit, very hot instructions. Her brain spent the night in overdrive. She napped throughout the morning, but by noon, she was up and moving. She straightened her living room and bedroom, including fresh sheets for her bed. Her full-size bed that could never compete with the behemoth of a bed Ronan had in his room. She looked at her apartment and wondered what he'd see. Then she pushed the thought away. She doubted he would be taking too much time to investigate. He didn't care about what she filled her shelves with—he was coming over for sex, plain and simple.

But not so simple. He'd promised to do whatever she asked. The problem was that she didn't have an automatic list of items to check off. She wasn't sure she cared a whole lot about how it went down as long as it did. She checked her phone. No call from Mom.

Then Chloe remembered how she'd left things yesterday.

Not calling to harass her was her mother's way of giving her the cold shoulder. Chloe sighed and dialed.

"Hello."

"Hi, Mom. How are you?"

"Fine."

"Look. I'm sorry about how I stormed out yesterday. I was just frustrated. For so many years, you've been saying snippy things about Ronan, like he's this horrible guy, but he's not. I f —screwed up that night." She took a breath to keep her thoughts clear. Drop an f-bomb and Mom would stop listening. "I was sixteen. I thought I loved Brendan, but we were never going to last forever."

"But the drinking and the car, Chloe."

"*I* took Garrett's car, not Ronan. I went to the party and chose to drink. It was a stupid mistake. One that Ronan paid for because he was trying to take care of me."

Her mother snorted.

"He could've just walked away. Left me at the party. *That* could've ended badly. Anything could've happened to me. He protected me." The night was still a blur for her. She remembered wandering through the party, drinking from any cup that had been pressed into her hands. Plenty of guys were paying attention to her, and it felt good. Who needed Brendan anyway? Then the way Ronan came along and manhandled her. Dragged her from the party grunting and mumbling at her.

"What about all the other trouble he's been in?"

"He's had a hard life. Everyone makes mistakes."

"He's been to jail." Her mother's voice dropped to a near whisper as if she was spilling some state secret.

"Do you know that? Or are you believing neighborhood gossip?"

"I heard Ann talking about how he'd been arrested. We all witnessed it when he was a teen. I'm sure he got worse as he aged. Troublemakers usually do."

"First, being arrested is not the same as hard-core prison. And now he's a superintendent at a job in a career he's been in for years, and he owns a house. Looking at that, he's doing better than I am." She said it to shed some light for her mother, but the words sank into her chest. The neighborhood troublemaker was more adult than she was. How the hell had that happened?

"Why do you keep defending him? What do you care what I think of him?"

"Because it's just wrong. He's a good guy who even came over to build his mom a new porch. I feel bad that your impression of him was developed from my poor choices."

Her mother tsked. "My opinion of him started long before then. He's always had somewhat of a reputation. I didn't want that to affect you."

"Reputation doesn't rub off. It's not contagious like a cold."

"That's where you're wrong, Chloe. It absolutely is. More so for a woman than a man."

"But it shouldn't. If I had a best friend who was an alcoholic, you wouldn't expect me to abandon her, would you?"

"Of course not. But alcoholism is a disease. Getting into fights is a choice. Committing crimes is a choice. Sleeping around is a choice."

At least he was being honest with who he was. He did things out in the open. Other men looked good on the outside but held nastiness the world didn't see.

"I see your point, but as far as I know, Ronan has settled

down and isn't doing those things anymore." Except for the sleeping around part, thank goodness.

"Or he's just gotten better at hiding them."

Chloe laughed. She wasn't sure if her mother was trying to be funny, but it was. Then Mom joined in her laughter. "I'll give you a call later in the week. Maybe we can have lunch."

"That would be nice."

"See? Having a job at a bar has its perks. If I worked at an office, I couldn't make plans for lunch with my mom."

"You're still not going to convince me that that job is the best you can do. But seeing as I promised not to make any comments, I'll be shutting up now."

"Thanks, Mom. Love you."

"Love you, too."

They disconnected and Chloe got ready for work. She didn't like it when her mom was mad at her. In general, it bothered her when anyone she cared about was upset with her.

When she got to the Rose, it was slow as was typical before the after-work crowd showed. She double-checked the schedule to make sure Johnny was working. Johnny was the head bartender, so he usually closed if she wasn't. While she wouldn't call him in so she could leave early to get laid, if he was already here, she wouldn't feel guilty about taking off if they were slow enough. Johnny was coming in at six. Excited, she considered texting Ronan, but she didn't want to jinx anything. It would be her luck to tell Ronan she would get off early and then they'd be slammed with a random party of fifty people.

She verified the bar was fully stocked and checked in with the kitchen staff. Then she made her rounds to chat with the regulars. "Hey, Donny and Neville. How's life treating you?"

"Always good when there's a Guinness in front of me," Neville joked. He said the same thing every time she asked.

"Stop flirting with the girl. She's too young for you."

"Age is just a number. Isn't that right, Neville?"

"You got it."

"But Cecelia is the real reason you would never flirt with me."

"I do all I can to stay on my wife's good side. How're things with you? How's the family?"

"They're good. We all went to church together yesterday. Garrett was giving Mass."

"He's a good boy."

Chloe just nodded. What could she say? Her brother was a priest. But to her, he was like any other big brother, vows notwithstanding.

Her phone rang in her pocket and she said her goodbyes before answering. "Hi, Erin. What's up?"

"Please tell me you apologized to Mom for yesterday."

"What did I have to apologize for?" It didn't matter that she had. Erin was asking for a reason.

"She wants me to come over after dinner and I don't want to spend my whole night hearing about what an awful daughter you are."

"I talked to her earlier. We're good. At least as good as normal."

"Why do you insist on pushing her buttons?"

"Because sometimes it's necessary. Like I told her, the way she reacts to Ronan is wrong. He's a good guy."

"Oh my God. Are you dating him?"

She hesitated for a second too long. "No."

"The block party wasn't everything, was it?"

"We've bumped into each other a few times over the last couple of weeks. That's all. Chatted over drinks." It wasn't a lie. If this conversation happened tomorrow instead of today, she'd have to lie.

"Hm-mm. Methinks you protest too much."

"Not quite how the quote goes, but what do you want me to say?"

"You were almost rabid in your defense of him yesterday."

"Mom needs to let go of what happened back then. I explained to Mom a little more in-depth about how Ronan had protected me from myself that night."

"One good deed doesn't make him a good guy. He's done a lot of bad stuff. Assault. Or battery. Whichever one means he beat the crap outta some guy. I'm sure there was more."

Everyone knew Ronan had always been quick with his fists, but it was typically in defense of himself or someone else. He didn't go around starting fights. "Which is also all in the past."

"And you're still going to say nothing is going on between the two of you?"

"We're friends." It was sort of true. Just then, Danny Cahill came through the door. "Look, I'm at work, so I have to go. Have fun with Mom."

She disconnected and met Danny at his table. Maybe she'd be able to bring some more information to Ronan tonight. "Hi, Mr. Cahill. What can I get for you?"

"Coffee. And a scotch, neat."

"I'll be right back."

Danny always had company when he was here. She watched the door as she went to the bar to get the drinks.

She returned and asked, "Need a menu?" It was a silly offer since he probably had the menu memorized.

"Can you bring two? I have a couple of men from my crews stopping by."

"Dinner with the big boss, huh?" She wondered if one would be Ronan. The thought of his heavy stare on her while she worked, knowing they planned to spend the night together, made her thighs twitch.

She greeted and seated a few more customers before making her way back to Cahill's table with the menus. By the time she got there, two guys were already sitting, neither Ronan. They were much smaller than him. Placing the menus on the table, she asked, "Can I get you gentlemen anything?"

When she met their eyes, she realized that they were the guys Ronan had working on his mother's porch. Leroy. She never got the other guy's name.

"Hey, again. You work here?" Leroy asked.

"Yep."

"You know each other?" Cahill asked.

Turning her attention to him, she said, "I was getting my hair cut while they were working on Mrs. Doyle's porch."

Oh, shit. Was it bad that she said that? He probably knew that Ronan had done that as part of the off-book job, but was she supposed to know? Of course, she would know. The whole neighborhood saw the new porch. But she hadn't said she knew it was off-book. Thoughts skittered through her head.

"Seems like everyone knows everyone in that neighborhood."

She nodded. "It's pretty tight-knit."

Leroy and the other guy ordered beers, which allowed her

to escape. She hadn't planned for something like this. While pulling the beer, she took a deep breath. Just treat them like any other customers.

She delivered their drinks and took their order. Once she put the ticket in at the kitchen, she hovered in the area, cleaning tables, trying to listen to why Cahill would be having dinner with these two guys. They weren't management level and Cahill wasn't the kind of man who spent time with the nobodies. Chloe had been around long enough to know that Danny hadn't come up through the ranks of the company. He wasn't one of the boys.

This had to be about Ronan.

Cahill was asking about how things were going on various jobs. The guys were pretty quiet. Maybe they were intimidated by being with the owner of the company. This man signed their checks, so they wouldn't want to say the wrong thing. Plus, they had to know this was weird.

Just as she was about to step away to check on their food, Cahill asked, "What do you think about Ronan as a supervisor?"

"He's good," Leroy said.

"Not afraid to jump in and get dirty like the rest of us," the other said.

"We can all appreciate a harder worker," Cahill said. "How did the weekend job work out last week?"

"Oh, uh..."

"You boys aren't in any trouble. Neither is Ronan. I know he had you working on his mother's porch. I'm just making sure he took care of you."

"Oh," Leroy said. "Yeah, yeah. He paid us good. No complaints. Extra cash is always good."

Since it seemed like both workers were on Ronan's side,

she went to pick up their food. She delivered it and asked if they needed more drinks, but they were fine.

"How is the camaraderie on the crew? Is Ronan interacting with everyone?"

Maybe this was a routine performance evaluation. What better way to know if a supervisor was doing a good job? The guys at the bottom of the food chain would have a definite opinion.

"Sure. We all get along okay."

"He's got some of the old-timers on your crew though."

"I guess." Leroy lifted a shoulder. The other guy said nothing but shoveled his burger in his mouth.

"Does he spend a lot of time talking to the old guys? Give them special treatment?"

"Not really. Ronan's not much of a talker, you know?"

Yeah, she knew.

"And the old guys, yeah, he gives them lighter loads, but like, they did their time. He doesn't want them to get hurt or have a heart attack or something." He paused and then added, "But none of us care. It's like a rite of passage. One day, we'll be the old ones."

"Okay. That's what I like to hear. We're the kind of company that takes care of their own. You boys enjoy your dinner." Cahill stood and placed some bills under his cup. As he passed her, he said, "Get the boys whatever they want. If they exceed what I left, just let me know."

"Will do, Mr. Cahill. Have a good night."

Danny seemed in good spirits, like he was happy with what the guys said about Ronan. That was a good sign. She wondered if she should talk to Leroy. Considering that option, she made her way through the bar, checking on customers and the waitstaff alike.

If she talked to Leroy, he might tell Cahill she'd asked. Then again, how often was Cahill going to interact with these two? Back at their table, she scooped up the money Cahill left. "Can I get you guys something else? Maybe another drink?"

Leroy looked over his shoulder toward the front door.

"Mr. Cahill took care of the bill. You can have another beer."

"Hey, you want to join us?" he asked, spreading his arms on the back of the booth.

"I'm working. But I'll go grab those beers." When she returned with the fresh drinks, she asked, "I haven't seen you in here with Mr. Cahill before."

"Doubt you will again," the other guy said.

Chloe wiped her hand on her jeans and then extended it. "I don't think we met before. I'm Chloe."

"Tanner," he said, shaking her hand. "We weren't introduced because Ronan made it clear we shouldn't've even been looking."

"That's not...We're old friends."

"Riiight," Leroy said.

Ignoring the slight jab, she asked, "Why don't you think you'll be back?"

"Cahill doesn't usually bring the help out to dinner. He was fishing for information. Kind of like you are right now."

Tanner was quick. She'd figured a nice smile and a beer would allow her to fish freely.

"I'm just keeping an eye out for Ronan. Like I said, we're friends. I heard Mr. Cahill asking you guys about him."

"No worries here. Ronan's one of the good ones," Leroy said.

"Yeah, I know. Enjoy your beer."

Ronan at least had the loyalty of his crew. That meant something. But it might not be enough if Danny caved to his father's pressure.

RONAN MANAGED TO GET THROUGH HIS ENTIRE WORKDAY WITH only being distracted by thoughts of Chloe a few times. He got home to find that Declan had cleaned all the debris from the kitchen as Ronan had asked. Admittedly, Ronan had had his doubts. Declan was smart and could work hard when he wanted to. The problem was he rarely wanted to. Ronan grabbed a beer as Declan was coming in from the backyard.

"You're gonna need another construction bag out there. A dumpster would've been better."

"No room for a dumpster. Plus, a dumpster draws attention and seeing as I'm not about to pull a permit to work on my own damn house, the city can suck it." He popped the top on his beer.

"I was thinking about what Chloe said last night about needing a woman's touch. I don't agree with her. This is your kitchen. It needs to be functional for you."

"And?"

"Let me design it. I think custom cabinets in here would look a lot better than what you'll get at some supply house."

"What do you know about making cabinets?"

"I've worked with you on plenty of installations, and there's was a cabinet maker I apprenticed with for about six months. I can do this."

Ronan blew out a heavy breath. He wanted to support his brother. If it were any of his other siblings, he would have immediately agreed. But this was Declan and his track record mostly revealed his lack of follow-through. On the other hand, Ronan had barely used the kitchen since moving in, so did it matter if it took Declan a long time? If he flaked, Ronan could just order cabinets. "Draw something up. Price materials. Then we'll talk about it."

"Really?"

"Were you blowing smoke up my ass or do you want the job?"

"I want the job. I just didn't think you'd agree."

"I didn't agree. Yet."

"Cool. I'll work on it." He grabbed a beer and joined Ronan in leaning against an empty wall. "Want to order pizza or something?"

"Sure. I have plans tonight, but it's not till later."

"Plans with Chloe?"

"What makes you ask that?"

"Dude. The sexual tension last night was pretty crazy. Are you guys a thing?"

"She's helping me with something. So, no we're not dating."

"I bet she's helping with *something*." Declan executed a hip thrust as if Ronan didn't know what his brother was talking about.

"This is why I don't tell you people anything."

"In all seriousness, though, thanks for letting me crash."

"How long you planning on staying?"

He shrugged, and Ronan knew there wouldn't be any more information. Ronan handed his brother some cash and his truck keys. "Go pick up a pizza. I'm going to shower."

"Cool. Anchovy and pineapple it is."

"You fucking buy that bullshit and you'll be sleeping in the yard." They laughed together because that was what their dad had always threatened them with when they couldn't agree on pizza toppings. Sometimes he forgot how good it felt to be with someone who had shared memories like that. He'd isolated himself from his family for so long because of the negative shit that he'd forgotten the positive.

Declan left, and Ronan texted Brendan. You're an asshole for sending Declan here.

It was your turn. He's crashed with all of the rest of us.

Damn. How long had Declan been homeless? What's going on with him?

Who knows? He's too busy cracking jokes and having fun to answer anything.

He wants to build me custom cabinets. If he fucks it up, I'm blaming you.

So what? You blame me for everything.

Ronan made his way to his bedroom. He figured the conversation was over, but then his phone lit up again.

How'd things go with Chloe?

How the fuck was he supposed to answer that? Fine.

Which was it? Fighting or fucking?

Neither.

Liar.

Declan was here when she drove me home.

Cockblocked by the little brother. What a shame.

But you sent him here, so again — your fault.

Brendan followed with a gif of someone laughing and falling over. Ronan plugged his phone in to charge and went to take a shower. Now he could let his mind wander to Chloe and all the dirty things he wanted to do to her.

After his shower, he texted Chloe to see if it would cause problems for him to spend the night. While he didn't want to give her the impression that this was a relationship beyond sexual, they were both adults. He'd spent the night with women before even though it was just about sex.

Pack a bag. I should be getting off work by 9.

She sent him her address and he shoved some clothes and toiletries in a bag. He was too old to be doing a walk of shame right before going to work in the morning, and he definitely didn't want to listen to Declan.

Declan returned with the pizza and another case of beer. Ronan sat in the recliner and Declan sank to the floor.

"There's a box or something you can sit on if you want."

"Nah, this is fine. What time are you leaving?"

"About eight-thirty, and I won't be back, so you can have my bed tonight if you want."

"Cool."

They ate in silence for a bit. "I guess you're not working again."

"Yeah. I haven't had a lot of luck finding something I like and a boss who isn't a total asshole."

"Sometimes you need to suck it up and deal with the asshole."

"Life's too short for that shit. I don't want to slave away, being miserable every day, and have nothing to show for it. I'd rather wander and enjoy myself." He reached for another slice of pizza.

Declan had a point. Ronan had a nest egg and a house. He enjoyed his job, but it was a means to an end. A way to find answers. But what then? He hadn't thought about whether he'd stay with Cahill Construction once he found his answers. He guessed it would depend on the answers. If the Cahills had had a hand in their father's disappearance, there might not be a company left. He let the idea roll around in his head for a bit.

"For the kitchen, anything off-limits?"

"Like what?"

"I assume you want a natural wood look, but open shelves? Glass front on the doors? Granite countertops?"

"Good wood. Nothing fancy. Regular wood doors. Probably oak. I'll figure out the counter after we have a plan for the rest. How long do you think it'll take you?"

"A day or two to come up with a plan. If you like it, another day or so to price materials."

It sounded like a plan. But Declan wasn't much of a planner. "What kind of job are you hoping to find that will make you happy?"

"Not sure."

"You're offering to build me cabinets. You want to work with wood? Do construction?"

"I don't need you to give me a job."

"I wasn't offering." The last thing he needed was to expose another person to the mess he might be stirring. "But I know a lot of guys."

"Let me do your kitchen first and see how that goes. I've been toying with starting my own business. Be my own boss."

"Thought you said you didn't want to work for an asshole," he said with a smile.

Declan threw a balled-up napkin at him. "Fuck you." After another swig of beer, he said, "Haven't you ever thought about it?"

"Starting my own company? Sure. But it's a lot of work, hustle. Right now, my paycheck is pretty much guaranteed. They go out and get the jobs. I just have to show up to do the work. Having my own company would mean doing it all."

Declan nodded, taking in Ronan's words.

They finished dinner and cleaned up. A little after eight, Ronan's phone pinged with a text.

Home earlier than expected. I'm here whenever you want to show up.

Impatient?

A little. You made all sorts of promises.

That he did. Now it was time to deliver.

CHAPTER
Ten

Chloe had cold beer in her fridge and she stood in her bedroom far longer than she should've trying to figure out what to wear. While she wasn't planning to dress up, she wanted something sexy. But fancy lingerie might make Ronan think she was placing undue importance on this. She shook her head, grabbed a pretty matching bra and panty set, and slipped into a tank top and shorts. That way, she wouldn't feel awkward if he wanted to have a drink first. And if fucking was first, these clothes could be quickly discarded.

She paced her living room. He didn't live that far, but he might've been busy with Declan. She settled on her couch with her cross-stitch and let the pattern calm her. Of course, the project she chose to work on was not a Bible quote. This one said, "*Thighs make great earmuffs.*" She was debating if she should include a pair of women's legs or just leave the saying. She focused on the thread and not the words because she kept picturing Ronan's bearded face looking up from between her legs. Lord, she wanted that.

If his kisses were any indication, he knew how to use his mouth. She shifted. Clear head. Sew the pattern.

A sudden knock on her door had her dropping her hoop. She jumped up, picked up her project, and set it in her basket. A deep, calming breath, then she went to the door. She swung it open.

"You don't even ask who it is?" Ronan asked.

"I was expecting you."

"The lock on the exterior door is busted."

"We've already called the landlord."

He grunted. It should've irritated her, but it just made her hot again. He dropped a beat-up duffel bag beneath her coat hooks and shoved the door closed. He made a point of flipping the deadbolt. The loud snick made the point that it had not been locked before she let him in.

"Can I offer you anything?"

One brow winged up.

Her cheeks warmed. "Like a beer or something."

"Or something."

He closed in on her and part of her wanted to step away. Not out of fear—well, maybe a little fear—but because he was so much. She planted her feet and waited for him to be right up to her. She had to crane her neck to maintain eye contact.

"Did you do what I told you to do last night?"

She swallowed and nodded.

"What did you come up with?" He stroked a finger down the side of her neck.

"Just like that? You'll do anything I want?"

His chuckle was low and dark. "I can't imagine I'd have anything off-limits for you."

Her thighs clenched. She stepped to him and rose on tiptoe to press her lips to his.

"Mm-mm. I want the words. Tell me."

"I want you to fuck me and make me come."

"That the best you can do? You were full of dirty talk last night."

She smirked and stepped back. Another challenge? Dirty words didn't scare her.

"I want you to kiss me all over." She unsnapped her shorts and lowered the zipper. "Then I want you to settle your face between my legs and worship my pussy." She slid the shorts over her hips and shimmied until they dropped. The muscle in his jaw twitched, but he didn't speak, just stared at her movements. "I want to come so hard that I won't be able to stand."

She kicked the shorts away. "Then I want you to grab me and shove your thick hard cock into me and see if you can hit the right places to make me come again. Make me useless."

One long step and his hands were on her. His large hand gripped her jaw. "I've got uses for that mouth."

She laughed. "Only if it's on my list."

"Yeah, you got a mouth on you."

"So make me shut up."

And he did. He plundered her mouth with his. She was dizzy from the effect. Or maybe it was the lack of oxygen. Either way, she didn't care. He backed her up to the wall and slid his hands under her shirt, pulling it up. He lowered himself and kissed across her chest and the swell of her breasts. She yanked the shirt over her head and tossed it on the floor to join her shorts.

He slipped her bra strap from her shoulder and licked a

line to her collarbone. Then he peeled the cup down and sucked her nipple. Her head thunked against the wall.

"You okay?"

"Oh, yeah."

He moved to her other nipple and gave it the same treatment. Then he sank to his knees and kissed wet, open-mouthed kisses down her stomach. He nuzzled her mound through her panties and she whimpered.

"Wait," she rasped.

He gave her that same cocky look.

She smiled. "I want to be sitting for this."

He rose to his full height. "Like the way you think. Unrestricted access."

She glanced at the couch beside them. That wouldn't do. Not nearly enough room for him. She tilted her head. "Bedroom's that way."

He took a half step back. Enough so she could move, but not so much that she could escape his touch. Once she turned the corner, she reached behind her and flicked the clasp on her bra. Her boobs were heavy with lust. When she got to her bed, she took off her damp panties.

Then she turned. "Where do you want me?"

EVERY-FUCKING-WHERE. PRETTY LITTLE CHLOE STOOD IN FRONT of him bare-assed naked asking him where he wanted her. It had to be a dream. But it wasn't. He still felt the silk of her skin on his lips.

"Sit on the edge of the bed."

Her sweet ass made contact, a small dip in the mattress, but she kept her legs together. At first, he thought she was being shy, but then he realized she was so fucking turned on she was flexing her thighs.

"Spread those knees wide. Let me see what I need to worship."

Her skin flushed all over. Pretty shade of pink.

He knelt and pressed his palms against her knees. "I'm bigger than that."

"Aren't you going to get undressed?"

"Clothes aren't in my way for this." He lowered his head and kissed her inner thigh. He smelled her arousal and his mouth watered. Worshipping this pussy was not going to be a hardship.

Chloe leaned back, arms stiff to hold herself up. She wanted to watch. He swiped his tongue over her, lapping her up. She released a shaky sigh and her head lolled back. He swirled the tip of his tongue over her clit and her hips jumped. He pressed his tongue as deep inside her as he could, coating himself with her juices. She tasted phenomenal. Thrusting his tongue in and out, he bumped his nose against her clit.

Her thighs trembled. He took his time getting her even more worked up. He licked and sucked every part of her, except her clit, which was poking out seeking attention. He massaged her inner thighs and stroked her with his thumbs.

"Please," she whimpered.

Such a sweet sound. "What? I'm worshipping."

"Make me come."

One finger circled her entrance and she thrust her hips up, forcing him in. "So impatient," he murmured against her. Then he gave her what she wanted and sucked hard on her clit while fingering her.

"Yes." Her hips rose off the bed as she sank back on her

elbows. Her eyes were glazed over with pleasure. Her lips parted as she panted.

He used his left hand to spread her wide. He alternated licking and sucking, crooking two fingers deep inside her.

"Fuck, yeah," she moaned, her eyes fluttering closed.

He kept going until her moans turned to screaming his name. His hard dick pressed against his zipper painfully. When her legs went lax, he stood and licked his lips. He gently undid his jeans and released himself, snagging the condom he'd tucked in the pocket.

Chloe's eyes opened a fraction. He yanked off his shirt. Her eyes opened more.

"Your body is damn near perfect. It's not fair."

"Come work construction and you can look like this, too." He opened the condom and rolled it on. "Damn shame though. I don't think I'd be attracted to you if you looked like me."

She laughed.

He sat down on the edge of the bed. "Come here."

She forced herself up but was taking too long for him. He wrapped an arm around her waist and pulled her over. She straddled him easily.

Bracing herself on his shoulders, she held herself up while he lined up with her entrance. When she sank onto him fully, Ronan's brain short-circuited. He gave her a moment to adjust. Or maybe he was giving himself that time. But then she started rocking and he couldn't hold back.

He gripped her hips and moved her up and down in the rhythm he wanted. She didn't fight him, just went along, digging her fingers into his shoulders, his biceps, anything for purchase. As he got close, he slowed and fondled her tits again, sucking hard on her nipples.

He stood and flipped her on her back on the bed. Her legs immediately wrapped around him, but he grabbed her ankles and held them up, resting against his chest. She was so fucking tight around him. Using his thumb, he stroked her clit. She began to tremble again. Her muscles clenched around him, milking him, and he lost it.

Growling, he released her legs, braced his arms on the mattress, and drove into her relentlessly seeking his own release. He came so hard his vision was gone for a brief moment.

Chloe's sweat-slicked, sticky thighs slid away from him and flopped wide on the bed. She stroked his beard. He lowered and kissed her.

"You taste like me."

"Good, isn't it?"

She smiled. Chloe was nothing like he'd imagined all these years. Not that he'd spent too much time thinking about what she'd be like in bed. But she was prim and proper. He'd never expected her to be this hot. He rolled off her, and she whimpered.

"Did I hurt you?"

"No. Just the opposite. I wasn't ready for you to go."

He took off the condom and left the bed on wobbly legs to throw it out. He found his way to the bathroom and cleaned up. Her scent was all over him. The bathroom door opened.

"Sorry. I think I should shower."

He tracked her movements as she started the water and adjusted the temperature.

"Uh. I gotta pee, too."

The bathroom wasn't built for two, unlike his, so he left. He shouldn't be thinking about Chloe in his bathroom. This was supposed to be it, right? Fuck the tension away. Except he was pretty sure once wasn't going to be enough. He went to the kitchen and helped himself to a bottle of beer. He considered joining her in the shower, but the thought of trying to squeeze in the small space put a damper on that. Next time, they'd try his house. His shower had ample space.

Next time? They hadn't discussed a possible next time. This was supposed to burn this out of their systems. His dick disagreed with the idea of one and done. He guzzled his beer and filled a glass with water to take back to the bedroom. If Chloe only planned to give him tonight, he was going to make the best of it.

She was finished in the bathroom and they met in the hall.

"You're staying the night, right?"

"Unless you tell me to leave."

"Hell, no." She stepped closer and took the glass of water from him. After a quick sip, she said, "I want to go again."

The quiet words had his dick perking up again. "Did you have more things on your list that I haven't done?"

"Well, I did say I wanted to come so hard I wouldn't be able to stand. That I'd be useless." She swept an arm down the front of her glorious, naked body. "I'm still standing."

"It's like that, huh?"

She smiled in challenge.

She wanted to be useless? He'd scramble her brain for a week.

CHAPTER
Eleven

Chloe lay in bed, her head on Ronan's chest, stroking his pecs. She really didn't think she'd be able to stand. Her muscles were numb, but her nerves were still tingling with the pleasure of repeated orgasms. She'd been with men who'd bragged about how often they could make a woman come, but rarely would one follow through. There was no bragging from Ronan, just a determination to fulfill his promise.

"I'm guessing from your silence that you're finally useless."

"Hmm...maybe." No need to let him get a big head. He already had one of those.

He pinched her ass. "Didn't your mother teach you it's rude to lie?"

She laughed and then kissed his chest. "Fine. You win. You more than successfully completed my list."

Silence hung between them, a pause of uncertainty.

Finally, she couldn't take it anymore. "So, do you plan to make a list for me?"

"Are you saying you want to do this again?"

"Who would be dumb enough to say no to multiple orgasms?" Relief washed over her at his response. They hadn't discussed this being an ongoing thing, but why not? She hadn't had a regular hook-up in a while.

Her loose body melted against Ronan and she fell asleep.

When the barest hint of light was glowing into her bedroom, Chloe sat up. She heard the shower running and checked the clock. Six am? What the hell? She stumbled out of bed, pulled on an oversized T-shirt, and went to the kitchen to make coffee. She'd never gotten around to telling Ronan about Danny Cahill coming to the bar yesterday, and she figured he should know.

He came into the kitchen fully dressed. "Sorry. I didn't mean to wake you."

"You didn't. At least I don't think so. I don't know what woke me up."

He moved to the couch and bent to shove his feet into his boots.

"Coffee's about ready if you want some."

"Sounds good."

She reached up and pulled two cups down from the cabinet. Ronan was suddenly behind her, hands on her hips, mouth against her neck. "Walking around like that is gonna make me late for work."

She shivered and closed her eyes. "As much as I'd love to seduce you, going to work late might cause you more problems than you think."

He released her, but she still felt the imprint of his fingers on her flesh. "What do you mean?"

"Danny Cahill came into the Rose yesterday." She filled

both cups and handed him one. "He had two of your guys meet him for dinner. Tanner and Leroy."

Ronan set his cup on the counter and crossed his arms. His biceps bulged and she remembered the flex of those arms while she rode him last night. "Unusual company, huh?"

"Let's put it this way. You said you were only invited once you were promoted. He was pumping them for information."

"They're good guys. I don't have anything to worry about."

"You're right. They told him you're a good boss. The weird part was that he was asking them about the old guys you have on your crew. He wanted to know if you talk to them a lot and give them special treatment."

That earned her a grunt.

"They knew he was fishing for something, but they didn't know what or why. But they like you."

"Good to know."

"Danny is following Alan's orders to keep an eye on you."

"Yeah." He picked up his cup and drank the coffee.

They stood in silence, drinking coffee. Not quite awkward, but not comfortable either.

"You can come by tonight if you want."

"I could probably do that. I have to check in on the work Declan is doing."

"Will you have enough time to make me a list?" She wagged her eyebrows at him.

He set his cup down again and stepped closer. He caged her in against the counter. "I think we can reuse your list. It was a pretty fucking good list."

Her smile spread quickly. "Yeah, it's a good start. I think I might want to add an addendum."

She reached between them and stroked his crotch. "I don't think you made full use of my mouth last night."

He ground against her hand. "Fuck." Then he pulled away quickly and adjusted himself. "Thanks for the coffee."

She laughed as he left the room to gather his things. There was no kiss goodbye, no romantic comments as he slipped from her apartment. As far as hook-ups went, this one was pretty damn good. She left her coffee on the counter, questioning why she even pretended as if she planned to stay awake. She crawled back into bed and dreamt of the things she'd like to do with Ronan before he grew tired of her.

RONAN GOT TO THE JOB SITE, WHICH WAS ONE OF THE WORST jobs he'd been given since starting at Cahill. It was an office build-out, but the actual construction was done. His crew was given the task of assembling cubicles and office furniture. He hated every minute of it, but with any luck, they'd be done within a couple of days.

He walked into the open space and flipped on the lights. Skids of materials sat along one wall. Next to the door, they had a table set up with the prints so Ronan could tell his guys where to install everything. Some guys loved these jobs. They required little thought and the work was easy.

Ronan hated it. The monotony was horrible. These were normally staffed by crews of older guys, the ones who couldn't heft bundles of shingles up a ladder or haul a bag of concrete on each shoulder anymore but still had some years left till retirement. Neither of which described Ronan.

He studied the print and began to question if he'd pissed Cahill off somehow. He'd been given this assignment before Danny spoke to Leroy and Tanner, so it wasn't that. Knowing the Cahills, this was another test. He'd just make sure there was no question about how good he was.

The door opened and Tanner came in.

"You still got fifteen if you want to grab a coffee," Ronan called.

"I'm good." He lifted a cup in response. "I wanted a chance to talk to you before the guys get here."

Ronan straightened from the print and crossed his arms. "What's up?"

"Mr. Cahill asked me and Leroy to meet him for dinner yesterday."

"Okay."

Tanner shook his head. "I know he's the boss and all, but he was fishing for dirt on you and I didn't like it. We told him you were a good boss, but I got the feeling that wasn't what he wanted to know."

Ronan already knew the answer, but he asked anyway in case Chloe missed something. "What did he ask about?"

"He wanted to know how you treat the old-timers. How much you talk to them. Whether they get special treatment."

"Okay."

"He played it off like he wanted to make sure that you took care of the old guys, but it was like he didn't trust that they were here. Like why would anyone want to work with them."

"They have experience and knowledge that can teach young guys like you things you can't learn in a classroom or from a book."

"Hey, man, I know. I got no problem with guys on the crew. Mr. Cahill, though, he was suspicious."

"Thanks for the heads up, but nothing funny going on here."

Tanner finally cracked a smile. "You might want to work on that because as soon as Cahill walked away, your girl Chloe was on us asking questions, too."

Fuck. She left that part out.

"Really?"

"I don't know if she was the second wave of digging for Cahill or if she was worried about you."

"You don't have to worry about Chloe. She's good." Ronan reached for his phone. "Go finish your coffee. We have an exciting day of office furniture assembly."

"Yay," Tanner said with zero enthusiasm.

Ronan walked outside of the small industrial office space to the back of the building and called Chloe.

"Hello?" she mumbled.

Shit. Was she asleep?

"Hey," he said.

"Ronan?"

"Yeah. Tanner just told me about his meeting with Cahill and he said you started questioning them, too."

"Uh, not really."

He heard rustling on her end and he pictured her sitting up and moving blankets around. "Listen, Chloe. That's all you're supposed to do. Not ask questions or investigate or any other bullshit you think you're doing."

"They're your guys, Ronan. I didn't know if they would tell you. I wanted to see what I could find out if they didn't tell you."

"Not your problem."

"Whatever. Danny was already gone, so it was fine."

Anger bubbled up in his chest because she didn't get it. "And what if Tanner didn't come to me about this, but he went to Danny? Then what? You could lose your job." Or worse.

She sighed. "I heard them defend you as a good boss. I went with my gut. It was fine."

"No, it's not fucking fine. This was why I didn't want you involved."

"Look. As much as I'm enjoying this reprimand you have going on here, I'm tired and I'm going back to sleep."

It wasn't until that moment that he realized that she wouldn't normally be up at six in the morning making a pot of coffee. She worked nights. She'd gotten up for him. Now he felt like an ass. "Thanks for the coffee this morning. You didn't have to get up."

"I wanted to tell you about Leroy and Tanner."

"You could've told me that last night and then slept in."

She chuckled in that raspy, throaty way she had. "You distracted me last night. The last thing I was thinking about was Danny or your guys."

"Glad I could be of service. Go back to sleep and stay out of trouble."

"Could say the same to you."

They disconnected, and he was still irritated by her recklessness. Even he didn't know what the Cahills were capable of. They could easily get her fired and he didn't want that on his conscience.

He went back into the building to get the crew started. He still needed to prove to Danny that he should be here. The fact that they had this easy-going job that would give him ample chances to talk to some of the older guys who knew his dad was a bonus. It wouldn't be suspicious at all to be talking while assembling some bullshit furniture.

By the time four o'clock rolled around, he was more

pissed off. The chairs this company had bought were beyond cheap, missing parts and containing instructions in every language but English. Not that a crew of carpenters should need instructions for basic chairs. The cubicle partitions supposedly snapped together, but when they tried to make the sections click, they more often than not cracked.

His idea of having this job done within a couple of days? Gone. The chance to talk to some of the older guys? Non-existent. He'd spent most of his day talking on the phone to the manufacturer, the client, and the office. He couldn't wait to escape the site. Unfortunately, escaping to the peace and quiet of his house wasn't in the cards either.

He walked into his living room and heard cursing and mumbling from the kitchen. After a day like today, he didn't have it in him to deal with Declan. Then he heard a female laugh. Shit. He'd known, in the far back of his head, that if he invited one sibling into his house, they would all eventually make their way in. He dropped his keys on the table beside his recliner and went to see what his family was doing in his house.

"Nessa." He nodded at his sister. "What are you doing here?"

She pushed away from the refrigerator where she'd been leaning. "Well, since you never invite anyone over, and Declan mentioned that he was staying here to work on your kitchen, I thought I'd stop by to say hi."

Ronan looked at Declan who was hunched over a card table with a stack of papers and a ruler. "What are you doing?"

"Drawing you a diagram of the kitchen."

"You know we mostly use computers for that shit, right?"

"Yeah," Declan said with his usual snark. "But I don't have

a computer and even if I did, I've never used those programs. Once I have ideas you like, I'll have the guys at the home improvement place do it on the computer."

Ronan huffed. This project was getting bigger by the minute.

"I was just telling Declan that I think one of those prep islands would be a good use of the space in here. It's just you, so you don't need a big ass table."

"What the fuck do I need a prep island for?" He crossed his arms and leaned on the doorframe.

"It's a selling point. I figured you planned to flip it. It's a lot of room for one guy."

Yeah, it was. "I got a good deal on it. My original plan was to sell, but it's growing on me."

"Or..." His sister offered one of her trouble-making smirks. "Chloe is the kind of girl who probably cooks and bakes and stuff. She would probably really appreciate a prep counter."

"You have a big fucking mouth," he said, turning his attention back to Declan.

Declan shrugged. "You know Nessa. She's nosy. She started asking all kinds of questions about what you do with your time."

"No comment, dude. That's all you gotta say."

Nessa, ignoring the conversation between him and Declan, sidled up to him. "So what's going on with Chloe? I never would've thought she'd act on her bad boy desires."

"What?"

"Come on. I've seen that girl at some neighborhood bars. She's always checking out the guys that look like..."

He stared down at his sister, waiting for her to finish. He waved his hand when she didn't.

"You know, guys who are rough around the edges."

"So she checks out your dating pool."

"Pretty much. The difference is, I've been in those waters a long time. She doesn't fit."

Maybe you don't know her any more than I do. But he knew her much better after last night. He was beginning to think that Chloe wasn't just visiting and exploring her wild side. Maybe she'd always been that way and people just didn't see it.

"Are you dating her? Cleaning up your bad boy image?"

"She's helping me with a project and we're having some fun on the side. That's all." He pushed off the doorframe. "Besides, it's not like her family would ever be okay with me dating their daughter. I'm hitting the shower."

He walked away, hoping for some peace.

"Hey, I'm picking up dinner. You have a preference?" she called from the kitchen.

"Whatever you want is fine." He texted Chloe that he wouldn't make it tonight. Siblings.

As he scrubbed away the day's frustration, he considered the information from Chloe and Tanner. If the Cahills were concerned about the guys on his crew, that must mean one of them knew something.

Wouldn't they have said something by now if it was something obvious? He couldn't imagine any of those guys intentionally keeping a secret like that. Not one that had to do with his dad.

That meant that someone knew something and they didn't even know it was important.

Now he just had to figure out who and what to ask.

It had been a couple of days since Chloe had seen or heard from Ronan. Since he'd called to yell at her Monday morning. Although she didn't think he was still mad at her for asking some simple questions, she'd thought she would've heard from him by now. They'd made plans to see each other again.

Sure, they were vague, tentative plans, but plans nonetheless.

She had no new information to share with him. Danny hadn't spent much time at the Rose this week. Part of her wondered if he had gotten suspicious of her listening in, but she hadn't done anything to make him suspicious.

Thoughts of Ronan had bombarded her for hours when she'd tried to sleep in. She'd been horny but saved herself for meeting with him. Now, she was regretting that choice because her period showed up like clockwork. She was irritable and both her staff and the customers were rubbing her last nerve today. All she wanted was to curl up on her couch with a pint of ice cream, a bag of potato chips, and some feel-good TV.

That desire doubled when one of her new servers called in sick at the last minute. So she plastered on her best customer service smile and tried to remember that midweek wasn't usually busy. She could fake it through the dinner rush and then beg Johnny to close tonight. Two hours in and she was cursing Kristi for calling off. Chloe's cramps started and bloating made her feel like she was a waddling whale. How could her body turn on her so fast?

A family of six came in and Chloe tried to pass them off to Julia, but her section was full. She walked the family to the only table on her side where they would fit. "Can I start you all off with some drinks?"

"Water all around," the woman said. "Milk for the kids. A glass of whatever white wine you have available for me."

Chloe nodded and looked toward the two men who were in deep conversation.

The woman, who was struggling to wrangle a toddler into a high chair, added, "Get them each a Guinness."

"I'll be right back with menus." She grabbed menus and silverware from the host station and delivered them.

As she waited for the drinks at the bar, she watched the harried woman play with her toddler while talking to the two other kids. The men continued to ignore the commotion and did nothing to help her. Chloe felt sorry for the woman.

She delivered the drinks and took their dinner order. The woman had ordered for the entire family. She knew exactly what everyone wanted and wasted no time waiting for input from any of them. She could've been a drill instructor as rapid-fire as the ordering went.

The toddler started banging a spoon and shredding a

napkin while the other two kids bickered. The mother sucked down her wine as if she were parched in a desert. Chloe delivered another glass with a smile.

"On the house," she whispered. "Looks like you could use it."

"Thank you."

Just then, one of the two boys pulled his straw from his cup of milk and sprayed milk all over Chloe.

She sucked in a breath of surprise.

"Oh my God. I am so sorry," the mother said. "Peter. Apologize to the nice lady."

Peter looked up at Chloe with a shit-eating grin. "Sorry."

Then his brother said, "How'd you do it?"

Before Chloe could step back, he'd figured it out and sprayed her from the other side.

"Michael," the woman said sharply.

Through clenched teeth, Chloe simply said, "It's fine." She brushed at her arm and her shirt with a napkin. "Your food will be ready soon."

In the kitchen, she washed her hands and arms up to her elbows to get rid of the milk and she blotted at her shirt. She was feeling really bitchy right now and she needed to let it go. She checked on her other tables and then circled back to the kitchen for the family's food.

As soon as she set the dishes down, both Peter and Michael began to complain about what their mom ordered. The men were laughing at their end of the table, still offering no help or input. How did this woman not go off on her husband? They had to be married or at least a couple. Why else would they all be together like this?

"Let me know if you need anything else."

The woman began cutting up food for the kids. One man

waved at Chloe and pointed to his pint glass. She delivered two more beers to the table. The woman still hadn't had a bite of her food. *This poor woman.* The toddler played with his food while his brothers shoveled theirs in their mouths. Chloe couldn't imagine living that life. Was that the extent of her mother's life? Or Erin's? There to serve and order and direct? Chloe wondered why she'd thought such a life was a good idea for her. She glanced at the men and realized either of them could've been Tim.

This could have been her life. The thought made her stomach turn. Or maybe it was another round of cramps.

An hour later, the kids were done with being in a restaurant and the mom was trying to keep them occupied, but the men had just ordered another round. Chloe made her way to the other end of the table to see if the woman needed anything else—like the check, maybe—as the toddler began wailing. He pushed food away and slapped at his mother's hands.

Chloe had babysat her nieces and nephews. She was pretty good with kids. She lowered herself to the toddler and asked, "What's wrong?"

He hiccupped and then projectile vomited on her.

The mother jumped up and shoved a handful of napkins at Chloe. "I can't believe this." Turning to her husband, she said, "Dave. We have to go. The baby just threw up on our waitress."

"Oh, damn. Is he okay?"

"I don't know. Just pay the bill, please."

Chloe straightened and wiped at her shirt. She pulled the bill from her apron and handed it to Dave.

He peeled bills from the cash in his pocket and handed them to her. With a wrinkled nose, as if it wasn't his kid that just puked on her, he said, "Keep the change. Sorry for the inconvenience."

"Thank you. Have a good night. I hope your son is better."

They shuffled out and Chloe looked at the cash. A ten-dollar tip. She reeked of milk and puke and he'd given her ten bucks. She bussed the table, muttering to herself. At least the dinner rush was over. When she walked past Johnny with the tray of dishes, he looked at her and cringed.

"I think me and Julia can handle this. Maybe you should go home."

"Thanks. I can't even with this." She pulled her shirt away from her. It was sticky. Her own stomach rolled at the thought of what she was wearing.

She rushed through closing out what she needed, her thoughts focused on a nice, hot shower. On her way home, she remembered that her landlord had promised to install a new showerhead today. He'd texted her this afternoon to say that he'd get it done. That lifted Chloe's spirits a bit. While it wouldn't make up for being puked on, it would at least be better than her usual shower.

In her apartment, she peeled off her clothes and shoved them in a bag so they wouldn't contaminate the rest of her laundry. She gathered a fresh towel and her comfiest clothes and went to the bathroom. Her heart sank. Her new showerhead was still in the package on her sink.

"Fuck. What's one more letdown on this crappy day?" She texted her landlord to find out what happened and started the water for a shower. Once the water was warm, she stepped in and suddenly water pressure was almost not existent.

She washed as quickly as she could, given the trickle of water she was dealing with. Then the pipes began to rattle and the showerhead came crashing down, thunking her on her head and then smacking her toes.

"Motherfucker!" she screamed. She twisted the knobs and called her landlord to leave a scathing message about what happened. After getting dressed, she stomped through her apartment and debated what to do. She needed to clean her smelly clothes, but she wasn't in the mood to tromp to the basement right now.

When her phone rang, she assumed it was her landlord returning her call. "Hello."

"Chloe?"

Ronan's deep voice rumbled across the line.

"Oh, hi. What's up?"

"I was calling to see if you wanted to get together when you get off work."

Emotion swelled in her chest. Of course, she wanted to see him, but not like this. She swallowed hard. "I'm already done for the night. It's not a good time."

"What's wrong?"

"Nothing." Her voice was too high and an idiot would be able to tell she was lying. But the last thing Ronan would want was to be exposed to her rampaging emotions. She rummaged through her freezer, yanked out a bag of vegetables, and pressed them to the rapidly-forming lump on her head.

RONAN KNEW A LIE WHEN HE HEARD ONE AND ALTHOUGH HE had no place in pushing for answers, he did. "What happened?"

"What the hell didn't happen?"

He waited, but she didn't continue. "Tell me."

"It doesn't matter. I won't be good company tonight. I'll call you in a few days."

"I might be able to turn your night around. We have a list, right?"

Her chuckle this time wasn't sexy. It was irritated. "I'll need a raincheck on that."

"Oh." Maybe she was good with it being a one-time thing after all.

A shaky breath wavered in his ear. "Look. I've had a shitty day. I got my period, so sex is off the table. I had to cover for a waitress who called in sick. I had a horrible night at work where a couple of kids spit milk at me and then their baby brother puked on me. And I only got a lousy ten-dollar tip from the family. Then to top it all off, my landlord was supposed to change my showerhead today. Not only did that not happen, the old one had messed up water pressure and then actually fell off and smacked me on the head. So, I feel like crap, probably don't smell much better and although I might be horny, period sex isn't my thing."

He listened and understood everything she said, but the message he got clearly was no sex and she was miserable. He should just give her the space she was asking for, but he felt bad that he hadn't called her since they slept together. Casual or not, he should've called. All he'd done was yell at her while she was half-asleep Monday morning and sent a text to cancel plans.

"Okay. Sorry you had a crappy day."

"I'm sorry, Ronan."

"You don't owe me an apology. We'll talk soon." He disconnected and grabbed a tool bucket and filled it with some basic plumbing tools.

On the way to her apartment, he made a quick stop at the store. It was late on a Thursday, so her street was pretty crowded. He ended up parking down the block from Chloe's place. Grabbing his stuff, he trudged up to her building. The front lock was still busted. Someone needed to have a conversation with the landlord. This was bullshit.

He knocked on Chloe's door.

"Who is it?"

At least this time, she asked without just swinging her door open. "Ronan."

She opened the door. "I told you I—"

He didn't wait for her to finish. He handed her the grocery bag and pushed past her. "I'm not here for sex, Chloe."

She wore some soft-looking flowy pajama pants and a tight tank top. Her hair was piled on her head. She definitely hadn't been expecting company. He pointed toward her couch. "Go back to watching whatever sappy stuff you have. The shower will be fixed within the hour."

Instead of going to the couch, she followed. "First of all, that's *Criminal Minds*. Nothing like a good serial killer show when you're feeling murdery. Second, I didn't ask you to fix my shower."

"I know you didn't." And it irked him a little. This was what he did for a living—fixing shit, building shit. Her not asking sent a pretty clear message. In the bathroom, he surveyed the damage. She hadn't even picked up the broken showerhead.

"You don't have to do this," she said from behind him.

"I know." He unboxed the new showerhead and took out his tools.

She grunted, but finally gave up and stomped off, grocery bag rustling as she moved.

Ronan had the old plumbing taken apart and prepped for the new parts when Chloe came back. She set a bottle of beer on the sink.

"You brought me chocolate ice cream and cheesy popcorn."

He shrugged. "I've been around women. I took a guess. Salty and sweet foods are usually a safe bet."

Chloe reluctantly smiled. "Thank you. That was thoughtful."

"You had a shitty day." He attached the new showerhead and tightened it. When he turned around, she was gone again. He probably managed to screw that up, too. He stepped from the tub, took a swig of beer, and then turned the shower on. Water flowed without issue.

His boots had left mucky footprints in the tub, so he let the water run a minute. Then he looked under the sink for something to clean his mess.

"Oh my God. You don't have to clean my tub," Chloe said from the door.

"My boots left dirt everywhere."

"You clean the tubs of all your customers?"

He turned off the water and stood. "You're not a customer. You're a friend, right?"

She crossed her arms. "You clean your friend's tub?"

He laughed. She had him there. "No, I'd tell him that I just did him a favor and he should clean his own damn tub. But like I said before, you had a shitty day. I was making it better, not worse."

"I don't need to be taken care of, Ronan."

"Didn't say you did."

They stared at each other, unmoving. The heat and attraction were still rolling between them, but there was more. An uncertainty.

Finally, she dropped her arms. "Thank you."

"You're welcome. Want to take it for a test drive? See if there're any problems?"

She chuckled. "Can't possibly be worse than having it fall on my head." She rubbed a spot on her scalp.

"It really hit you?"

"Yep."

"Your landlord's an asshole."

She lifted a shoulder. "He's okay."

Ronan moved around, gathered all the trash, and put his tools away.

"You want to stay for a while?" she asked. "I mean, I know you have to get up early for work, so if you need to go, that's fine. I just thought maybe you might want to share some ice cream and watch murderers be brought to justice."

Chloe was rambling. She was cute.

"I can stay for a while." He was all for justice being served.

Her face lit up. "Give me ten minutes. I want to try the new shower. Make yourself at home."

He left the bathroom and threw away the packaging. He sat on the couch and drank his beer. Last time he was here, he hadn't paid much attention to the apartment. He'd been too focused on getting Chloe naked, but he looked around now. She didn't have a lot of stuff in her living room. More furniture than he had, but not too much else. She had a few family photos on the table beside her TV. Next to the couch, she had a bag of yarn and stuff. A tray on the table had more yarn and a hoop thing that must've been one of her projects. He laughed just as Chloe came back into the room.

Her scent hit him hard, and that combined with the message on her project gave him a flash of last Sunday. "Thighs make good earmuffs, huh?"

Her cheeks were pink, but it might've been from her shower.

"You tell me." She took the hoop from him and replaced it on the table. Her hair was wrapped in a towel.

"Does your mother know you sew things like that?"

When she laughed this time, it was the raspy sexy one. She pulled the towel from her head and let her hair fall to her shoulders. "Hell, no. She'd have to go to church daily to pray extra for my soul. This is my hobby. I sell them online. Dirty messages sell a whole lot better than homey platitudes."

She sat next to him and ran a comb through her hair. He couldn't help but lean over and take a deep sniff. "Much better than milk and puke."

She stretched her arms over her head, her tank skimming higher on her torso. "That shower was like magic. I can't wait to play with it more and see all the things it can do."

For someone who he always considered a good girl, this woman made everything sound dirty and sexy.

"Really? Not even a reaction? You're a tough crowd, Doyle."

"There's a reaction, all right. But you made it clear sex was off the table. I might be an asshole, but I respect what a woman wants."

"I like that about you." She rose, took a drink from his beer, and then straddled him. "There's some room between nothing and sex, wouldn't you say?"

She kissed him and then slid off his body until she was kneeling on the floor between his legs. She reached for the button on his jeans.

He grabbed her hands. "You don't have to do this. I didn't come over here looking for anything."

"That's what makes it hotter." She undid his button and he lifted his hips to allow her to pull his pants off. She shoved them to his ankles but left them there. She stroked him with a firm grasp, just the way he liked. "I don't swallow."

"Okay." He thrust his hips up into her fist.

"Just putting it out there." She lowered her head and swirled her tongue over his tip.

"Fuck." He closed his eyes and fisted his hands on the couch, as she took him in her hot mouth.

"You gonna tell me what you like?" She stroked him again.

"You're doing fine. Hand and mouth. Pressure."

She licked the line between his balls and he gripped his own thigh. She laughed as she trailed her tongue up his length. "You can touch me."

"Didn't want to freak you out."

"I don't scare that easily. You can even pull my hair a little if you want."

He growled and thrust his fingers into her hair. The moan he received in return pulsed in his cock. Her mouth was perfect and it didn't take him long. He released her head. "Off," he grunted. Then he grabbed the towel she left on the couch from her hair and cleaned up.

She rocked back and swiped at her lips with a pretty grin.

"Come here." He held out a hand to help her up and back onto his lap. With his left hand, he cradled her jaw and brought her in for a kiss. His right hand gripped her ass and scooted her close until she was notched against his dick.

She gasped at the contact.

"Use me. Ride me," he said gruffly.

She shifted slowly, rubbing herself against him. She took his mouth as she ground her hips, her fingers digging into his shoulders. He felt her heat through the soft cotton of her pajama pants. He held her close as she panted and buried her face in his neck until she shuddered her own release.

They clung to each other for long minutes after. The uncertainty from earlier gone. Whatever this was between them was there and wasn't going away.

CHAPTER

Thirteen

Chloe kept her face against Ronan's neck, breathing in his scent, feeling the soft scrape of his beard along her forehead and cheekbone. What was wrong with her? She couldn't just have the man hang out in her house without jumping him? But it had been hot and pretty amazing. She'd wanted to give him a blowjob. Wanted to make him feel weak. She hadn't counted on him turning the tables on her. *Use me.* His words caused another shiver to run through her.

When her heartbeat returned to normal and his heart was a steady beat beneath her palm, she pushed up and away from him. She stood. "I'm going to go freshen up," she said as she pointed in the general direction of her bathroom. He nodded and began the process of tucking himself back into his pants.

After cleaning up in the bathroom, Chloe looked at herself in the mirror. One very satisfied woman stared back at her. She couldn't remember the last hook-up she had that was this good. A little voice in her head whispered, "Hook-ups don't bring presents and fix stuff."

She shook that thought away, blaming it on her hormones. He'd wanted to get together and when she brushed him off, he became creative. Points for that. Leaving the bathroom, she wondered if he planned to stay.

But there he was, still sitting on her couch, legs sprawled in front of him, drinking his beer.

"Can I get you another?" she asked from behind him.

"I can stay for one more."

She went to the kitchen and grabbed a beer for him and a glass of water for herself. After handing him the beer, she sat on the couch, which suddenly seemed much smaller than usual. "Thanks for coming over tonight. And the snacks. And the shower. It was really thoughtful."

"No thanks for the orgasm?" he said, his voice a quiet rumble.

"I figured we were even on that score," she answered with a smile. She pressed play on the TV remote and her episode of *Criminal Minds* started.

Ten minutes in, Ronan's only response was, "This is fucked up."

"So what have you been doing all week? Besides work, of course."

"Sorry I didn't call sooner. I meant to, but I got caught up working on something with Brendan."

That made her sit up. "Have you figured something out?"

"Based on the questions Danny asked Tanner and Leroy, we're thinking that one of the older guys on my crew knows something or has some information about our dad."

"It's been twenty years. I'd think if they knew something, they would've said something."

"That's what I thought. But it could be that they don't know something directly related to my dad, but information that might lead to something else."

"How are you going to figure out who knows what?"

He sighed. "I have six men on my crew that I hand-picked because they were working for Cahill at the same time as my dad. The company was smaller back then, but there were still multiple crews. There's no way to know who knew my dad without just asking them."

"Yeah, I see how that might be suspicious on the job. But what about after-work drinks? We have regular crews that come to the Rose. Not Cahill's, which seems weird, but other guys."

"Cahill likes to hold court at the Rose because he's *important*." Ronan said the word with air quotes without moving his hands. "He isn't the kind of boss who mixes with the guys at the bottom."

"So you just need something social." She paused and thought. Then she shot up. "Host a barbecue. You have a backyard. Invite your guys over. Like team bonding."

He stared at her with his beer midway to his mouth. All of his features were pinched as if she'd just suggested he offer his crew a striptease.

"What? Burgers and hot dogs on the grill. Cold beer. They appreciate you as a boss. Danny will think you're just trying to get kiss-ass points as the new boss. Nothing suspicious. Brendan can even come and ask about your dad."

Ronan shifted, more relaxed. "Brendan might've even worked with a few of them."

"Brendan worked for Cahill?"

"Briefly. One summer after my dad went missing."

Every time he said that, her heart broke a little more. She

couldn't imagine not knowing. Her family wasn't perfect, but she liked knowing they were always there.

"What the fuck do I know about hosting a party?"

"What's there to know? You own a grill?"

"Yeah."

"I know you have a refrigerator. Buy some salads and chips and dip. Throw meat on the grill. Keep it simple."

He nodded, and she saw his brain working. "I'll run it by Brendan and see what he thinks. Might work."

She wanted to offer to help, but that would cross the line of their current agreement. She settled back on the couch and focused on the BAU hunting a killer. They watched in relative silence, except for Ronan's variations of "That's fucked up."

When the episode ended, he stood. "I need to get going."

"Thanks for coming by. It definitely turned my day around."

He bent over and gave her a kiss that said his day went better than expected, too.

They separated and he said, "Lock me out."

She rolled her eyes but followed.

"And call that fucking landlord again and tell him to fix the front door."

She tried not to read anything into his concern, but she smiled. She held the door open as he grabbed his tools. "FYI, we should be open for business by Sunday. Monday at the latest," she said waving a hand over her uterus. One bonus of being on the pill was that her periods tended to be short.

"Hm. I'll keep that in mind." He pressed another quick kiss to her lips and left.

Chloe locked the door, cleaned up their mess, and

crawled into bed. Spending time with Ronan was nice. She enjoyed being with him and the orgasm was a nice bonus.

Settling under the covers, she said aloud, "Not the plan, Chloe. Ronan is not looking for a girlfriend. Stop thinking about him outside of the bedroom."

She hoped that hearing the words would make them sink in.

RONAN'S HEAD WAS FILLED WITH TOO MANY THOUGHTS. HE HAD more fun last night with Chloe than he thought when he'd headed over there. He hadn't planned on getting laid, and he wasn't about to complain about her taking the lead and offering a blowjob. But the rest of their conversation about his crew and her investment in his investigation about his dad did a number on him. He hadn't ever had anyone to talk to about this. He had no business sharing with Chloe. But she made it easy.

Brendan said he was going to look into the guys he'd chosen to be on his crew, but he hadn't gotten back to Ronan with any more information.

For the first time in years, he felt like he had forward motion in finding out what happened to his dad, but he still didn't know anything. He was hopeful and frustrated all at once. He texted Brendan and asked him to come over to his house after work today so they could figure out their next moves.

It was strange not only talking with Brendan regularly again but actively working together on something. As young kids, they'd been close. Irish twins, barely a year apart, they'd been inseparable. Everything changed after their dad went missing. Ronan had been angry and acted out; Brendan searched for answers. By the time Ronan wanted answers, Brendan had shut down, which just made Ronan act out more.

Their relationship was far from perfect, or even back to where it used to be, but these past few weeks had taught him how much he'd missed his older brother.

In the kitchen, Ronan found Declan hunched over the same card table with his pages and Ronan's laptop. "Help yourself to my shit."

"It's not like it was password protected. And I told you I don't have a computer. I didn't think it would be an issue."

"It's not. Just have a lot on my mind and I'm not used to other people being around." Speaking of which, he should probably get rid of Declan before Brendan showed. Brendan's arrival would be suspicious enough, but if Declan overheard their conversation, he would tell the rest of the family.

"Lucky for you, I have plans tonight," Declan said.

Dodged a bullet there. "Date?"

"Nah. Just hanging out with Tyler. He's finally moving back. He's staying with his sister and from what I got from his texts, she's driving him nuts."

"I know the feeling," Ronan countered.

Declan flung a pencil at Ronan. "Fuck you. I stay out of your way. I even bought beer and food for the fridge."

"I was kidding. You don't irritate me too much more now than you did when you were ten. What time you heading out?"

"'Bout a half hour. The bar has happy hour wings."

Ronan set his keys on the table. "You can take my truck as long as I can trust you not to drive drunk."

"Really?"

"It'll be cheaper than Uber and faster than the bus."

"Cool. Thanks, man. I have the list of materials and a plan for the kitchen. Maybe tomorrow we can go over it."

"Sounds good. Have fun. Tell Tyler I said hi." Ronan went to shower and change. By the time he returned to the kitchen, Declan was gone. He opened a beer and scanned the contents of his fridge to figure out dinner.

Declan's idea of buying food was questionable. He did get milk, probably because Declan could practically live on cereal. There was a loaf of bread and jelly. The man still ate like a twelve-year-old. Not liking those options, he texted Brendan.

I'm ordering dinner. You want in?

Sure. Whatever you get is fine.

Ronan called in an order at the pizza place down the street. He didn't want to try guessing what Brendan would like and pizza was always a safe bet. Then he cleared Declan's mess from the table and pulled out his notes.

Over the past few weeks, he realized that all of the information he'd kept in his head was a jumbled mess, so he began writing it down so he could look for connections. When the bell rang, he answered the door to find Brendan and the pizza guy on his porch.

"I have the best timing," Brendan said. "Pay the man."

"Already paid, asshole."

"In that case," he turned to the delivery driver and said, "I'll take this." Then he pushed past Ronan into the house.

Ronan handed the man a tip and closed the front door behind them. "Take it to the kitchen."

"Love what you've done to the place," his brother said as he set the pizza down on the table and his bag on the floor.

Ronan gathered his pages and stacked them on the

corner of the table. Then he grabbed a couple of beers from the fridge.

"How are things going with Declan?" Brendan asked.

Ronan shrugged. "He's working on something for this kitchen. It's taking him a fuckton of time to figure it out, so I guess it's a good thing I'm not in a hurry."

"See? It was good that I sent him over. Where is he now?"

"Hanging out with Tyler. It's probably good that he's not here getting involved in this." They each reached into the pizza box and grabbed a slice.

They ate quickly and in silence, which didn't bother Ronan. When they had their fill, he closed the box and pushed it to the corner of the table, opposite of where he stacked his papers. "I didn't know how to organize the information I have. Most of it isn't even concrete, just feelings and impressions I've gotten. But it's led me here and something is starting to shake loose."

"How do you mean?"

"Even though Danny Cahill tried to convince his father that I'm just a stellar employee, he brought in two of my guys to question them."

"You're a new supervisor. Not that out of the ordinary."

"It is when he asks about how I treat the older guys on the crew. You know, the ones I picked because they've been at Cahill for twenty years?"

"So you're making them nervous. What about the old guys?"

"What about them?"

"Have they told you anything?"

"I haven't had opportunities to ask them questions without it being suspicious." He thought about Chloe's idea. "Chloe suggested I host a barbecue here for the crew. Get them away from the job site and then I can pump them for information."

"That's a good idea. They'd be relaxed and it wouldn't be their boss asking questions, just a guy wanting to hear stories about his dad."

"You could come, too. They might know you."

"When are you planning on doing this?"

"Sunday?"

"Like in three days?"

Ronan shrugged.

"Some people have lives. They might already have plans. And two days isn't a lot of time for you to get it together."

"What's there to get? Meat for the grill, beer for the fridge, and some sides."

"Do it next weekend. That way people can plan for it." He drank his beer. "It also gives it time to get back to Cahill."

"Is that a good idea?"

"Who knows?" Brendan grabbed some of the notes Ronan had made. "Let's see what you got." He bent over and pulled a file from his bag.

"Nice purse," Ronan said.

"Fuck you. It's a briefcase."

"Nope. Briefcases are hard-sided. That's a man purse."

"Some of us have jobs that require us to carry things to and from the office."

"I carry things. I just do it with a toolbox and toolbelt." He'd forgotten how much fun it was to push his brother's buttons. "What does your fancy file say?"

"It says you're an asshole."

Ronan laughed. "We knew that already."

"I tried to make a list of guys that I worked with that summer at Cahill, but it's sketchy because I was a kid who didn't pay attention to last names. But from what I could recall and with checks I've done, I've got about five guys. I found a few more that aren't working at Cahill anymore." He spread pages out on the table.

Computer-printed photos and biographical information on Cahill employees. John Mulroney was one of them. "Old Man Mulroney knew Dad. We've talked. Nothing specific, but he talked about how much I look like Dad."

"Okay. So we make sure to hit him up at the party." Brendan slid him to the side.

"Joe McKinley is on my crew, and so is Nick Jordan. The other two I don't know at all."

"Three out of five isn't bad. You make sure they show up next Sunday. I'm going to start running down these other guys. Do you know any of them?" He handed Ronan the stack.

There were a lot, but that wasn't surprising, given that construction typically had a high turnover rate. Some guys weren't cut out for the physical demands of the job. Some hated the uncertainty of work. Others moved to other companies because they didn't like Cahill.

Brendan went to the fridge and grabbed two fresh bottles of beer. He popped the tops on both while Ronan flipped through the pages.

"Since they've been gone for a while, I don't know if I know any of these guys. If they were working with Dad and then left, there's no way I know them."

"Go to the back of the pile. Those are newest."

Ronan flipped the stack over. He glanced at the first one. "Shithead. Won't know anything. Pissed off all the Cahills. Don't know how he made it there as long as he did. No one liked him." He discarded the page.

"Let's not discount him. If he pissed them off, he might know something."

"I doubt it. All he ever did was complain and hurt himself. Then he'd get some money out of them."

"So not just a shithead. A scammer."

"Yeah, that's the consensus."

"What about these three? I remember them from my summer before I got fired."

"I think they're retired."

The doorbell rang and Brendan looked up. "Expecting someone?"

"No." Then his phone lit up with a call from Danny Cahill. "Fuck. It's Cahill."

Brendan started gathering papers.

"Hello?"

"Ronan. It's Danny Cahill. I'm at your front door. Are you home? I saw your truck and assumed."

"Uh, yeah. I'll be right there." He disconnected, looked at Brendan, and said, "Cahill's at the door."

"I'm moving. Give me a minute." He scooped up all of the papers they'd been looking over and his beer and went up the back steps that no one ever used.

Ronan went to the front door and opened it. "Mr. Cahill. What are you doing here?"

"I had something come up that needs to be taken care of this weekend, so I'm hoping you can handle it. Can I come in?"

"Of course." He opened the door wide and stepped aside to let Cahill in. Bosses didn't show up to their employees' homes unexpectedly like this. Ronan was even more suspicious of the man. "Sorry. I don't usually have company and I've been renovating. I have a couple chairs in the kitchen."

He led the way into the kitchen and pointed to the chairs. "Can I get you something to drink? Or a slice of pizza?" he asked, gesturing to the box.

"No, thank you. I won't keep you long. Alderman Ekhart has a situation in his backyard. A fence needs to be moved to be correctly placed on the property line. He's been fighting with his neighbor about it for months, and he needs to address it this weekend. Can you handle it?"

"I don't see why not."

He pulled a thick envelope from his interior coat pocket. Setting it on the table, he added, "There's the money for the job as well as a copy of the plat of survey." He looked around the kitchen. "What are you planning in here?"

"My brother Declan wants to take a stab at building cabinets for me. He's in the process of designing something."

"Really? Is he any good?"

"Like I said, he's taking a stab. We'll see if he's any good."

"Well, you know we always have an open door for good employees. Let me know if he's looking for something."

"I will. Was there anything else?"

"No. This job just popped up and I wanted to give you as much time as possible to get a crew set, rather than dropping it on you on a Friday."

"Will do. Thanks for the opportunity." He walked Cahill to the front door and locked up. When he got back to the kitchen, Brendan was once again at the table.

"First of all, what the fuck with that staircase?"

"I think you're the first person to use it since I bought the place."

"Clean that shit up. Second, is that his normal MO? Show up at your house to give you a side gig?"

"Not at all. The side jobs usually come through the

project manager Thomas Walsh and then I meet Cahill at the Rose for cash."

"So we're making him nervous."

"Someone's nervous. How do you think they'll react when I throw my barbecue next weekend?"

"Don't know, but it should be interesting." Brendan took pictures of Ronan's notes and then shoved his phone back in his bag. "I'm going to try to reach out to these former employees to see what I can find."

"I'll let you know if I can get the old guys to my house next Sunday."

"You might want to give Chloe a heads up so she can keep her ears open."

"Her ears are always open." He was still concerned for her job. If Cahill thought she was feeding them information, he'd get her fired.

She would probably hate Ronan then. That bothered him more than he wanted to admit.

Chloe hadn't spoken to Ronan since he left her house the other night. Although it was Sunday and she'd told him they'd be clear for sexytimes, they hadn't made plans. But Mrs. Adamos across the hall had stopped her at least five times to ask if Chloe could have her friend with the tools stop by to fix her door. All summer she'd been dealing with the swollen wood, but often she hadn't been able to lock it.

A request like that was beyond the boundaries of her arrangement with Ronan. It was one thing for him to fix something in her apartment, but this wasn't something she knew how to ask for. So here she was, wasting her perfectly good day off stressing about making a phone call. Finally, at lunch, she dialed his number.

"Hey," he answered.

"Hi. I know it's Sunday, but are you busy?"

"I'm actually on a job right now."

"Really?"

"Side job. Why, what'd you need?"

"It's not me, but my neighbor. She asked me to see if you could maybe fix her front door. It sticks real bad and our landlord..."

"Is an asshole," he finished. "Yeah, I can come by after I'm done here. You working today?"

She smiled broadly, even though he couldn't see it. "Nope. I have the whole day and night off."

"When I'm done here, I'll go home and change then come to you."

"You could come straight here. When you're done with the door, I can wash your work clothes. You can try out the amazing new showerhead in my bathroom."

"Amazing, huh?"

"Yeah, it's that good."

"Will you be joining me for that shower?"

"I might be able to arrange that. We can come up with a payment plan for the work."

"Sounds good. I gotta go finish this fence. See you in a couple hours."

A couple of hours turned into more like four hours, but Chloe did let Mrs. Adamos know that Ronan would be by sometime this afternoon, so she was satisfied. Chloe spent that time cleaning her apartment and doing some more cross stitch. She had orders to package and prep for shipping. Her online shop was building. While she wasn't getting rich off it, it had become a nice side hustle income that would allow her to splurge on things she normally wouldn't.

When a heavy knock hit her front door, she was surrounded by envelopes and mailing labels. She carefully shifted the piles so she didn't confuse anything and went to the door.

Ronan stood there grimy and sweaty, which should've been a turnoff, but damn he looked good.

"Hi."

"Sorry it took so long. The fence was more involved than we thought it was going to be and it had to be done today."

"No problem. Mrs. Adamos is thrilled that you said you'd try to fix it." She pointed across the hall. "She's over there."

Chloe took a step forward, but he made no move to go to Mrs. Adamos's apartment. Instead, when he stepped closer, he grabbed her hip with one strong hand, lowered his mouth to hers, and kissed her. It was hot and demanding, and nothing she had been prepared for.

Then suddenly, he released her and stepped away from the door for her to lead the way across the hall. She stumbled around him, a little dazed by the power of his kiss. "Wow," she said quietly.

"Been a few days and you're looking downright edible in those shorts."

She glanced down at her outfit, which she'd given zero thought to this morning. They were the same shorts she wore all the time. She knocked on Mrs. Adamos's door.

"Coming!" The announcement was followed by the knob turning and thumping and rubbing of the door.

"Step away from the door," Ronan said. "I'm going to shove it open."

"Okay."

He turned the knob and rammed his shoulder into the door.

"Unf." The sexual sound came from Chloe's throat without warning.

Ronan shot her a look over his shoulder, one raised brow to call her on her reaction.

Her cheeks became warm, but she smiled.

Mrs. Adamos was on the other side of the door. "You see? It's like this all the time in the summer."

"Mrs. Adamos, this is my friend Ronan."

Ronan wiped a hand on his dirty jeans and then extended it to the older woman.

"Ronan? What kind of name is that?"

"Irish, I guess."

"Sounds like a good, strong name." Pointing to the door, she said, "Can you fix it?"

Ronan stepped into the apartment and swung the door. Then he closed it as far as he could until it stuck. "I think so. Shouldn't take long."

He left the door open and stepped around Chloe to grab his bucket of tools that he'd left by her door. Chloe leaned against the stair rail and watched him pull out tools.

"You can go back to your place."

"You sure?"

"Why? Is your neighbor a serial killer or something?"

She chuckled. "No. You need anything?"

"Nope."

"Okay." She moved back to her place. Before settling back on the floor to pack her orders, she went to the kitchen and grabbed a bottle of beer for Ronan. She popped the top and set it next to his bucket.

"Thanks."

As she backed away, she watched the muscles of his forearms flex. His biceps bulged as he shaved the edge of the door. Watching him do his job should not act as an aphrodisiac, but her hormones argued otherwise. Reclaiming her space on the floor, she stuffed envelopes and affixed labels.

She heard the occasional grunt or bang from the hall, but otherwise, Ronan kept busy.

When she had her box ready to take to the post office, she got off the floor, her butt sore from sitting there so long. She stretched and went to the kitchen to see if she had something she could make for dinner. She hadn't gone grocery shopping for a while since she ate at work most nights. Yeah, nothing of substance appeared.

A thump at her door had her rushing over. She swung the door open to see Ronan balancing a dish in one hand and his bucket of tools in the other.

"Hurry up and let me in before she comes up with another job."

Chloe stepped back. "What do you mean *another*?"

He dropped his tools near her coat hook. "Look. Your neighbor is nice. Sent me off with a plate of food that smells delicious, but holy shit she wanted me to work for it."

Chloe cringed. "Sorry."

"No big deal. Now we have dinner."

"That's good because I have nothing to cook here. I was about to order something."

He set the dish on her counter. When he turned back, she wrapped her arms around his waist. "Thank you. I really appreciate it."

He put a hand on her shoulder. "I'm really grimy between the dirt from the job and sweat. You don't want to rub up on this."

"Then put that dinner in the oven to stay warm while we shower. We'll get you all cleaned up." She backed away from him and pulled her tank top over her head.

RONAN FUMBLED TAKING OFF HIS BOOTS AS HE WATCHED CHLOE
strip on her way to the bathroom. He wanted to tell her to
watch herself around the Cahills, give her a similar warning
to the one she'd given him. But seeing her sweet ass walk
away from him made all thoughts of the Cahills disappear. In
the bathroom, he dropped his dirty, sweaty clothes in a pile in
the corner.

Chloe already had the water running, but she stood near
the sink, waiting for him. He stepped into the tub and under
the spray. The showerhead was nice but not nearly as good as
the view of her standing naked outside the tub.

"You coming in or what?"

"I was just wondering how we're both going to fit in
there."

"I'll make room." He soaped up quickly.

She stepped into the tub. She'd pulled her hair up into a
pile on her head. The water splashed off his shoulders and
into her face, causing her to squint. He angled the water a
little more. "Come here," he said, pulling her against his
warm skin.

He kissed her deeply, cradling her ass in his palms. She
moaned into his mouth. They played with each other's
bodies, toying, teasing, but he realized that unfortunately,
one of them would probably end up hurt if they tried to fuck
in the small space. Her fingers wrapped around his dick and
she stroked him. He spun them and pressed her against the
wall. With one hand, he pinched a nipple and his other
sought out the wet heat of her pussy.

They drove each other over the edge and stood panting,

bodies brushing as the water grew cold. He reached behind her and twisted the knob to turn off the water.

"Next time we shower together, it'll be at my house where I have room to maneuver."

"Who said there'll be a next time?" she asked with a saucy grin as she stepped from the tub and wrapped a towel around herself.

"We both know that we're not done with each other yet."

"Good point. I would offer you something to wear, but," She waved a finger at him. "I doubt I have anything that would fit. Use a towel and I'll run these to the laundry."

He wanted to protest. It seemed silly that she should do his clothes, but the idea of climbing back into those smelly things didn't appeal to him at all. "Thanks. I'll get dinner set up."

She disappeared into her bedroom and returned wearing a fresh T-shirt and shorts and carrying a laundry basket that already had clothes in it.

"I'm not sure it's a good idea to mix my work clothes with your stuff."

"Why? Do you have cooties?"

"I don't want your clothes to get ruined."

"It's just my work clothes. Jeans and Black Rose shirts. A little dirt won't do any damage. I'll be back in a minute."

He walked out of the bathroom with a fluffy towel wrapped around his hips. In the kitchen, he pulled the dinner from the oven and went into the cabinets to find plates. He served up the kabobs that smelled amazing. His stomach rumbled and he popped a piece of tender meat in his mouth. Damn, that was good. If Chloe didn't hurry, he might devour all of it.

He heard the door click shut, so he carried their plates

into the living room so they could sit on the couch. He nudged a box of packages out of the way. "What's this?"

"Those are the cross-stitch orders from my online shop I need to ship out."

He handed her a plate and held the knot of the towel as he sat.

"What do I owe you for fixing Mrs. Adamos's door?"

"You don't owe me anything."

"I'm sure she didn't pay you. She asked me to have you come over as a favor."

"It was a favor."

"No. Fixing my shower was a favor. Doing work for my neighbor is something you should get paid for."

He shrugged. "It wasn't a big deal. Plus, she fed us dinner."

"Are you sure? I feel like I was taking advantage."

"So what? I've taken advantage of you working at the Rose. It's what you do for friends, right?" He had to keep reminding himself that that was all they were. Friends. Fuck buddies. He'd never fit into her life. Not with her family.

"If you say so."

"Speaking of your eavesdropping—"

"Did something happen?"

"Kind of. Danny Cahill showed up at my house the other night."

"I take it that's not normal?" She slid a hunk of meat and a pepper from her skewer and bit into them.

"About as normal as it is for him to take guys from my crew out to dinner."

"So he's acting all kinds of weird. Why did he come over?"

"He said it was because he had this off-book job that had

to be done this weekend. The fence I was working on yesterday and today."

"It was a real job, so why are you suspicious?"

"Those usually come down from through supervisors and project leads. Danny doesn't go around handling it. Other than the cash. We think he's getting suspicious."

"We?"

"Brendan was over. He hid so Cahill wouldn't see him. But I wanted to warn you. If he's getting suspicious of me, and he suspects you're listening in on his conversations, it could cost you your job."

"I'm just doing what I always do. Don't worry about me."

But he did worry about her. He didn't want to be the one to bring her down.

CHAPTER
Fifteen

onan's week was packed with work and meeting with Brendan to compare notes. Between those meetings and having Declan at his house, he'd seen more of his family in the last month than in the last couple of years. As much as he'd enjoyed hanging with his brothers, it didn't leave him time to see Chloe. They talked on the phone a few times, but their schedules didn't match up.

When he'd told her that he was having a barbecue for his crew, she was happy that he'd taken her suggestion. Although he'd wanted to invite her, part of him wasn't ready to have their relationship—whatever it was—on display to be scrutinized. More important, though, he couldn't risk Cahill seeing them together. Although Cahill was aware they knew each other if he knew they were fucking, he would curb his meetings in front of Chloe.

Early on Sunday, he went grocery shopping and stocked up on everything he could possibly need. Except in his search, he realized that he never threw parties, so he didn't have things like coolers for the beer or extra bowls for chips.

As much as he hated the thought, he knew he needed to call for reinforcements. He loaded all the food into the cab of his truck and considered his options. Mom would probably be his best bet.

He checked the time. Church would be over, so instead of calling, he drove straight there. It wasn't until after he parked that he considered that he might run into Chloe if she went to church with her family. The McCarthys went to church every week, always had, but he didn't know if Chloe joined them. She was the type of girl who would just to make her parents happy.

He got out of his truck and went to his mom's front door. Before he had the chance to knock, it opened.

"Ronan. What are you doing here?"

"Were you expecting someone?"

"No, but you rarely stop by on a Sunday."

"I need some help."

She stepped away from the door and he followed her in.

"I'm having a barbecue for my crew today and I realized I don't have some stuff like bowls and coolers. Can I borrow some?"

"Having a cookout and you didn't invite your family?" she asked over her shoulder as she made her way to the kitchen.

"It's a work thing."

"But Declan will be there." She reached up into a cabinet and pulled down the same big plastic bowls they'd had for most of his childhood.

"Declan is staying with me."

She turned to him with a smile. "I know. And I like seeing my boys together again. Maybe we should do that here. Have everyone over for a cookout."

Ronan was proud of himself for withholding the groan

that rose in his chest. He loved his family, but all together, they could be overwhelming. "Baby steps, Ma."

She shoved the bowls at him. "Coolers are in the garage. What else do you need?"

"You still have the extra lawn chairs in the garage, too?

"Of course. Make sure you bring 'em back in one piece."

"Will do. Thanks." He bent and kissed her cheek as he scooped up the bowls. In the garage, he grabbed two old coolers and five folding lawn chairs that had seen better days. Everything needed to be cleaned. Looked like Declan would be working for his food today.

He hauled the chairs and put them in the bed of his truck. Then he loaded in the coolers. He glanced over at the McCarthy house. He didn't see Chloe's car on the block, so she must not be there today. He shouldn't care. He knew her family didn't like him and he'd lived with it for a long time without it mattering one bit.

But Chloe was starting to mean something to him, even if they remained nothing more than friends. He just didn't think he'd ever get any kind of acceptance from her family.

After he had everything in his truck, he went back inside and said goodbye to his mom, who was on the phone. He waved to her, but she held up a finger to get him to wait.

She pulled the phone from her ear. "Nessa said she can bring you dessert for your party."

"I'm fine. It's not a party, just a work thing. And she's not trying to be generous. She wants to check out who I'm inviting."

"She wants to know what time to come."

"Never," he said and waved as he left.

He knew Nessa was going to show up anyway, which made not inviting Chloe an even better decision. It was bad enough having his siblings know he was sleeping with Chloe. They certainly didn't need to be interacting with her.

On his way home, he called Declan and told him to drag the hose out to the alley so he could spray down the chairs and coolers. One advantage to having Declan there was that it would free Ronan to go buy the ice for the beer. He pulled up in the alley behind his garage and Declan was waiting for him.

When he hopped from the truck, he said, "Stop telling Nessa my business. This is a work thing for me. I don't need all of the Doyles crashing in."

Declan threw his hands up. "She asked what I was doing today and I told her. I didn't exactly invite her."

Ronan pulled out the coolers and handed them to his brother.

"It just feels like you're finally back with us, you know?"

Ronan did know. He'd been doing his own thing for so long that the constant companionship of family was almost foreign to him. It seemed to shift so suddenly though. "Even when I was gone, I wasn't that far."

"You made it clear you wanted distance." He took a lawn chair from Ronan's hand and stared him in the eye. "We all missed you."

"It was better that I wasn't around."

"Better for who?"

"Everyone." But he knew Declan was hinting that the distance was selfish. It hadn't been like he dropped off the planet. He checked in with his siblings and his mother, and he visited. He just avoided big gatherings like family parties because it had been too hard to handle. "At least let me ease back into the family thing."

"We're Doyles, man. We don't make anything easy."

Wasn't that the truth?

Hours later, Ronan had the grill started and beer chilled. Declan had been surprisingly helpful in setting up. Nessa, of course, showed up, but she helped, too. For a change, Ronan wasn't feeling overwhelmed by the prospect of having his house and yard run over by people.

The younger guys showed up first, probably so they could get their fill of free beer. Ronan and Brendan discussed approaching the older guys while Nessa and Declan introduced themselves to Ronan's crew.

Before long, he had a full backyard. Nessa had brought a speaker and hooked her phone up to it for music. He stood over the grill, cooking up meat. He pulled out his phone and snapped a picture of his yard and sent it to Chloe.

Your idea is a hit. Thanks.

Looking up from the screen while waiting for her response, he was surprised to see Danny Cahill standing on his back porch. He shoved his phone in his pocket and tapped Declan on the shoulder. "Watch the grill."

Then he made his way to the house, his heart thumping. What the fuck was Cahill doing here again?

"Hey, Mr. Cahill."

"Ronan," he said with a nod. "I hope you don't mind my intrusion. I heard you were throwing a barbecue for your crew and I like the idea. I think more crew leaders should be doing things like this. Good way to keep morale up."

"Would you like a beer or something? Food should be ready soon." He sure as fuck didn't want the man to stay, but he couldn't tell him to go.

"No. I'm not staying. I just wanted to contribute. Say thank you for doing a good job." He handed Ronan an envelope.

Ronan knew the envelope held cash. It was the same type of envelope he dropped off last weekend. "I don't need you to pay for anything."

"Take it. Feeding everyone costs money. It's worth it for me to contribute because a happy crew works harder. I benefit from that. Thank you." He extended a hand.

Ronan tucked the envelope in his back pocket. "Sure you won't stay for a beer?"

"No. Your crew wants to relax and they won't do that with the big boss around. Just make sure no one overdoes it tonight. Works still goes on tomorrow."

"We'll be good. Thanks."

Cahill nodded and waved and made his way back through the house. Ronan walked him out and stood by the front door as he climbed in his car and drove off.

Brendan came up behind Ronan. "What the hell was he doing here?"

"If I had to guess, he's nervous about me being social with my guys."

"Good sign."

"Is it?" Ronan asked. It was another shift, but at the moment, it didn't feel all that good. His phone buzzed in his pocket. He pulled it out and checked the text.

Glad my idea worked. Have fun. Hope you can find some answers.

Brendan read over his shoulder. "Why the hell isn't she here?"

Ronan moved the phone away from his brother's prying eyes. "I didn't invite her. And with Cahill showing up, I'm glad I didn't. He'd probably assume she was spying and get her fired."

Brendan slapped his shoulder. "Cahill's gone now. You should tell her to come by."

"She's probably working."

"Won't know unless you ask."

"What's your interest in what we're doing?"

His brother lifted a shoulder. "You're obviously into her. It's good to see you invested in something other than Cahill."

Ronan took a deep breath and turned his phone over in his hand. Then he gave in to the urge that might not have been the best idea.

If you're free, you should stop by. Food's on the grill and the beer is cold.

CHLOE STARED AT THE TEXT FROM RONAN. WHEN HE'D TOLD her he was hosting the barbecue, she'd been a little hurt that he didn't invite her, but then she reminded herself it was a work thing. But part of her old insecurities rose and hinted that maybe he didn't want to be seen in public with her.

She was closing at the bar tonight, but she had a few hours until she had to go in. Take a nap or hang out with Ronan? She shot off a text. Need me to bring anything?

Nope.

Of course, she should know better than to think Ronan would offer some flirtatious banter via text. She considered herself lucky when she got full sentences out of him. She grabbed her purse and keys and headed out. She stopped at the bakery for a box of cookies. Even though Ronan had said he didn't need anything, she was raised to always bring something to a party.

It took four times of circling Ronan's block to find a place to park. She didn't think he'd invited all that many people. Maybe this was just the kind of neighborhood where people were home on a Sunday afternoon. With her cookies in hand, she walked down the block to Ronan's house.

Such an odd thought. The one guy from their neighborhood that most people would've placed bets on to be a total loser, and he was a homeowner. His neighborhood was mostly quiet, but she could hear people in their yards enjoying the warm late summer weekend. It was very homey.

When she got to the front of his house, she heard talking and laughter coming from the backyard. Given his lack of furniture, the yard seemed like a safe bet. She flipped the latch on the gate and entered the yard. People, mostly guys from his crew, were sitting on lawn chairs scattered around. Ronan stood at the grill, his back to her, so he didn't see her. Brendan, however, did.

"You made it," he said as he neared. "I told him to invite you."

"Really." So Ronan had no intention of having her participate in his party.

"It's not like that. He was worried about Cahill causing trouble for you. As it turned out, Ronan was right. Danny Cahill already stopped by. I doubt he'll come back. That's why I suggested the invitation."

"Hmm-mm." She wasn't buying it. Maybe she should just leave.

"Come on," Brendan said. "Let's get you a drink." He put an arm around her shoulder and led her deeper into the yard.

"You don't have to do this, Brendan."

"Do what?"

"Force this. If Ronan had wanted me here, he would've asked on his own."

"He did. He was texting you before I said anything. I saw your text and asked why you weren't here. Trust me. He wants you here."

She sighed. "Is there a table or someplace I can put these cookies?"

"Hey, Ronan. Look who's here."

When Ronan turned, his expression went from curious to heated when his eyes landed on her. Then his face broke into one of those rare smiles she loved.

"I'll take those," Brendan said as he reached for the box of cookies. Then he nudged Chloe closer to Ronan.

"Hey," Ronan said, his deep voice a rumble across her nerves.

"Good turnout. Any luck on the information front?"

He took a pull from his beer and shook his head. "Not yet. Waiting until they drink more. Can I get you a beer?"

"I have to go to work tonight, but I'll take a drink of yours." She took the bottle from his hand, her fingers caressing his as she moved. Then she wrapped her lips around the bottle and took a drink.

"You trying to torment me?"

"How so?"

"You just told me you're working tonight, so I know you can't stay. Then you do that." He pointed at her mouth.

"Don't know what you're talking about. I was just a little thirsty," she said with a flirty smile.

He cleared his throat and turned back to the grill. She watched in silence for a few moments while he flipped burgers and rotated hot dogs. "Brendan said Cahill showed up here."

He grunted.

"He also said that was why you didn't invite me earlier."

He looked down at her over his shoulder. "If Cahill saw you here, he'd get suspicious. He might stop talking in front of you. And if he thought you were feeding me information, he might try to get you fired."

Chloe took a moment to digest those words. She couldn't decipher if he was worried about her or just worried about losing his informant.

He took the food off the grill and faced her. "I don't want you caught up in the middle of this. I don't know how ugly it'll get."

"I'm a big girl. Danny Cahill doesn't scare me."

"Maybe he should." He took a breath and closed his eyes as if he needed to search for patience. "I don't want you to get hurt. I know we're keeping it casual, but that doesn't mean I'd be okay with something happening to you."

"Hey, man. We're hungry," a voice called from behind Chloe.

Chloe turned and saw Ronan's sister Nessa reaching for the platter of food, but she suddenly stopped.

"Hey, Chloe," she said with all the innuendo of a little sister. "Nice to see you here."

"Good to see you, too."

Then Declan bounded up behind Nessa. "Hey, Chloe." He bumped Nessa out of the way and wrapped Chloe in a tight hug. "I'm glad you're here."

Chloe chuckled. Declan was feeling good because he'd had a few to drink. "Good to see you again, Declan. How's the kitchen coming?"

He pulled back from the hug but stayed in her personal

space. "We haven't started work yet, but I've given Ronan all my plans. Do you have any ideas? I could add to what I have."

"Uh, no. I'm pretty sure Ronan should decide what to do in his kitchen."

"I figured you might be here more often and...you know."

She smiled. "Even if I do come by more often, I don't cook."

"You have really pretty eyes, you know that?" Declan said, pressing closer to her. Then he winked at Ronan. Such a trouble maker.

"Go feed people," Ronan said to his sister, shoving the platter at her. "And make sure he's the first to get food."

Nessa poked Declan with her elbow. "Come on."

He followed her without another word to Chloe.

"Your brother is cute."

"Uh-huh." Then Ronan took Chloe's hand and pulled her across the grass and up the stairs to his house. He pushed through the kitchen door and closed it behind them.

"What?" she asked.

"I didn't invite you at first because I am worried about you. I don't want Cahill to cause trouble for you because of me. I also don't want my siblings to gossip about what we're doing and get you in trouble with your family."

"Oh."

"But know this. I wanted you here. I like spending time with you."

Her heart raced. She forced her brain not to read too much into it. "Okay," she said on a shaky breath.

He caged her against his refrigerator. "And I won't stand by while you flirt with my brother—any of them—to piss me off. I'm not playing games."

"Hey. He hugged me."

"Then you told me he was cute."

"Well, he is." She ran a hand down his T-shirt-clad chest. "I'm a little old for cute, though. I like what we have going on here."

"Me, too." He lowered his lips to hers in a hungry kiss.

She didn't let him get carried away, though. "You have guests. And a job to do."

"You're distracting."

She smiled. "I'll try hard not to be. What can I do to help?"

"Grab the salads from the fridge and put them on the table outside. I need to cool off." He stepped away from her, adjusted his crotch, and moved toward the bathroom.

Chloe swallowed her giggle and opened the fridge. They did have a good thing going. But unlike with other guys she had fun with, Ronan wasn't the bad boy he had been. She froze in front of the refrigerator. It had been easy to want Ronan when she believed he was like every other player she'd ever been with. But he just admitted he cared. It mattered to him that he might cause trouble for her. He wanted her safe.

Pulling the salads from the fridge, she let that thought settle over her. She'd spent a long time counting on only herself to feel safe and secure. She didn't know what to do with Ronan.

Keeping her heart out of it might be harder than she thought.

Ronan moved through his party, offering drinks, and passing plates of food. Chloe chatted with everyone. She was a natural host, making it all seem effortless. He and Brendan had decided to divide the crew to search for information. Brendan would take Old Man Mulroney and Ronan would take Joe and Nick.

Just as he pulled up a chair to join Joe and Nick with a fresh beer, Chloe wandered over to say goodbye. She ran a hand across his shoulders as she leaned down to kiss his cheek. "I have to head to work."

"Thanks for coming."

"Have fun."

As she walked away, Nick said, "You got yourself a good woman there, Ronan."

Too good for the likes of him. "Yeah, she is."

"So how do you like being the boss?" Nick asked.

"A lot more fucking paperwork than swinging a hammer."

Nick pointed toward the house. "Your hands get too many papercuts to do the real work at home? The place is rough."

"I'm working on it. It'll get there." He was surprised he hadn't taken more ribbing about the state of his house.

Joe was uncharacteristically quiet.

"Something wrong, Joe? Can I get you something else to eat?"

"I'm good." He peeled at the label on his bottle. "When you invited us, I thought it was just the crew, you know?"

"That was my plan. I want you guys to know that even though I'm the boss, I'm still one of you."

Joe leaned forward, elbows on his knees. "But you collect those envelopes now, don'tcha?"

Was that jealousy from the old man? Did he want to be a crew lead?

"I still just do what the boss tells me. We all know how that works. Do the little side jobs so we can get the contracts for the big jobs. Greasing palms is how business is done."

"Like father, like son."

"Hey, now," Nick said.

Ronan held up a hand. "What's that supposed to mean?"

Joe leaned forward and lowered his voice. "Them envelopes is what got your dad in trouble. You're heading down the same path."

"What do you mean? I know my dad did the off-book jobs. Brendan over there and I held our first hammers on those jobs."

"I'm not talking about those envelopes."

Ronan stood and shifted his chair closer to Joe. "What are you talking about?"

Nick intervened again. "You shouldn't go there."

"He should know who he's in bed with."

"I'm not in bed with anyone."

Joe's attention swiveled back to him. "I saw Cahill hand you an envelope tonight. As soon as you accept that, you're in bed."

Joe didn't like that Cahill showed up to their party. But why? "I didn't invite Cahill. I don't even know how he knew about the cookout. He gave me money to pay for this. He said he thought it was a good idea."

"I'm sure he did." Joe settled back in his chair.

"Why didn't you ever move up to management?" Ronan asked. "You're one of the most experienced guys around. Why keep busting your hump?"

"The envelopes. I work my forty and that's it. I refused to let the senior Cahill dictate any part of my life. So I'll only be crew."

"Tell me about the other envelopes. I don't know what you're talking about. I've gotten cash to run the off-book jobs. That's it."

Joe was quiet again and took a long pull on his beer. Nick pointed at Joe with his near-empty bottle. "This ain't gonna end well." Looking at Ronan he said, "He thinks he knows shit, but he's not sure. And speculation could cost you. That's all I'm sayin'. I'm going for a fresh beer."

He shoved off his chair and walked away. Ronan waited patiently for Joe to continue.

Joe cocked his head to the side. "He's right. I've got no proof of anything. Just more'n twenty-five years of working here."

Ronan needed to pull the information from Joe, give the man a reason to confide. So he told the truth. "To be totally honest, Joe, the main reason I've been working for Cahill has been to get answers about my father. He was there one day, and then he was just gone. It never sat well with me. As a kid, the rumors about a mistress pissed me off, but as a man, I just want the truth."

"There was no woman," Joe said definitively. "I wasn't friends with your dad, but all he did was talk about his family. He didn't have a straying eye."

"It would be easier if that was it." Even though he spoke the words, Ronan couldn't believe the relief he felt. A mistress would be a convenient reason, but then he'd have to come to terms with the fact that his father didn't want them. Want him. But his gut had always been right.

Joe leaned forward again. "Look, I don't know what all the other envelopes are about. It's not on the up-an-up, not like a job. Back then, the senior Cahill was going all political, all kinds of back-alley deals. And Danny?" He turned away and spit. "He was a good for nothing piece of shit. Drugs and trouble. That's all he was."

Drugs? Ronan had never caught wind of that. He glanced over at Brendan and wondered if he knew. As FBI, he would know if Danny had a record.

"What does that have to do with my dad? I don't get it."

"I don't know what happened to Michael. I just know he was taking a lot of extra envelopes and running errands most nights before he disappeared. No one's running a night crew for construction, so it was something else. If I was you, I wouldn't trust a damn thing any Cahill says." He stood. "Now I'm ready for another beer."

"One more thing."

Joe looked down at him.

"Why stay? If you hate them and don't trust them, why keep working for them?"

"Back then, because they had all the power. Got all the

big jobs. Guaranteed work year-round. Then I got old. Nobody wants to hire an old man." He patted Ronan's shoulder. "Get out while you can."

"Thanks, Joe. That was more than anyone has told me in years."

"Keeping your mouth shut is the best way to keep your job. But again, I'm old and I just don't give a fuck anymore."

"You'll have a job with me as long as you want one."

He nodded and walked over to the cooler to grab a beer.

Ronan sat back in his chair to digest the information.

For another hour or two, he put thoughts of his father to the back of his head and enjoyed time with his guys. No, they weren't friends, but they spent a lot of time together day in and day out. Maybe they could be friends if he gave them a chance.

By nine, the sun was gone and so was his crew. They all seemed to have a good time. If nothing else, they enjoyed free food and beer and the chance to give him a hard time about his house looking worse than any of their sites.

Brendan stayed and once the yard was clear of people, they worked together to clean up. Declan was in bed, where Nessa deposited him before heading home. Right now, Ronan was happy he'd gotten a mattress and tossed it on the living room floor for his brother. He was too old to be sleeping on the floor, and he might've felt guilty sticking his drunk ass brother on the floor.

"You have any luck with Mulroney?" Ronan asked.

"Some. How about you?"

"Oh yeah. As much as it bothers me that Cahill crashed the party, I think that was just the right amount of motivation for Joe to talk. Let's get Mom's chairs stacked in the garage and we can go over everything inside."

When the yard was mostly put back together and the trash shoved in a can, Ronan and Brendan grabbed the remaining beer and filled the fridge. They both took one and sat at the card table to debrief.

"Before we get into what we got from the guys, what the hell was Cahill doing here?" Brendan asked.

"I'm not sure. He said he heard about the party and he liked the idea of crews bonding or some shit. He gave me cash to help defray the cost."

"But?"

"My gut says he's worried and came to snoop."

"That's what I think. They're definitely hiding something. Mulroney agrees. He said that Alan Cahill was doing some shady shit back then. He didn't have any proof, but it was almost an open secret that Cahill was looking to buy his political career, from alderman straight to mayor."

"What could that possibly have to do with Dad? He had no political aspirations that I've ever heard of." He took a long pull on his beer.

"What did you get from Joe and Nick?"

"Nick didn't say much of anything, so I have no idea what he knows. But Joe was pissed that Cahill showed up. Like he doesn't belong. Which he doesn't because the man has never worked a hard day in his life that I know of. But he saw Cahill give me the envelope and he commented on that. He said that Dad was taking a lot of extra envelopes and running errands for Cahill when he disappeared."

"Side jobs?"

Ronan shook his head. "No. These were different. He said the same thing about Cahill being political, but he also said that Danny was a piece of shit drug addict."

"Well, now." Brendan rocked back in his chair.

"Does he have a record?"

"Yes and no. There was juvie stuff that was sealed. But just because there's no record doesn't mean he was clean. Alan might've been cleaning up his messes." He took another drink. "It's another path to follow. All these years, I've been focusing on Alan. Danny was never on my radar. I didn't ask people about Danny. He wasn't working for his father back then. To me, he was just the boss's son."

"He's been running things for years. I don't know when he got to the top and took the reins from Alan, but that'll be easy enough to find out."

"You think he has the reins?"

"For most of the day-to-day operations, yeah. Alan still has his hand in things, but Danny is in charge." Ronan crossed his arms. "Probably the only reason I have a job. Alan doesn't seem to like anyone with the Doyle name."

Brendan shoved up from his chair. "Looks like we turn our focus on Danny. You talk to the guys and see what you can find out about when he started working for Daddy Cahill. I'll call some neighborhood cops I know and see if any of them can give us insight on Danny."

"Sounds good." Ronan rose, finished his beer, and tossed the bottle in the trash.

"One more thing," Brendan said. "I think we need some-place else to meet besides your house."

"Why?"

"First, this place is a mess. There's nowhere to work. But more important, Cahill has made it obvious that he has no problem dropping in on you unexpectedly. If he gets any nosier, it could spell trouble."

"Your place?"

"We can try that."

"I'll need your address then. I've never been to your place."

Brendan nodded as if acknowledging how far apart they'd been. "I'll text it to you. I'm heading out." He slapped Ronan's shoulder. "Talk to you as soon as I have something to share."

"Me, too. See ya."

Brendan let himself out and Ronan took in his kitchen. His brother was right. There wasn't anywhere to work here, but even if there was, it was risky given Cahill's random appearances. They were definitely onto something. Ronan just hoped they would finally find the answers they needed.

IT HAD BEEN A FEW DAYS SINCE CHLOE HAD SPOKEN TO RONAN. They texted occasionally, but she could respect that as a casual thing. She had no rights to his time. She'd closed every night this week, so she was happy that they weren't terribly busy tonight, which allowed her mind to daydream about Ronan. Every time she remembered him dragging her from the party, her blood raced. While they agreed to keep things casual, he'd admitted that he wanted to spend time with her. She didn't know what to do with that. The man was infuriating. They had chemistry in abundance. That was the only obvious thing.

He rarely spoke, but then he came to her apartment to make her feel better with food and a shower. He didn't invite her to the barbecue—that had been her idea—but then he admitted it was because he worried about her losing her job.

And to top it all off, he got jealous that she hugged his brother? What the hell?

For a guy who supposedly wasn't looking for a relationship, he was borderline possessive. Lucky for him, it wasn't over the top or creepy.

She was inexplicably drawn to him. More than the sexual energy, she wanted to spend time with him, too. She wanted to help him find the answers he sought.

Would finding those answers change who he was? Would he then be looking for a relationship? Chloe didn't know how she felt about that. She couldn't imagine finding everlasting love. At least she never allowed herself to consider it with someone like Ronan. He was there for a good time.

Could they ever build something more? Would she want that? She'd always pictured Ronan as a love-'em-and-leave type. That was who she looked for. They were safe in a way nice men weren't. Bad boys didn't play pretend. Nice guys that her mom pushed on her had expectations she might never meet.

Ronan had no such expectations.

Maybe that was why she liked him so much. They just enjoyed each other.

As she sat in the office creating the schedule for the next two weeks, she decided to not work until closing as often as usual. Ronan always had to wake early for work, so her schedule wasn't conducive for seeing him other than when she had a day off. She would still be needed on the weekends, but she could let Johnny take on a little more responsibility.

Like tonight. Even though it was Friday, she was for sure leaving early. It had been a long week of closings. Even if Ronan didn't want to meet up, she could do some cross-stitching to add to her shop. Sitting at the booth beside the one considered to be the Cahills', she texted Ronan. I'm getting off early tonight. Want to meet for dinner?

While she waited for his response, she fiddled with the schedule.

Can't. Meeting with Brendan.

I could join you. I'll bring dinner and stay after he leaves.

Bubbles popped up and disappeared. Chloe rolled her eyes. Then she added, But it's fine if you rather I didn't.

We're not meeting at my house. We'll be at Brendan's.

Oh. Well, that kind of defeated her purpose for wanting to come over.

Bubbles lit her screen again. Brendan says bring some wings from the Rose.

You sure? I don't want to crash.

It's fine.

Not exactly a resounding invitation. She continuously felt like his siblings pushed him to spend more time with her than he planned. It was especially weird coming from Brendan given their history.

An hour later she was driving to the address Ronan had texted her, a variety of hot wings stinking up her car. The neighborhood was more upscale than where they'd grown up. Tall apartment buildings and condos lined the streets. Trendy restaurants sat on corners. She pulled into the parking garage and found a visitor spot.

She could've just told Ronan to come to her apartment when he was done. Why did she offer to meet here?

She sighed. She wanted to help. Juggling the food, she walked up to the front door of a six-story building and scanned the bells for Brendan's name. Using her pinky, she rang. A moment later, the door buzzed and she pulled it open. By the time she reached the elevator, the doors slid open and Ronan stepped out.

"Hey. I came to help." He reached for the bag of food and

turned to catch the elevator door, but was too late. He pressed the elevator button again.

He didn't say anything else, so she asked, "Why are you guys meeting here?"

"Cahill keeps showing up unexpectedly at my house. We can't risk him seeing our research."

"What do you mean *keeps* showing up?" The elevator arrived and Ronan held the doors as she stepped in.

"He showed up the first time Brendan and I were comparing notes. The same night I told Brendan your idea for the barbecue. It was weird but it was about a side job. But then he showed up at the barbecue."

That she knew about. It was why he'd been glad she hadn't been there from the beginning. They would lose their edge if Danny Cahill saw her hanging out with the Doyles.

The elevator stopped and Ronan led the way to Brendan's door.

"Do you think he suspects you're digging into your father's disappearance?"

Ronan opened the door and held it with his foot as she followed. "We have to assume so."

"Assume what?" Brendan asked.

"That Cahill's onto us."

Brendan grabbed the food from Ronan. "I haven't had these in years." He winked at Chloe. "You're proving to be more useful than I thought."

"That's me. Bringer of hot wings." She scanned the apartment. The building was on the new side and Brendan had a fully furnished apartment. It was a striking contrast to Ronan's run-down, bare house.

Brendan paused in tearing open the bag at his breakfast

counter. "I'm sure you're much more than that." He stared pointedly at Ronan.

"Of course." The look Ronan gave her was filled with heat.

Her cheeks warmed. "So what have you learned?"

The guys loaded paper plates with wings and they all sat around a small round dining table.

"Aren't you eating?" Ronan asked.

"I ate at work."

He opened his mouth but then quickly closed it without comment.

"We got some information about the Cahills," Brendan said. "Twenty years ago, Danny was an addict and his father was a dirty politician."

None of that seemed too surprising. "What does that have to do with your dad?"

The brothers shared a look for a minute, and she thought they weren't going to tell her. It was Brendan who tilted his head as if to get Ronan to spill.

Ronan put down the wing he'd been gnawing on. "We think Cahill was bribing people to get votes. He probably used our dad to deliver the bribes."

Her brain rapid-fired possibilities. Had he taken money and run? Had the wrong people found out? But why do something to Michael Doyle? She shook her head. This wasn't a cable TV show. This was real life. While she never really thought their dad ran off, money was a good motivator. "Do you think he stole from them?"

Ronan's mouth formed a grim line. "No, we don't. We're still trying to figure out how it all fits."

"What can I do to help?"

She didn't think it was her imagination when his face

softened. While Ronan and Brendan ate, they rehashed the conversations they'd had with the older guys on the crew. Besides the warnings they'd received, they also heard some stories about their dad. They recounted those tales and laughed. It was such a different side to Ronan. She loved seeing it.

Her heart lurched at the thought. No. There would be no love here. She knew it. He knew it.

Now she just needed to make sure her heart knew it.

CHAPTER
Seventeen

Ronan had no idea why he'd listened to Brendan and told Chloe to meet him here, but he was glad he did. Not only was she an objective outsider, but he also loved hearing her laugh. And she did it pretty often. Even amid the ugly nature of what had brought them together, she was light and happy. He couldn't remember ever having her level of sunshine in his life. It was a little unnerving, but part of that might've been because he was afraid of getting used to it.

The conversation had been derailed by Ronan and Brendan sharing stories about their dad. It all felt so natural. But the board Brendan had set up in his living room loomed over them as a reminder that something had happened to Michael Doyle. And now Brendan and Ronan were old enough to push for answers. For the first time in over a decade, Ronan started to feel better about his chances of finding those answers.

"Would it help to find the other politicians and campaign workers from Alan's run?" Chloe asked.

"What would that tell us?"

"Alan started as an alderman. That's all neighborhood bound. His opponents and his volunteers would all be from his neighborhood." She sipped her beer. "Think about it. If his neighborhood is even half as connected as ours, people would talk. Gossip mills run everywhere."

Brendan shifted and narrowed his eyes. "Might work. Gossip isn't something we can use to build a case, but it might get us somewhere."

"Like I give a fuck about building a case," Ronan said. "I just want answers."

Brendan leaned forward with his elbows on the table. "And what are you going to do with those answers?"

"I guess it would depend on what we find."

"Exactly." Pointing to the board, he said, "So do we know anyone from back then?"

"Finding who ran against him should be a simple Google search," Ronan said.

"Google won't give us the dirt."

"The Byrnes would know," Chloe said. "They're good friends with the Cahills, which is why Alan and Danny act like they own a corner of the Rose."

"Are you sure they don't?" Brendan asked.

"What do you mean?"

"Maybe they do own a piece of the Rose."

"Why does that matter?" Ronan asked.

"If they own the Rose, the Byrnes are in bed with them."

"I don't think so, but I can find out," Chloe said. "I mean, I can find out if they're legally part owners. If they have a hidden agreement, I won't be able to find it, but I have access to all of the books for the Rose."

"Does Alastair work anymore?" Ronan asked.

"He's mostly retired, but he's around. Has a hard time staying away. I talk to him often."

Brendan snorted. "What are you gonna do, just say, 'So who worked for Alan Cahill twenty years ago when he was running for office?' That's not suspicious at all."

"Give her some credit. Chloe's not stupid." Ronan was angry on her behalf.

She blushed and looked at Brendan. "I figured we could come up with a plan together. That's why I'm bringing it up."

"For the record, I don't think you're stupid." Brendan sighed. "Sometimes my frustration gets the best of me. This would've been so much easier if someone had done this digging twenty years ago."

"Why wasn't it done?" Ronan asked. "Don't you have any insight into that?"

"I tried getting information when I first started at the FBI. No one knew anything. No one would talk. A lot of time had already passed. When we were teenagers, I talked to the cops assigned the case. They weren't doing anything. They were convinced Dad ran off."

"Do you have the case file?"

Brendan stood, grabbed a folder from a box on the floor, and tossed it on the table.

Ronan stared at the folder, afraid to open it. Chloe's hand patted his thigh, and then she reached for the file. She flipped it open on the table between them. He could see the report, but he didn't want to read the words.

Chloe picked up the top page. "There's almost nothing here. The report your mom filed saying your dad was missing. They interviewed a few people in the neighborhood and Alan, who said he didn't know anything, except that Michael didn't show up for work. No mention of him asking Michael to do anything. Meg Donnelly said she'd heard rumors of Michael having a girlfriend. No evidence of an affair was found."

She closed the folder and slid it away from her. "That's bullshit. They didn't do anything."

In his gut, Ronan had always known that, but to see it in black and white was even more disheartening. If someone had cared enough to really look for his dad, it wouldn't have taken two decades for them to have answers.

"Don't you have any cop friends?" Chloe asked.

Ronan groaned. "Cops and I were never on the best of terms."

Brendan shook his head. "I don't know anyone well enough who would've been around back then."

Ronan had a thought. One that he didn't dare to explore when he'd been younger. "What about Mr. O'Malley?"

"What about him?"

"He was a uniformed cop his whole career, but I bet he'd have some insight into the detectives who were on Dad's case. Jimmy's a detective now. He might be able to find some answers."

"You want to ask the O'Malleys for help? How is that going to keep this quiet?" Brendan asked.

"The O'Malleys were never big on gossip. Besides, who are they going to tell? It's not like they're friends with the Cahills."

"Jimmy's a good guy," Chloe said. "If he could help, I bet he would."

Ronan sighed. "Maybe you should talk to Mr. O'Malley," he said to Brendan. "You're more his kind of people."

"Nuh-uh. He's old-school police. He'll dislike me for being a Fed. But Jimmy's cool."

Thinking back to the block party last month, Ronan said, "Not sure about that, either."

Chloe smiled and tapped his thigh. "Jimmy left Truth or Dare because you asked about the statute of limitations on a crime. If you admitted to something, he would have to arrest you, so he left. He's good people."

"You talk to the O'Malleys and I'll run down people who might've worked the campaign," Brendan said.

"What about me?" Chloe asked. "What can I do?"

"Nothing," Ronan said at the same time Brendan answered, "Talk to the Byrnes."

Ronan shot his brother a glare. "Didn't we just talk about how that wasn't a good idea? The point here is that she doesn't get fired."

Chloe scoffed. "He won't fire me. I'm good at my job and I never bitch."

Ronan stared into her eyes. "But if he says something to Cahill..."

"He won't. I'll talk to Mrs. Byrne. I'll bring her one of my cross-stitch projects and talk over tea."

"Hit up the wife who probably won't talk to Cahill. Good idea," Brendan said.

Ronan still didn't like the idea of it. The more questions she asked, the more trouble it could cause her.

As if reading his mind, she said, "It's fine. Mrs. Byrne and my mom are old friends. I'll have my mom set it up. If I give the gift to my mom, she'll insist I deliver it myself. It shows what a good daughter I am, which in turn shows what a great mother she is. No one will suspect a thing."

They cleaned up the dinner mess and Ronan walked Chloe to her car.

"Want to follow me home?"

"I didn't bring clothes."

She smiled. "Do you need them?" Then her smile slipped. "Do you have to work tomorrow?"

"No. It's a rare weekend off for me."

"Spend the night. Then you can think about visiting Mr. O'Malley." She ran a hand down his torso. "I've missed you. And being naked with you."

He didn't want to admit it, but he missed her, too. "You make a really good offer."

"One that you can't refuse?"

No, he couldn't refuse her. "Let's go. The faster we get to your place, the faster we can get naked."

CHLOE WAS THRILLED THAT RONAN HAD AGREED TO GO HOME with her. He was so hard to read. She didn't feel like they'd run their course yet. It was a weird feeling because they weren't a couple, but they weren't a one- or two-night stand either. Fuckbuddies and friends? She shook her head as she let herself into her apartment. They didn't need to label it. They could just keep having a good time.

She beat Ronan there, so she took a few minutes to freshen up in the bathroom. Then he knocked on her door.

"When is the fucking landlord going to fix the lock downstairs?"

Interesting way to enter her apartment. "Uh, I don't know. I keep my door locked. It's fine."

"No, it's not. Anyone can be lurking in the hall and push their way in when you get home. Especially with the late hours you keep."

Creepy thoughts all around. "I'm fine. If it'll make you feel better, I'll call him again tomorrow."

"This time tell him you'll withhold part of the rent until it's fixed. That's a safety concern."

She would never not pay her rent. She couldn't deal with the conflict it would cause. But she nodded and took his hand. "Let's go get naked."

"Wait," he tugged her hard enough that he pulled her off her feet and she stumbled into him.

All in all not a bad place to land. He caught her effortlessly.

"Yes?" she asked, staring up into his dark blue eyes.

"I still don't like the idea of you asking questions about the Cahills."

"What's the big deal?"

"It's one thing when you're just listening. They're talking in a public space. But asking specific questions could raise suspicions. What will you do if word gets back to Cahill?" As he spoke, his arms came tighter around her to hold her body to his.

"I don't have to do anything. Maybe he'll demand another waitress wait on him. Boy, that would break my heart."

"What if you lose your job?"

She rolled her eyes. "This is my seventh job in like five years. Yeah, I've had this one longest, but that's because I like it." He frowned. "However, it's not like there aren't a million bars in Chicago. I'm pretty sure I can find another job if I have to."

Even though she would hate leaving the Rose, she would do it if it got him answers. This was the first job since college that she felt at home and enjoyed going to work. But it was still just a job.

"I don't like it."

She stroked his jaw, enjoying the feel of his beard. "I want to help."

"Why?" he whispered, almost as if he hadn't planned to ask.

"Because you deserve answers. It's something that obviously has weighed on you for years and has influenced many parts of your life. If I can help get you answers that will give you peace, how could I not help?"

"You know you're too good for me, right?"

"Nah. You've seen my naughty cross stitch."

"You know what I mean."

She stepped back from his arms. "No, I really don't. We're two consenting adults having a good time."

"Except your reputation is that of a good, wholesome girl who doesn't get into trouble, goes to church, and sits down for family dinners. I've been arrested more times than I care to think about, haven't gone to church since my dad's disappearance, and my family is...not like yours."

She smiled. "I like your family. You guys have the freedom to be honest and you say what's on your mind to each other. There are no games or passive-aggressive jabs."

He chuckled and the sound reverberated through her. "No, we're just aggressive-aggressive."

"But there's no mistaking how you feel. I wish my family was more like that."

"What are you talking about?"

"In my family, there's a lot of emphasis placed on how things look and being polite and nice to everyone. It's exhausting. At least for me. My good girl reputation? It takes effort and I have it because my mom would have it no other way."

It was the same reason she'd stayed with Tim so long. They were supposed to be perfect for each other. "My ex was like that too."

She stopped herself, not wanting to think about Tim, and stepped closer to Ronan again. He wrapped his arms around her waist. "That's why I like being with you. I don't have to filter what I say."

"Like what?"

"For example, my family would die—literally keel over—if they heard me tell you that I want you to take me to bed and eat me out until I scream. Then I want you to fuck me until I pass out."

"I could see how your mom might find that inappropriate."

"But you don't."

"Not at all. I like explicit directions."

"Oh, I can be more explicit than that." She pulled him toward her bedroom and showed him how explicit she could be.

Ronan rolled over as the sun streamed across his face. Although he'd never been a natural morning person, after years of working construction where his job was dependent on daylight hours, he usually woke with the sun. But unlike most days, he had a warm, naked woman curled up beside him. Chloe's soft skin was enough for him to want to lounge under the covers much longer. He stroked his fingers up and down her back. She burrowed her face in his neck.

"Too early," she murmured.

"Yeah. Go back to sleep. I couldn't help touching you." He kissed the top of her head. As far as mornings went, this one was pretty amazing. Maybe he'd sneak out and grab them some breakfast before he headed home and then to the O'Malleys. But that would require him to leave the bed, so instead, he chose to lounge, holding Chloe.

He didn't know how long it had been, but her phone began buzzing and then within minutes, there was a knock on her front door. "Hey, babe," he said, giving her a little shake. "Someone's at your door."

"Huh?"

"Your phone buzzed with a text and now someone's knocking."

She sat up and grabbed her phone. "Shit."

Another knock, followed by, "Chloe. I know you're home because you're never moving this early."

"Damn it. It's my mom." She flung the covers off and hurried around the room pulling on random clothing items. She ran her fingers through her hair and sighed.

He climbed from the bed and reached for his jeans.

"Uh. Can I ask you a huge favor?"

He looked at her and waited.

"Please stay in here until I get rid of her?"

He wouldn't mind waiting here for round two. Sounded like a damn good idea.

"I can't deal with her right now. Especially if she sees you."

So it wasn't about round two, but about keeping him a secret. His jaw reflexively tensed, but he held back the grimace. "Sure."

She hustled out of the room and closed the door behind her. He hopped into his jeans and moved closer to the door.

"Hi, Mom. What are you doing here?"

"Nice way to greet your mother."

"It's early and you know I work late."

"This is a respectable hour to visit someone."

"Not when that someone often works until two in the morning."

"I did call repeatedly and you didn't respond. I was in the area running errands, so I popped in."

"Can I get you some coffee?"

The fuck? He was supposed to stay in hiding while they shared a cup of coffee?

"That's not necessary. I wanted to check in on you. I know your date with Lance didn't go as you had expected, but Tobin McLachlan is back in town. I saw his mother the other day."

No wonder Chloe didn't want her mother to see him. It might ruin all of her matchmaking possibilities.

"No, Mom. I went on the date with Lance against my better judgment. Please stop trying to fix me up."

At least she had the courtesy to not accept a date while he was still half-naked in her bedroom. He pulled on his T-shirt.

"I want you to be happy. Have a full life. Is that too much to ask?"

"I am happy, Mom. I like my life."

"But the future. Who will take care of you?"

Ronan had the sudden urge to open the door and demand that her mother see that she could take care of herself, and if she needed help, he was there. He wanted to care for her. But he stopped himself with his fingers wrapped around the knob. Her mother would never see him as an acceptable anything.

"Look, Mom. I'm not trying to be rude. But I'm tired and I'm not looking for a husband. I appreciate that you care about me, but I'm fine."

There was silence for a moment and Ronan strained to hear anything.

"I'll be going then. Lunch tomorrow?"

"Yes, I'll be there for lunch. Before you go, I have a cross-stitch for Mrs. Byrne. Can you give it to her?"

"You should deliver it yourself. She said she hasn't seen you in ages."

Damn. His girl was good.

No, not his girl. She was making that painfully obvious. He heard them saying their good-byes, so he finished dressing. Chloe came back just as he was tying his boots.

"Sorry about that. She drops in unexpectedly on occasion. Wait. You're not leaving, are you?"

"Yeah. I should get my day started. Lot of ground to cover."

"Do you at least want to stay for breakfast?"

He wanted to tell her to go have breakfast with Lance or Tobin, but the hopeful look in her eyes had him sighing. She was just living by the rules they'd set up. He had no claim to her. "Sure. What do you got?" he asked as he stood.

"Well...I'm not sure," she answered, crinkling her nose.

"So you invite me to breakfast, but you don't have food?"

She took his hand. "I invited you to stay because I want to spend more time with you. I bribed you with nonexistent food."

Her smile was bright and as he'd realized last night, he couldn't refuse her. "Get dressed and we'll go out to eat."

CHLOE GOT READY IN RECORD TIME BECAUSE SHE HAD A FEELING Ronan would come up with some excuse to leave her. It was wrong of her to keep him in the bedroom when her mom showed up, but how was she supposed to explain that? She liked Ronan. But her mother didn't. She was tired of being a disappointment in her mother's eyes.

Plus, she wanted to keep what they had as something

special. She knew they wouldn't be a real couple with everyone else they knew, but here, in her apartment, it was real enough for her. Her mother knowing about them would ruin that.

She pulled her hair up into a messy bun and slipped on her gym shoes. "I'm ready."

He sat on her couch, scrolling through his phone. When he looked up, he didn't appear as irritated as he had when she'd gotten rid of her mom. He rose and followed her to the door. Before unlocking it, she said, "Look. About before with my mom—"

"It's fine. I get it."

She searched his eyes to see if he was lying. Would she know?

"You sure?"

"Yeah. Let's go. I'm hungry."

She opened the door and when they stepped through, she reached for his hand. If he was mad, he wouldn't walk with her hand in hand, right?

"Maybe you should go on one of those dates your mom is pushing for," he said when they hit the sidewalk.

She pulled up short and dropped his hand. "What?"

She didn't want to go out with anyone, much less someone her mother deemed worthy.

"Won't she get suspicious if you never date anyone? If people see you dating, they won't suspect us."

"I suppose." She turned and started walking toward the diner on the next block. The sun was warm and the breeze cool on her face. The end of summer in Chicago was both glorious and bittersweet. "But the guys she picks. Ugh."

Ronan put an arm around her shoulder. "Can't all be as hot as me, babe."

She laughed. "Ain't that the truth?" They walked for a bit and she liked the feel of his big, warm body brushing against hers. "The real truth is that she keeps hoping I'm going to settle down with one of these guys that she picks out. I have no desire to do that."

"To settle down? Or settle for one of them?"

She wrinkled her nose as she thought. "Maybe both? I don't know. For sure, I don't want one of the *nice* boys she picks out. But there was a time that I thought I'd be married by now."

That seemed so long ago.

"Weren't you engaged to one of those nice boys?"

She licked her lips and nodded. Did she want to talk about Tim with Ronan? She never wanted to talk about Tim at all. "I thought you didn't pay attention to my life. I'm just a girl from the neighborhood, you know."

He groaned at her throwing his words back at him. "People in the neighborhood like to talk. I don't remember anyone talking about why you broke up though."

That's because no one knew. She let them all believe she was a flake. It was easier than admitting everything else. Plus, who would believe her? Tim was supposedly the perfect guy. He'd almost had her convinced it was all in her head. "Just didn't work out. That's all."

He huffed. "That's a bullshit answer. It's like saying irreconcilable differences. No one's to blame."

They arrived at the diner. Ronan slid his arm away from her and held the door for her to enter. They sat in a booth and each picked up a menu from behind the napkin holder.

"So he cheated on you," Ronan suddenly said.

"What?"

"The ex. Why wouldn't you want people to know he cheated? He's the idiot."

"He didn't cheat. Not that I know of." She focused on the plastic-coated menu as if she didn't know exactly what she wanted.

"You cheated?"

She looked up from the menu. "No. I would never." No matter how tempting it had been. She'd longed to be with someone who would make her feel good. Like Ronan did.

Ronan stared at her, studying her. Her skin flushed under his scrutiny and she fidgeted. The waitress came to the table. "Do you need some more time?"

"I'm ready," she answered quickly. "Are you?"

He nodded.

"I'll have French toast and a side of bacon. And a pot of coffee."

"Ham and egg sandwich," Ronan ordered.

He sat quietly until the waitress delivered their coffee. As he poured them each a cup, he asked again, "If there was no cheating, what was it?"

"Haven't you ever just had a relationship not work out?"

"Sure, but never after asking someone to marry me. At that point, I'd expect we knew each other well enough—all the dark and ugly parts—that you loved the person enough to want to spend your life with them."

Dark and ugly parts she had discovered in spades. "Some people don't reveal those parts early on and it takes time to uncover them."

"Did he hurt you?"

Chloe sucked in a breath. She hadn't meant to let him get that close. This was a difficult question. She knew what he was asking—did he hit her—but she was no less hurt. "Someone always ends up hurt when there's a break-up."

He reached across the table and wrapped his fingers around her forearm. "That's not what I'm asking."

"I'm aware. And I think you're smart enough to realize that I don't want to talk about it."

"Chloe." His voice was soft but held a hint of warning.

"Ronan," she countered. "Let's not do this. We agreed that we're casual. We don't need to share deep secrets. But to put your mind at ease, he never laid a hand on me."

Although it was the truth, it felt like a copout. But she couldn't bring herself to explain how Tim had made her feel small and stupid and worthless.

He dropped it then, even though she could tell he didn't want to.

"Want to help me think up ways to pump Mrs. Byrne for information about Cahill and his old campaign?"

"You shouldn't be doing that."

"Mrs. Byrne loves me. I do my job so well that her husband can feel comfortable faking retirement. Whenever she makes plans, he's there because he trusts me with the bar. Besides," she said with a broad smile, "I'm such a sweet girl."

"Yeah, you are." His voice was husky and she knew he wasn't thinking about her sweet personality.

The waitress delivered their food and they dug in.

As she cut her French toast, she asked, "Any exciting plans this week?"

"If you consider looking at kitchen counters exciting, then yes. How about you?"

"Just work. But I'm not closing every night, so if you're not busy, we could get together."

"Sounds good. I like getting together with you. Just shoot

me a text when you're free." Half of his sandwich was already gone. "I appreciate all the help you're giving us. You are, in fact, a very sweet girl, Chloe McCarthy. As bad as it might be to say, I'm glad your ex fucked up."

That made her laugh. "I'm glad, too."

CHAPTER
Nineteen

Ronan walked Chloe back to her apartment and had a hard time leaving her. He'd wanted to crawl back into bed with her, but they both had things to do. It had been a rough morning, but as long as he remembered his place within Chloe's life, they'd have a hell of a good time. He thought about the little she'd said about her ex. Nessa'd had a similar response when he'd asked about Tony and how he'd treated her. He didn't understand why women would put up with shit like that. Chloe shifted the conversation pretty quickly, reminding him yet again that they were casual. Part of him was getting too invested and he knew it was a mistake.

He'd never in his life cared about what Laura McCarthy thought of him and his family. Not since the night they'd had him arrested. But what she thought mattered to her daughter, no matter how much Chloe might pretend it didn't.

When he walked into his house, he heard the echo of a saw whirring from the backyard. Declan was up and working before eleven a.m.? Ronan went straight to the kitchen to see what kind of mess he was dealing with.

Declan came in through the back door carrying a sheet of expensive plywood. "Hey." He smirked. "Walk of shame?"

"No shame here."

"Stride of pride?"

Ronan grunted.

"Just got laid parade?"

"Enough." Even though he wasn't wrong on either count, Ronan wasn't about to encourage him. "How are things going here?"

"Good. I've got everything laid out and I'm cutting in the yard to minimize mess, but building in here."

"You're measuring twice?"

Declan rolled his eyes. "I know what I'm doing. I might not have listened to everything you and Brendan tried to teach me, but I do remember to measure twice, cut once."

"Good. 'Cause I'll beat your ass if you waste perfectly good wood."

"That's what she said."

It was Ronan's turn to roll his eyes. "Grow up."

He left the room to shower and change. Then he planned to go to the O'Malleys to see if he could find anything out there.

Stopping at the coffee shop near the O'Malleys, he texted his mom to see if she had any idea of what he could bring Mr. O'Malley. She reminded him that the old man was diabetic and that Jimmy would kill him if he gave Seamus sweets. Black coffee it was.

He arrived at the O'Malley house and parked. He probably should've called, but it seemed like a weird conversation to have over the phone, so he was taking his chances like this. Seamus O'Malley had been retired for years and even Ronan knew he rarely went out anywhere. He rang the bell and waited.

Tommy O'Malley answered the door and his face filled with shock. "Ronan?"

"Yeah. Sorry to show up like this, but I was wondering if your dad was around? I'd like to talk to him."

"Shit. He's always here. Come on in."

Ronan held both cups of coffee in one hand and opened the screen door with the other. Tommy disappeared into the house.

"Hey, Dad. Ronan Doyle is here to see you." Then he turned to look at Ronan. "He's in the kitchen. Go ahead. I'm getting ready for work. See ya." He ran up the stairs, taking two at a time.

Ronan made his way to the kitchen where he found Mr. O'Malley sitting at the table reading a newspaper. An honest to God, real newspaper. Ronan didn't even know they still sold them.

The old man looked up from the paper and squinted at him. "Haven't seen you in years. I'm not a cop anymore, so if you're in trouble I ain't the one to talk to."

Ronan shuffled forward and set the coffee in front of him. "It's just black coffee. And no, I'm not in trouble. Been staying out of it for a long time now. Can I sit?"

Seamus nodded at a chair and pulled the lid off the to-go cup. "What do you want?"

"I was hoping you'd be willing to talk about the summer my dad went missing. You were a cop back then." Ronan sat in the chair across from him.

"Wasn't my case."

"I know, but you knew the people who were in charge and you knew my dad."

"Why the hell are you dredging this up now? It's been what? Twenty years?" He folded the newspaper and put it to the side.

At least Ronan wasn't being summarily dismissed. He sighed. "It has been twenty years and I've been searching for answers for at least half that time, but we have no answers. No matter where I looked or who I talked to, I found nothing, but in my gut, all roads led to Cahill Construction. So I got a job working for them and now I'm running a crew."

Seamus grunted. "You think Cahill had something to do with your father?"

"They know something, whether they did something to him or not. They know. I just can't figure out how to find what I'm looking for. Last weekend, I had some of the guys over to my place and Joe McKinley told me that the cash envelopes are what got my dad into trouble. He said my dad was running all kinds of errands for Cahill back then for extra money. Cahill was doing back alley political deals and Danny was into drugs."

"All sounds about right. I never saw the case file on your dad, but you know this neighborhood. Everyone had an opinion. Back then, it was mostly mob talk. Cahills are connected. I don't know why they would've gone after your dad, though. He wasn't nobody special."

"Is it possible he saw or heard something that he wasn't supposed to?"

"Sure. But we're not talking mob hit. They'd blackball him. He'd never get a job again. That was worse than anything. Especially for a man with a house full of mouths to feed." He sipped his coffee.

Ronan let those thoughts tumble around in his head. "Do you know anyone from back then who might know anything? Someone who had more knowledge than gossip?"

Seamus shrugged. "I only knew cops back then. Most are probably retired. You should ask Jimmy. He's there. Has access to case files. He can get you names."

"Thanks." Ronan wasn't so sure that Jimmy would help him. He might if Brendan asked though. One cop to another. "Can you give me Jimmy's number?"

The old man shifted in his seat and pulled out an old flip phone. He opened it, pressed a button, and passed it to Ronan.

"I didn't think they even made these phones anymore."

"I only got the damn thing because Norah made me. Bossy one."

Ronan copied the number into his contacts and closed the old phone. "Thanks again. I appreciate it."

"If Jimmy doesn't come up with anything good, let me know. I can see if any of the old guys are still kicking. I liked your dad. He was good people."

Ronan nodded and stood. On his way out to his truck, he texted Brendan Jimmy's number. He was so tired of all of the supposition. It was like everyone knew the Cahills were shady as shit and knew something about his dad, but no one had any kind of proof.

As he drove back home, he considered whether he could live with knowing the truth but not being able to prove it.

CHLOE RAN A HAND OVER HER HAIR AND SCHOOLED HER FACE TO look like the respectable girl she was supposed to be. When Mrs. Byrne opened the door, her face lit with a smile. "Chloe. What a surprise!"

"I made you a cross-stitch and my mom suggested I deliver it myself."

"Come in, come in. I just put some tea on."

Chloe followed her into the house and the smell and feel of the living room reminded Chloe of her grandmother's house. Even though Alastair and her father were friends, something about the Byrnes always felt older. She made her way to the kitchen while Mrs. Byrne chatted about an upcoming visit to Ireland she planned to take.

When Mrs. Byrne pointed to a chair, Chloe sat and put the cross stitch on the table. This one read, "*Now faith, hope, and love remain—and the greatest of these is love ~ Cor13:13.*"

"Oh, that's lovely," Mrs. Byrne said. Then she busied herself pouring tea. "How are things going at work?"

"Good. I enjoy working at the Rose. We've been steadily busy."

"I'm glad. I keep trying to get Alastair to fully retire. I think it's time to sell. I want us to enjoy our golden years."

Sell the Rose? She hadn't considered all of Mrs. Byrne's talk of retirement would lead to that. "Don't any of your kids want to run the bar?"

She shook her head. "No. They appreciate what their father built, but they have their own lives now." She reached across and patted Chloe's hand. "But don't you worry. We'll make sure you're taken care of. If Alastair finds a buyer, they'll need help. Someone to show them the ropes."

Shoving panicked thoughts from her mind, Chloe said, "While I'm here, I was wondering if you might have some information about Chicago politics. You and Alastair worked on Alan Cahill's campaign back in the day, right?"

"Oh, yes." She waved a hand. "But that was eons ago."

"I have a friend considering getting into politics and she asked if I would be interested in helping run her campaign. I don't know anything about that, but I'm good with people. Do you remember who was in charge of the Cahill campaign? Or maybe some of the workers whose brains I could pick?"

"That was twenty years ago. I helped Alan because Alastair said it would be good to see one of our own in office. I mostly made coffee and phone calls." She sipped her tea.

"You know me, Mrs. Byrne. I can talk to anyone. But the money is the part that worries me. My friend asked me because of my business degree, but I don't understand campaign finances. It seems like it would be complicated." She took a drink of tea, even though she didn't want it. Not enough of a kick, but she'd be sociable.

Mrs. Byrne chuckled. "You know what they say about Chicago politics. I don't know how much has changed over the last couple of decades. Back then, there was a lot of money changing hands." She pursed her lips. "And not all on the up and up."

"I don't want to do anything illegal."

"As you shouldn't." She sighed and leaned forward. "I suppose it can't hurt to—how do the kids say—spill some tea after all these years."

Chloe smiled. She couldn't imagine her mother ever trying to use modern slang.

"As I said, things were different back then. Someone with money and power could pretty much buy whatever they wanted."

Chloe sat back and couldn't hide the surprise. "Are you saying that Mr. Cahill bought the election?"

She lifted a shoulder and tilted her head. "I'm saying that he had a vision about what he could do for the city and he needed to be in office for that. He was willing to do anything necessary." She waved a hand again. "And here I am running off with stories and not answering the question you asked."

"Sometimes stories are worth the detour."

Mrs. Byrne squinted one eye. "If I remember, it was one of the Nolan boys who ran the campaign. Alan had a hand in everything. He didn't like to let up control."

"Still doesn't. He's at the Rose at least once a week to talk to Danny about the construction company."

"That sounds like Alan. You could ask him, but of course, he won't be talking straight like this. He's still got some politician in him."

"I don't want to bother him. I thought you might know someone who was in the trenches, so to speak. Either way, it doesn't sound like a job for me." She sipped her tea and tried not to look antsy. She had a feeling that something about this conversation would help Ronan and Brendan.

Mrs. Byrne picked up the cross-stitch. "This really is lovely. Thank you so much for thinking of me. Would you like some more tea?"

"No. I actually should get going. I have some errands to run before work." Work at a job she genuinely loved. And Mrs. Byrne wanted to sell? It shouldn't bother her. She'd just told Ronan getting another job was easy. She briefly wondered what it would take to own a bar, but then pushed the thought aside.

They both rose and Mrs. Byrne walked her to the front door.

"Thanks for the stories. It was fun."

"Kind of you to say."

"I'm not saying it out of kindness. I truly enjoyed myself." And she did. The fact that she had one more piece that said Alan Cahill was crooked was a bonus.

Ronan hadn't seen or heard anything from Danny or Alan Cahill, so he felt okay with having Brendan meet Jimmy O'Malley at his house. He had no idea what Brendan had said to him, but Jimmy agreed to gather all the information he could find and bring it to them. Chloe had also texted him to say her conversation with Mrs. Byrne had gone well, too. Things were falling into place and he was beginning to have hope that they would actually find some answers.

Thankfully, Brendan showed up first. It wasn't that Ronan didn't like Jimmy. It was more that they traveled in different packs, made decisions that led them to different places. Jimmy was a little too goody-two-shoes for Ronan. Which made sense knowing he became a cop like his old man. Jimmy never looked down on Ronan for getting into trouble over the years, but he did avoid him.

Brendan set a pizza on the table and leaned against the cabinets as he popped the top on a beer. "Are these gonna collapse?"

"Very funny. Declan did a really good job building and installing these cabinets." Ronan grabbed a slice of pizza. Declan had surprised him with his work ethic. He was still working on the doors, as they required more skill than building the boxes, but it was a good start.

"You think Jimmy's got something good?"

Brendan set his bottle down and helped himself to a slice. "He must have something. Not sure if it's good. If he had nothing, he'd tell me so over the phone. The face to face makes me think he found something."

"I'm going to meet Chloe later to hear what Mrs. Byrne said. The Byrnes have been friends with the Cahills forever. Someone's gotta know something."

"And time tends to loosen lips." Brendan took another drink of beer. "Chloe doesn't spend the night here? Still don't want her around your family?"

Ronan huffed. "First, we're not in a meet-the-family relationship. Second, would you bring any woman around Declan?"

Brendan smiled. "Got a point."

The doorbell rang and Ronan went to let Jimmy in. They greeted each other with a nod and Ronan said, "Brendan's in the kitchen. We have beer and pizza."

"I already ate, but I'll take a beer."

He held a small folder at his side and Ronan couldn't help but think it wasn't much.

Jimmy and Brendan shook hands while Ronan grabbed a beer from the fridge. After handing the bottle to Jimmy, he moved the pizza box to balance on top of the cabinets where his counter should be. "Sorry for the mess. Redoing some stuff here."

"No worries. I get it." He set the folder on the table and

they all took a seat. Jimmy sighed. "I wish I had something more concrete for you."

Fuck. If he came up empty, why was he here?

Jimmy opened the folder. "I talked to the cops who ran the case. My dad was right, they're all retired, but they were more than happy to talk to me. There's nothing official, but they think Alan Cahill made your dad disappear."

Whoa. That explained why Jimmy didn't want to put that in a text.

Brendan leaned forward with his arms on the table. "Made him disappear how or why?"

"That's the thing. No one had a solid answer. The things they did agree on are that your dad was loyal to Cahill, and Cahill trusted him. Your dad did a ton of off-book jobs, whatever Cahill needed. They also all agreed—again without any proof—that Cahill bought the election and your dad knew it. Maybe had some proof."

"Our dad didn't care about politics," Ronan said. "I doubt it would matter to him if Cahill was a dirty politician."

"I agree," Jimmy said. "These cops also said that right after your dad went missing, Danny Cahill did, too. To rehab. His parents covered it up. Made it seem like he was on vacation. They looked at him to see if he was somehow involved, but they couldn't get near him."

Brendan stood. "Are you thinking that Danny and our dad got into something? Alan found out, killed our father, and shipped his son off to rehab?"

"No clue." Jimmy shook his head. "But there's something there."

"Danny would be the weak link," Ronan said.

"But there's no pressuring Danny without Alan catching wind. The man already hates you," Brendan pointed out.

"Unfortunately, there's not enough here for anyone to spend man-hours on this cold case. If we had a new lead or trail to follow, I could run it up the ladder," Jimmy said.

"So another dead end." Ronan couldn't keep the disappointment from his voice.

"No," Brendan said. "Just another thread. We keep pulling at the strings and things will fall apart. Someone will talk."

Jimmy tapped the folder. "I don't know where to send you. Although it's a different time around here, things haven't changed that much. Alan still has a lot of friends."

Brendan nodded. "That's why I could never work here. Not for the city. It's too dirty." His eyes widened. "Obviously, not everyone."

Jimmy held up a hand. "No offense taken. This city's always been a mess. The old guard is still on the way out. It just takes time. And they're not all bad. These guys were frustrated. They couldn't tie Cahill to anything, and they tried. But he's good."

"He's an old motherfucker who needs to come clean," Ronan said.

"If he did what we suspect...there's no statute of limitations. He'll know and he won't talk."

Ronan stared at Jimmy. "You can say it. We think he killed our father."

Saying it out loud, giving voice to the dark thoughts he'd had for years was both freeing and heavy.

The words carried weight. His chest tightened as he thought of all the missed years with his dad. He looked to his brother for some kind of reassurance.

Brendan's grip on his bottle tightened, but he didn't say anything. Didn't refute Ronan's words.

Jimmy stood. "I wish I had more for you. If you find something else for us to go on, let me know. I'll do what I can."

"Appreciate it," Ronan said, forcing gratitude past the rock in his chest.

Brendan walked Jimmy out. While they were saying goodbye, Ronan looked at the notes Jimmy left. Official reports were barely filled out, but the handwritten comments Jimmy added spoke volumes. Cahill might be slick now, but twenty years ago, he might've made mistakes. If no one knew where to look, they couldn't find them.

"So what do you think?" Brendan asked when he came back into the room.

"I think we have to go back twenty years and retrace Dad's steps, know what Cahill was doing. I think he messed up somewhere and we just need to find it."

"It ain't gonna be easy. It's all been buried for twenty years."

Ronan stood. "I've got a strong back made for digging."

"I'm not just talking about the hard work. I mean the repercussions of whatever we find."

"Cahill's gotten away with it for too long."

"Cahill's not the only one who will feel the consequences of the truth coming out. You'll get your answers. But what about what it'll do to Mom?"

"Mom will be fine." Their mother was the strongest woman he knew. "How could the truth be any worse than not knowing?"

"If we're right about Cahill, it'll hit her hard. She trusted him." Brendan shook his head. "And what about the rest of us?"

"Are you saying you want to drop this now? Because it might upset the balance of your perfect fucking life?"

"My life will be just fine. You'll lose your job. But we haven't mentioned any of this to our family. This will blindside them."

"So we tell them." Ronan's irritation grew. They'd come further along lately than he'd been able to in years.

"Tell them what? We're investigating the possibility that Alan Cahill killed our father? What happens then? We have no proof. Hell, we don't even have a body."

"At least they'll know."

Brendan sighed. "The more people who know make it more likely word will get back to Cahill."

Ronan closed his eyes and held tight to his frustration.

"Hey," Brendan said. "I'm just thinking out loud."

Ronan looked at his brother. "It feels like you're talking in circles."

"I am, I guess. We know Cahill is suspicious of you. If he thinks we're on to him, he might try to cover up whatever remaining tracks he might've left. Right now, he's gotten away with whatever he did to dad. Probably never looked back. Who only knows what he's done in the decades since. We all know the power he's wielded for years."

"And you don't want to give him reason to look back now. I get it."

"It's more than that. Someone that dirty doesn't just stop. They get a taste of getting away with shit and they keep going. We could be unraveling a mountain of secrets."

"I'm not walking away. For the first time in years, I feel like I'm on the edge of something."

"We are. It's just a lot of grunt work that's gonna take time."

More fucking time. As if twenty years hadn't been enough.

"I'll take Jimmy's notes and combine them with what I have. Go see your girlfriend."

He was about to say that Chloe wasn't his girlfriend, but what else would he call her? "Let me know if you find anything. I don't know where else to look."

"We'll find the next lead. See you later."

He grabbed the file and his keys and left. Ronan put the leftover pizza in the fridge for Declan. He stuck a note to the door telling Declan to make sure the counter was ordered for the kitchen. Then he went to see Chloe.

They agreed to meet at a bar. It might've almost been a date if he hadn't already told her to date other men. What the hell had he been thinking? That she didn't want a relationship with him. That was why her family couldn't know. Why she'd asked him to stay in the bedroom when her mother showed up.

He arrived early, but there were plenty of people around. He went to the bar to order a beer, still bitter about the lack of leads from Jimmy and thinking about Chloe keeping him a secret. So when a pretty blonde sidled up beside him and asked if he would buy her a drink, he obliged.

"I'm Tiffany."

"Ronan." He shook her hand as she gave him the once over.

When their beers were set down, he asked, "How about a game of darts?"

"I'm not good, but I'll play."

He led the way to the back of the bar.

"I've never seen you in here before," she said.

"I'm meeting a friend."

"Girlfriend?" she asked coyly.

"She's female, yes. But not my girlfriend." He didn't like

the way it sounded, like a lie, but he reminded himself of the rules he and Chloe had chosen. It wasn't like he was going to take Tiffany home. It was a game of darts.

He pulled the darts from the board and handed her a set. They played a practice round and she was terrible. He tried not to laugh as her last dart landed in the wall beside the board. She giggled.

CHLOE WAS RUNNING A LITTLE LATE GETTING TO THE BAR, BUT she saw Ronan's truck outside, so she knew he was around somewhere. She ordered a couple of beers to apologize for running late, and then she wove her way through the crowd looking for him. When she got to the back room, she found him.

He was playing darts with a woman who was obviously hitting on him. Jealousy and anger bubbled up, but she took a deep breath. She had no claim to him. They were casual, right? He'd told her to go out on the ridiculous dates her mother pushed on her. Oh, damn. Was he getting even with her?

She stood in the back and watched for a few moments. The woman was flirty and quite touchy-feely, but Ronan was just being Ronan. When he finally turned and his eyes met hers, she felt it burn through her, an immediate desire. What the hell was wrong with her?

He said something to the woman, who then patted his chest, and offered a little laugh.

Keep it light, Chloe.

When he neared, she handed him a bottle of beer. "Sorry I'm late. Got hung up at work."

"No problem." He pointed to a nearby table.

"Make a new friend?" she asked, with a glance toward the dartboard.

Ronan shook his head. "Not really. She was looking for someone to buy her drinks and take her home. I was biding my time until you got here."

He sat down and took a drink. "Jealous?"

"No more than you were hearing my mom offer me up for dates."

He grunted and she didn't know how to interpret that.

"I went to see Mrs. Byrne and she spilled some tea."

"Really?" He leaned back in his chair as if he was relaxed, but every ounce of his attention focused on her.

"She said that Alan bought the election. One of the Nolans ran his campaign, but Alan had a hand in everything. Nothing was being done behind his back. Whatever happened, he knew about it."

"Anything about my dad?"

"I didn't ask about him specifically. I thought that would be too suspicious. I came at it from the politics. I can reach out to the Nolans. My parents know at least one of them."

"I don't know if it would matter. Jimmy O'Malley has come across similar information. Cahill is dirty, but no one can prove it. We're still not sure how it ties to my dad." He drank his beer and sank into silence for a bit.

Chloe wished she knew what to say or do, but she had nothing, so she just drank her beer and watched as Ronan's darts partner picked up another guy to drink with. She felt Ronan staring at her. Returning her attention to him, she asked, "What?"

"I'm wondering what exactly we're doing. We got into this being casual, but it's not feeling that way anymore. You're over there watching Tiffany as if she might crook a finger and I'll go running."

Chloe swallowed hard and lifted a shoulder. "I'm just interested in seeing what your type is."

"My type?" He leaned close to her across the table and spoke with narrowed eyes. "You're my fucking type, Chloe. You're in my head and I can't get you out of my system."

His words shouldn't have made her happy and she definitely shouldn't get turned on, but she was. "If I'm your type, why bother with her? You could've sat and had a beer by yourself. You made sure I saw you with her. What were you hoping for?"

He slid back in his chair. "Not a damn thing. I understand what I am to you."

At least he didn't deny he'd been flirting with the woman. He didn't feign innocence or make her feel like she was imagining things. But she didn't like the way his comment sounded like an accusation. "And what exactly is that?"

"I'm your fuck buddy that you keep as a dirty little secret."

"That's not true."

"Yes, it is. But you can't get jealous that some other woman has my attention. I've been playing by your rules. I know my place."

Her heart sank. She opened her mouth to refute everything. To explain that the problem was with her. That she was afraid to have a relationship even though he made her want to, but the words didn't come.

He rose, polished off his beer, and said, "Thanks for the info. I'll let Brendan know about the Nolans and see what he thinks."

She wrapped her fingers around his forearm. "You're just gonna leave?"

"I'm not really in the mood tonight."

"That's not what I meant. We can have another drink, talk..."

"I don't have anything else to say."

He walked away and she sat stunned for a minute. They'd been having a good time. And she really did like him. She pushed her fear down and ran after him. Outside on the street, she looked to where his truck was parked.

"Ronan!"

He paused and turned. She jogged across the street.

"Wait. Just give me a minute." She hated the weakness in her voice. She took a deep breath. "I like what we have. I like you. More than like you, and that sucks because I wasn't looking to fall in love."

She sucked in a shaky breath afraid of how he'd interpret those words. She wasn't even totally sure what she'd meant by them.

He crossed his arms over his broad chest. She wanted those arms around her.

"What do you want me to say, Chloe? I wasn't looking to get involved with you. You pushed into my life. You got us here, and it's like I don't have a right to want more."

She licked her lips. Her heart thundered and as scary as it was to admit, she pushed forward. "I want to be able to give you more. Give us more."

He didn't look convinced. She stepped closer and touched his cheek, loving the feel of his beard on her palm. "This started out as fun. I thought you were the perfect guy to keep things simple with. The bad boy of the neighborhood surely wouldn't want a relationship."

"I'm not that guy anymore."

"I know. I like this guy even more."

He grabbed her wrist. "Where do we go from here?"

"I don't know."

Pulling away, he said, "Let me know when you figure it out."

"You're still just going to walk away?"

"I don't know what you want from me, Chloe. I can't do this. I've got too much on my mind to play games."

"I don't want this to end. This matters to me. I know you're dealing with a lot. So let me help you take your mind off your troubles." She smiled. She might not be able to commit to giving him everything he wanted, but she could give him this. "Let me ease some of your frustrations."

She pressed closer to him. Ran her fingers across his chest. Slid her leg between his. Then she rose on tiptoe and whispered in his ear, "We can figure out the rest later. Tonight, we can make each other feel better."

He growled and spun her to press against his truck and his mouth crashed down on hers. His hard-on prodded her and she stroked him through his jeans.

"Follow me home," she said.

"Fuck that. Get in the back of my truck." He clicked the button to unlock the door. Then he scooped her up and tossed her on the back seat.

She laughed. "I think we're a little old and you're a little big to do this."

"Watch me." He unbuttoned her jeans and slid his hand inside to stroke her.

Within a minute, her eyes were rolling back in her head. She shouldn't want to have sex in a truck in a parking lot where anyone could walk by, but it only turned her on more. "God, yes." She rocked against his hand and wanted more.

As soon as she came, he yanked her jeans off. Then he

muscled his way into the truck, sliding her further into the cab, and sat beside her. He pulled a condom from his pocket, sheathed himself, and pulled her onto his lap. It was fast and hard and so, so good. Chloe braced her hands against the roof as he drove up into her. She was trembling again and he sent her over the edge with a grunt of his own.

They sat interlocked, sweaty and panting. Chloe was afraid to open her eyes. She knew he was going to send her on her way, and she wanted a few more minutes of him. She heard him fumbling around near the door. She finally opened her eyes so she didn't land on her ass if he literally tossed her out.

He held a tiny pack of tissues. He eased her off him, removed the condom, and then cleaned her up. His hands were gentle and his voice soft as he asked, "You okay?"

"I'm good." She reached for her clothes and sat beside him while she untangled her pants. Once they were both dressed, she said, "Tell me what you want."

"I want you. All the time. Without the sneaking around. The rest of my life is up in the air, but you're this one good thing I have. And no one is supposed to know."

"I think..." What the hell did she think? She liked him. He'd seen all the parts of her few others ever paid attention to. Could this work? "I think I'd like to try."

"Really? With me."

She laughed. "Of course with you. But I need some time to figure out how to deal with my family. Can you give me some time?"

"I can do that." He leaned over and brushed his lips over hers. "I need to get home to bed. Early day tomorrow."

"Sure you don't want to come over?"

"If I come home with you, we both know we're not going to sleep."

She huffed dramatically. "Fine. Be that way. Move your ass so I can get out." She shoved his shoulder, but he didn't budge.

"Let's go out to dinner. A real date."

"Take me dancing and it's a deal."

One eyebrow winged up. "Do I look like I dance?"

"Might be fun."

"Doubt it." He opened the door and held her hand as she climbed out. "I'll call you tomorrow."

They kissed again and he stood watch over her as she walked to her car. He didn't get back into the truck until she pulled out of the lot.

For weeks she'd been questioning what she'd gotten herself into with him and now, it looked like a relationship. She should be scared, but she was oddly relaxed. With Ronan, she never felt like she had to hide parts of herself. He liked her for who she was. She was smiling like an idiot all the way home.

Tomorrow she'd think about her family and how they might react, but for tonight, she was enjoying being wanted by a man she was falling for.

RONAN HELD TRUE TO HIS WORD AND HAD TAKEN CHLOE OUT to dinner on a real date. When she texted him yesterday to say she'd made plans for their second date, he only responded with: I don't dance.

It gave her a chuckle because part of her wanted to see him dance. But he'd be one of those guys who'd stand at the edge of the dance floor, arms crossed, stubbornly refusing to move.

She just hoped he wouldn't be so stubborn about tonight's date. She wanted to do something fun, so she found a coupon for a couple's art class. Neither of them were artists, so they could suck together. Besides, it was a BYOB activity. How bad could it be if they could drink while painting?

When she got to Ronan's house, she rang the bell and Declan answered.

"Hey," he said, pulling the door wide. "Ronan's changing. He'll be out soon."

She stepped into the living room. "How's the kitchen coming?"

"I got the cabinets in. Wanna see?"

"I'd love to." She followed him to the kitchen. The new cabinets were beautiful. "You made a prep island. Very fancy. This is amazing." She ran a hand over one of the doors. "Did you actually make these?"

He nodded.

"They're stunning."

"They're not even done yet. They need another coat of stain and poly." He blushed. This grown man, who spent most of his time joking around, had a hard time taking a compliment.

"Really, Declan. If I owned a house, I'd hire you in a minute."

"Whoa," Ronan said behind them. "What do you think you're hiring my brother for?"

"These cabinets are beautiful."

"Yeah, he did pretty good, but let's not give him a swelled head. You ready to go?"

"Yep."

"You gonna tell me where we're going?"

"Nope."

Declan burst out laughing. "She really knows how to drive you nuts. I love it."

Ronan growled at his brother.

Chloe looped an arm around Ronan's. "Trust me. It'll be fun."

Since she didn't want him to know where they were going, she drove. He, of course, grumbled about the size of her car the whole time. When they arrived at the art studio, she parked and reached into the back for the six-pack of beer.

"Bringing your own beer? What the hell is this?" he asked.

"Trust me, okay? Keep an open mind. It'll be fun."

He climbed out of the car with only one small grumble. The man definitely didn't like surprises.

When she held the door open for him, he paused, looking around the room. "You didn't sign me up to be a nude model, did you? I'm not stripping."

She laughed but had no idea what made him think that because he was blocking her view of the room. "No, it's a BYOB couple's painting night."

He stepped aside to let her through. The room was filled with middle-aged women sipping wine. Their eyes were glued to Ronan.

She nudged him to a couple of open easels and handed him a beer. "So I guess I misunderstood the couple part. They only sold tickets in pairs."

"Uhhuh." He took a swig of beer. "You know my brother Gavin is the artist. I don't have any artistic talent."

"You're not supposed to. This is just for fun."

He sighed and settled on the stool in front of the easel,

and Chloe smiled. She'd come to realize that Ronan grumbled and bitched a lot, but he'd do this for her. Even though it was outside his comfort zone, doing something he probably wouldn't like, he'd do it anyway. It made her like him even more.

A few minutes later, the teacher came in, looking like a made-for-TV movie hippie. She wore a long, flowy gown, and the wild curls around her head poked out everywhere.

"Good evening. I hope you're all prepared to search your soul, open wounds, and bleed onto the canvas."

"If this is some kind of fucking cult, I'm gonna have issues," Ronan muttered.

Chloe stifled a laugh.

"Before we pick up our tools of paint and brush," the teacher continued, "I want you to close your eyes for a moment." She put on some instrumental meditation music and lit an incense stick. "Let the music free your mind."

Ronan grunted. Chloe snickered. The teacher shot them a look. Chloe grabbed Ronan's hand and closed her eyes.

The teacher went on. "I don't want you to think about what you want to paint. I want you to feel it. Consider the people in your life. What colors do they remind you of? What shapes do they bring to your life?"

The room fell silent. Then the teacher rang a bell. "Open your eyes and begin painting."

Chloe released Ronan's hand. He opened his eyes. She hadn't expected him to play along. She leaned close and said quietly, "Sorry. I didn't know it was going to be this weird. That's what I get for using a coupon online."

He shrugged. "We're here. Might as well paint. But you owe me."

"I will happily pay up later."

RONAN HAD NO IDEA WHAT THE FUCK HE'D GOTTEN HIMSELF into with Chloe. Dancing was beginning to look not so bad. He had no clue how to paint. Fuck. He didn't even know *what* to paint.

Chloe had already picked up her brush and was painting lines. He leaned over to peek at her work, but she scooted and angled her canvas. "Eyes on your own paper, Doyle. No cheating." She winked as she teased.

He continued to stare at the blank canvas. He didn't know what his face said to the teacher, but she made her way across the room to him.

"Need some help?" she asked.

"I have no idea what I'm supposed to do. I need more direction."

"No, you don't. You just need to let go of what you think it's supposed to be. As I said at the beginning, paint the colors and shapes you feel."

He barely refrained from rolling his eyes. He didn't feel in shapes and colors. This whole thing made him feel stupid and incompetent.

Then he looked over at the women across the room chatting and joking as they painted. His gaze landed on Chloe. She'd tucked her hair behind her ears and she was deeply focused on the brush stroke she was making.

Her concentration was cute.

He picked up his brush and began to paint. It was ugly, downright hideous even, but the teacher said to paint how he felt. Lately, he'd been a ball of anger, frustration, and resentment.

Except for the time he spent with Chloe. She was the one thing in his life that made him feel better rather than worse. He continued to paint until the teacher rang the bell again.

He was deep into his second beer when Chloe slid off her stool. "Ready to share?"

He stared at the mess on his canvas. "I guess."

She turned her easel toward him. The entire space was filled with geometric shapes, all evenly and perfectly drawn, all linked together, except one, near the bottom right corner.

He took another swig of beer. "I don't want to show mine. It looks like a preschooler did it. Especially compared to yours." He pointed to the triangle slipping away from the other shapes. "Why is that one trying to escape?"

Her brow furrowed. "Escape? Huh. I hadn't thought of that. The triangle is me, a little unmoored compared to the other people in my life."

He hated that she felt so out of place and disconnected. He wished he could fix that for her.

"Your turn," she said expectantly, as she scurried over to where he sat in front of his canvas. She leaned her arm on his shoulder and looked at his painting.

Her sweet scent wrapped around him and he pulled her closer.

She studied the blobs on the canvas. "It's kind of dark."

"That's my life—messy and dark."

Then she pointed to the thick, yellow stripe across the top of the canvas. "What's that?"

"That's you."

She stiffened in his arms and then turned to face him. "What?"

"The mess at the bottom is all the shit I'm dealing with. But you're this wide stretch where I get to feel good."

Her eyes got teary and he didn't know what to say. He knew he should've kept his mouth shut. He could already imagine Declan berating him. *"What woman wants to be compared to a paint splotch?"*

He opened his mouth to apologize, but her lips crashed onto his. He held her hips as they kissed.

When she pulled away, she simply said, "I love it."

"You do? It looks like shit."

She turned in the circle of his arms again. "It's not every day that I'm told that I'm someone's sunshine and happiness."

He rested his chin on her shoulder. "You should. Because you are."

They cleaned up their empty bottles and carried their paintings to the car.

"Where to now? Chloe asked.

"Your place. You owe me for that freak show."

She burst out laughing but took his hand. "Deal. Thanks for not running away. I know that was weird for you. But it was fun, right?"

He just shook his head. He'd do pretty much anything for her, even if it meant pretending to like painting.

Twenty~One

Ronan worked long hours over the next few days, but they went by fast because most nights, he and Chloe would hang out, even if it was just for a while. They had been on a few real dates—no dancing involved—but she spent the night at his house or he spent the night at hers. While not perfect, they were making it work.

Tonight, however, they would only be able to have dinner together. With Brendan. Brendan had an update that required more than a text, so Chloe offered to pick up dinner and meet him at Brendan's. She was almost as invested in the information as he was. He rang the bell and he was surprised to see Chloe open the door.

"Hey. I beat you here."

"How are you?" he asked as he bent to kiss her.

"I'd be better if I didn't have to go back to work in an hour. Three people all called in sick, so there's no way for me to get out of it." She grabbed his hand and pulled him toward the dining room. "Brendan and I have been plotting."

"Plotting what?"

"I talked with Joe Nolan, who had a falling out with Alan Cahill years ago. He said Cahill stole the election. He bribed and paid everyone in sight to make sure he won," Brendan answered.

"And?"

"And he said that Danny was the weak link for Cahill. Alan was always cleaning up Danny's mess. Danny got arrested, Alan paid off the cops to pretend it didn't happen. Danny owed his drug dealer, Alan paid the tab. Anything to make it look like Danny was a good boy."

"What does any of that have to do with Dad?"

Brendan handed him a beer and they sat around the small dining room table scattered with papers and pictures.

"Nolan said Dad was Cahill's errand boy. He knew everything. Dad was the one who delivered the payoffs."

"You think Dad threatened to expose him?"

Brendan shook his head. "No. Errand boy paid well. I don't think there was any incentive for him to try to blackmail Alan."

"You think Dad was skimming?"

Brendan shrugged. "Don't know." He took another drink. "Anything's possible."

Ronan's phone buzzed repeatedly with a bunch of texts. Brendan's did the same. Family chat was the worst creation ever. Their mom started the firestorm of texts.

Nessa's birthday is Saturday. Party in 2 weeks. I need a head count and volunteers to bring food and set up.

Declan already responded that he'd bring dessert, which was always the cheapest option because he'd bring a package of cookies and call it a day.

Killian said he'd bring the keg, and Kieran volunteered for plates and cups.

Ronan looked up from his phone. "Isn't she a little old for a party?"

"It's her twenty-fifth. And you know Mom."

Ronan shook his head. He hated the family parties. Mom always invited everyone she could imagine, family, friends, and neighbors.

"What?" Chloe asked.

"Nessa's birthday."

Before he could even think what to type, Brendan responded for both of them. Ronan and I will bring meat.

"What the hell are you volunteering me for?"

"Because you've skipped out of most parties for years. If no one can eat unless you show, you won't blow it off."

Chloe laughed. "Can I help?"

Staring at the texts, he said, "No. We're good."

Then he set his phone down and ignored his irritation at his family. "Back to Nolan. You think Mom might know something? She'd know if there was extra money coming in, right?"

"Wouldn't she have told us?" Brendan asked.

"She wouldn't have had a reason to. Maybe it seemed insignificant."

"I haven't gotten to the best part yet. Nolan said he'd help. He's willing to confront Alan. He just needs to know what questions to ask, how to push him."

"How will that help us?"

"We can plant a wire at Cahill's table and look for leads."

"I can do that," Chloe said.

"No." Ronan turned his attention to her. "It's too risky."

Chloe stared at him for a minute and then stood. "I

guess you don't need me for anything then. I have to get back to work. Let me know if there's anything I *can* do to help."

"I thought you had some more time," Ronan said.

"Not really. You guys seem to have your hands full. I'll talk to you later."

"Wait. I'll walk you out."

"I'm fine." She touched his arm. "Go back to planning. We'll talk later."

He watched her walk out as the door closed quietly behind her. Did he do something wrong? His face must've shown his confusion because Brendan said, "I think she was waiting for an invite."

"For what?"

"Nessa's party, asshole."

"Why the fuck would she want to come to that?"

"Because she's your girlfriend and that's what couples do."

He hated when his brother talked to him like he was stupid. It hadn't even occurred to him to invite Chloe. The party would be at his mom's house. Right across the street from her parents. "We're not there yet. She said she needs time to deal with her family. They don't like me."

"You don't get women at all. Even if she decides it's not a good idea or she won't come because of her family, she wants to be invited. She wants to know you want her there."

"She knows."

"You sure?"

He thought so. Hadn't he made his feelings clear? Dropping the topic altogether, he asked, "How are we going to get Cahill to tell Nolan anything about Dad?"

"I think we should have Nolan show up at the Rose when

both Danny and Alan are there. Then he can threaten to blackmail Alan."

"But if he just asks about Dad, Alan has no reason to say anything. We have no leverage to give Nolan."

"Nolan's presence will get them to talk with a bug at the table. When they talk, we'll hear it."

"First, I know you're the FBI and all, but isn't that illegal? And second, you can't ask Chloe to do that. She'll lose her job."

Brendan huffed. "Yes, it's illegal. Do you care? Cahill's been doing illegal shit for decades. If we listen in, we can get the leads we need. Then we can work backwards to find it another way. It's easier to find a new path when you know where you're going."

Ronan sat with that a minute. He couldn't care less if what they did was illegal, but Brendan should. "If we get caught, you'll lose your job. And, like I said, so will Chloe."

"Someone would have to prove we did it. I bet Cahill has a lot of enemies."

"What does Nolan think happened with Dad?"

Brendan shook his head. "He leans toward him getting caught for skimming, but he doesn't know."

"You think Cahill would murder someone skimming? Lightening that envelope is almost expected in this business. It doesn't add up." Ronan rubbed his forehead. "I'm going to talk to Mom. See if she has any ideas."

"You're gonna tell Mom about Cahill?"

"I'm going to ask her what she knows about Cahill."

"I'll touch base with Nolan again and see if he has any good ideas."

They finished their beers and Ronan stood.

"Make it right with Chloe," Brendan warned.

"Chloe and I are fine."

Brendan sighed, and Ronan did what he could to ignore him. As he left, he considered Brendan's words. Chloe was the one who asked for time. Bringing her to Nessa's party would be outing them to her family. There'd be no sneaking around there. They might as well make out on the corner.

And as much as he might enjoy the actual kiss as well as watching her mom get her panties in a bunch, he knew Chloe had to do this her way.

CHLOE WORKED ON AUTO-PILOT. THE BAR WAS BUSY, BUT NOT overwhelming, which left just enough time for her to think about Ronan and why he hadn't planned on telling her about Nessa's party. As the night wore on, and business slowed, she allowed her irritation to boil into anger. When it neared closing time and only a few regulars were sitting at the bar, Chloe took a seat in the corner of the bar to do some paperwork.

She waved Johnny over. "I need a drink."

"Sure thing, boss. What'll you have?"

With a sigh, she answered, "Something to make me forget."

He smiled wickedly. "I got just the thing."

While he went off to mix up some magic for her, she studied the night's receipts, but her thoughts continued to turn to Ronan.

If she hadn't been there when the texts came in, he wouldn't have mentioned it. How could he think that not inviting her was having a relationship? She'd told him she wanted to give it a try. And the first chance he had, he was still keeping her separate. He said he hated sneaking around like he was her dirty little secret, but he didn't want her at a family party.

Fuck that.

Johnny delivered a slim glass filled with a harmless-looking, frothy pinkish-purple liquid. "I call it Amnesia. Let me know what you think."

So Johnny thought she couldn't handle some hard liquor. One more man who underestimated her. She took a full drink and was pleasantly surprised. Sweet with a hint of tart, but the burn of alcohol was there. Still didn't think it'd give her amnesia, but it tasted good.

She'd put herself out there for Ronan, allowed him to see all the parts of her she kept separate. She was falling for him and believed his words, but his actions told a different story. Everything from Brendan asking for her help to not inviting her to a birthday party. He was keeping her at a distance.

Johnny wiped down the bar and pointed to her nearly-empty glass. "Like it?"

"It's better than I thought it would be. Thanks."

"Want to tell me about it?" He leaned his forearms on the bar in the classic bartender pose.

"What?"

"You've been pissed off all night. Friendly to the customers, but I could see the anger bubbling up."

"Just personal stuff." She waved him off.

"I'll be back in a minute. Let me close these guys out and you can vent a bit."

She smiled and shook her head. Johnny was a good guy, but she didn't feel the need to spill her guts to him. He moved around behind the bar, letting the regulars know it was time to go.

When the guys were done, they tossed a few bills down for Johnny. He scooped them up and collected their glasses. Chloe slid from her stool and walked the customers out, locking up behind them. She returned to her seat to find a fresh drink waiting.

Johnny smiled as he rinsed a glass. "So what's going on?"

Chloe sipped the drink and then looked around as if someone else might be listening. "There's this guy I've been seeing. I thought we were getting serious, but I don't think it's the same for him."

"Ooo...juicy. Anyone I know?" He wagged his eyebrows.

"I don't think so. But it doesn't matter. He was supposed to be a quick fling and things got complicated."

"How so?" he asked as he swept behind the bar. She had to give him credit—he was good at multi-tasking.

"I had some information he needed and I bartered that for fun."

"I never pegged you for a naughty girl."

Chloe smiled. "Most people don't. I come from a nice Catholic family, and I've always done what was expected. I wanted my parents' approval, so I was a good girl. But it never fit, you know? It was natural for me. I just put on a bright smile and swallowed down my instincts."

She drank some more, enjoying the buzz of alcohol singing through her. "Anyway, the thing with this guy went from being a quid pro quo thing to something more. He said he wanted more. This was his idea, but now he's backing off, keeping me at a distance."

"That doesn't make sense."

"Right?" She slapped the counter. "I was totally fine keeping it casual."

"No, I mean, are you sure you're reading things right?" He stopped sweeping and kind of leaned on the broom handle.

"How can I not? There's a family party that he not only didn't invite me to, but he wasn't even going to tell me about it."

"The thing is, I've never met a man who says he wants something more unless he really does. If he brought it up, not in response to you—"

She waved her hands. "Totally him. His idea."

"Then you're misreading or something else is in play."

She scanned her memory for other reasons for him to not invite her.

"Unless he's into drama," Johnny added.

Chloe burst into a fit of laughter. Ronan? Drama king? The man didn't even like to talk to people. He was the most isolated person she'd ever met. He'd told her that he'd kept his distance from his family because it was hard for him to be around all of them.

"I'll take that as a no then. Why else would he keep you at bay? To protect you from something?"

That sobered her. It started with him rejecting Brendan's idea of her planting a bug. He'd been trying to keep her out of all of the business with the Cahills and his father. But she didn't need his protection. People had been telling her what to do her whole life.

She was capable of making her own choices and decisions. After leaving Tim, she promised herself no one would ever make her feel that way again.

She was making her decisions now, so she pulled out her phone. The blurry screen made her squint. "How much alcohol is in these?"

Johnny chuckled. "Enough to make you forget."

She blew out a breath and opened her eyes wide as if that would help her focus. Texting was out of the question, but she could make a call. She scrolled to Brendan's name and tapped.

As soon as it was ringing, and she had the phone to her ear, Johnny looked up, horrified. "Stop! What are you doing? Who are you calling?"

She made a face at him that she hoped said, "Shut up," because Brendan picked up.

"Chloe?" he asked, kind of muffled and gruff.

"Oh, shit. How late is it?" She looked around the bar before remembering they didn't have clocks because they wanted people to lose track of time.

"What's wrong?" he sounded much more alert.

Johnny reached for her phone, but she pulled back.

"Nothing. I just wanted to let you know that Ronan doesn't make decisions for me. In fact, I'm done with his bullshit."

"What are you talking about?"

"Come on, Chloe. Give me the phone," Johnny said.

"Who's that?" Brendan asked.

"No one," she answered, still waving Johnny off. "That thing you mentioned earlier that I could do for you? I'm in. I don't care what Ronan says."

"Are you drunk?"

"Maybe a little. But that doesn't matter. Stop by my place tomorrow and show me what I need to do."

Johnny made another grab for the phone. "You shouldn't call dudes when you're drunk. Don't you know that?"

She started to laugh and she wanted to explain that this was Brendan, but when she shifted to keep the phone away from him, she lost her balance and fell off her stool. The phone skidded out of her hand as she thumped on the floor. In the back of her head, she knew she should register some pain, but all she could do was curl up in another fit of laughter.

"Ah, hell. I knew the second one was too much."

Through her teary eyes, she saw him grab her phone. "Chloe'll call you tomorrow." Then a pause. "I'm a friend." He huffed and held out the phone. "Tell grumpy dude that you're fine."

"I'm fine, Brendan. I'll talk to you tomorrow," she yelled since it seemed like Johnny and her phone were far away. A moment later, Johnny's hands were under her arms and he hoisted her off the floor.

He held her shoulders for a moment. "You okay?"

The way he stared into her face, with his eyes bugged wide almost sent her laughing again. She bit her cheek and nodded.

"Give me a few minutes to finish cleaning up and we'll get you home."

She waved a hand, which set off a wobble in her whole body, so he caught her arm again. "I can call a car."

"I'm not sending you home with a stranger and hoping you arrive. I'll drive you."

She smiled. "Thanks, Johnny. You're a good guy."

He helped her sit down again. "Let's see if you're still saying that tomorrow morning."

Twenty~Two

Ronan rolled over to the sound of his phone. He cracked an eyelid to find it still pitch black out. What the fuck?

"Hello?"

"Hey, you might want to check on your girl."

Ronan scrubbed at his face and sat up. "What?" He held the phone away from his face, saw that it was Brendan, whose voice registered even as he was checking. Then he scanned for missed calls or texts. Nothing.

Putting the phone back to his ear, he heard Brendan saying something. "Repeat that, man. I was sound asleep."

"I got a call from Chloe. She was drunk and with some guy."

He jumped out of bed and reached for his jeans. "Where was she? And why the *fuck* was she calling you instead of me?"

"Stop!" Brendan's voice startled him. "She wasn't in danger. The guy said he was a friend, *she* said she was fine, but she was drunk. And pissed off at you."

"Pissed off at me for what?"

"She didn't say, but I'm guessing it's because you didn't invite her to the party like I told you."

He really didn't need Brendan's smug *I told you so.*

"I'm suggesting that you check in on her, that's all. I'm sure she's fine."

"Yeah, thanks." He disconnected, beyond irritated that she called Brendan. He dialed her number as he finished getting dressed. Of course, she didn't answer. He grabbed his keys and texted. Are you okay?

He was in his truck before he got a response.

Fine.

He started the engine. Chloe, who always had something to say, sent him a one-word text. He didn't know if that meant she was pissed or if he should be worried. Without thinking, he drove to her apartment. Finding parking this late wasn't easy, so he ended up parking on the main street and walking down the block. As he neared her apartment, he heard her laughter echoing down the street.

The streetlights were dim, but he could make out two figures on the sidewalk in front of her building. He sped his pace and forced himself not to overreact. Maybe it wasn't her. Maybe it wasn't some guy practically carrying her.

He was in front of the neighbor's house when he heard her say, "The lock's still broken. Just turn the knob."

"Chloe," he called.

The man with his arms all over her shifted so they both turned to face him. "What're you doing here?" she asked at the same time he said, "Who the fuck are you?"

"Nunya business," she slurred.

The guy sighed deeply. "Look, dude. I work with her and I'm just giving her a ride home."

She patted his chest and then pressed a finger to her lips. "Shhh!"

"Come on," Ronan said, holding out a hand.

She curled tighter to the guy. "I didn't ask you to come here."

"No. You called my brother."

"Damn Brendan." She wrapped an arm around the guy's waist. "Johnny is taking me up to bed."

One look at Johnny's pained expression told Ronan everything he needed to know. She was playing games.

"Fine. You have fun with Johnny."

"What?" she screeched, shoving away from Johnny.

"You obviously decided that what we have isn't important. You get drunk and are more comfortable calling my brother than me. Then you have Johnny here take care of you. Looks like I'm not needed."

"I called Brendan because he lets me make my own decisions. He doesn't tell me what I can and can't do. I'm a grown woman. If I want to help a friend by doing something that's not totally legal, that's my choice. If I want to get shitfaced, my perog—prerog—decision." Her entire body wove back and forth.

"You're right, Chloe. You can do whatever the fuck you want, but I won't be part of it. I can't take the blame for your bad decisions. Once was more than enough for me."

"No one's asking you to. And you can't tell me you're out. I'm out. I told you this wasn't supposed to be a thing. So you don't get to break up with me."

"Hey, maybe you should wait till tomorrow for this conversation before you say something you'll regret," Johnny said.

Ronan shook his head. "That's okay. She's right. We're not supposed to work out. She's made that clear."

He turned to walk toward his truck. He shouldn't have pushed a conversation in the middle of the night with a drunk woman, but she had a way of pressing every one of his damn buttons. He also knew that drunks didn't make shit up. More often than not, their truth came spilling out, so he doubted Chloe would have any regrets tomorrow.

He, on the other hand, already felt the heartache settling in. He'd known that Chloe would probably never be his for good, but he'd believed he'd have longer than this. He climbed in his truck and pointed home.

Chloe McCarthy had been nothing but trouble for him his whole life. Why the hell did he think that sleeping with and falling in love with her would change that?

He swerved over the line with the thought. Damn. He was more tired than he thought. Love? He had feelings for Chloe. But they hadn't been together long enough for anything so serious.

That was his story and he was sticking to it.

THE POUNDING CREATED A LEVEL OF PAIN CHLOE HAD NEVER even dreamed about. Why would her dreams cause her pain? She eased an eyelid up and the blinding light from the window stabbed her brain.

She rolled over and discovered there was nowhere to move because she was on her couch. Her stomach flipped and her brain revolted against the movement. "Oh, God."

Then the pounding happened again and she realized it wasn't in her head.

"Chloe. Open up."

She drew in as much air as she could and held it as she levered herself off the cushion. She stumbled to the door, carefully released the breath as she moved. She could handle her liquor. She would not throw up.

As she grabbed the doorknob, a sticky note stared at her. *Don't hate me. You said you wanted to forget, but you might want to call the brooding hulk that showed up last night. – J*

Another quick rap on the door. Chloe clenched her jaw and swung the door open, but even that little movement took all her energy and she leaned on the slab of wood.

Brendan stood on the other side. He took one look at her and cringed.

"Thanks." She turned to go curl back into a ball. "What're you doing here?"

"You told me to stop by and tell you how to install the bug at Cahill's table."

Parts of her night flooded back. Yeah, that conversation was why her ass was sore right now. She rubbed her right ass cheek and collapsed on the couch.

"Are you okay?"

She nodded slowly.

"Why don't you go take a shower and I'll make some coffee?"

The thought of anything going down her throat threatened to make her puke. "I'm fine."

"No, you're not. And you stink like a barroom floor."

She sniffed. Her eyes rolled shut.

"Come on." He held out a hand and pulled her to her feet. "I've got the best hangover fix."

"I'm not hungover. I can handle a few drinks."

"Sure you can. Go wash off the stink."

"Whatever." But she shuffled to the bathroom. A shower couldn't hurt. Brushing her teeth. That needed to happen first. The inside of her mouth felt like a carpet. An old seventies shag carpet. She leaned heavily on the sink and managed to brush her teeth with only gagging twice. Then she stood under the hot spray of the shower. Her head went from a full thump to a nagging throb. Good enough.

Now she could try to piece together the last part of her night. After pulling on a pair of shorts and a nightshirt—because she sure as hell was going back to sleep after Brendan left—she went to the kitchen where he had a cup of coffee poured and a breakfast sandwich made. Like made—not bought.

She took a bite. It was the exact right amount of greasy and filling. After she swallowed, she moaned.

Brendan leaned against her counter and sipped coffee with a wicked grin on his face. She wondered if he knew how much he and Ronan looked like each other when he did that. "How are you not married yet?"

"Haven't found the one. Why aren't you?"

She sighed and sank to a chair. "I'm not the right type for marrying."

He laughed. "You're definitely the marrying type. Maybe you're shopping in the wrong stores."

Her head hurt too much to try to analyze metaphors. "Why are you here again?"

"To give you this." He pulled a small box from his pocket and lifted the lid. A small black button sat inside. "Take this and stick it to the underside of the table."

She made a face at that. Tables could be gross.

"Unless Alan always sits in the same spot and there happens to be a plant or something next to him. It has to be in a position to pick up his conversation without being drowned out by other customers."

She took another bite of the heavenly sandwich and closed her eyes. There was a pillar behind where Danny usually sat. But nothing next to Alan's seat. And they always sat in the same places. "I think it's going to have to be under the table." She chewed thoughtfully. "Or, I can add new centerpieces and tuck it in there."

"Don't do anything that will make them suspicious. A new thing on the table might trigger them."

"We used to have small plastic flowers on the table, but I made Mr. Byrne throw them all away. They were older than me and so gross. It's been a few months, but since we had something on the table for decades, I don't think they would suspect."

"I trust your judgment on that. Only do what you can without being noticed."

She smiled sadly. "Easy enough. Waitresses are usually unnoticed. I'm good at it."

"Once it's in, shoot me a text so I can make sure it's working."

"Okay."

"I have to get to work. Call me if you have any questions."

"Will do."

"Seriously, Chloe. If anything doesn't feel right, walk away. Ronan will literally kill me if anything happens to you."

She rolled her eyes, which still hurt like a motherfucker. "First, nothing will happen. What's Alan going to do? Second, Ronan won't be an issue."

"I doubt that."

She didn't remember everything from last night, but she did remember him showing up and being bossy and they broke up. "He showed up here last night and things didn't go well. That's part of why I didn't think you'd be here today. I figured he would've told you to stay away."

"He can be pushy like that, but it's usually with the best intentions."

"Doesn't feel that way. Thanks for trusting me to do this."

"No. Thank you. This might finally get us some answers."

She nodded and opened the front door for him. "You might not want to mention to your brother that you gave me the bug. It'll probably start a fight, and I don't want to be the cause of a rift between you."

"We're big boys, Chloe. Don't worry about us."

"Talk to you later."

She closed and locked the door. Then she ate a few more bites of the sandwich before crawling into bed. Her brain hurt and talking about Ronan and last night made her heart hurt.

But something about her breakup with Ronan hit her harder than when she left her fiancé, which made zero sense. It must've been the alcohol still muddling her brain. No way could her brief fling with Ronan Doyle mean more.

As sleep pulled her under, she was reminded of the lesson she thought she'd learned a long time ago: she didn't need a man.

Chloe tried not to be nervous—or at least not show her nervousness. She'd spent the last two days making new centerpieces for the tables. Mr. Byrne thought they looked nice, and he liked that they were cheap even better. She went with small black vases because between the color and the natural shade from the lighting, the bug would be camouflaged. Then she added some cute silk flowers.

She was setting each of the tables and she'd already texted Brendan to test the wire. It was working fine. They decided tonight would be the best night because Alan and Danny often had dinner together to go over construction company business.

She busied herself with routine bar and dinner prep to ease her nerves. She'd thought for sure by now Ronan would've reached out. She supposed she could've called him to apologize for her behavior. She'd been angry but to try to make him jealous was childish. Johnny had accepted her apology and said he hadn't been used to make a boyfriend jealous in a long time.

Danny arrived first, as usual. The more she thought about how much time the man spent at the Rose, it made her consider what his family life must be like. Did he not like them? Or did they all just do their own things? Until she was in college, she saw her parents every night. Most of the time, they had dinner together. She supposed Danny might eat dinner with his family. He usually just had a couple of drinks and held meetings. She texted Brendan to let him know Danny was here.

Brendan said he needed to be nearby to listen to the conversations. Chloe almost offered to let him set up something in the office. Mr. Byrne didn't spend too much time there, but she wasn't sure if she was willing to take that kind of risk. Mr. Byrne and Alan were still friends.

At Danny's table, she said, "Hi, Mr. Cahill. What can I get for you tonight?"

"Just a Guinness."

"Will your father be joining you?"

"Yes. He'll be here any minute, I'm sure."

"Would you like me to bring some menus, then?"

"I think we'll be having dinner," he said with a smile. "Sort of a celebration. But we won't need menus." He pulled out his phone and began scrolling, effectively dismissing her.

A celebration? She wondered what they'd be celebrating without their whole family. Not a birthday or anniversary. Must be something with the business then. As she headed to the bar to get the beer, she saw Alan Cahill walk through the door. Her heart sped up a little as the old man took his seat across from his son. As soon as he sat, he shifted the small vase over.

She delivered Danny's Guinness and asked Alan what he wanted.

Alan smiled at her and she suddenly realized that if she didn't know what the Doyles had told her, she would find him charming in that cute old man way. "I'll have a scotch. Neat. My son says we're celebrating something, but hasn't mentioned what."

She shrugged with a smile of her own. She hoped Danny wouldn't say anything until she returned. At the bar, she texted Brendan again. Danny says he has good news for Alan. On your way?

Be there soon. Listen in if possible.

She took the small glass of whiskey to the table. Danny had a creepy grin on his face.

"Do you know what you'd like for dinner?" She pulled out her order pad.

Alan leaned back in his seat. "I haven't had the shepherd's pie in a while."

"And for you?" she asked Danny.

"I'll have the filet mignon. Rare. Mashed potatoes."

She scribbled on her pad. "Anything else?"

The men shook their heads. She hurried to put in the order and then spent time cleaning the tables near the Cahills in an attempt to listen. Danny was damn near whispering, though. Not much of a celebration if it was a secret.

She moved one table closer.

"I've got the support," Danny said.

"But not the reputation," his father countered. "Why now? You've never shown any interest."

"The kids are older. The business is healthy. I'm ready to make my mark on the city just like you did. I thought you'd be happy."

"I'd be happy if you had a functioning brain cell."

Ouch.

Alan continued. "Do you have any idea the rigorous vetting that goes into even thinking about an election?"

"I've already talked to a strategist. She thinks that as long as I come out ahead of anything and talk about my addiction and sobriety, people will respect it."

Alan practically growled. "So you can drag me through the mud telling the world how I covered up all of your fuck-ups?"

"It won't come to that. The narrative reads that I'm a neighborhood boy who succumbed to his vices, but I ultimately cleaned up. I'm an upstanding citizen, father, businessman, and son of a former mayor."

"You plan to ride on my coattails. I should've figured."

"It doesn't matter if I want to exploit that or not. That's your legacy."

Chloe couldn't believe what she was hearing. Danny wanted to run for office?

"What about the rest of your ... transgressions? How are you going to skirt around those?"

"As far as anyone knows, my addictions were the only problem. I've been keeping an eye on Doyle. He's turning into quite the company man. He's quick to take on extra work for cash like his father. No suspicions."

"You don't know a damn thing. There are hundreds of companies that he could get a job with. Why come to us? Why now?"

As much as Chloe wanted to stay and listen to Danny's theory, she knew their food would be ready soon, and there were only so many tables she could wipe down in this section. On the way to the kitchen, she stopped in the hallway to text Brendan. Did you hear any of their conversation?

I just parked and set up. What'd I miss?

Danny is planning to run for office. He wants to follow in Alan's footsteps.

Fuck.

Chloe didn't know how to interpret that, so she went to check on the Cahills' order. When she carried the plates back to the table, she immediately recognized that Alan was even angrier. She set the plates down and simply asked, "Can I get you anything else?"

"No, thank you, Chloe," Danny said stiffly.

Dismissed again, she busied herself with her actual job, even though her curiosity was getting the better of her.

Every time she checked on the Cahills, the tension at the table had increased, but their conversation dropped to angry mutters and whispers. Alan was bent out of shape at the thought of Danny running for office.

They finally finished their meal. Alan left first and Danny had another drink by himself.

"How are you doing?" she asked.

Danny stared at her with expectant eyes.

"Not to be nosy, but you said you were celebrating something. Your dad didn't look too enthused."

"No, he wasn't. Don't know why I thought he would be. He still sees me as his young son who can't do anything right. He can't see that people grow and change."

Chloe nodded. She understood that a little too well. "Give him time and he might come around." Even she didn't believe that. "Let me know if I can get you anything else."

"Thank you." He downed the rest of his drink, tossed some bills on the table, and left.

As she cleared the table, she couldn't help but hope that this new turn of events would help the Doyles find answers. Yeah, *the Doyles*, as if her mind wasn't strictly on Ronan. She was still irritated with him and she didn't know where they stood anymore.

TWO DAYS AND RONAN WAS STILL MOPING AROUND. AT LEAST that's what Declan had said when Ronan walked into the kitchen to help install the countertop.

"Brendan said you pissed Chloe off. What'd you do?"

Ronan huffed. "Fuck if I know. When I saw her last, she was falling down drunk bitching about how I can't tell her what to do. Brendan thought she was pissed that I didn't invite her to Nessa's birthday party."

"Why didn't you?" his brother asked as he neatly leveled the counter.

"It's going to be at Mom's house and she's not ready for her family to know about us."

"Did you tell her that?"

"I didn't get the chance. She was too busy telling me that she called Brendan because he lets her make her own choices." Ronan itched to step in and make sure Declan was installing the counter properly, but he locked his knees. Declan had pulled through on the entire job.

"Shit. You should know better than to tell a woman what she can't do. Have you met our sister?"

"She's being reckless."

"With what? What're you trying to stop her from doing?"

Ronan paused. At some point, they'd have to come clean with their siblings. "Keep this between us for now."

He waited until Declan paused work, rose, and turned to face him. "Sounds serious."

"It is." He inhaled deeply and offered an abridged version. "Brendan and I have been working to find out what happened to Dad. We think Alan Cahill was behind it, and Chloe has access to him because she works at the Black Rose."

"Whoa." Declan raised a hand, then said again, "Whoa. You're doing what now?"

"It's complicated and we don't have all the info yet, but we know the Cahills are dirty. We're just trying to figure out how dirty. And Chloe keeps taking risks that could cost her her job." He reached into the fridge and grabbed a beer.

Declan sank to the floor. "Dad?"

Ronan passed him a beer.

"Brendan's been pressuring Mom to have him declared dead for years. Where is this coming from? I thought Dad just took off."

Ronan joined his brother on the floor. "I never for a minute believed he ran off—alone or with a woman."

"I just thought you said that because you didn't want to believe it."

"He's dead. I want to know the where and how." He took a pull of his beer. "No. I *need* to know."

Declan sat, stunned. "So Chloe knows, but you haven't told the rest of us? That's kind of shitty." He drank. "Unless you told the rest and it's just me you left out."

"No one knows. We can't afford word spreading. You know how that neighborhood is. Gossip is like water during a drought."

"Then why tell me now?"

"You asked. And I think we're getting close. To something, anyway. But don't go blabbing to everyone else. Not yet."

After another drink of beer, Ronan pushed up off the floor. "Come on. Let's get this done." He held out a hand to pull Declan to his feet.

"What do you think? I did better than you thought, right?"

"You did. I figured I'd be in here in a couple months finishing what you didn't. I would say that I could get you on a crew, but depending on how this shakes out, I might not have a job much longer."

"I could see how Cahill might have a problem with you causing trouble. What'll you do then?"

The thought had been nagging at him for a while. What would he do? He'd been focused on working for Cahill for so long, he hadn't considered anything else. But it was time.

"You could start your own company. I might consider working for you," Declan said.

"I would require you to not only show up every day but to be there early. There's no starting at ten o'clock."

Declan laughed. "When you're the owner, sure there is. What difference does it make what time I start as long as the job gets done?"

"Most customers don't want a carpenter hanging out in their house all night."

"You don't mind." He crawled back under the counter to make sure everything was fastened.

"I'm not a paying customer."

Declan bolted up, smacking his head in the process. "You're not? I'm working for free?"

"Room and board, man." Ronan lifted his beer with a smile.

"You're an asshole."

"Yeah, but you love me anyway. Besides, you know I'm kidding. You'll get paid." Now that the cabinets were almost finished, Ronan could see how good Declan was. He hoped paying him well would be enough of an incentive to get him to grow up and get a job. The man was a little old to still be couch surfing.

His phone buzzed in his pocket. When he checked it, hoping it was from Chloe, he saw a message from Brendan.

You need to come over. Chloe planted the bug and I got news.

"What the fuck? I'm going to kill him."

"Kill who?"

"Our oldest brother. He did it anyway. He used Chloe."

"Uh, not to be on the receiving end of this shitstorm, but I think I should point out that you've already said Chloe wanted to make her own decisions. I don't think Brendan made her do anything. If she's pissed, she'd do it just to spite you. Think Nessa."

Declan was right and he knew it. "I told him it was too risky for her."

"Sounds like she feels the risk is worth it." He thumped Ronan's shoulder. "Maybe she thinks you're worth it."

"She dumped me, remember?"

"You fought. She was mad and now she's proving a point." He dropped his empty bottle in the trash. "Dude, you should be paying me extra for teaching you about women."

"Yeah, sure. Add it to my tab." He finished his beer and held his phone, trying to figure out what to text Brendan.

I told you to leave Chloe out of this.

She wanted to help and we need all the help we can get.

You're an asshole.

I know.

Ronan put his phone away and looked at Declan. "Are you good here? I'm going to head over to Brendan's."

"Depends."

"On what?"

"If you're still planning on murder, I might need help. If you're just going to talk to him, I'm good."

Ronan shook his head. "If I planned to kill him, would I tell you?"

"Good point. If you punch him, though, get a picture. Video would be better. I'd like to see."

Ronan didn't what to say to that, so he left. He drove to Brendan's apartment and thought about what Declan had said. Chloe had a stubborn streak, so maybe she was just making a point. It didn't make him feel better or worry less about her.

By the time Brendan buzzed him in, he was calmer and much to Declan's disappointment, not likely to hit his brother.

Without even saying hi, Brendan said, "You're not going to fucking believe this."

"What?"

"Danny Cahill is planning to run for alderman in the next election. He broke the news to Alan today. Unfortunately, that part of the conversation happened when I was en route to the Rose to listen in, but Chloe heard it."

"What does this have to do with us?"

"It's the way Alan reacted. He didn't come right out with a confession, of course, but he berated Danny, talking about how the vetting process will dig up all of his transgressions. Then he drilled him on why you were working there. We know Alan doesn't trust you, but now Danny admitted that part of the reason for your promotion was to keep you close. Keep you happy, and just a little dirty, so you don't get suspicious."

"I guess he wasn't counting on me coming in with my suspicions."

"This election bid is just what we need. Danny needs to stay clean, so if his father did something to Dad, he'll want to distance himself. If Danny was the culprit, he'll be working double-time to make sure nothing sees the light of day."

Now Ronan saw where Brendan was going with this. "You think sending Nolan in to push a few buttons will work."

"I think if Nolan hits the right buttons, it'll send them both over the edge."

"How do we figure out what those buttons are?"

"Dad. He's gotta be the trigger. Danny was openly discussing his addictions with his father. He plans to get out in front of that. Make himself seem more average Joe, someone people can relate to since he's overcome his addictions."

"And if his focus is split between keeping an eye on me and looking pretty for the public, he won't see Nolan coming."

"Exactly. Now we just need a plan."

They spent the next couple of hours searching out information about Danny and his election aspirations. Other candidates were filing and announcing this week. Ronan never paid much attention to local politics, but seeing it laid out like this made it obvious that Danny was waiting for the perfect time to let the city know that the Cahill legacy was in play.

Ronan wanted nothing more than to take them down.

Chloe mostly got used to the bug being at the Cahills' table. She wasn't really nervous about it anymore. The bar had been buzzing since Danny announced his run for alderman. The clientele looked at him like he was a celebrity as he strode through the Rose smiling at his constituents.

Brendan started showing up to listen in even when Alan wasn't there. He seemed to think Danny's election bid was a new lead. She hadn't seen Alan in a few days and it had been even longer since she'd seen Ronan.

She felt shitty about the way she behaved but didn't know what to do about it. He acted as though they were done. It hurt, but she'd known what she was getting into.

Brendan had texted earlier in the day to let her know he'd convinced Joe Nolan to come to provoke the Cahills. Since she didn't know Nolan, she wasn't nervous about giving anything away.

Danny was at his table when she checked on other customers. "Hi, Mr. Cahill. What can I get for you tonight?"

"Just a Guinness."

"Anyone joining you this evening?"

"My father should be here soon."

She got his beer from the bar and delivered it. When she turned, she saw Alan Cahill walk through the door. Actually, it was more of a shuffle. His face was flushed and his bright blue eyes sparked.

"Hi, Mr. Cahill. How are you?" she asked as he neared.

"I've been better."

"You're looking a little flushed. Let me get you some water."

"Only if it's with a whiskey." He winked at her, but he didn't look well.

She brought his whiskey but added a glass of water to her tray. Alan was already grumbling at Danny when she set the glasses in front of him.

"If you need anything else, just give me a holler."

She walked away and only heard Danny ask, "What does he want? He hasn't worked for you for years."

Chloe assumed they were talking about Joe Nolan. She'd never met Nolan, so she didn't know what to expect. She pulled out her phone to send Brendan a text about the tension at the Cahill table, but then she realized he was probably listening. She'd never make it as a spy. Too many moving parts to keep track of while putting on a face of innocence. She'd take restaurant work over that any day.

That made her think about everything that Ronan was dealing with. He was interacting with his family again while still digging for answers about his dad. The face he had to put on each time he had to deal with the Cahills must've been difficult. He certainly didn't need additional pressure from her.

Since the bar was quiet in this pre-dinner hour, and her only responsibility was the Cahills, she waved to Johnny to let him know she was taking five and she stepped out back to call Ronan. The phone rang three or four times and she was about to hang up, assuming he didn't want to talk to her.

"Hey," he said.

Just like that. Like it had only been a few hours instead of days since they'd spoken.

"Hey." All of a sudden, her heart filled and her chest became tight. Just from hearing the sound of his voice. Her emotions choked her and the words wouldn't come.

"Chloe? You still there?"

Swallowing quickly, she said, "Yeah, I'm here. It's good to hear your voice."

"Yours, too."

"Look. I'm sorry about the other night. I don't know what got into me. I felt like you were pushing me away and trying to control me all at once, and then Johnny made these drinks that knocked me on my ass. So I was mad and wanted you to be too. But it wasn't fair."

"Babe."

The single word had her sucking in a breath.

"You're rambling," he said.

"I don't want you to be mad at me. I don't want to fight."

"Neither do I."

"Can you come over when I get off work so we can talk?" she asked hesitantly.

"You can drive me home."

"Where are you?" She looked around as if he'd be there.

"Sitting in Brendan's car listening to the Cahills."

He was here. "I wish I could see you sooner."

"It won't be too long."

Before she could say anything else, he was talking to someone else, probably Brendan.

"Nolan is coming down the block, so you'll need to get back to work."

"See you soon." She hung up, tucked her phone in her pocket, and went back to the bar.

Although she didn't know who Nolan was, when a tall, older man came in and waved Jana, the hostess, off, Chloe figured it was him. Then he made a beeline for the Cahills. The man looked sketchy, peering over his shoulder like he was being watched. She didn't want to look like she knew where he was going, so she waited a minute and then approached the table.

"Hi. Can I get you anything?"

Alan waved her off. "He won't be staying long enough to finish a drink."

"Okay." She tried not to sound too cheerful in covering up her shock at his abruptness. While Alan was often brusque with Danny, he'd always been polite to her. "How about either of you? Need refills?"

"No, we're good, Chloe. Thank you," Danny said.

She walked away and restrained herself from looking back to watch the drama unfold.

RONAN SAT IN BRENDAN'S CAR BESIDE HIS BROTHER, THE conversation inside the Rose coming across the laptop speaker clearly. He leaned back in the passenger seat in an attempt to stretch his legs.

"Why the hell did I need to be here for this? It doesn't take two of us to listen," Ronan grumbled.

"Because if Nolan doesn't make them panic enough, I'm going to go in for a beer and make sure both Nolan and the Cahills see me. Let them know I'm onto them. I need you here to keep listening."

He definitely wasn't cut out to be a cop. All the sitting and waiting was horrible.

"Besides, aren't you glad I dragged your ass along? Now you get to have Chloe take you home."

"Or I could've just driven to her house later when she gets off work. And used this time to do something productive."

"Like what?"

"Anything has to be better than sitting here." His ears perked up at the sound of Chloe's voice as she asked Nolan if he wanted to order.

As Alan brushed her off, Brendan said, "Old man's already irritated. That's a good sign."

"Do you know what Nolan said to him to get him to take a meeting?"

"Something along the lines of 'We've got a problem.' I didn't ask."

They dropped into silence and waited to hear the conversation.

"Well?" Alan asked.

"Brendan Doyle came to see me. Asking questions about twenty years ago and the election."

"What about it?"

"He asked who worked on the campaign, if I was aware of anything shady going on." Nolan paused. "He asked about whether his father worked the campaign."

"What did you tell him?"

"Nothing. But he's FBI."

"Doesn't matter. Even if he digs something up, the statute

of limitations is passed. Nothing he can do. It's not worth his time. In fact, you should tell him so."

"What about his father?"

Brendan smacked Ronan's arm. "This is it."

"What about him?" Alan asked.

"Where'd he go?"

"How the hell should I know?" Alan's voice was sharp.

"Look, I don't know the details, but we both know there was a lot done back then that isn't covered by the statute running out."

Nolan was met with silence.

Ronan's heart sank. This plan wasn't going to work. It was their only shot. "Fuck," he whispered.

"You look here," Alan said. "Keep your mouth shut. You'll be taken care of like always. Doyle's got nothing and we'll keep it that way."

"Are you going in?" Ronan asked.

"Nah. My presence isn't enough of a threat if he thinks I'm chasing him for election fraud."

"Taken care of how? I'm ready to retire. You gonna make that happen?" Nolan pressed. "And now Danny here is following in your footsteps. How much covering up are you gonna do to make that happen?"

Alan's voice was a harsh rasp. "Stop being a weasel. I'll get you some cash. You keep your mouth shut."

"I guess we'll see how much you think my silence is worth. It'll be a lot harder to get Danny into office. The wrong people start asking the right questions and not only will he not get elected, but they'll come looking for both of you."

Alan began to sputter, but the shuffling led Ronan to believe Nolan left. Sure enough, the front door to the Rose opened and Nolan strode out. A moment later, Brendan's phone rang. Brendan stepped out of the car to talk.

Ronan continued to listen to Alan berate Nolan in his absence.

Finally, Danny spoke up. "What are we going to do about Doyle?"

"Not a fucking thing. That family has been a boil on my ass for twenty years. Let him dig. He doesn't even know where to look."

"Dad, calm down."

"Don't tell me to calm down. You made this mess and I keep having to clean up after you!" Alan was full-on yelling now. "I told you this would happen. Putting yourself in the public eye. Thinking you could be me."

Then there was nothing but chaos. Danny was yelling at his dad, dishes sounded like they were being thrown, someone screamed to call nine-one-one. Ronan was halfway out of the car when Brendan grabbed his arm.

"What's going on?"

"I don't know. All hell's breaking loose in there."

Brendan picked up the laptop to listen.

Ronan took off toward the bar. He ran inside and looked around. A crowd had gathered near the Cahills' table. Then he saw Chloe talking on the phone. She was fine. All of the other sounds fell away and he focused on her voice. As she spoke, he realized Alan Cahill had a heart attack.

He returned his attention to Cahill's table. As the crowd shifted, he saw Alan on the floor, Danny holding his hand and talking close to his father's face.

How could things possibly get worse? He moved closer to the bar and leaned against the counter as his heart rate returned to normal.

Sirens wailed down the block announcing the arrival of the ambulance. Within minutes, paramedics rushed through the door. Chloe ushered customers back to their tables and called over to the bartender to get everyone more drinks. Then she noticed him and hurried over.

"What are you doing in here?"

"I heard everything going to hell and needed to make sure you were okay."

Her eyes were wide and when she spoke, her arms were flailing. "Alan was yelling at Danny and then he just fell over. He didn't look good when he got here. He's been worked up pretty much the whole time."

"Hey, Chloe," someone called from behind them.

"I have to get back to dealing with this."

"I'll be here."

Relief crossed her face and gave him no small amount of satisfaction. He looked over her head as the paramedics wheeled Alan out, Danny on their heels. His gaze met Ronan's, but his expression was blank like he didn't even recognize him.

His phone buzzed in his pocket. Brendan.

"What the fuck is going on?"

"Alan collapsed. Chloe said he wasn't looking good when he got here. They're taking him out now."

Danny and his father were tucked into the back of the ambulance and the vehicle screamed away from the bar.

"Well, fuck," Brendan said.

"What now?"

"I'll find out what's happening to Cahill. You want me to drop you off at home?"

"No. I'm going to stay here. Find out what Chloe saw. Get her perspective."

"Grab my wire while you're in there. No sense in leaving it where it might get found."

"Call me when you know something."

"You, too."

Ronan took a seat at the bar and ordered a beer. Once Chloe had the Cahills' table cleared off, Ronan walked over there and took the booth. His gaze tracked Chloe's movements as she wove through the tables checking on customers. Her smile was bright but phony. Alan Cahill had rattled her, but she wasn't showing it. Not to people who didn't know her. He noticed the stiff line of her shoulders and the frozen curve of her lips.

He hated seeing her like this. Knowing that he was the cause of at least part of that weighed on him. This was why he didn't want to involve her. He and Brendan were stirring up a hornets' nest and she was stuck in the middle. The voice deep in his head berated him for being here, for not staying away from her, for wanting to be with her no matter what.

But at this point, he wasn't sure she'd still have him.

CHLOE WAS BEYOND OVERWHELMED. SHE'D DONE WHAT SHE could to calm customers who witnessed Alan collapse. A few regulars were sweet and tried to check on her, but she couldn't think about how any of the events from tonight might affect her. So she just kept moving. As much of a distraction as Ronan usually was for her, his presence bolstered her. He didn't have to say anything, but she felt his watchful gaze on her. She was a little surprised when he moved to take the Cahills' table, but then she realized he was probably removing the bug.

And of course, right now, no one else wanted to sit there, as if the booth had caused Alan to keel over.

After the wave of customers who had been present during the emergency had left, things settled down. Fresh faces filled the bar, people who had no clue about the excitement from earlier. As things slowed down, her adrenaline finally started to wane. She called Mr. Byrne to let him know what happened. The man would be worried about his friend. Mrs. Byrne immediately yelled at him for not telling Chloe she should close early and send everyone home. She assured them that the bar was fine now and the current customers were unaware of the emergency.

The conversation went on for a few minutes and her hands began to shake. She sank to the chair behind the desk in the office, suddenly feeling weak.

"Chloe? Is everything okay?" Mr. Byrne asked.

"Yeah. I mean, I'm feeling a bit off now that the chaos is over. I think I'm going to head home a little early if that's okay. Johnny is here to close."

"Of course. Whatever you need."

"Thank you." She disconnected and rested her head on her hand propped on the desk. A wave of wooziness hit her. What the hell was going on?

A knock sounded at the office door. Crap. Couldn't she just get like five minutes of peace to get her shit together? "Yes?" she called, straightening.

The door cracked open and Ronan's face poked through the space. "Hey."

"Oh, it's you." She sank back, not feeling the need to feign politeness.

"Can I come in?"

She just waved.

Once he was through the door, he took one look at her and rushed over. "Are you all right?"

"I'm fine." She took a deep breath. "Just a little overwhelmed from everything and my body is letting me know it's stressed. I'll be okay in a few minutes."

He reached for her hand. "You're freezing." He rubbed her hand between his. "Can I get you something to eat or drink?"

"Actually, I'm going home."

"You ready to leave now?"

"Yeah. I just need to let Johnny know he's closing." She stood and wobbled a bit.

Ronan steadied her. "How about *I* go tell Johnny and then we'll go?"

She plopped back onto the chair. "Sounds good."

While he was gone, she rifled through the desk drawer for a snack. Maybe a hit of sugar would help. She found a bag of M&Ms and poured a handful into her palm. Her mouth watered and her stomach grumbled. Then she remembered that she hadn't eaten dinner yet. She'd planned to grab something from the kitchen after the Cahills left for the night.

With a deep breath, she stood. She was a little steadier on her feet. They could stop and grab some food on the way to her place.

Ronan came back into the office. "Whoa."

"I'm fine. I just realized part of my problem is that I haven't eaten. With knowing about Nolan and everything..." She sighed again. "We can pick up something. I'm fine." At his skeptical look, she added, "Really."

She gathered her things and waved goodbye to Johnny. At her car, she unlocked the doors, but then Ronan gently took her hand and removed the keys.

"I'll drive." He opened the passenger door for her and she got in.

"I'm fine."

"I know." He closed the door and walked around the car. He squeezed behind the wheel and adjusted the seat and mirrors. "I'll feel better having something to do. I've been stuck all night with my hands tied."

She didn't put up a fight. She was tired. Tired of the Cahills and tired of fighting with Ronan. Just everything.

"About the other night..."

She held up a hand. "Can we not? I don't have it in me for a big discussion or a fight. Can we just let it sit until later?"

He nodded. He hit a drive-thru on the way to her apartment and ordered a mountain of food.

"How many people are you feeding?"

"You're not the only one who skipped dinner." He set the bags on the floor behind her.

When they got to her building, she trudged up to her apartment. Ronan still hadn't said anything. They ate their food in silence, tension filling the air until she couldn't take it anymore.

"What are we doing?"

He looked at her with confusion. "Eating dinner."

"You know what I mean. Why are you here? Trying to take care of me."

"You said you didn't want to talk about it."

"Sitting here in silence is worse than talking about it." At least she hoped. It couldn't possibly be worse than the other night.

He pushed back from his food. "It was brought to my attention that you might've been upset that I didn't mention Nessa's party to you."

She raised her eyebrows. He needed that pointed out to him?

"I should've explained."

"What's there to explain? You said you wanted a relationship, but then you didn't invite me to a family party. It's just a birthday party. It's not like it was a wedding or anything."

He huffed a sigh. "It's a party that will be in my mother's backyard. Right across the street from your parents. There would be no keeping this from them if you're at our house."

"Oh." Now she felt shitty all over. "I'm sorry. I totally read that wrong."

"I could've explained. I figured you knew. I didn't want you to feel pressured into telling them before you're ready." He inched closer to her. He slid his hand along her jaw. "But know this. I would never be embarrassed or ashamed to be with you. I don't care if the world knows."

And just like that, all the tension weighing on her melted away. She pressed forward and kissed him. When she pulled back, she said, "I still don't like you telling me what I can and can't do."

"I don't want my crap to ruin anything for you. I've fucked up enough in my life. I don't want that to touch you. Plus, your parents already don't like me. I don't need to give them more reason."

"They'll have to get over it because I like you very much."

"You make it sound easy."

"Loving someone should be easy. Don't you think?"

"Don't know. This is new territory for me."

"Me, too. But I haven't felt this good about being with someone in a long time."

"And Johnny?"

"What about Johnny?"

He just stared at her, waiting for an explanation.

"I was mad at you and wanted to make you mad, too. Nothing was ever going to happen with Johnny. I was in no shape to drive and then you were there and it made me mad all over."

He lowered his face again to stare directly into her eyes. "No more games."

She smiled. "No more being bossy."

"No guarantees."

"I guess sometimes a little bossy is okay."

"Yeah?"

She stood. "Yeah. Like in the bedroom. A little bossy there is good."

"That I can do." He rose. "Lead the way."

Ronan woke to the sound of his phone. Chloe's body was wrapped around him and he didn't want to move. He loved the feel of her against him, but the only person who would call this late was Brendan. He shifted and eased out from under Chloe. Then he sat up and took his phone to the other room.

"Yeah?"

"Cahill's dead."

"What?"

"Massive heart attack. He got to the hospital and they worked on him. He was stable for a little while but then had another attack. He's gone."

Ronan sank to the couch as the full meaning of Brendan's words hit him. Alan Cahill was gone and he was the only lead they had to find out what happened to their father. "Fuck."

"That about sums it up."

"What do we do now?"

"Give me a couple of days to regroup. Alan might've been

hiding something, but that doesn't mean no one else has information."

"It's a hell of a roadblock."

"I'll let you know if I find anything." His brother disconnected and Ronan tossed his phone to the side.

"What happened?" Chloe asked from the doorway.

"Alan Cahill died." He leaned his head back and closed his eyes.

"What did we do?"

He sat up. "We didn't do anything."

"We set up Nolan to come and rattle him."

"You said he didn't look good when he got there."

"But then Nolan got him upset."

Ronan stood and took Chloe's hand. "He was an old man. None of this is on you."

"It might be. You don't know that. That plan might've pushed him over the edge." Her eyes were filled with genuine concern for a man they knew was far from good.

"If he hadn't been hiding illegal activities, maybe he would've been healthier. Hell, if he hadn't participated in those activities, he might still be here. I'm not the bad guy here." He wasn't going to try to muster regret for what they'd done. In the grand scheme of things, they were barely pressing.

"I'm not saying you are. But a man is dead."

"From a heart attack. It's not like we murdered him. Maybe his time was just up."

Her shoulders slumped. "I still feel bad."

Once again, she was proving she was too good. The only reason this news upset him was because Alan took all the information with him. "Come on. Let's go back to sleep. You can go to church and light a candle for him." The old man could use all the help he could get.

"My mom would like for me to join them for Mass other than when my brother is doing it. It would probably help if I believed lighting a candle would make a difference."

Ronan had nothing to add to that. He wasn't a church-goer or true believer, so he didn't hold out hope a candle would save Alan's soul. He led her back to bed, but sleep eluded him. His mind raced trying to find new possibilities. Would people be more likely to talk now that Cahill was dead? Or would they all continue to keep his secrets?

He lay there for hours replaying every conversation he'd had with Danny Cahill. Nolan had sworn up and down that he didn't know what had happened to his father. But he'd always suspected Alan knew more.

Did Danny? Danny was an adult when their dad went missing. Mom had never mentioned Danny, only Alan. And the old-timers led Ronan to believe Danny spent more time high than anything. Ronan wondered if he would've paid attention to anything his father did. Would it hurt to ask?

He could lose his job.

Possibly be branded as a troublemaker and get blackballed.

It would tip their hand.

He eased out of bed again and got dressed. Looking at Chloe peacefully asleep, he knew he wanted to have more with her. Build a life. A normal life. But he wouldn't be able to do that until he put the rest to bed. If things blew up any more, he didn't want her in the blast radius. He had no doubt she would stand by him, but he wouldn't risk her.

After gathering his things, he picked up her phone and took it with him to the living room. Then he left her a message to explain as best he could. She'd still be pissed. But at least he wasn't telling her what to do.

CHLOE WOKE THE FOLLOWING MORNING AND RONAN WAS GONE. He hadn't said anything about having to go early. She'd been so knocked out that she hadn't even felt him leave. She went to the kitchen to make some coffee and call the Byrnes to give them an update about last night. She picked up her phone to call Ronan first and then the Byrnes, but she saw she had a couple of missed calls from her mom and a voicemail from Ronan. Why would he call in the middle of the night? Was that when he left?

She put the phone on speaker and hit the button to listen to the voicemail while she readied coffee.

"Hey, Chloe. I couldn't sleep, and I didn't want to disturb you. I'm spinning out right now. All the work. All the digging. It all led to Alan and now he's gone. I need to keep searching for answers. I need a little space. Not a lot, and I'm not walking away from us or what we could have. I want all of it with you, but I need to finish this first. I hope you understand."

She stood there with a scoop of coffee in one hand and stared at her phone. What the hell was that? Last night they'd talked about wanting to be together. A real relationship and he couldn't even make it through the night? She dumped the grounds into the coffeemaker and replayed the message. Without caffeine in her system, maybe she misunderstood the message.

The second time was only a little better. This time she focused on the positives of what he'd said. He wanted to be with her. Last night she'd thought he was being a little callous about Alan's death, but now she was seeing it differently. He and Brendan had been holding on to the hope of getting their answers from Alan. What would they do now?

She picked up her phone again to call the Byrnes, but a knock on her front door stopped her. She opened the door, hoping it was Ronan, but her mother pushed her way in.

"Are you okay? You're awake but didn't answer the phone or return my call. I heard about Alan Cahill. You were there? It must've been awful."

Chloe barely had the door closed before her mother had gripped her shoulders and stared into her face.

"Are you in shock? Should I call the doctor?"

Chloe blinked. "I'm fine, Mom. It was a lot to handle last night, but I handled it. The ambulance arrived and took Alan to the hospital."

Her mom pulled her into a hug. "Oh, honey. You don't know. Alan died last night."

She wasn't sure why her mother was hugging her, as if Alan had been a friend or something other than a regular customer. She pulled out of her mother's embrace. "I'm okay, Mom."

"You look awful."

Chloe turned so her mom wouldn't see her eyeroll. "It was a rough night and I just woke up. Do you want some coffee?"

"That would be lovely. But let me get it. Go sit down."

Chloe sat and waited until her mom returned with two cups. "How did you find out that Alan died? What happened?"

"Mrs. Byrne called me first thing. She'd gone to the hospital last night to be with the family. Alan had another massive heart attack in the middle of the night. Danny is so distraught. Everything rests on his shoulders now."

"Why? He's not an only child."

"His mother will lean on him. He's already running the construction company. Now he'll have to handle everything. I don't know how he'll be able to continue his campaign."

"What about the rest of the family?"

"I don't know what his older brother is doing, His sister died a few years ago. Cancer. She did have children though. Two daughters, I think." Her mom shook her head. "I'm sure they have nothing to do with Alan's businesses. They must be about your age. Probably have their own lives and careers. Families."

Chloe filed that tidbit away to relay to Ronan and Brendan. Her mom laid a hand on Chloe's wrist.

"Are you sure you're all right?"

"Yeah, Mom. Thanks for checking on me."

"I told you you should get a new job."

Chloe closed her eyes and took a deep breath. "Where I work has nothing to do with what happened. If I worked in an office, one of my co-workers could drop dead in the cubicle next to me. Stuff happens. No one can control that."

Her mother didn't respond. Chloe knew there was no convincing her. They sat in silence, drinking their coffee. Chloe considered how to tell her mom about her and Ronan. Maybe blurting it out would be best. Inhaling deeply, she braced herself.

Then her phone rang. Part of her hoped it was Ronan. It would give her a way to bring it up, but it was Mr. Byrne.

"Excuse me, Mom. This is Mr. Byrne." She stood and walked into the kitchen. "Hello, Mr. Byrne."

"Hi, Chloe. Sorry to bother you so early, especially after

last night. I'm calling because the Cahills are planning Alan's funeral. They want the funeral to be a small family affair, but since he was so well known, there needs to be a public event. I offered to host a wake at the Rose. We'll be open regular hours today and tomorrow, but Tuesday we'll be closed to regular business after three. Word will go out immediately, so we need to have all hands available for the mourners. We won't be serving a full menu. Drinks and appetizers for the guests. I expect hundreds of people to stop by."

Chloe leaned against her counter and pulled a pad of paper in front of her. "Okay. Do you have a list of appetizers? I'm sure you don't want to offer everything on the menu. And are we just keeping food out for guests, or are we allowing them to order?"

"I haven't had a chance to go over the details with the Cahills, but I prefer to just have a buffet set up with appetizers. I'll leave the selection up to you. Soft drinks will be no charge, but everything else is a cash bar. The Cahills have enough to deal with without having to worry about a bar tab, and I know this neighborhood. If they think they drink for free, they'll break the bank."

Chloe smiled as she took notes. "I'll develop a menu and send it to you for approval. Then I'll create signs to keep on the tables and one for the door to let people know we're closed for regular business. Is there anything else I can do?"

"Not that I can think of right now."

"I'm sorry for your loss, Mr. Byrne. I know Mr. Cahill was a good friend."

"Thank you for everything, Chloe. You're a godsend."

They disconnected and Chloe took her pad back to where her mother sat waiting. "Sorry about that. Mr. Byrne wants to have a wake for Alan Cahill at the Rose. I have a lot of planning to do today to get ready."

"I guess that's my cue to head home." She rinsed her cup in the kitchen sink and then hugged Chloe. "You're a good girl."

Yeah, when I'm not being a disappointment. "Thanks, Mom. I'll talk to you later."

After taking a shower and getting dressed, Chloe sent a quick text to both Ronan and Brendan about the wake for Alan. She didn't know if it would matter, but in her experience, drunk people liked to reminisce and talk about the dead. Someone might spill and talk about things they shouldn't.

Neither of the Doyle men responded. Of course. She didn't have time to stress. Mr. Byrne was counting on her to pull off a wake, so she had a lot to do. Even as she made her to-do list, though, she added a mental item to talk to Ronan about his cryptic message.

RONAN AND BRENDAN AGREED TO GO TOGETHER TO TALK TO their mom. She believed Alan was a good guy who helped her out after Dad disappeared. Even though they believed she was being naïve, she considered him a friend. Brendan was already there waiting in his car when Ronan parked his truck. They met on the lawn.

"What? Afraid to go in without me?"

"Funny," Brendan answered. "I thought we should do this together."

Side by side, they walked up the front steps. Brendan

knocked but didn't wait for an answer. He twisted the knob and they strode in. "Hey, Mom. You up here?"

She came from the kitchen and looked at them oddly. "What are the two of you doing here?"

"We need to talk," Brendan said.

She settled on the armchair in the living room. Brendan sat near her on the couch. Ronan chose to stand.

"What's happened? Who's hurt?" she asked quietly but firmly.

"Alan Cahill died," Brendan said.

Ronan stared at their mother, watching her reaction. Her hand slowly moved to her mouth and pressed against her lips.

Before she said anything, Brendan continued. "He had a heart attack."

She lowered her hand and pinned Ronan with a look. "And why are you here delivering this news? I'm sure as soon as I step outside, someone would be talking about it."

"We think—" Brendan started.

"We more than think. Alan had something to do with Dad going missing. Brendan and I have been working to find some answers."

"I told you that the Cahills didn't have anything to do with it."

"Why do you think that? Because he gave you money? They think they can buy their way out of everything."

She rose and stared up at him. "You don't understand. There are a lot of things you don't know. Things were different back then, but Alan was never evil."

"Evil or not, he was shady as fuck." Ronan's voice rose as his mother's quieted. They expressed anger so differently, but they recognized when nothing was changing.

He waited for her to reprimand him for his language. Instead, she sucked in a sharp inhale.

"You're going to keep pushing the Cahills, aren't you?"

Brendan finally stood. "We have to, Mom. Someone knows something."

"At least have the decency to leave them alone in their grief." Then she turned and walked back to the kitchen.

The brothers watched her leave and then stared at each other as if to ask if they should follow.

"Shit. You pissed her off. I'm not going in there."

Ronan shook his head. "I'm pretty sure that was her way of telling us to leave her alone. Come on."

They left the house and stood outside his truck. "Why does she keep believing in him?" Ronan asked.

Brendan sighed. "We were kids. We didn't know anything other than Dad was gone. We never considered what it was like for her." He paused. "What it is like for her."

"What?"

"She lost her husband. She's held her shit together for all of these years. Think about it. Did you ever see her fall apart?"

Ronan shook his head. Their mother was made of nothing less than steel.

"She did that for us. And now we're here telling her that the support system she had—no matter how shitty it was—is the cause of everything."

A stab of guilt jabbed into Ronan's chest. He was an idiot. He couldn't imagine his mom not being okay. She just handled things, did what she had to do. He'd never thought that she considered Alan a friend.

"See you at the wake?" Brendan asked.

Ronan looked at him. "You're coming to that?"

Brendan huffed. "Just because Mom thinks we should leave them alone, doesn't mean we should. I want Danny to know we're still here looking for answers. Nolan asking questions was just the beginning."

"You're an asshole."

"Takes one to know one. And you like me this way."

Ronan shook his head. He did like his brother. He'd missed him over the last few years even if they did butt heads constantly. "See you there."

Ronan met with Thomas Walsh and the other superintendents at the Cahill office. They all looked and felt out of place. Alan and Danny kept a small office storefront not far from where they lived, but everyone knew that the real business was always conducted at the Rose. When Danny needed to talk to one of them, it was either at the Rose or he came to the site. With the exception of the day they were hired, Ronan doubted any of them had spent any time in this office.

Thomas cleared his throat. "For any of you who haven't heard the news yet, Alan Cahill, Danny's father, died last night. Danny is stepping away from daily operations for the week as he deals with his family affairs. Most things won't change. Your jobs will continue as usual. If anyone is interested in paying their respects, there is a wake being held at the Black Rose tomorrow afternoon into the evening. The family asks that we assemble then. They want to keep the funeral small and we are not invited to participate in that."

Ronan looked at the other guys. No one said anything.

What was there to say? Although they all knew Alan, except for a few old-timers, Danny had been their boss since hiring. Thomas dismissed them and they filtered out to their respective trucks. Ronan moved on autopilot once again. Brendan had no new ideas when they spoke yesterday.

When Chloe had texted about the wake, he wanted to respond. He wanted to talk to her, see her, hold her. But once again, he felt stuck in his life. For him, Chloe was movement forward, toward a new future. He just couldn't see that future until he found the answers he'd been searching for.

And it felt like they were close. At least closer. On the brink of getting somewhere. Until now. Then again, maybe it had all been in his head.

He went to the job site and shared the information with his crew. The attitude of the older guys shifted. Ronan saw their realization of mortality. Sure, Alan was older than any of them, but he had been younger once. He had worked on the crews, unlike his son. It was part of the reason so many people respected him. He was a man of the people.

Ronan knew it was bullshit. It didn't matter how a man got his money. Once he was rich, he was like every other rich asshole out there. Only out for number one. Somehow, Danny Cahill knew something or played a role in his father's disappearance. He was sure of it now. But for the life of him, he couldn't think of any next steps.

Instead of spending his day telling everyone else what to do, he joined his crew in doing the heavy lifting. He needed the physical exhaustion to keep his mind quiet. By the time he was heading home, he was sweaty and dirty and beat.

He parked in the first spot on the block he saw because he didn't want to circle the block to look for parking closer to his house. He grabbed his tool belt in case he couldn't sleep and wanted to do more work at home. His brain was foggy, so it took a full minute for him to realize that Chloe was sitting on his front steps. At first, he thought it was a mirage. As he got closer, she stood. For the first time all day, he was able to breathe deeply. The tightness in his chest loosened. His muscles relaxed.

"Hey," she said quietly.

"What are you doing here?"

"I know you want some space, but I didn't think you should be alone right now."

"My asshole brother didn't let you in?"

She smiled. "I don't think Declan is home. No one answered when I knocked."

"With him, that doesn't mean anything. He might be taking a nap. Or just ignoring the knock."

She took a deep breath, stepped closer, and moved to wrap her arms around him.

He jerked away. The shocked look on her face made him feel like an even bigger asshole. "I'm gross from work. You don't want to touch me right now." He reached for her hand. "Let me take a shower and then you can hug me all you want."

He led her up the stairs. "Shouldn't you be at work?"

"I spent the day planning Alan's wake. I'm going to be there running things all day tomorrow. Being here was more important."

His chest thumped at her words. He couldn't remember the last time someone treated him as important. "I'm glad you're here."

Inside, he dropped his tools near the entryway. Then he peeled off his shirt. "Grab yourself a beer and get comfortable. I'll be out in a few."

"I'm going to order some dinner. What do you want?"

He turned and smiled at her. "Whatever you want is fine. I might not be great company tonight."

"I don't care. I want to be with you and it doesn't matter how much you try to push me away. I know you want to be with me."

His lungs froze. He didn't know what to say to that. She was right on every count. He crossed the room. With his left hand, he cradled her jaw and lifted her lips to his. He kissed her deeply and the contact relaxed every racing nerve in his body. A sense of peace wafted through his brain.

When they separated, whispered words fled from his mouth. "God, I love you."

As soon as they were in the open, he froze again. Waited. Did he just fuck up a perfect kiss?

Her eyes fluttered open and her gorgeous lips curved up.

"You don't have to say anything. I'm going to take my shower." He pulled away, not wanting to hear that she wasn't ready or that she wasn't there yet, and might never be. He'd wash his regret down the drain.

"Wait." She tugged his hand. "I love you, too, Ronan. I wasn't expecting to be ready to say it right now. But it fits. It feels right." She stood on tiptoe and pressed her lips to his again.

This time as he stepped away, their eyes remained locked until he got to the hall to turn into the bathroom. He had no idea what he'd done to deserve to have a woman like Chloe in his life at all, let alone have her love him, but he had to make sure he didn't fuck it up.

CHLOE WENT TO THE ROSE FIRST THING IN THE MORNING TO make sure everything was ready for the wake. She was tired but felt great. Her giddiness over Ronan's declaration last night hadn't faded. She'd known he had feelings for her, had cared about her, but she hadn't expected him to say that he loved her. But as she had said to him, it was right. For the first time in years, she was happy. She felt safe and loved.

No, they weren't perfect, but they were working through things. They both needed to learn to trust a little more and open to each other even when it was difficult. She had yet to talk to him about her relationship with Tim, but she knew she needed to. She had to find the words to explain it—once she figured out the words for herself. She had too much going on right now.

At the Rose, after she had things moving in the kitchen, she had servers rearranging the tables to allow for people to sit in larger groups. She also made room at Alan's table for a small memorial. The family had a poster made and there were flowers ready to go.

Johnny came up beside her as she was studying the placement of the flowers and the picture.

"Gotta love an Irish wake, huh?"

"These guys like to drink. They'll act like Alan Cahill was such a great guy."

"Was he?"

She shrugged. "In my experience, people are rarely as good as their fans make them out to be. He was a politician at heart."

"I hear you. I don't trust politicians either."

She smiled. "I've got the full staff coming in for the evening rush. The family is keeping the funeral low-key so I'm guessing most of the neighborhood will turn up here."

"Plus, we have the alcohol."

"You know it. You need any help behind the bar before the others get here?"

"Nah. I'm good. Fully stocked. Why don't you go take a break? You probably won't get one later."

"I will. I just want to make sure everything is set up." She shifted the flowers over a bit and stepped back again.

"So...I, uh, I've been meaning to ask. Everything okay with your boyfriend?"

She started at the question because she was so used to her relationship with Ronan being a secret. Sometimes she forgot that there were people who knew. "Actually, yes. We're really good."

"I'm glad. You deserve to be happy."

"Thanks."

Johnny went back to the bar and Chloe puttered around, rolling more silverware into napkins and running through her checklist. Ronan had been right about one thing: she had to talk to her family. Not about Tim. He no longer mattered in her life. She wanted to tell them she and Ronan were a couple. Nessa's party was happening on Saturday and she planned to be there. Her parents would have to get used to the idea.

Her stomach turned over. What if they didn't?

She sat down at the table where she'd been setting up. Her family loved her. She knew that. But she'd spent her whole life afraid of disappointing them, worried about what they thought of her. Somehow, they saw the disappointments as phases she was going through like she would just come around one day. She'd made it clear there was no chance she was getting back together with Tim once she left, and her mother seemed to be coming around to the idea that she enjoyed managing the Rose. Could she expect them to accept her love for Ronan? What if they assumed it would pass?

What if it didn't?

They wouldn't cut her off or disown her. No matter how mad her mom may get, she always cooled off. And her siblings never cared about who she dated. What was the worst that could happen? Her mother would continue with snarky comments? Chloe was beyond used to that.

But she wouldn't stand for her mom to make Ronan feel bad. If Mom couldn't be nice to Ronan, she wouldn't bring Ronan around the family. The stress lifted from her chest. The anxiety she carried about telling her parents about her feelings for Ronan slipped away.

She jumped up and texted Ronan. I'm going to talk to my parents on Saturday before Nessa's party. I want the world to know we love each other.

She knew he was working, so he might not see the text, but she wanted him to know she was committed.

They would make this work.

By the time afternoon hit, Chloe needed the break Johnny offered. Between prepping for the wake, fielding calls from the Byrnes, and making sure they'd have enough staff, on top of the secrets she was keeping was enough to drain her emotionally. She let Johnny know she was going home to change before the wake. While it was a break she desperately needed, she had also been raised to know that wearing her usual jeans and T-shirt were not appropriate attire for a wake. She pushed through the front door of her building, climbed the first three steps, and froze.

Danny Cahill was standing in front of her apartment. Her heart thumped. What the hell was he doing here? How did he know where she lived?

"Uh, hi, Mr. Cahill. Um, can I help you with something?" She made no move to get closer, knowing she could run out the door faster than he could get down the stairs.

"Hi, Chloe. I'm sorry to show up like this, but I needed to speak to you."

"I just came from the Rose. Everything is set up for your dad's memorial. I just came home to change."

He waved a hand and came down a few steps. Leaning against the wall, he said, "It's not about that. I'm sure you have it handled. This is about Ronan Doyle."

She hoped it was confusion he saw on her face and not shock or fear. "Ronan? What about him?"

"He was there. At the Rose after my father collapsed."

She blinked rapidly. She wasn't prepared for this. Should she lie?

"I saw him, but it didn't register at the moment, you know? I was so worried about my father."

"Yes, he did come in right after all the commotion with the ambulance."

"Why?"

"Why what?"

"Why was he at the Rose?"

"He, uh...came to ask me out." It wasn't a total lie. She shook her head and rolled with it. "He said he'd been thinking about me and wanted to go out on a date."

"What did you say?"

"That it wasn't a good time."

The man came down a few more steps. Chloe backed down and held the bottom of the rail.

"He's trouble, Chloe. I don't know how well you might've known the Doyles growing up. I know you all came from the same block, but I'm not sure he can be trusted. You're a good girl. I wouldn't want you to get hurt."

Chloe paused, her heart and mind racing. Part of her wanted to believe that he was just giving her dating advice, but she knew it was more. It was a warning. A threat of some kind. She just didn't know what it meant.

She gripped her keys in her hand, the pinch of metal in her palm reassuring her. "Thank you for your concern, but I'll be fine."

He nodded. "Make sure you know what you're getting into."

She held her ground as he stepped down to leave. She would not let him know the effect he had on her.

As he reached the door, she asked, "If he's so much trouble, why did you hire him?"

Danny looked over his shoulder at her. "My father always said if someone is working under you, they can't sneak up behind you."

He opened the door and left.

Chloe shook with nerves. Brendan and Ronan had suspected he knew they were looking into him, but this was proof. She raced up the stairs and let herself into her apartment. She sat down and pulled out her phone. Her hands were shaking. What the hell was wrong with her? She wasn't really afraid of Danny Cahill. Was she? What could he do to her?

But there was something so subtly dark about his visit. She wanted to call Ronan and tell him, but he would not react well. He would go after Danny and that would ruin the progress they'd made. But they had to know that he was onto them.

She called Brendan.

"Hey, what's up? I thought you and my stupid brother made up."

"We did."

"Then why are you calling me?"

"Because if I tell him what just happened, he'll do something he might regret."

"What are you talking about?"

"I just came home from setting up the Rose for tonight and Danny Cahill was at my apartment."

"What? Why? How did he know where you live?"

"I don't know how he knew, but he came to ask why Ronan was at the Rose when his dad collapsed."

"Fuck. What did you tell him?"

"I told him that Ronan came to ask me out. Then he warned me away from Ronan. Said the Doyles were trouble."

"He ain't wrong."

"It's more than that, Brendan. He knows. I'm not sure he knows I'm with Ronan, but he knows you guys are looking for information."

"Good. I had Nolan tell him that I was asking questions. I want him to know."

"I think he might've been suspicious for a while. I asked him why he hired Ronan if he didn't trust him and he basically said it was to keep an eye on him."

"Keeping his enemies close, I guess."

"I didn't like it."

"Are you okay?"

"I guess. He didn't do anything. And if I didn't know what you guys suspect about everything with Alan and Danny, I would think he was just an older guy giving out fatherly advice. But I do know, and it gave the conversation a different twist, if that makes sense."

"It does."

"Anyway, I have to get ready. I just wanted you to know. Don't tell Ronan. Not yet. I'll tell him after tonight."

"Be careful."

"You too."

She disconnected and went to get ready to continue playing her role of naïve neighborhood good girl. But first, she was calling the landlord to make him come out to fix the lock that should've been taken care of weeks ago.

CHAPTER
Twenty-Seven

Ronan didn't want to go to the Rose to pay his respects. He was pissed that Alan died before he could get the information he was sure Alan had been hiding. He couldn't even say that he truly respected the man. But to not show up would raise red flags, so he showered and changed and headed to the Rose. At least he'd be able to see Chloe.

She had a way of making him feel better even when he didn't expect it.

The bar was already crammed when he got there. Good. Then it would be unlikely anyone would notice if he ducked out. It didn't look as though the Cahill family was in attendance, not that Ronan knew any of them except Danny. Brendan said he'd be here, but Ronan wasn't sure he'd spot his brother in the crowd. He sat on a stool at the bar.

He saw Johnny, the bartender who drove Chloe home, checking him out. He waved to him, hoping to convey there were no hard feelings. "Can I get a beer?"

"Sure." As Johnny poured the drink, he said, "Chloe

mentioned you guys got things straightened out. I'm glad. She seems happy with you."

"Me, too." He took a sip of his beer. "Is she around?"

"She's running crazy right now. The turnout is even bigger than she expected and she planned for a lot. Give her a minute and I'm sure she'll be flying by." Johnny wiped down the bar. "We're not serving the full menu, but there are appetizers in the back room if you're hungry."

"Danny Cahill here?"

"I haven't seen him. But that doesn't mean much." His attention was pulled away at the end of the bar.

Ronan picked up his glass and walked the perimeter of the bar, taking in the crowd. How many of these people knew Alan? Or any of the Cahills for that matter? He saw a few of the guys from work huddled together at a table, and he nodded a greeting. As he neared the Cahills' usual table, he saw the shrine for Alan. The picture was old, maybe from a campaign poster. Certainly not the octogenarian he was.

Lingering against the back wall near the booth was Brendan. Ronan edged over to his brother. "Why did you think coming here was a good idea?"

"I want to see who shows."

"A lot of nobodies. This is open to the public so anyone who ever voted for the man might show."

"But so will the people who were once close to him. The people like Nolan who aren't close enough anymore to go to the actual funeral. Those are the people I want to see. The ones who know where to find the skeletons."

Ronan flinched at the statement. Even though he knew Brendan was speaking figuratively, they both knew Michael Doyle was dead. His would be among the skeletons somewhere. He took a drink of his beer and that was when he noticed Brendan raising his phone and snapping a picture.

"What are you doing?"

"You think I know who all these people are? I'm taking their pictures to figure it out later."

"Have you seen Chloe?"

"Yeah. She's been through here a few times. Checking on food. Making sure the customers are happy. Doing her thing."

Moments later, the crowd shifted. Not physically, but the tension and attention in the room changed. Then Danny Cahill pushed his way through, shaking hands and accepting condolences. He looked tired. When he got to the table, he paused, staring at the photo of his father. The man shrank, his shoulders hunched in grief.

Part of Ronan felt sorry for him, but then he remembered that he never really got the chance to grieve his own father. He'd spent so much time waiting and hoping his father would come back that by the time he realized Michael wasn't returning, Ronan had just been angry.

He wasn't sure he'd ever left that phase.

Danny straightened and turned to the crowd in the room. "Thank you all for coming. My mother isn't able to be here tonight. She's too distraught, but I wanted to let you know that your showing up means a lot to the Cahill family. My father loved this city and its people. And knowing that so many Cahill Construction employees are here would flatter him. He built the business from the ground up and managed to touch a lot of lives."

"Not always in a good way," Brendan mumbled.

"Leave the man his grief. He's not his father."

"Yeah, his father would be a prick to your face. Danny is a snake in the weeds."

Ronan paused, wondering what Brendan meant.

Danny continued, "My father left a great legacy behind him, a strong belief that this city was the best. As you probably know, I'm following my father's path in running for office. It feels even more right to do so now. To finish the work he started years ago." Turning to his father's portrait, he raised a glass. "Here's to you, Dad."

Everyone followed suit and Danny disappeared back into the crowd, glad-handing as if he wasn't getting ready to bury his father. Damn politicians.

As conversations around them picked back up, Ronan asked Brendan, "What'd you mean about Danny being a snake?"

"There's more than we've seen in reports and incidents about Danny. When Alan said he'd been cleaning up after Danny his whole life, he wasn't kidding. There's some other stuff, but now's not the time."

Ronan wanted to press, but he knew Brendan wouldn't talk now. There were a lot of ears all around and they didn't know which ones were loyal to Cahill. He drained his glass as he digested what his brother said. From all accounts, Danny was hopped up on drugs back then, so Alan hadn't let him be part of anything. Not the construction company and certainly not his campaign.

But he also straightened out and got clean right after their dad went missing.

He turned to his brother.

"So Danny knows more about our father than we gave him credit for. Whether he was there, or Alan filled him in later. He knows something." Brendan raised his phone and snapped a few more photos. "He's nervous. Even now with his dad's death, his focus is on covering up."

Ronan opened his mouth, but Chloe finally dashed by. As she passed, she didn't notice him, so he called out her name. She turned, looking a little harried, but smiled when she saw it was him. That little hitch, the curve of her lips at seeing him, was enough to make him want to scoop her up and carry her home. She held up a single finger to let him know she'd be back.

"I don't know how you lucked out with that one."

"Me neither," he said. "You had your chance years ago."

"Nah. Not really. We didn't belong together. I just saw it before she did. Chloe would've broken my heart."

Chloe joined them then. With a hand over her heart, she said, "I would never have broken your heart, Brendan Doyle. I'm a sweet girl."

Brendan chuckled. "Sure you are."

"How's your night going?" Ronan asked.

"Insane. I knew Alan had a long history here, but I wasn't prepared for this. We've been packed since we opened." Her face softened as she touched his arm. "How are you guys doing?"

"Intel gathering," Brendan said. "This isn't over."

"Let me know if there's anything I can do." She glanced over her shoulder. "As much as I'd like to stay and chat, I need to get back to it."

Ronan kissed her on the cheek and let her go. He continued to track her movements through the room. Now that he knew where she was, it was like she had a homing device on her. He couldn't not look at her. "So how are we going to get information from Danny?" he asked without turning to Brendan.

"I don't know if we can. Maybe in a weak moment, while he's grieving, he might be willing to talk about Daddy's dealings, but something tells me Alan trained him better than that. We might have to keep looking for other people. Maybe those who knew Danny's dark side. They might know more."

"You have a line on someone?"

"Not yet. But I will."

They stood there, watching the crowd, not talking. Brendan occasionally took another photo. The crowd continued to grow instead of dwindling as time wore on. Ronan couldn't take it anymore. He needed to go home and have some quiet. He'd lost sight of Chloe as new groups had filled the space, but he wouldn't leave without saying goodbye. He wanted her to come to his house when she was done.

"I'm going to find Chloe and then head out."

"Don't forget Nessa's party on Saturday."

"I won't. Chloe is coming with me. Plus, I would never hear the end of it if I didn't bring the food you signed me up for."

Brendan pointed across the room. "There's your girl now."

Ronan turned and saw Chloe stiffen. He knew that look. She was about to lay into someone. He made a path for himself through the throngs of people.

"I'm sorry, but you've had enough. This is a private event," she said.

"No, it's not," the guy slurred. "It's for Alan Cahill. Open to the neighborhood. I'm payin' my respects."

"Then maybe you should be more respectful and not be drunk and obnoxious. I'll have a server bring you some water. Maybe try something to eat."

"Is that an invite? I'd like to have a taste of you." He slid an arm around Chloe's waist, and as she pressed a hand against the guy's chest, Ronan grabbed him by the collar and yanked him back.

"I think the lady asked you to back off."

"Get the fuck outta here. She's flirting with me."

"You need to go. Now." Chloe waived one of the bouncers over.

The guy twisted away from Ronan and took a swing. Ronan blocked it easily enough, but a crowd huddled around them.

"Oh my God. Please stop." Chloe stood in front of Ronan.

"I'm not doing anything. He swung on me."

The gathered crowd began chattering loudly, drawing more attention. Rather than backing down, the drunk took another swing. Ronan shifted Chloe out of the way and the man's fist made contact with Ronan's jaw. His head snapped back and without thinking he punched the guy, knocking him off his feet. Brendan was tugging Ronan back from going after the guy again.

Then Danny Cahill pushed through the crowd. "You," he said, pointing to Brendan. "I should've known you'd be in the middle of trying to ruin my father's wake. It's your fault he had a heart attack. Asking questions and casting doubt. You're not welcome here." His gaze shot to Ronan. "Get him gone, or you won't have a job."

As if working for Danny Cahill mattered to him. His fists flexed.

Chloe put a gentle hand on his wrist. "It's time to go."

The bouncer was already peeling the drunk off the floor and dragging him out.

"I warned you, Chloe," Danny said as he disappeared back through the crowd.

"I'm sorry," Ronan said, looking into Chloe's eyes. "I didn't come over here to start a fight."

"But you also didn't trust me to handle my job on my own. I don't need someone to swoop in to rescue me."

"I didn't mean it like that."

"I know. I can't deal with this right now. Please go."

"Will you come over tonight?"

"I don't know. I might be here late."

She was pissed and she probably needed time to cool off. He took the extra key he had made out of his pocket. "If you decide to, let yourself in."

"How will you get in?"

"It's an extra." He hadn't planned on letting her know he had it made for her, so she could come and go as she pleased. A crowded bar was not the place to move their relationship to another level. He glanced over his shoulder at Brendan. "Let's go."

He kissed Chloe's cheek. "Sorry about the trouble."

CHLOE'S FRUSTRATION WITH RONAN FUELED HER FOR THE REST of the night. Just like everyone else, he didn't trust her to handle things. As if she were feeble and weak-minded.

She thought back to Ronan's painting. He'd said she was his happiness.

That thought—the feeling—contradicted his actions.

She began wiping off tables so they could get everything done quickly. As she locked up behind the cleaning crew that just arrived, she realized that the contradiction was what made her crazy.

It was like living with Tim all over again. Feeling underestimated. Her feelings being dismissed.

But Ronan never made her feel small and useless.

Fuck. She threw the rag she'd been using against the table. Tim was still fucking with her head, making her doubt herself and Ronan.

"You okay?" Johnny asked.

"Yeah, just frustrated and tired."

"Head home. You've had some long days. I'll finish up here."

"You sure?"

"Yeah. The cleaning crew will handle most of it. Get some rest."

"Thanks. I appreciate it." She grabbed her things and hustled out. She didn't bother calling Ronan first. She just drove to his house and hoped he'd still be awake.

She rang the bell and Ronan answered, wearing low-slung shorts and nothing else. Her mind went blank.

"Hey. I gave you a key," he said, stepping back from the door.

Caught up in all her thoughts, she'd completely forgotten about the key.

"I gave up. I didn't expect to see you tonight."

She entered the house and looked around his living room. "No Declan?"

"We moved the mattress upstairs so we both have more privacy."

"Cool. Can we talk?"

"Sure. Let's go to my room."

She followed him to his bedroom. He sat on the bed and patted the mattress beside him.

"I'll stand."

"That doesn't sound good. Look. If this is about tonight and me hitting that guy—"

"It is. But not really." She blew out a breath. "I was really mad that you stepped in. I felt like you didn't think I could handle the situation, which is literally my job."

Ronan opened his mouth, but she held up a hand.

"The thing is, once I thought about it, I realized that my reaction was a little over the top and that has nothing to do with you." She licked her lips and walked the length of the room while searching for the words.

She stopped in front of his window and stared blankly outside into the dark. "My ex, Tim, didn't treat me well. He never hit me, but he made me feel small and stupid all the time. At first, it was minor comments here and there about how I didn't do something right. Then it got worse. He would outright call me names and when I'd call him on it, he acted like he didn't or that I was overreacting."

Ronan let loose a low growl but said nothing. She turned to face him. His hands were fisted on his thighs and his blue eyes were stormy as he stared at her.

She took a steadying breath and sat beside him. "It took a long time for me to realize he was gaslighting me all the time. He made me doubt every part of myself."

Ronan opened his hands and refisted them. Chloe placed her hand on top of his.

"I'm okay," she said quietly.

"He deserves an ass-kicking."

"I doubt it would do any good." She unfurled his fingers and held his hand. "I'm not telling you this to get you all worked up. I realized tonight that my experience with Tim colors how I react to things. I'm so afraid of letting that happen again—of losing myself—that sometimes I *am* going to overreact."

Every line of his body, every muscle was tense. Anger rolled off him, but she wasn't afraid. She wasn't even uncomfortable.

He scrubbed a hand over his head and then gently sandwiched her hand between his two giant palms. "I would never intentionally do anything to make you feel bad about yourself, and I want you to promise me that if I ever say or do anything that affects you that way, you'll say so. I didn't get involved tonight because you couldn't handle that asshole. You shouldn't *have* to. And I couldn't bear the thought of him laying hands on you in any way, especially to hurt you."

She smiled. "I know."

"You'll have to accept that I'm a little possessive and protective that way. So I can handle you telling me when I'm out of line, but you need to know that I will always step in between you and anything that will hurt you."

"Okay." She wrapped her free hand around his wrist. "On that note, there's something else I have to tell you."

The muscle in his jaw flexed, but he waited.

"First, know that I'm fine. Nothing horrible happened." She inhaled deeply. "This afternoon, when I left the Rose to go home to change, Danny Cahill was waiting at my apartment."

"What?" He started to jump up, but she pushed him back.

"He suspects you're working with Brendan. He didn't say as much, but he asked why you were at the Rose the night his father died."

"Damn. I knew he saw me, but it was like it didn't register. I didn't think he'd remember."

"He does. I told him you came to ask me out."

"Smart thinking." The corner of his mouth lifted in a partial smile.

She shouldn't want to bask in the pride on his face, but she did. "Anyway, he warned me that you were trouble. It made me a little uneasy, but he wasn't...really threatening. I asked him why he hired you if you're trouble and he said his father taught him to keep an eye on people so they can't sneak up behind him. He's watching you as much as you're watching him."

"Let him watch. Are you sure you're okay?"

"Yeah. He rattled me. Nothing like walking in to a surprise visitor. Part of me thinks he wanted me to give you the message."

"I hate that you're caught up in the middle of this."

"I'm not. It brought me you."

"Can't complain about that."

She surged forward and kissed him. It quickly became heated and they fell back onto the bed together.

Yeah, they weren't perfect, but they worked.

By the time Saturday rolled around, Chloe's mind was focused on how to tell her family about her and Ronan. Depending on how that went, she might want to spring her new career plan on them. One step at a time.

Nessa's party was in a little while, so Chloe headed to her parents' house to talk to them before going across the street to the party. She didn't want her relationship to be discovered through the rumor mill. She wasn't nervous, which surprised her. The last week with Ronan had been eye-opening. Once she let go of the imagined consequences of their relationship, she relaxed and settled into it.

She hadn't even freaked out about Ronan making her a key for his house.

Declan had given her a hard time, though. It was almost like having an extra brother.

She parked in front of the house and grabbed the two containers of cookies she'd made. One for the party and one for her mom. After locking her car, she noticed her sister's car. Great, now she only had to have this conversation once.

Walking through the front door, she called, "Hey, Mom, Dad."

"Chloe," her mom said as she came from the kitchen. Her father was at the dining room table, reading the paper.

"What are all those for?" Mom asked pointing to the containers.

"This one's for you."

"You baked?" Mom asked, surprised.

"Yes." Chloe tried to keep the sarcasm from her voice. So the cookies came from a tube of dough. She did do the actual baking.

Erin came in from the kitchen carrying two cups of coffee. "Hey, Chloe. There's a fresh pot of coffee if you want some."

"Cool. Have some cookies." She set the container on the table.

Her mom continued to talk as Chloe went to the kitchen. "I heard there was a problem at the wake the other night. Ronan Doyle punched someone, causing a scene."

Chloe didn't even get to pour her coffee. She returned to the dining room. "Yes, he did punch someone. The guy was drunk and put his hands on me. When Ronan told him to back off, he swung at Ronan. Twice. There wasn't much of a scene."

"The neighborhood has been talking about it as if it were a brawl."

"Well, it wasn't."

"Ronan was defending your honor?" Erin asked.

Their mom scoffed. As if Ronan was incapable of doing anything honorable.

Anger bubbled up in her chest. "As a matter of fact, he was. He didn't like seeing some other guy wrap an arm around me because we're seeing each other."

Erin let out a whoop and her mother froze. Even Dad looked up from the paper.

With all eyes on her, she swallowed. "No, we're more than seeing each other. We're a couple and we're in love."

She held her breath after the last words rushed out, waiting for a reaction.

Nothing. They just looked at her for a few seconds. Her dad opened the cookie container and grabbed one.

"Well," her mom said. "There's something to be said for a man who would protect a woman he cares about."

"What do you mean?" Erin said. "That's downright hot."

Chloe stifled a laugh as Mom said, "Erin."

"What? We're all adults here."

Mom simply shook her head and sipped her coffee. Chloe waited. She knew better than to think this was over.

"Are you happy?" Mom asked.

"Yes."

"That's all that matters, then. I can't make decisions for you. Would I choose such a man for my daughter? No. But he works a job and seems to care for his family."

"He does." She nodded. "I'm going to get a cup of coffee now."

"Good. Then you can fill us in on the details of this secret relationship you've been having," Erin said.

In the kitchen, as she filled her cup, her father walked in. He set his cup next to hers for a refill.

"Does he treat you right?" Dad asked.

"Yes."

"Then I guess he's better than Tim."

Her father didn't talk much, and she hadn't thought he considered anything about her breakup with Tim. But thinking back now, she realized that he had been happy when Tim was gone.

"You know about Tim?"

He picked up his cup. "I know that when you were with Tim, the light in your eyes was dimmed. Like your mother said, we can't make choices for you. But lately, I see your bright eyes again, and that's enough for me."

He left the room and Chloe took a shaky breath. For so long, she'd been keeping so much of herself hidden out of fear. But the people who cared about her saw through. It was time to be herself. She wasn't quite ready to tell them what happened with Tim. After talking with Ronan, the next time would be easier. But today wasn't the time.

When she took her seat at the table again, she said, "I'm going across the street for Nessa Doyle's birthday party. That's what the extra cookies are for."

"Is there anything else?" her mom asked.

"I've been thinking about my job."

"You're finally getting a new one?" her mother asked hopefully.

"Not exactly. As you know, Mr. Byrne is semi-retired. Mrs.

Byrne wants him to sell the bar. I wanted to talk to you about helping me buy it."

Her father put his paper down again. Her mom followed suit with her cup of coffee.

"You want to buy the bar?" Mom asked.

"Yes. I know you think the job is beneath me, but a business owner is a step up, right?" she said with a smile. Then she sighed. "I love it there. And since it's an established business, it's not as risky as starting a new venture. I know almost everything about running it."

Her parents were silent.

"I don't need a decision this second. But I'd like it if you'd think about it. I don't need your help running the business, but I'll need a co-signer for a loan."

"It would be a good investment," her father said. "I'll talk to Alastair and see what kind of numbers he's thinking."

"Really?"

"We'll have to talk some more, but we can look into it."

Chloe smiled. That's more than she'd been hoping for.

"Are the surprises done now?" her mom asked.

Since she asked, and Chloe was on a roll, she went on. "Actually... you know the cross stitches that I do?"

Her mom nodded as Erin said, "Oh, no."

"I have a pretty successful shop where I sell completed products and patterns."

"Why haven't you ever told me? I would send all my friends to buy from you."

Chloe smiled. "These are not the kind of crafts your church friends would enjoy."

She pulled out her phone and opened her online store. Then she turned the screen to her mom.

"You should've stopped while you were ahead," Erin murmured.

"I need to stop hiding parts of who I am. I'm not a perfect woman or a perfect child."

"I never expected you to be perfect," her mom said. She slid the phone across the table. "And as for your shop, I think you underestimate the foul minds of my friends. You can be a nice Catholic woman and still be subversive to undermine the patriarchy. Lenore has a print in her office that says, 'A woman once said Fuck this shit, and lived happily ever after.' It makes me smile every time I see it."

Erin snort-laughed. "You never swear. That sounded all kinds of wrong coming out of your mouth."

"I choose not to curse. That doesn't mean I can't appreciate a well-placed *fuck* on occasion." She took a cookie from the bin. "I've never expected perfection from my children. I want you healthy and happy and able to function in the world. And to visit on occasion."

"Okay. I'm all of those things, Mom. I thought you didn't approve of anything about me."

"You don't need my approval. I worry about you. That's what mothers do."

She was getting full of emotions she couldn't process at the moment. Luckily, Erin switched the subject to ask about the bar and Alan's wake.

Chloe hung out with her family until the party across the street had started. She didn't want to be the first to show. Standing, she said, "I hate to spill and run, but I have a party to attend."

Erin stood. "I'll walk you out."

Chloe grabbed the second container of cookies and rolled her eyes. She knew Erin wanted more details.

Out on the porch, her sister said, "Quite the bombshells you were dropping in there."

"They handled everything better than either of us thought they would."

"Yes, they did. They've always been so proper and...nice. I guess we don't give them enough credit."

"They did raise us."

The sisters laughed.

Then Erin lowered her voice. "Please tell me he's as hot and sexy as I've always imagined those Doyle guys to be."

Chloe laughed. "Yes, he is. And then some."

As she crossed the street, Chloe listened to her sister's laugh echo down the block and her mother's admonishment for being so loud.

She'd definitely underestimated the importance of family.

Twenty-Eight

When Ronan got to his mother's house to help set up for Nessa's party, Chloe's car was already parked across the street. She'd said she was going to tell her parents about their relationship today. She was making it real to the people she cared about. He fought the urge to go over there to stand with her.

Besides, it was time for him to do the same. He lugged his groceries through the gangway straight to the backyard. When he bumped the gate open, he saw most of his siblings already setting up tables and chairs. Killian was priming the keg. Declan was shoving a cupcake in his mouth while he tried to tell Kieran where to put the long table their mom would use for the food. Gavin was pouring charcoal into the grill.

"Hey," Declan said with a mouthful of cupcake, frosting still on his lips. "Hope you brought good meat. I'm starving."

"You're always starving." He set the bag on the small card table near the grill. "Can I talk to you guys for a minute?"

They all paused and looked at him suspiciously.

"So...Chloe McCarthy from across the street will be coming to the party." His comment was met with confusion. "As my date."

A chorus of "oh"s rang out. Then Gavin said, "We already knew about that. You want to keep secrets, never let Nessa and Declan hear 'em. We've known for a long time."

Ronan looked at his little brother.

"What?" he asked with his arms up. "You didn't say it was a big secret."

"I think I said exactly that."

"Well, for strangers, sure, but this is family. We don't keep secrets."

In general, he'd like to believe that, but both he and Declan knew that they'd been keeping a secret. Unless Declan hadn't. "Does that mean—"

Declan backed away until he was standing behind Kieran. "I might've told them that you and Brendan were looking into Dad's disappearance."

Ronan shook his head. He shoved the irritation down. Ultimately, it didn't matter because he and Brendan had already decided to talk to the whole family after the party. "You need to learn to keep your mouth shut when someone tells you to."

"We have a right to know what happened with our father, don't you think?" Kieran wanted to know.

"When I started, I didn't want to get anyone's hopes up. I didn't know if I'd be able to find anything out."

"And now?" Killian asked.

"Not much more. But it'll keep until after the party. Let's have fun with Nessa, and Brendan and I will lay it all out after."

The gate opened then, and Brendan came in with more

bags of food. As they continued to set up, he filled Brendan in on his conversation with everyone else.

Before long, haphazard decorations were hanging on the garage. The yard was filled with friends and family. Food was cooking on the grill. People were laughing and talking and drinking. Ronan suddenly realized that he missed this more than he ever thought he could.

Chloe came into the yard and he went to her. "How did things go with your family?"

"Really well," she said. "Better than I could've imagined. They all just want me to be happy."

"Even if it's with me?"

"Yep. My dad was okay with it and Erin wanted details."

"What about your mom?"

"She was surprisingly accepting. Not like she was jumping for joy or anything, but she accepted everything I said without any complaints or threats or anything." She laced her fingers through his. "I even told her about my naughty cross stitch."

"Wow. So you went all out. I planned to tell my family about us, too, but Declan and Nessa already told them."

She smiled up at him. "Family, right?"

"Let's go eat and get some drinks."

"I brought cookies."

"You didn't have to do that."

"I wanted to. Everyone chips in, right?"

They stopped by the food table to drop off the cookies. Ann was there, mixing salads and shifting bowls around. She took the bin of cookies and set them near the end of the line of food.

"Chloe. It's so good to see you. How's your family?"

"They're all good."

"I'm so glad you and Ronan aren't sneaking around anymore like a couple of teenagers. Since being with you, he's come back to the family."

"I can't take credit for that."

"Hush. You might not have prompted it, but being with you has given him balance that he'd been lacking for years." Ann pulled her into a hug. "Thank you for bringing my boy back."

Ronan smiled. The Doyles had always been pitied as a family as if since Michael went missing, they lacked something. They never needed pity. Whenever they were together, even at the height of bickering, they were full of love and friendship. How could anyone see that as lacking?

He'd stayed away for too long not because he found them lacking, but because they had been overwhelming. A reminder of what he'd been missing. Now, it just felt right. He was happy to be home.

THE PARTY LASTED LONGER THAN THEY PLANNED, WHICH WAS par for the course for a Doyle family party. Nessa hadn't been surprised, not that any of them fully expected her to be. She danced across the lawn, flirting with every guy she encountered, regardless of whether he'd come with a date.

Chloe handed Ronan a fresh beer as he stared at his dancing sister. "How much has she had to drink?"

Ronan took a swig and shook his head. "The thing is, I don't think she's drunk. Just happy."

The song on the radio switched and Nessa yelled. Then she cranked the volume before grabbing Declan's hand. "Come on, big brother. Dance with me."

Declan, like the rest of the boys, didn't dance. But he

stood and held their sister's hand as she shimmied and twirled.

From the porch, Ann yelled, "Nessa Doyle, it's gettin' late. Turn that down before someone calls the police."

In unison, the Doyle boys all called, "Is it even a Doyle party if the police don't show at least once?"

They laughed and joked. Nessa did turn the music down at the end of the song. As people began to say their goodbyes, Ronan reminded each of his siblings to stay after so they could talk about their father.

Chloe helped Ann pack up the food, and he and Brendan began stacking chairs. By the time Nessa hugged her last friend goodbye, most of the yard was put to rights. Nessa went to each of her brothers and kissed them on the cheek. "You guys might be the biggest pains in the ass, but you sure know how to throw a great party. Thanks."

"Since you came solo, is it safe to assume the douchebag Tony is out of the picture for good?" Ronan asked.

Declan answered for their sister. "He's been gone for a while."

"He still deserves an ass-kicking."

Declan narrowed his eyes. "Why?"

Nessa held up her hands. "Doesn't matter. He's gone. I've moved on. Let's not ruin a good night. What do you and Brendan want to talk about?"

"Let's take it inside," Brendan said.

Chloe held Ronan's hand. "I'm going to head home."

"You can stay."

"It's a family meeting. You should be with your family."

He kissed her full on the mouth. "At least go back to my place. I shouldn't be too much longer."

"Okay."

"And I want you to think about moving in."

Her eyes widened.

"Not immediately. I want to get some more work done on the house first, to make it a little more livable."

"It's kind of fast, isn't it?"

"I don't see the point in wasting time. I love you, Chloe McCarthy."

"And I love you, Ronan Doyle."

They kissed again, this time amidst hollers and yells from his siblings to get a room. Nessa was right. They were giant pains in the ass, but they were his.

ONCE THEY WERE ALL IN THE HOUSE, SETTLED IN WITH DRINKS around the dining room table, Brendan began.

"As you all know, just over twenty years ago, Dad went missing. Ronan and I have both been working different angles to try to find out what happened to him. We agree that he's dead." Brendan paused and let that sink in. It was something they all knew but never spoke of. "We also agree that there had to have been some kind of foul play. With the digging we've done, we're convinced that if Alan Cahill wasn't behind it, he at least knew something and covered it up."

Ann sucked in a harsh breath.

"Mom?" Ronan said.

"I've been thinking ever since you were here last after Alan died. There's something I need to tell you. Something that I've never told any of you." She glanced at their faces around the table. "That summer when your dad went missing, he'd been working extra odd jobs for Alan Cahill. It wasn't unusual. Any time we needed some extra cash, he did that. The medical bills for Killian's broken arm or sending Gavin to the arts camp. He'd do anything for you kids." Her lips pressed together into a tight line before she spoke again. "For me."

She took a deep breath. "I was pregnant again. That summer. He was working extra to prepare for the baby." Her eyes filled. "I lost the pregnancy after he went missing. I didn't tell anyone. It had been early on."

Ronan took his mother's hand. Why would she have kept all of this from them? Carried this burden on her own.

She patted his hand. "I was distraught. Worried about all of you. When Alan came offering his help, I never considered..."

Tears spilled down her cheeks.

"Are you saying you think this was guilt money?" Brendan asked.

"I don't know. I thought he was being a good man, looking out for family. Your father had worked for him from the beginning."

"Maybe that's all it was," Declan offered.

Ronan shot Brendan a look. They knew better. It was hush money from a man who was entering the Chicago political scene.

"There's more. Yesterday, I received a certified envelope from Alan's lawyer." She rose from the table. "I'll be right back."

When she stepped away, Ronan stared at his siblings. They were all dumbfounded. When Ann returned with an unopened manila envelope, she handed it to Brendan.

"Did the fucker put us in his will?" Nessa asked.

Brendan pulled the papers out. He read a letter from the lawyer that stated that Alan's will dictated that this letter be sent upon his death. A smaller envelope contained a hand-written note.

"I know your family is looking for answers. There are none. Michael Doyle is dead. Declare him so and move on. Let the dead stay dead."

"That's it?" Ronan asked. "No deathbed confession? No information about what happened or where his body is?"

Brendan turned the paper over as if there might be some other clues. Then he tossed it on the table. "Nothing."

"But we were right. He knew. And now he took that information to his grave." Anger boiled through Ronan. They had been close.

"If he did it, why not just confess now? He's dead. Nothing can happen to him," Killian said.

"He would never risk ruining his name," Ronan bit out.

"Or," Brendan said, "he wouldn't take the blame for something someone else did. He's not going to point a finger, but he wanted to close the book on that chapter in our lives. So we could finally lay him to rest and stop searching for answers. We know he's gone."

Ronan shoved away from the table. "It's not answers, though."

Ann stood beside him. "We might never get those."

"I think we should lay him to rest. Have him declared dead," Brendan continued.

Kieran and Gavin both said, "I agree."

The others looked back and forth between Ronan and Brendan. The two oldest, at odds again.

"I thought you wanted answers, too. Now you're just giving up?" Ronan asked.

"Not one fucking bit. But if we let them believe we are, they'll let their guard down. Then we'll get our answers."

Ronan didn't like it, but as a conniving plan, it made sense. "Where do we go from here?"

Killian grabbed a bottle of whiskey and a handful of glasses. "Tonight, we toast our father."

They poured drinks and raised glasses.

"Your father would have loved seeing you all like this. Together," Mom said.

"Drinking," Killian added with a smile.

She narrowed her eyes at him. "Laughing. This right here is everything Michael Doyle wanted in his life." She raised her glass. "To family."

They drank and then quiet fell over the group until Brendan cleared his throat. "I remember when I was about twelve, I wanted a Nintendo so bad. All my friends were playing video games, but Dad said if I wanted it, I had to earn the money."

Ronan snickered because he knew that exact line. He'd suffered the same fate when he asked for a new bike.

"He took me on a side job to build a small deck. I thought it'd be cool learning to build with dad. Except it wasn't about learning to build. He had some guys from the job working for him for cash, but man, he beat me down with the labor. He had a dump truck show up and pour a mountain of rocks on the woman's lawn. All I did for days was fill a wheelbarrow in the front and dump it in the back. I don't think I ever hauled so many rocks in my life. My back still hurts every time I think about it."

Ronan tilted his head. "I don't remember ever having a Nintendo." And he'd know because even if Brendan had paid for it, his parents would've made them share.

"That's because I didn't buy it. I worked three more jobs

with him on the weekends to earn that money. When I had it, I decided the game system wasn't worth all that."

"He always wanted you to know the value of hard work," Mom said, a little misty-eyed.

"That explains what happened to Declan, then," Nessa called out with a hoot of laughter."

"Shut the hell up. I know how to work. I just don't feel the need to be a slave to society's expectations."

Nessa leaned forward. "That's his way of admitting that he hates to get up early."

They all laughed and the floodgates of memories opened. They all shared stories about their father, describing their individual connections with a man who had been gone for two decades. Ronan couldn't imagine ever leaving such a permanent mark on others' lives.

But in this moment, he was glad they had each other. He was happy to finally be home.

Epilogue

Ronan tugged at the tie that strangled him. This was why he'd never considered a job that required wearing a suit. He stood with his family at a bogus grave as they finally said goodbye to their father. Most of the neighborhood had turned out. Some just for the gossip, but most because they wanted to support the Doyle family.

Chloe stood by his side, holding his hand as the priest said prayers. Even the McCarthys were in attendance and they hadn't given Ronan one dirty look. Mr. McCarthy shook his hand and Mrs. McCarthy offered a smile, stiff as it might've been.

Many of the old-timers from Cahill came to the service. Ronan watched them from behind his sunglass and wondered if any of them would now come forward with more information. He tuned out the prayers and responses and just studied the people in attendance.

When it was done, he stood beside Brendan and his mother, shook hands, and accepted hugs. He nodded as people told him what a beautiful service it was and how they should finally find peace. As Gavin and Killian walked their mother to the car, he and Brendan stayed back by the grave.

Chloe went to pull away, but he held her tight. "You can stay. You've been in this since near the beginning."

"And it's time now for you guys to step back," Brendan said.

"Fuck no."

Brendan blew out a slow breath. "You're moving on. Starting a fresh life with each other. It's my turn to take the reins of this now. I don't want this to continue to hold you back. We lost you for a long time and now that you're back, we want you to stay. I'm asking you to trust me to see this to the end."

"You think I'm just going to walk away? Keep working for Cahill knowing his father had a hand in something that took mine from me?"

"I'll keep you in the loop, but no, I don't want you to keep working for Danny if it's going to cost you. You've done enough. Let me take over."

Ronan kicked at the soft earth. "I don't know that I can just walk away."

"If you don't, you might lose more."

"What about you?"

"My life has been my job. I haven't done anything to cause me to lose that."

Suddenly Ronan was struck by how lonely his life had been before he began dating Chloe and let Declan move in. Having people in his life had helped with the struggles of searching for answers. He nodded. "I'm here whenever you need anything. And I'll stick at Cahill for a while longer. Danny thinks he's watching me, but he's the one who'll be in the public eye running for office."

"I know. And when I need your help, I'll ask."

"Or demand. That's usually your method."

"Comes with the territory of being the oldest."

"You're barely a year older than me."

Chloe squeezed his hand. "Trust me. There's no arguing with the logic of the oldest siblings. Let him believe he runs the world. Let's join the rest of your family."

Ronan and Chloe walked to his truck. "How's everyone else handling all of this?"

He looked ahead to where his siblings were all piling into cars. "I'm not sure. Declan is having a hard time and he knew before the others. When I told him I believed Dad was dead, it hit Declan hard. For some reason in his mind, Dad ran off. I don't know if somehow that was easier to believe or what. But knowing that it wasn't Dad's choice to leave us...he's struggling with that."

"It's gotta be hard. Regardless of what they thought, to have confirmation makes it real."

"Nessa is probably handling it best. She was so young when he disappeared. She lived her whole childhood without a father. The twins aren't saying anything. At least not to me. But they've always been like that. They turn to each other first."

"What about Gavin?"

"Gavin's quiet too. He's probably pouring himself into his work. We'll turn around one day and Gavin will pop up with a museum's worth of art. He processes things with his hands."

She hugged his arm. "You know, for someone who supposedly stayed away from his family for years, isolating himself for whatever strange reason, you know them all really well."

"Yeah, I guess I do. They're all I've got."

"That's not true. Now you have me, too. We're in this together."

"I love you." He wrapped his arms around her and held her close. She was definitely the best addition to his life.

DECLAN WALKED THROUGH HIS BROTHER'S KITCHEN AND admired his handiwork. Ronan hadn't believed he could build and install the custom cabinets. But they looked damn good.

And he got them done just in time. Although Ronan hadn't said anything, Declan knew that he wanted Chloe to move in. He hadn't told Declan to move out, even though Declan pretty much had just become a squatter. But with all of the information that had come to light recently, he knew it was time to go.

He had his duffel packed and sitting at his feet. He snapped some pictures of the finished product as proof of what he was capable of when he put his mind to it.

Chloe and Ronan came through the front door discussing something in loud tones. Not an argument really, heated, but in a light way. He put his phone away as they came into the kitchen carrying bags of groceries.

"Declan, can you please tell your brother that there's no way that oatmeal cookies are better than chocolate chip. Everyone knows that chocolate chip is the universe's best cookie."

"Never argue with your woman over inconsequential shit," he said to Ronan. "Looks like I still need to give you lessons on how to treat a lady."

"I do just fine." Ronan's gaze landed on Declan's bag. "Going somewhere?"

"Yeah, I figure it's about time for me to get out of your hair. Cabinets are officially done. All the doors are attached and shelves installed."

"And they look phenomenal," Chloe said.

"Thanks."

"I know I give you a hard time, but you can stay," Ronan offered.

"You have your thing going on. Chloe's here. You don't need me lurking around."

"Where are you gonna go? You still don't even have a job."

"I'll be fine. I always land on my feet. Luck of the Irish, I think."

"Don't be ridiculous. You don't have a place to go to. Stay here till you find one."

"Thanks for the offer, but I need to go. I have to figure things out."

"At least stay for dinner," Chloe said. "We have pizza coming."

"That I can do. Hard to say no to pizza."

The doorbell rang and Chloe went to grab the food from the delivery guy. Ronan pinned him with his big brother stare.

"Aren't you tired of running around? It's time to grow up."

Declan nodded. "I know. That's why I can't stay."

Those were words he knew Ronan could respect. As someone who had distanced himself from the family while he figured out his shit, Ronan would understand where Declan was coming from.

"You don't need to worry about me. I have friends I can

crash with until I figure out what I want. Someone's always looking for a roommate."

"We're here if you ever need anything."

"Thanks, man." He turned and looked at the cabinets again. "And thanks for trusting me with this."

"You have real potential there. If you want to do this, I can make some calls."

"I'll let you know."

"Come on, boys. Grab the beer. Pizza's here."

They took three bottles from the fridge and went to the living room, which was newly furnished. Declan wasn't the only one who was changing his stance on how he'd been living life. "Chloe's a good influence on you. 'Bout time you got real furniture."

Ronan chuckled. "This coming from the guy who doesn't even have a house. He's gonna criticize my lack of furniture."

Declan laughed. It was good to have his brother back in his life. As tempting as Ronan's offer to stay was, Declan knew that if he stayed it would be too easy. He'd been taking the easy way for years. He had convinced himself that it was the only way to live life. If he buckled down and became responsible, he'd grow to resent it and run off like his father had. Now he had to re-evaluate everything about his life.

The first step was figuring out who he was.

***

Keep reading for an excerpt of Declan's book, *In Fine Form*.

In Fine Form

EXCERPT

Declan Doyle rolled over on the couch and tried to find a better position. He'd been sleeping in his best friend Tyler's living room for a week, and the springs in the couch were killing him. At least at his brother's house, he had a mattress—that his brother bought, but still. He'd left Ronan's house knowing that he needed change, but going without a plan wasn't working so well.

When Tyler offered to let him stay, Declan assumed it would be as a roommate, as in having his own bedroom. Tyler had just moved back to Chicago from Ohio, so Declan thought he wanted a roommate to help with costs. He failed to mention that he already had a roommate. It explained how he managed to move out of his sister's house so quickly.

Declan gave up on sleep and sat up, running a hand through his hair. Tyler bounced from his bedroom.

"Hey, man. Glad you're up. I have an early start at the shop, and I wanted to talk to you before I head out."

"What's up?" He stood and stretched.

"Frankie is getting a little irritated with you being here.

He thought you were staying for like a day, and that's on me." Tyler pressed a hand to his chest. "I thought I made it clear you needed a place to stay. I'm sorry, but I got something else for you."

"Look, I appreciate the place to sleep." Not so much the uncomfortable couch. "I can make my own way."

"No. Really. This is a win-win situation."

"What is?"

"My sister needs some help with that crappy house she bought. She was driving me crazy when I was there because she needs all this work done, but she can't afford a lot, and I'm not into construction. Give me an engine to work on, and I'll do it all day. But a piece of wood or drywall? Hell, no."

"Are you telling me that Rennie wants me to move in?"

"First, you know she hates that you call her that."

He did know. That was why he did it. If he couldn't treat his best friend's older sister like his own, what was the point?

Tyler continued, "Renee needs someone to guide her through what she should do first, and if that someone can do some of the work for cheap, say free room and board...She'd really appreciate it."

Declan laughed. "Your sister doesn't appreciate anything about me. I don't think she even likes me."

"She likes you just fine. Except when you call her Rennie."

It was a silly childhood thing. He'd known Tyler since the third grade and Rence was in seventh. She was too cool to hang out with them, so they felt it had been their duty to try to torment her. "Why did she buy a crappy house if she doesn't have the means to fix it?"

Tyler shook his head. "Ever since the divorce, everything that happened with Graham, she needed to start over. The divorce pretty much bled them dry because Graham's an asshole, and crappy was what she could afford. But it's livable. And you'd have your own bedroom."

"I don't know. I need to get a job. How am I supposed to fix her shit and work a job?"

"Do some of her stuff while you look. Anything's an improvement. Plus, Sadie adores you."

"I am pretty adorable. That's why all the ladies like me."

"Yeah, whatever. So you'll do it?"

Declan shot his friend a look. "What's in it for you?"

"Besides you getting off my couch? It gets her off my back. Like I said, win-win."

"The idea of win-win isn't supposed to be about you."

"I take what I can." He pulled out his phone. A moment later, Declan's phone pinged. "That's her address and number."

Declan narrowed his eyes. "Did you already tell her I'd do this?"

"Maaaybe."

"Asshole. What if I said no?"

"I had faith that I'd talk you into it. I was prepared with pics of Sadie and everything." He waved his phone in front of Declan.

"Like a cute little kid would make me change my mind."

"What time should I tell her?"

"You mean I'm supposed to go now?" Declan looked around the room, where his few belongings were scattered.

"She works from home, so why not?"

"Fine. Tell her I'll be there by lunch. I want to shower and get my stuff together."

"Cool. Meet for beers tonight?"

"You're buying." He grabbed a T-shirt from the arm of the

couch and sniffed it.

"You got it." Tyler grabbed his keys and left.

Declan sank back to the couch, T-shirt in hand. Working on Renee's house couldn't possibly be that bad. He'd just survived a couple of months living with Ronan who didn't cook, rarely had groceries in the fridge, and had no furniture. Renee might be a cranky chick, but he knew she'd have the basic comforts. And it would afford him time to figure out his next moves while giving him more experience. Living with the wicked witch wouldn't kill him, would it?

***

Renee scrolled through the spreadsheet double-checking her figures. She knew it was right. This was more like triple-checking. Her phone bleeped with a text from her brother. Declan will be there by lunch.

He better be able to really do the work. I'm not playing.

Do you ever play? He grew up with brothers who do construction and he just redid Ronan's kitchen. He's the best you can afford.

She made a face at her phone even though he couldn't see her. She didn't like the truth he was spewing. She sighed and looked around her kitchen. She'd love to redo this room first, but she wasn't sure if it was the best use of her limited funds. She wasn't thrilled with the state of her new house, but it was hers. Graham had no part of it and there were no memories of him in it. So no matter how rundown it was, it was worth it.

The thought made her smile.

A moment later, Sadie came running into the kitchen. "Can I have a snack?"

Renee sighed. Growth spurts were going to kill her. Sadie was back to eating nonstop. "You can have an apple or grapes. It'll be lunchtime soon."

"Grapes."

She gathered a handful of grapes and put them in a bowl for her daughter. As she handed Sadie the bowl, she said, "Declan will be here around lunchtime. Remember I told you he might be coming to stay with us for a while?"

"He's funny." She snatched the bowl and ran back to the living room.

Funny. That was one way to think of Declan. Renee closed her laptop and checked in the fridge to decide what to make for lunch. "Hey, babe. What do you want for lunch?"

"Chicken nuggets!"

She should've guessed. Sadie was in a pattern of eating the same food over and over for days on end. Renee was fine with it, but she had no desire to eat chicken nuggets again. She turned the oven on and grabbed the chicken and a pizza from the freezer. While the oven preheated, she pulled out her notebook where she kept all of her ideas and thoughts about the house. She wanted to be able to have a starting place for Declan.

As she thumbed through the pages, she created a mental list of work she needed to finish by the end of the week. It was hard to believe that her baby was starting kindergarten. When Sadie was an infant, it felt like it would take forever for her to get to school age. Now, she was there, and Renee wasn't sure she was ready to let go.

When the pizza and chicken nuggets were ready, she set plates on the table and called Sadie. They settled in for their usual lunch routine, where Sadie told her about her morning as if Renee hadn't been there with her. It made sense when Sadie was coming from preschool or one of her classes when she was on her own.

But Renee let her chatter on about the cartoon she

watched or the game she played with her toys or the city she built with her Legos. Mostly, Renee just needed to smile and nod and ask an occasional question.

"School now?"

Renee sighed. "I told you, school on Monday."

Sadie bounced in her seat in excitement.

"But we can go pick out a backpack today if you want." Renee had already bought all of the other school supplies and painstakingly wrote Sadie's name on every little thing. She almost hadn't because who cared if someone stole a pencil or crayon? But she knew Sadie would notice if other kids had their names on everything, so Renee followed the instructions the school had emailed.

She checked the clock. Still no word from Declan. Was she supposed to sit around all day and wait for him?

She sent a text to Tyler since no one had thought to give her Declan's number. He's still not here. I have shit to do.

So go do it. He'll get there eventually.

She gave him until she had lunch cleaned up and Sadie ready to go. No Declan, so they went to the store. Sadie had to try on nearly every backpack before settling on the first one Renee handed to her.

"Can I wear it home?"

"You can wear it until we check out and you can hold it in the car. It can't stay on your back. It's not safe like that."

Sadie squinched up her face and nodded. They held hands as they walked through the store toward the registers. After paying for the bag, they drove home, Sadie playing with the zippers on her bag, testing them repeatedly.

"Who's that?" Sadie asked as Renee was parking.

"Who?"

"On our steps."

Renee put the car in park and looked through the window to their front porch. Sure enough, a man was lying on the stairs, legs outstretched, his head resting on a bag. A moment of panic hit her, but then she remembered Declan. She honked the horn. He sat up and pushed his sunglasses to the top of his head. He squinted at her and smiled.

"It's Declan."

"Yay!" Sadie unbuckled herself, grabbed her bag, and flew out the door. "Declan!"

How the hell did a guy who they hadn't seen in over a year get a reception like that?

Renee climbed from the car and locked up. By the time she reached the house, Sadie was showing Declan how awesome her new backpack was. He looked different than how she remembered him. He was one of those people who were frozen in time in her mind. Although she'd seen him in recent years, he was always seventeen in her head. Cute, but annoying like a little brother.

He looked at her over Sadie's head and shot her a grin. That smile had always been a killer and seeing it on a guy who was definitely more man than boy was quite the hit.

"Hey. How are you? It's been a while." He stood and leaned over to kiss her cheek.

For some stupid reason, it made her blush. "I'm doing okay."

She pointed to his scruffy jaw. "That's—" *Sexy.* "New."

He rubbed his hand over the close-cut beard. "Yeah. Ronan had one for a while because he didn't want to look like our dad. I figured I'd give it a try."

She couldn't remember ever meeting his dad. Then again, they were all kids when he went missing. Now, she wasn't sure if it was a sore subject. "Ty said you were gonna be here by lunchtime."

He shrugged. "It's only like one-thirty. That's still lunchtime, right?"

She sucked in a deep breath. "Let's go in and get you settled." She looked around. "Is that it?" she asked pointing to the duffel he'd been resting on.

"Yep. I travel light."

She walked past him to the door, unlocked it, and ushered Sadie in. "Go put your backpack away. I'm going to show Declan around."

Declan followed them in as Sadie ran off to her room, bag thumping at her side.

"Your room is this way, toward the back of the house on the other side of the kitchen." She led the way, looking at her house the way he might see it. It was a little dingey and had an old lady vibe, but she was working to change that. "Here you go."

She gave the bedroom door a shove and stepped back toward the kitchen. He tossed his bag on the bed and turned in a circle.

"Nice place."

"If you say so."

"I slept on Ronan's attic floor. This is furnished and everything."

"Your brother made you sleep on the floor?" She couldn't keep the shock from her voice.

"He lives alone and didn't have much furniture to begin with. But he bought a mattress, so I wasn't on the bare floor." He lifted a shoulder again as if he didn't have a care in the world.

To be so laid back.

"Should we see what needs work?"

"We will. But first, some ground rules."

"Shoot." He sat on the edge of the bed and gave a bounce. Then he patted the mattress beside him. "Take a seat."

She waved him off. She was better when standing. "First, no parties, no women."

"You mean here, right? Like you don't expect me to be celibate. Just don't bring them here."

"What you do out in the world is your business."

"I would never be so disrespectful to bring another woman into your house. What do you think of me, Rennie?" He put a hand over his heart and looked at her with wide eyes.

"Second, do not ever call me Rennie. It annoys me."

He huffed out a breath. "I'll try."

"Three, you're welcome to eat or drink anything in the fridge. I cook or pick up dinner most nights. I'm willing to get you something specific when I do the grocery shopping—within reason."

"Whatever you have, is good with me. I'm not picky."

"Four, I expect you to treat this like a job. No sleeping all day and then working at midnight. Sadie has a regular bedtime and I don't want work noise to keep her up. Plus, she's starting school next week, so her routine is shifting. It's going to be hard enough without adding lack of sleep. Any problems?"

"Got it. Don't be a douche. Get the work done."

She cringed. "And maybe try to curb the language. I don't want to have to explain to a five-year-old what a douche is."

"Again, I can try." He stood up. "My turn."

"For what?"

"My rules."

Note to Readers

If you could spare a moment, I would appreciate you leaving a review of this book.

If you'd like to stay up-to-date on my releases and have the chance to win some prizes, click here to join my newsletter.

Between Love and Loyalty

Meeting His Match

<u>Hot & Nerdy Novellas</u>

Her Best Shot

Her Perfect Game

Her Winning Formula

His Work of Art

His New Jam

His Dream Role